ROOKS NEST

Also by June Barraclough

THE HEART OF THE ROSE

ROOKS NEST

A Novel by
JUNE BARRACLOUGH

ST. MARTIN'S PRESS
New York

ROOKS NEST. Copyright © 1986 by June Barraclough. All rights reserved.
Printed in the United States of America. No part of this book may be used
or reproduced in any manner whatsoever without written permission except
in the case of brief quotations embodied in critical articles or reviews. For
information, address St. Martin's Press, 175 Fifth Avenue, New York, N.Y.
10010.

Library of Congress Cataloging-in-Publication Data

Barraclough, June.
    Rooks Nest.

    I. Title.
PR6052.A716R6   1987   823'.914   87-15560
ISBN 0-312-01083-4

First published in Great Britain by George Weidenfeld and Nicolson
Limited.

First U.S. Edition

10   9   8   7   6   5   4   3   2   1

CONTENTS

Some hang above the tombs,
Some weep in empty rooms,
I, when the iris blooms,
    Remember.

I, when the cyclamen
Opens her buds again,
Rejoice a moment – then
    Remember.

Mary Coleridge

One

HARTSEDGE HALL

When I was a child I had a recurring dream : I would be standing in a meadow by a lake whose surface was still and glassy. I looked into the lake and saw there the reflection of a great mansion whose contours wobbled slightly with the faintest movement of the water. I knew instinctively there was danger around me but I had no idea why. I tried to move away from the lake but my feet would not budge and I remained standing there as, without warning, the waters began to move. At first they moved in slow motion and the reflection of the house moved too as though the stones were dizzy. I tried to turn round to see the real mansion behind me but some stones began to fall silently over me into the lake, disturbing the waters and ruining the reflection. It was the silence which was so awful. When the stones had all soundlessly fallen except for those from the top of the roof, I waited for the roof to crash. When the pediment fell into the lake and joined the other stones there, the waves began to moderate, and then became quiet – and then were once more little ripples. There lay the lake before me again with the reflection just as it had been at first. Now I knew I could look round and I turned to find the house whose reflection I had been watching. There was nothing there! Only a meadow with waving grass : no stone house, no roof! Just a blue sky and a line of trees. I found I was now able to walk away from the lake, and I stumbled on the roots of brambles. At this point I always awoke from my dream, the sensations of dread still with me but receding slowly. Sounds came back – the Grandfather clock on the landing outside my bedroom and a branch tapping irregularly against the mullion.

My dream had had no people in it and until I was sure that I existed and had not died in my dream I lay trembling, stroking my upper arms which were crossed on my chest.

In my waking life I rarely thought of my dream ; just occasionally I would remember it. But it was familiar to my sleeping self, for each time I dreamed it, perhaps once or twice a year, I recognized it and was frightened every time. Perhaps I feared that I too would be sucked away into the waters and would become a reflection on their surface of a person who was not there. In later years when I dreamed the dream, a garden was growing by the lakeside and its brilliant blue flowers crumpled when the waves began to move, and returned as shadow flowers when the storm was spent.

One of my first real memories is of standing on the 'ramparts' at Hartsedge Hall. I had named them ramparts – they were in fact the spaces in front of the battlemented roof of the Hall. I suppose the roof of that small Jacobean manor house was not very high, but it was the highest place to which I dared to climb. I didn't climb to the ramparts out of bravery but because I was afraid, for I had to force myself up the stone stair that led from one of the attic rooms to the roof. There was a little trap-door at the top and once I found I could push it open I made up my mind to crawl up and seat myself on the leads. My legs felt wobbly and my heart pounded and I felt rather sick but I did it – I proved to myself that I could conquer my fear. I sat there for a little while, knowing I could go down again as soon as I wanted, and then I stood up, leaning against a stone chimney stack. I dared not go near the edge of the battlements but from my position I could see all the countryside spread out below like the patchwork quilt that had been my Mama's and now covered my own bed. The Hall grounds were hidden from my view, except for the stone walls at the bottom of the garden. The bright green fields stretched out beyond, cut into irregular patches by the dark dry-stone walls. Near to the first field was the line of trees that marked the leafy lane we called Cow Lane. It curved round to the village, passing the fields of Wynteredge Farm whose roof I could see high up on the ridge. That and the few cottage roofs further on were a dark grey colour that turned black in the rain. Everything looked so different from my high vantage point. Which was the real farm – the one I passed on my walks or the one I could see from here? On the ridge beyond that, I could see tall square-towered Sholey Church, and further still, fold after fold of brown hills. Covering them all was a grey-blue sky with a few puffy clouds gathering. In the evening that sky would be pink and gold and later, when it had turned the colour of plum-bloom, the stars would come out, sharp and silvery. The stars over the Pennines were like crystal icicles, pointed and shining. On some moonlit nights the clouds would scud across the sky, and the moon, lighting them up, made them look like the cream cheese Mrs Hirst made up at the farm, and which her son Sam sold to us.

I liked to be on my own. In summer I would hide in a haystack and in winter under the big table in the school-room or in the attics. The attics were lovely: empty and quiet, with trays of apples, and eggs in waterglass, and strings of onions hanging from the rafters. They had tiny mullioned windows, uncurtained, and I would look out of them at the monkey puzzle tree in the garden. My best thoughts always came to me when I was alone. Often I couldn't remember afterwards what I had been thinking about; my mind seemed to go far away. It is all mixed up in my memory with the distant sound of cows mooing or dogs barking, mingled with the sound of the wind which brought all those sounds to me, or with the sight of a dancing sunbeam whose dusty motes hung like speckled gold aslant the walls.

Of course I didn't always want to be by myself. I believe I was on the whole a fairly cheerful child and I liked to sit at the big hearth in Martha's kitchen toasted on one side and frozen on the other, the treacherous wind snuffling under the old wooden doors and blowing the rag rugs as it licked the stone flags. My Aunt Juby had a smaller fire in her sitting room and the door closed better, and at Christmas-time I was allowed in there to sit in the dusky afternoon with a book. Sometimes there would be snow lagging the sills and turning the garden into a still white wedding cake and I would go out before sunset with Ellen the maid, reluctantly at first, to cut holly and ivy with the farm boys. On our return we would make toast and then my aunt would play her precious pianoforte with its candles in brackets, and as we sang hymns and wassails I would think that there was nowhere on earth as good and safe as Hartsedge Hall. Even though it was my home only because Aunt had adopted me when my Mama died, it *was* my home and I loved it.

I used to write to Papa at Christmas, for he was Abroad. My Christmas wish when we pulled the chicken wishbone was always 'Please let Papa come back to Rooks Nest before Twelfth Night'. I don't know why I stipulated Twelfth Night – it was as though, if Papa didn't manage to come before then, he would never come again and the New Year would be another without him.

Apart from the poky little cottages where the farmworkers

and weavers lived, and the old inns and farmhouses, there were only two kinds of houses in the district – the very old ones like our Hall with its stone mullions and round rose window and fancy porch and the date carved above in the stone; and the few larger and grander houses that were not so old, only about a hundred years, with their winding drives and lodges and 'landscape'. The Halls were scattered around for miles, even on the encroaching moorland and were not 'manufacturers' houses' as the others were called. They had always belonged to a sort of gentry, and when the gentry faded the Halls might be turned into farms or be divided up into cottages.

Although I loved the Hall it was Rooks Nest I longed for, the 'manufacturers house' a mile or two away where I had been born and which was now empty. Sometimes I could persuade Martha to take me near it when we walked down to Martha's mother's at Slead Syke. We would go down the old Coach Road – neglected now the new Turnpike Road had been built – where the high stone wall on one side of the old road was the boundary wall of the Rooks Nest property. When I was very small Martha would lift me up to look through the thick trees to the glint of a little lake in the parkland and I could just make out the outline of the square stone mansion.

Hartsedge Hall had never been divided up. Aunt Juby had inherited it and now she was going to make it into a school for the daughters of gentlemen and rich tradesmen. I wondered why they didn't make Rooks Nest into a school. It would have been far more suitable, to my way of thinking, for I was not very enthusiastic at first for the Hall to be overrun with strange girls.

Rooks Nest fascinated me because nobody ever went into it and because my Mama had died there. Martha had once worked for Mama and she would tell me all about its former glories. I only had to say 'Tell me about the grotto, Martha' or 'What was the conservatory like?' and she would start on her reminiscences. Then I would ask about Papa and when he would come back and Martha would always say 'Aye, he'll see what a grand lass you are when he comes', and then change the subject. Rooks Nest seemed to belong to a past that was not just a different past to that of Hartsedge Hall; it had a whole different feeling about it. The Hall was the older building but the other house, glimpsed through the trees, was magical to me. I had lived there for the first few months of my life and I felt there was a certain glamour to having been born there. I would pester Martha for an account of my birth, but she was silent on the matter. Her 'poor young lady' (that was my mama) had been buried far away on the coast where they had taken her so that the sea air might revive her, but it never did. When I asked about my early days, Martha always told me that Papa had asked Augusta Jewesbury, my Aunt Juby, to take me and look after me, because she was Mama's oldest friend. And Martha had come along too and had done most of the looking-after.

Aunt Juby never said much to me about Mama. It was Martha who hinted that there had been some sort of quarrel between Mama's and Papa's families before they married so that when Mama died they 'cut him out'. When she said that, I envisaged a large pair of scissors snipping at my poor papa.

'Don't ask your auntie – she has enough to worry about,' Martha would say. I would not have asked her in any case, not when I was a child, for although she was a good and kind lady I was somewhat in awe of her. She was tall with faded brown hair that was always escaping from its combs, and her steel-rimmed spectacles gave her an abstracted air.

There had once been a Mr Jewesbury, Martha told me, but he had died, and this did not seem to have been an occasion for great mourning. I always thought of my aunt as being unmarried and it was true that she had no children of her own, and I did not take her name when she took me; I remained Meta Moore.

Aunt must have found me a great worry when I was a baby. She always looked preoccupied, except when she was playing her pianoforte – then her face would light up and its usually anxious features relax. Perhaps she had been frightened that I would die when I was in swaddling clothes, but Martha had battled for me and I became quite healthy and reasonably strong, though subject to colds. 'Reared by hand you was,' Martha was fond of saying with pride in her voice. I wondered how other babies were reared till I saw Mrs Hirst the farmer's wife feed her own baby as a cow feeds a calf.

One morning after I had been out on my roof ramparts, I found Martha in one of her rushes. One pair of hands plus Ellen's were not enough and I was conscripted to the peeling of potatoes.

'Where've *you* bin, Miss Muddle?' she asked, turning round

13

from the big stone sink as I rushed into the kitchen. 'Ellen's bin callin' you – didn't you hear?'

'Yes – I came because I heard her. I was just thinking, upstairs,' I replied guiltily.

'Think about these taters then – I don't know, what with this school idea and all – what've we got to have *boarders* for?' grumbled Martha.

My absence was forgiven in the general atmosphere of hurry. I thought, perhaps no boarder would want to come and then we could all be cosy again but I didn't say this as it sounded selfish.

'Sharp now – you can have your dinner. There's a lass coming on Saturday to see about boarding. Your auntie's right churned up.'

'What's she called? Is she older than me?' I asked anxiously.

'Wait and see. Young Mr Rainer, your Dad's cousin – he recommended your auntie to her mother . . . Seems he might be letting yon Rooks Nest too!'

This was exciting news but it had happened before and nothing had come of it. Perhaps Papa had written to his cousin?

'Is Papa coming back?' I waited to ask when the potatoes had been peeled and I had helped to 'side' the cooking utensils.

'Nay,' said Martha briefly. 'Eat up now and we'll go for a walk this aft.'

That afternoon I persuaded Martha to walk down past Lightholme village and to continue on past the high wall of Rooks Nest which closed in the old Coach Road on one side. 'Does it still belong to Papa?' I asked as I skipped along. I had never thought to ask that question before. It had only just struck me that perhaps a house that had once belonged to you might be bought by someone else and that houses, unlike people, were not for ever.

'I don't reckon so,' replied Martha shortly, saving her breath for walking.

'Then – *who* then?' I pursued, struck with horror that the house might somehow have evaded me, slipped through my fingers. I stopped skipping. 'Papa – ' I began.

'Your Dad had other things to think about. I've an idea it's gone to his cousin.'

'You mean Cousin Rainer?'

'Nay – he's a *young* man, *son* of your father's cousin – though I

14

believe he minds your Dad's business for him. It's Ben Moore, Rainer's Dad. Your Dad was Old Moore's youngest grandson, see, and Ben was the eldest grandson. So Mr Rainer is your Dad's cousin's son.'

'Oh Martha – isn't it complicated? You are clever to know it all. I must write it down – that's what I'll do, so I'll remember. But Rooks Nest *was* Papa's wasn't it – it didn't use to belong to Mr Rainer's father?'

'No, lass, by rights it was your Dad's – came from your Mam – but it's a long story, not the sort of thing to bother your head over.'

Martha had grasped, I now believe, that my father had mortgaged the property to his cousin Ben and had set his son Rainer to manage it and my father's affairs. Of course I didn't understand all that then; I was concerned only with the feeling that Rooks Nest ought one day to be mine – even if it were a ruin!

We walked down by another farm on the left and round by Grassy Lane and Stoney Lane and then I said 'Please Martha, can we go back again by the Coach Road? Then I can have a good look over the wall. It's *so* beautiful when the trees are all orangey and yellow. Don't you think it's prettier in autumn even than in summer?' The beauty of the trees and the falling leaves always took my breath away and I wanted to share it with someone. It was the same with all my feelings – I could not keep them to myself, and the someone I usually shared them with at that time was Martha.

On our way back we turned into the old Coach Road. Martha usually let me have my way when we were out walking, though she grumbled a lot about her feet.

'Help me climb the wall, Martha – please!' I begged.

Martha sighed but hoiked me up and held on to my boots once I had scrambled to the top of the old high wall and could see over it at last. The rooks were cawing, going home, and the sky was pinky-grey. I stared and stared, trying to make out as much as I could through the trees – a chimney, a glitter of water, the curve of a sanded path.

'When can I visit it properly? Soon?' I asked as usual when I had had to get down from my vantage point, for Martha was now in a hurry to get back to the Hall.

'Perhaps when Mr Rainer comes back north,' she replied, as

she always did, and I had to be content with that for the time being. 'Or when you're grown up' she added.

'When you grow up' was a constant refrain in my ears. I imagined that time to be when I would step out into the big world, the world of newspapers and travel, Papa's world. I should become famous, though for what I had no idea. Perhaps I would become like Miss Lister of a neighbouring Hall who had travelled the world and written a diary and, they said, 'lived like a man'. Or like Papa who was in Germany from where he had sent me a picture of musicians. Or perhaps I would succeed Augusta when her school was famous, and everybody would send their daughters to sit at my feet. I would have them listen to my stories and my singing and my piano and take them out for walks on the moors and paint sunsets and I would be so good at it that the Queen would say 'Miss Moore, I entrust the Royal children to you.' Or, if not the Queen, then perhaps a duke or some nobleman.

It must have been the following Saturday that the girl of whom Martha had spoken, came on a visit with her mama to inspect Aunt's school. She did not in fact come to stay with us until six months later and by then other girls had arrived. But in my mind she was always the First Boarder. A Miss Barbara Stott she was, and that afternoon she and her mother were to take tea in the parlour.

The parlour was at the end of the house that looked into the 'stone garden', my name for the remains of a paved courtyard where horses could be tethered. Someone had once extended it with little low walls, enclosing turf. Harebells like those on the moor grew there and at the bottom of the slope there was a snicket leading to Cow Lane. The monkey puzzle tree was at the other end of the house outside the sitting room but the parlour was more private to my aunt. That afternoon I crept into it before the guests arrived.

The fire was glowing softly and the Turkey carpet matched it in colour and stretched itself out as though basking in its warmth. There were special shutters behind the mullions and two recesses at each side of the chimney-piece. Someone had tried to make the room look modern, with pictures and a low sofa and a round table but it still had an old-fashioned air. Aunt Juby had once told me the parlour was Jacobean, and the carv-

ings too, and also the big shiny wooden chair and one of the portraits, that of a woman with long curly black hair and big grey
eyes holding a peach cupped in her two hands like a globe. When
I was younger I had thought it was a portrait of Mama but of
course it was not.

I pressed my nose against the diamond panes and looked out
over the stone garden. The big carriages now came to the other
end of the house which really had no back or front. Farmers and
children went to the kitchen porch while those of higher degree
called at the front porch under the round rose window.

I closed the parlour door softly on its sneck and passed
through the schoolroom which was furnished plainly but neatly,
and the little room next to it where the family would eat and
where the girls were to have their suppers, and went through to
the only other room of any size on the ground floor, the sitting
room. About a hundred years before it had been stripped of its
oak panels and was now light and airy with big window-seats.
Some of the books had been moved to the schoolroom but I was
more interested in the books which had *not* been taken away. I
wondered whether the new girl, when she came, would like
reading.

I finished my walk round the house and, not wanting to go
back to the kitchen where Martha was busy, I went up to my
bedroom and washed my hands and face in the little bowl on the
dressing-table where the ewer stood with the clear well water. If
I stood on tiptoe I could see my face in the swing looking-glass
that stood there. The glass had once been Mama's and I liked to
imagine that one day when I looked into it Mama's face would
gaze back out at me. It was rather a frightening idea but I could
not let go of it. How often Mama's face must have looked out of
that mirror! I wondered if Mama, who they said was in Heaven,
could see me. But when I looked into the glass, all I saw was a
thin freckled face with dark grey eyes and cream-coloured
cheeks, surrounded by wavy brown hair. I blew out my cheeks
and patted them and wondered what impression I would make
on the boarders when they came.

'Mee-ta!' It was Ellen's voice. She shouted again, nearer now,
and I heard her stomping up the stairs. In she came, looking
harassed.

'Give me your hairbrush lass – you're to look clean and tidy
now, the missis says; 'ave you been practising your curtsey?'

'No, Ellen, I haven't. But I've washed my face.' She wielded the hairbrush as though it were a mop. 'Have I to curtsey to – to the girl?'

'Of course not – to her mam, when you're introduced. It's Mrs Stott, didn't Martha tell you? Married to him that owns the big new mill. What a carry-on – as though we haven't enough people in this house already!' She finished by yanking the brush through the tugs in my hair, spun me round, pulled at my sash, inspected my drawers to see they were not sliding down, spat on my shoes and cleaned them with the edge of her petticoat, and finally pronounced 'You'll do!'

When we arrived downstairs Ellen put her finger to her lips and tiptoed to the parlour door. I had not heard anyone come to the house – they must have left their carriage at the gate – but she said 'They're here,' and tossed her head, knocking rapidly on the door and depositing me inside the room in one impatient movement. 'Here y'are Mum!' she almost shouted. I saw that Aunt Juby was seated in her big chair and that a lady and a girl were perched on the sofa.

'Here's my – niece,' said Aunt, rather nervously. 'I think the children may be of an age, Mrs Stott.' I went up to the sofa, curtseyed to it and tried to smile at the lady, who was dressed in a bright green and purple costume. She inclined her head and I stood there, looking at her daughter out of the corners of my eyes.

'It will not be for some time then?' continued Augusta to the impassive Mrs Stott. 'Say next spring? We can easily accommodate Barbara then – or earlier if you wish. But of course if she is staying with your parents she may like to begin day-lessons sooner?'

The girl Barbara sat looking at the Turkey carpet. She still had her bonnet on and never once looked at me. The grown-ups went on talking and seemed to come to some arrangement.

'Meta, take Barbara and show her the schoolroom and the garden,' commanded my aunt. 'You may both come in for a cup of tea in about half an hour.'

The girl rose slowly and without a backward glance at her mother followed me out of the room. She was taller and plumper than me and I thought she must be older.

She followed me into the garden and I began: 'This is where I play and that's the apple tree,' but she interrupted me with:

18

'What's your name?'

'Meta.'

'What a peculiar name,' said the girl. She sounded like a grown-up lady. I wanted to like her, indeed I was determined to like her, so I replied: 'It's Margaret really – Meta's for short. Yours is Barbara, isn't it? That's a very *unusual* name. I like it.'

'How did you know my name?'

'I just heard it from my aunt.' (Augusta had in fact said previously: 'What a strange *Roman* name!')

Barbara sighed. 'Do you live here all the time?'

'Yes.'

'Where are your mama and papa then? Is that lady really your aunt?'

'My mama is dead,' I replied, with the coolness of long practice. 'And my papa lives abroad. Where is *your* papa?' I had only meant to be polite, thinking Barbara would be able to tell me her father was a rich man but she flushed and said: 'I don't know where he is at present. Mama and I have just come back from abroad.' This took me aback slightly.

Barbara seemed to have little more conversation so we went in to take tea soon after. I felt rather disappointed. Although I had not wanted to share my home with others I had been a little excited about meeting a new girl of my own age but Barbara had not seemed eager to make friends. Well, there was plenty of time, I thought. Some people improved upon acquaintance as Aunt was always saying.

That first meeting is etched on my mind and when I think of Barbara, I always see the child with the rather sullen, stubborn look and the dull eyes. She did not come to stay, as I have said, for another few months, but I did not forget her. I wondered later if her mama had taken her off abroad again.

In the meantime other girls had arrived, older girls whom I thought of as almost grown up. I still preferred to play with the Hirst boys from the farm or to sit reading by myself if I could not have a 'best friend', a girl, of my own age.

By the time I was nine there were seven pupils at our school and many more 'promised'. The first three were Viola, Frances and Matilda. One of the attics and a back bedroom had been swept and distempered and new beds bought for them. Aunt was always having workmen in at that time and I liked listening to them as they talked in their broad dialect, using words that I had never heard before, or only occasionally from Martha. *She* understood their language and enjoyed chivvying them and exchanging good-humoured jokes with them. The house always seemed to be full of workmen and girls. Aunt was so busy I hardly saw her except during lessons, and even Martha now had less time for me.

As the school began to be established I think Augusta realized she could not have me running round like a little hoyden, picking up dialect from the workmen and their children whom they sometimes brought with them. She felt she had neglected me a little, though it was all in a good cause and I myself was to inherit her school one day. So I was bought new pinafores and allowed to attend the little class of boarders and day girls of whom Barbara Stott was eventually a member.

After a few months with us, Barbara put on weight, grew her hair and seemed unapproachable. Viola and Matilda petted her as they had never petted me. 'Poor little girl', I heard them whispering together. 'Her mama's gone away and they say dreadful things about her.' But I could never find out what these dreadful things were, however much I eavesdropped. The other boarder, a cheerful fair-haired girl called Frances Green, was more to my liking. She was as untidy as me and groaned over the calico sewing, liked to read stories and swapped pressed flowers with me. After supper, which was normally about six o'clock, we would be allowed into the big sitting room to chat and read and play the piano and Frances would share her box of sweets with us. Her grandfather had built up a grocer's business in Bradford, which had expanded into other towns. Their speciality was sugar oranges and pears and peaches – sticky garish confections which I thought tasted like heaven. There was a little silver hammer to break them into mouth-size portions. Frances wore real silk dresses under her school apron and I would feast my eyes on the colours – mauve and green and rose-pink. Such dresses were rarely seen then, even in Halifax, our nearest town. Frances let me stroke the stuff of her sleeves as we sat by the fire and I took pleasure in our closeness and in Frances's beauty.

When Barbara had arrived at Hartsedge as a boarder, I had expected to befriend her and leave the older girls to their own studies. But Barbara was a difficult person with whom to have a conversation. Her favourite pastime was to sit with her doll Henrietta and commune wordlessly with her.

'Do you play houses with your doll and make up stories about them?' I once asked her.

Barbara lifted her heavy eyes and stared at me. 'No,' she replied.

'Well – what do you talk about to her, then?'

'I don't *talk* to her,' replied Barbara after a silence. 'She talks to *me*.'

'Well – I know – my dolls used to talk to me, but of course it's you really doing the talking isn't it?' I said.

'Henrietta tells me things. Papa gave her to me, so she talks about Papa.' This was the longest speech Barbara had so far made to me.

One day I heard from Martha that we were to have new teachers.

'We've got old Miss Shackleton and Aunt Juby and the Rev. Gurney for Divinity,' I said to Martha. 'Why do we need anyone else?'

'I hear your Auntie's getting a gentleman to teach pianny and she's advertising for French and globes.'

'But Aunt Juby's always taught French herself.'

'She's busy organizing and supervising,' replied Martha, using the two words my aunt was constantly reiterating.

The schoolroom was repainted during the year and a large new globe, three small tables and a big work-box for sewing purchased; several pictures had been hung, new shelves put up and new books were expected any day. I heard my aunt explaining to Miss Shackleton that the garden would 'do' for botanizing. The Reverend Gurney had been conscripted for 'Rithmetic, really that portion of mathematics beyond Miss Shackleton, and Martha herself was incorporated for plain sewing. All we needed now was a governess to teach French and perhaps other languages.

One morning nearly a year after I had first met Barbara in the parlour, I finally persuaded her to go for a walk round the bottom of the garden with me. Ellen was supposed to be 'supervising' both of us but was busy beating carpets.

We wandered over into the meadow on this lovely early autumn morning. The hedge of blackberries was beginning to ripen and the cows were still out in the next field, which belonged to Wynteredge Farm. We heard a muffled shouting from behind the hedge but paid no attention to it until Barbara said, 'Look – boys!'

'Oh, it's only the farm lads,' I said. 'Do you think the black-berries are ripe?'

A head poked itself over the gate next to the hedge.

'Hullo, Sam,' I said.

'Hullo, Meta. Who've you got with you then?'

'It's my friend Barbara,' I replied hoping the Lord would for-give me for a lie. I had been disappointed in Barbara and did not think of her as a friend but it would be more saintly to say she was.

Soon three boys had joined us.

'I'm going back,' said Barbara. 'They're dirty.'

I felt my cheeks go red with embarrassment.

'Aye – we're mucky,' said the eldest Hirst boy.

'Farmers have a lot of mud,' I said.

'Nowt wrong with mud,' said Sam. 'Who's Miss Maungy Face then?'

'Don't talk to me like that,' said Barbara. The boys seemed to have unlocked a flow of language.

'Go and play with your dolly,' said Sam Hirst.

Barbara turned tail and stalked off.

'I'm sorry,' I said, longing to stay and run around with the boys who often let me play with them.

'Eh – is it true her mam's a tart?' asked John Hirst.

'A what?' The boys began to shriek with laughter. 'How do *you* know anything about her?' I asked.

'A little bird,' said the eldest boy who was about thirteen, I suppose.

The boys seemed unkind that morning. 'Ask her what her mam does with her fancy man,' jeered John. I had never seen his face so bloated and cruel. They were rough boys but they had been my friends. I suppose I was too young then to grasp the import of their conversation. Sam, the nicest of them, was blushing and whispered 'Shurrup' to his brothers. 'Meta doesn't know what you're on about,' he said.

'She's only to look at t'bull and cow,' said one of his brothers brutally.

I felt myself tremble in a funny way. There *was* something queer about husbands and wives I knew, but what had it to do with bulls?

'We'll tell you one day,' said John. 'Or ask your friend Barb-ara.'

Just then I saw the tall form of Farmer Hirst striding across the field from the farm.

'Eh, up! There's Dad. Don't say owt, Meta. It were nothing.'

The boys scattered and I walked slowly back into the garden where I found Barbara hunched up on a stone seat.

'Why did you talk to those horrid boys? I wish I'd never come here. You're a dirty rude girl to talk to boys like that. I shall tell Papa to take me away.'

'Oh, please don't do that, Barbara.' What if Barbara had heard what they had said? Then the other girls' papas would take them away too and poor Aunt Juby's school would be ruined. But it wasn't wrong to talk to the Hirsts. They were not always rude and nasty. And there *was* something funny about Barbara.

Barbara must have said something to one of the older girls for Augusta called me into her parlour the next morning, her face long and frowning.

'Meta, I'm sorry I've had so little time with you recently but it'll all be easier soon,' she said as a preliminary. 'I wanted to tell you not to discuss her parents with Barbara. You'll understand when you are older. Barbara has had an unhappy life and I am determined to be charitable towards her. Matilda tells me that you took her to play with your friends over the hedge?'

'But, Aunt ... I often talk to them. It was because Barbara was rude to them that they were rude to her.'

'Never mind that, Meta. I want you now to promise me something. You know I shan't make a good school if people start gossiping. You're growing up now and I don't want you talking to the Hirsts any more. I know you mean well – and personally I have always wanted you to know that the world has many sorts of people in it. But I fear you have been a little neglected of late. I'm afraid ... children of the lower classes ... well they fight and use bad language, and you have to start to learn to be the sort of little lady your dear papa would wish you to be. You know, you do get rather dirty and untidy, my dear – and imitate the speech of the village people...'

'But Aunt, I don't imitate them – it's just that I like listening and learning words and...'

'Oh dear ... next thing we know you'll be fighting them. It's all got to stop. Did they say – anything – about Barbara?'

I knew that whatever else I blurted out I must keep quiet about bulls and cows. 'Oh they said Barbara's mama and papa did not . . . like each other . . . I think.'

'I see. Poor Barbara is the victim of circumstances. Do you understand, Meta – for all our sakes – we mustn't have you wandering round listening to low talk? In a few years you'll be a young lady and you'll want to know the right people and have a good reputation in the village . . . and then one day you may be able to travel and learn things we can't all learn here in Lightholme.'

I perked up at this. 'You mean abroad with Papa? Oh, Aunt Juby, has he written? When shall I see him?'

'I believe he is at present in France,' replied Augusta. 'But there may be a message from his cousin Rainer when he next visits . . . so, remember Meta, we're turning over a new leaf. Be kind to Barbara, no more rushing out into the fields – keep to the garden – ask Martha if you don't know what to do with yourself . . . you must be a credit to Martha, my dear, for she has mostly brought you up as I have every reason to know.'

'Aunt Juby, I'll try and do all you say. I'll be nice to Barbara. But promise me, promise me, you'll tell Papa to come back soon.'

'Of course I will, little one, but he has a lot of work abroad. We must always wait and hope. Now go and tidy yourself up and you may help Martha unpack some new books in the schoolroom.' The best thing about the new schoolroom was the large new collection of books. I wanted to read them all. I fled and spent a blissfully happy morning.

Martha, of course, had disliked Barbara from the start. She would not brook any sulks from her. 'What right has she to be such a sullen, stuck-up miss?' she said.

The excitement of the arrival of new pupils had not quite made up for me the shrinking time I could spend alone with Martha. If I had known the word I would have called it resentment – or even jealousy – that my home should have to be shared. But was it really my 'home', or just where I had been brought up? Wasn't Rooks Nest my *real* home?

When I was with Martha she insisted upon my doing plain sewing. 'Why should I learn to sew, Martha? I hate it,' I used to say over and over again when I pricked my finger or lost the thread from my needle for the thousandth time. 'What use is it

telling me to be patient? I shall never like it. I hate being neat.
Boys don't have to sew, do they?'

All this was put out of my head when one day in October a
letter came for Augusta from my father. In it was a little note for
me which I put under my pillow to hold every night before
going to sleep.

My dearest child,
You must forgive me for not having written to you for so
long. I am much occupied and cannot leave France for
England though I may have to go to La Suisse where there
are lots of lovely mountains. Be a good girl. I hear you are a
pupil at your aunt's. Work hard and don't forget your
loving papa.
P.S. Your second cousin, Rainer Moore, may call on your
aunt soon. He will bear my love to you.

Somehow, although the letter was precious, it was disappoint-
ing in a way I could not define. I was almost forgetting what
Papa looked like. It excited me to think he was there in France –
but if only he would take me with him! I imagined all the places
he might visit and made a special study of a map of France and
Switzerland and repeated the names of mountains as though
they were a spell to bring him back. Yet Papa seemed farther
away alive than Mama who was dead and buried in Scarborough.

The school seemed to be thriving even though no one had yet
come to teach 'proper' French, and the globes were still being
taught by Augusta. I enjoyed most of the lessons but was a little
disappointed that not all the new girls seemed to like me. I
wanted so much to be liked.

Months passed, months of rain and cold and then it was
another Christmas and most of the girls went home. Barbara
and two of the other boarders stayed, and even Barbara could
not dampen the magic of the season. Then, after Christmas,
which had included the procession of all the Hartsedge Hall
inhabitants, save Martha, to the tall square-towered elegant
church on the ridge, Aunt Juby announced that for a great treat
we were to be taken to the town in a carriage to see the new pantomime. 'Why didn't she tell us before – then I could have
enjoyed looking forward to it for a week or two?' I said to

Martha. 'Won't Mary and Julia and Louise and Jemima be envious! Just think, Martha, a pantomime!'

I was too excited; Martha feared the panto would be a disappointment, but then, *she* had never seen one. Chapel went in for sacred oratorios and discouraged its members from visiting the 'the-ater'. 'Don't build it up too much, love,' she warned me.

But she need not have worried. Everything lived up to and beyond my expectations, from the carriage ride in the afternoon with the skies already growing dark, to the theatre itself, recently refurbished in gilt and red with a dark crimson velvet curtain. And when the curtain lifted and *Cinderella* began, my joy was inexpressible. Not so much for the jokes, which were not really very funny, but for the actresses: the Fairy Queen in yards of white butter muslin and her magic wand tipped with a golden star; Cinderella, transformed after a touch of the same wand and an interval of darkness into a girl in a billowy pink crinoline glittering with silver; Dandini, the faithful messenger, in blue and silver, the actress's long dark hair swept up into a crown of curls. I knew the story of course, had always known it from the little book that had been Augusta's with 'translated from the French' after its title, and I had often played it myself in Martha's kitchen. The Prince though was a bit of a disappointment. He was a girl and the Ugly Sisters were men who didn't seem to bother pretending to be ladies at all.

But it was not the joking or even the glittering costumes which really stole my heart away, it was the music. In the little pit there was a pianist and two violinists and unaccountably a trumpet; from time to time everything would stop and Cinderella and Dandini and the Fairy Godmother – and even Cinders' father, the Baron – would sing sad songs. At least they seemed to me to be sad and I thought that they were looking especially at me as they sang them.

'It wasn't as good as the one I saw once in London,' remarked Barbara crushingly as we were borne home in Frances Green's father's carriage. I was still in spirit on the stage, seeing the spangles and the wand and hearing the songs. Barbara always seemed to want to spoil everything. There had been a moment when Buttons, played by a thin dark-haired young man, had sung a passionate song to the rag-clad Cinderella and it was Buttons of whom I was thinking when we turned into the Hall yard. After Cinderella's rags had been changed into her party dress no one

26

remembered Buttons any more, not even Cinderella. It was a shame: he had really loved Cinders, even when she was poor and in rags.

Buttons set me to thinking of Sam Hirst. Augusta had relented enough to offer one of the Hirst boys a job as a gardener and odd-job lad at the Hall, for we needed more help outside and Farmer Hirst's few acres did not need as much labour in winter when the ploughing was done and before the spring sowing. Sam had been sent over as garden boy for the time being and I told him about the pantomime. I thought about Cinderella and decided she was not really a heroine. She didn't *do* anything – just waited patiently for a fairy to change her life. I would rather have been a queen than a princess even though Cinderella had changed into something beautiful in her ball-dress. *She* was like a butterfly or a flower. But a Fairy Queen could give wishes to everyone and how nice that would be! When lessons began again I wrote about my Cinderella feelings but it was marked down by Miss Shackleton for being untidy. In the green book which Papa had sent me two birthdays ago, I wrote a long piece called 'Dream Queens' in which I allowed my imagination to roam. The dream queens all found their way to Rooks Nest where I imagined a great open air summer pageant by the lake. I clothed my dead mama too in the dress of the Fairy Queen and was half frightened, half proud of the gloriously sad feelings all these imaginings aroused in me. I hid the book.

The school went on growing and Martha told me that for the first time my aunt had ruled a black instead of a red line under her yearly accounts. But my father continued to be absent and I think it was at this time that I subconsciously gave up hope of ever seeing him again. Letters from him were few and far between, but on my twelfth birthday a remembrance card arrived for me, this time from an address in Switzerland.

One afternoon I was sitting alone in the empty barn with the black and white cat, Mewer, on my lap. I was feeling lonely but thinking with half of my mind of schoolwork and the hated embroidery which awaited me indoors and which I had run to the barn to escape from. Only the day before, Aunt Juby had warned me quite kindly of the dangers of story-telling. I had become a favourite at bed-time with the other girls for I 'embroidered' upon stories I had read, or made up, and got the others so excited they could not sleep.

'Why not read some Bible stories or some of the Greek myths – they're in the schoolroom. All these tales of ghosts and dead ladies frighten your friends,' she said to me. I am not surprised now, when I look back on my twelve-year-old self, that I was involved with stories of dead ladies who resurrected themselves at the touch of a wand.

'I'm sorry, Aunt,' I said. I knew it was an easy way to popularity and even Barbara would listen to me, staring fixedly with a strange expression on her usually secretive face. I should just have to keep my imagination to myself, in my green book, I decided.

'Miss Meta! Miss Meta!' It was Martha's voice. 'You're to come in!'

I brushed off the pieces of straw that had stuck to both me and Mewer, and the cat leapt off my lap and melted away to pursue her private life. I went cheerfully enough into the kitchen. I ought really to have been with the others on their visit to Halifax, for it was Saturday afternoon, but I was saving my money to buy *Jane Eyre,* which Matilda's elder sister had raved about on a visit to us.

Martha met me. 'It's Mr Rainer – at last – on a visit to your auntie. He's in the parlour.'

'Oh Martha – he hasn't brought . . . P-Papa?'

'No, lass, but he may have news of him. Let me straighten your collar, smooth down your hair. There now – go along then.'

I paused before the parlour door for a moment. This Cousin Rainer had been promised for so long. Perhaps he had bad news? For another moment I bent my ear to the door and heard: '. . . she puzzles me a little . . . so like her papa . . . scatterbrained.' Oh dear. I drew a deep breath, knocked, waited a moment, lifted the latch and stepped into the long, low room. With his back to the glowing fire stood a slim fair-haired man. Aunt Augusta was in her rocking chair and they were intent upon their conversation. For a split second I wondered whether in spite of all, the stranger *was* my papa – but no, of course not. This man was not as old as Papa. He must be approaching thirty, a grown-up – though curiously young-looking.

The man moved forward, let his coat-tails drop, and advanced to shake hands. I felt my face tense with eagerness and interest.

'This is Meta,' said Augusta flatly, not getting up. 'And this is your papa's cousin, Mr Rainer Moore.'

I devoured his face as though his being Papa's cousin would bring me closer to the idea of Papa.

He smiled. 'I'm sorry it's been so long,' he said in a friendly way.

I did not know what to say. 'Do I look like my papa?' I ventured after a silence during which the young man had been looking at me earnestly. 'When did you see Papa?' I went on, not waiting for his reply.

'Meta, don't overwhelm your cousin. Let him sit down and I'll have some tea sent in and then you can have a chat.' Augusta rose to see to this and the fair man and I were left, each in a high-backed chair on either side of the fireplace. The smell of a cigar was still in the air of the room and I sniffed it with pleasure, one of my favourite smells and not often found at the Hall.

'So this is the undisciplined daughter of Jonas,' he said. 'Still a little girl and certainly with a look of him.' I stared at him, half pleased at what he had said.

'I saw your papa a few months ago – he sent his love. He's sorry he can't come back to England but certain matters have delayed his return.'

'Money?' I asked, trying to sound adult.

Cousin Rainer looked at me. 'Partly – to do with business. It's better for him to be abroad.'

'Is he well?'

'I believe so.' Rainer hesitated. I suppose he was wondering how much you could tell a twelve-year-old of debts, mistresses, penury, projects, hopes nurtured and abandoned. But I knew none of this then and was thinking only of my papa's health.

'Tell me about yourself and then I can tell him . . . next time I'm on the Continent myself.'

I decided to plunge. 'I expect you have been told I am too imaginative?'

His face broke into a smile. 'I hear you love music, reading, painting and that you are doing well and keeping your end up with your aunt's pupils,' he replied.

I was surprised and pleased. 'I have piano lessons and drawing lessons but I'm not any good really. I hate sewing . . . but I do read a lot. Do you?'

'Why yes! Have you read any Carlyle?' He must have decided to treat me as though I were grown up. I had never heard of Carlyle.

'N-no . . . there's such a lot to read isn't there? I am so ignorant. I want to learn proper French, but Aunt Juby – Aunt Augusta, hasn't been able to find a teacher for us.'

'You should learn German too,' said this unusual man.

'Oh – and Latin, and Greek. If I were a boy the rector would have started me . . . but they always say it's not for girls.'

'Learning languages needs a deal of discipline,' he countered. 'But now you've made me talk like a schoolmaster myself.'

'Are you a schoolmaster?'

'Why, no, I was at Oxford. As a matter of fact I was going to be a clergyman – but I didn't!'

'Are you a businessman, like Papa?'

'No, Meta, not really. I do a *bit* of business and I write – and I report for a financial journal when I'm abroad. I am a hopeless case of indiscipline myself.' We both laughed.

'I may put your aunt in the way of a teacher of languages for you all. A friend of mine knows a lady from Ireland who may come to live in Yorkshire after living abroad and I believe she is looking for a situation. Then you could learn your French – and German too.'

'Oh that would be wonderful. You see Aunt says I shall have to be able to earn some money – if I don't get married – and I know she wants me to have her school one day. I don't want to be a governess, not because it isn't ladylike but because it sounds so dreary. What I want to do is go abroad and have adventures,' I said without guile, thinking only of finding Papa and staying with him.

'Do you really like learning?' he asked me.

'Oh, yes, of course – but I don't like being a girl. I want to travel and find out about things . . . and write about them.' I felt I could say anything to this Rainer Moore. He didn't laugh at me, or tell me not to be so 'enthusiastic'.

'You might make a good teacher,' he said, a little deflatingly.

'That's what my aunt thinks. So long as I don't have to teach Berlin work or gros-point.'

'Tell me,' he said, changing the subject, 'do you go for many rambles around here? I've just finished reading a book about local legends – there's a lot of interest in the old stones on the moors at the moment.'

'I love the moors,' I replied. 'I'm glad I'm called Moore! I could walk for ever up there, but we never get further usually than Sun Woods, or down beyond Slead Syke on the other side. And Aunt Augusta hasn't afforded a carriage of her own for a long time, or we could have started from up top and walked over the real country. But my favourite walk is to Rooks Nest. I used to go and look at it with Martha when I was little,' I went on. 'But of course – you have it now, don't you? Are you going to live there?'

'We only lease it from your papa,' he replied, not quite truthfully. 'I was not living in Yorkshire when your papa left and my father put in caretakers – it must be nearly ten years ago, now. But I have hopes – who knows – we might let it to someone!' I realized that he did not like to explain that my father had no more claims upon it.

Aunt returned to the parlour just as I was thinking what to say next.

'I hope Meta hasn't been tiring you out with questions? She often doesn't know when to stop,' she said. She paused, perhaps thinking she had sounded too critical of me, for she laid her hand gently on my shoulder, something she did not do very often.

'Not at all, Augusta. We were having a most interesting conversation. I have mentioned some of my plans – but I'm sure Meta can be very discreet when she wants.' His light blue eyes were upon me with the hint of a smile.

'Oh, Meta can be very discreet,' replied Augusta, and just then Martha came in with a tray stacked high with plates of buttered tea-cakes and scones, a teapot, cups, saucers and milk. She gave me a look which said 'I hope you're doing me credit, lass.'

'What wonderful skies you have here,' said my cousin politely when he had applied himself to Martha's cooking with gusto.

He looked out of the window and I felt a little cheated. I could not carry on a 'grown-up' conversation with my aunt in the room. The talk turned to wool merchants and the state of trade and some mutual friends. But I answered him when they stopped talking.

'I love the sky,' I said. 'It's best in autumn and winter. Do you know about the stars and all their names? Are you going to stay at Hartsedge? – then you could walk on the moors and they say there are grand views from the top ... that ... you might paint. I wish *I* could.'

'I can see we shall have to add astronomy to our syllabus,' said Augusta drily.

'You could have a competition to paint the landscape,' I was beginning . . .

But Augusta stemmed my enthusiastic ideas with 'Mr Moore and I have a few things to discuss after tea, Meta. Perhaps when you've finished you'd like to go round to the front and look at your cousin's carriage.'

Shortly afterwards Rainer departed, not without a warm handshake and a smile. I was left with a lot to think about. A new teacher! What would she be like? When would she come?

I did not see Cousin Rainer again for many months and I was thirteen when my aunt explained to me that it was unlikely Papa would ever return to England to live. There was also a hitch in the plans for appointing the languages lady so I consoled myself with reading my new discoveries, Shelley and Byron and Keats, and listening to our music teacher, Mr Robertson, playing the piano. He was an ardent lover of Mendelssohn and if he had had a face and figure to match his music, who knows but that I would have made a romantic hero of him. But he was middle-aged, short and stumpy, and no fit object for Imagination.

I felt a need for something to happen, for someone to love. Hartsedge Hall was too familiar, too bound up with the childhood I was leaving behind. Yet before I was fourteen something did happen – I ventured alone over the high wall of Rooks Nest and discovered the reality of my magical landscape.

Two

LAVINIA LOGAN

I suppose I had a healthy sort of upbringing. Since we had to be careful about money we still did not keep our own carriage, so we walked a good deal. Sam Hirst would take my aunt out in the gig if necessary. We kept a pony for that purpose and on Sundays I would sometimes accompany Aunt to Sholey Church in my best bonnet and gloves. I disliked having to pay attention to my dress. I was an untidy girl and my ribbons were always being lost and my stockings coming down. I was a trial to Martha, I believe, who still saw to my dress and had enough to do without that. Sometimes I would try to make amends by offering to relieve the parlour maid, Ellen, of the dusting. Dust seemed to collect like fine grain on our old furniture and I could never understand where it came from. Fortunately our old tables and chairs were of simple design and did not have the twirls and over-elaborate flutings of what was fashionable and up-to-date, but even so there was a lot of cleaning and polishing necessary in the house, apart from the blackleading and the scouring that went on in the kitchen. I was so glad that I was not a servant! But we gave work to women who did not want to go into the mills and I know that Aunt Juby was a good employer. They left us only if they married.

As I grew older, I often talked about marriage to Martha who was a realist in these matters and did not seem to regret that her life had not led her to a husband. The girls too talked a good deal about marriage at night when they and I were tucked up in bed or when we sat round the fire in the sitting room for a treat. Most of them seemed to think of marriage as the only possible end for a woman. I could not agree and felt a sense of rebelliousness about it. Unless we married very rich men we would spend our lives looking after houses and other people and having babies and would never have time to read and enjoy life. I could not see why any woman would want to get married and was scornful of the whole business. 'If only I were a boy,' I would think, 'what things I would do and be!' But I told myself sternly that I must prove myself to be 'as good as a boy'. I was sure my knowledge was equal to any boy's but I was not a good tree-climber nor adept at the 'dares' the Hirst boys had used to undertake. Still, if I were a boy I would probably have been sent away to school. I liked being at Hartsedge, so I resolved to make the best of it. I would be a famous unmarried lady, I decided, for after all my poor mama would probably still have been alive if *she* had remained unmarried. Aunt Juby did not seem to look back on her own marriage with any pleasure – indeed she never mentioned it. I thought women were slaves for the most part, and I wanted to be free – but I still dreamed of some soulmate with whom I might end my days; some man, even, with whom I might live in perfect harmony – or escape abroad with. This person might perhaps be a little like my idea of Papa. He would be amazed at my learning and my accomplishments and we should sail on into a romantic sunset united in our aspirations. But he was, as yet, a chimera and I did not think I would ever find him – some mixture of Robin Hood and Lord Nelson and Byron was to my taste and to have this hero love me was clearly unlikely.

I think I grew up slowly. It was not the case that one day I was a child and woke the next morning to adolescence; instead, I mingled childish pastimes and childish reading with more adult occupations, from one year to the next. I went out sketching with Julia, our Jewish boarder, and we would walk together over to the little valley which opened out on the one hand to broad meadows and on the other rose to hills and moors.

There was another old Hall in the valley, grander than ours, with Tudor beams and a latterly added tower. We would attempt to portray it in our sketch books – badly in my case, beautifully caught on the other hand by Julia. Sometimes groups of us would go for walks in the woods gathering wild flowers and collecting leaves and on these walks we would be accompanied by Miss Shackleton. When the weather was bad and we were confined to the Hall, I occupied much of my time trying to perfect my piano-playing under Mr Robertson's guidance, but the result always filled me with despair. Here again Julia shone, though she could not sing. For that we had Matilda who had a pure sweet voice and I used to wonder how such heavenly tones arose from such a prosaic girl.

On Saturdays my aunt would accompany some of the girls in a hired carriage to the town to shop but I hated these expeditions, except the one to the market which was held in an old stone court near the Piece Hall where the weavers still brought a few 'pieces' to sell. But most of the weaving was now done, in the mills and the town resounded to the sound of the clogs of the women and girls when they came out of the mills. We would be hurried back before dusk, for the town was ill-lit, and I was always glad to get back to Hartsedge and to the peace of the village and the surrounding hills with their farms standing etched against the sunset sky like distant magic paintings. I could sometimes escape to walk alone in the village. Most people knew me there and were friendly, and I felt the village was a safe place — unchanging and simple and tough.

Now that my childhood proper had ended, Rooks Nest might have stopped exerting its pull over me, but instead, it had seemed to come into focus. It was a real place and I might go there.

One Saturday in late spring I decided that I would climb over the wall into the parkland and gardens of Rooks Nest, notwithstanding a 'Trespassers Will Be Prosecuted' notice. Once my decision had been made it had not taken me long to walk to the point where Martha and I had often stopped when I was a little girl. This time I scaled the wall, with some scraping of my stockinged shins, and jumped down into the unkempt grass of the other side. Why I had not done it before I am not sure, except that for the whole of my childhood the place had seemed both near and far, real and yet part of a dream. Perhaps with one part of my mind I had felt that Mama might be waiting for me there but had feared to test my irrational conviction in case she were not.

I got to my feet and looked around. The thick elms and beeches hid the house from my view and I ran down the grassy slope and on to an overgrown path that wound through the trees. Soon the path came out into the open and skirted a field that lay long and sloping upwards on my right. I stopped for a moment. On my left the grass grew high and I imagined that no one had been there since Mama and Papa's time. Then I breasted the waving green stalks and found that my feet led me to a piece of cropped ground and suddenly there was the lake, its waters gently swept by a hovering breeze and with trees skirting its farther shore. I looked across it and saw a little wooded island. There was an old rowing boat pulled up on the bank. It didn't look as though anyone had used it to row across to the island for years.

I sat down on the bank and there was utter silence. Then a moorhen started up and then another and they floated off towards the island. I looked towards the other end of the lake and in the distance there seemed to be a stone rock under some willow trees veiled at a distance in the pale yellowy green of late spring. That must be the grotto. I got up and walked in that direction and soon saw the sweep of lawns. I left the side of the lake and climbed their slope, when suddenly the house appeared on my right and only a few hundred yards away. I shivered involuntarily. There was my birthplace waiting for me to renew its acquaintance. All these years it had been waiting and I stared at it, trying to feel that I knew it, but I did not. It was even larger than I had imagined, much larger than the Hall and built of one central block with two curving wings of a lesser height. Built of grey stone it was, and there was a paved terrace running the length of the ground-floor rooms with empty urns placed at intervals on the flags. As I drew nearer I saw conservatories at the far end in front of one wing, and more great lawns on the other side.

I came up to the terrace and passed a statue, grey and rain-pocked. On its plinth was carved the one word HOPE. There was still that utter silence as I came round the side of the conservatory by a great mass of lilac bushes. I stopped then and pulled down a swag and sniffed the blossoms. They were like turrets among the emerald leaves. The various bushes bore every colour of that gorgeous plant – pale mauve, dark purple-pink, bluey-purple and white. Then I saw in the middle distance a little pointed summerhouse and more statues. The grass around the little pagoda-like house was rather overgrown but it looked as though someone had made attempts to mow it now and again. As I walked, my feet stumbled against a stone and I looked down and saw there was a grave. The stone bore the name PUCK with a date twenty years before. I realized, almost knew, that it was the grave of a dog. Was it Papa's or Mama's family who had lived here then? What opulence! – having carved gravestones for your dogs! I looked back again to the house and saw that there were shutters on nearly all of the windows.

Then I remembered the caretakers and hoped that no one had seen me. Everything seemed to speak to me of a past that had nearly been mine. Oh why could Papa not come back and reclaim his lost realm?

I went round to the back of the house. It was vast. I counted twenty-six windows on the ground floor in addition to those of the kitchen. Why should they have built such an enormous place? The conservatories had some of their windows cracked but there were plant-pots with black earth still standing on ledges and the hot damp smell of a growing place. They must once have housed regiments of tomatoes and climbing towers of vines. I wondered what flowers had been grown there, for I loved flowers.

I was idly tracing my name in the dust of one of the panes when I heard a slight sound like an intake of breath. I looked up and there was a woman standing there, a woman in a dress of green silk. For one wild moment I thought it was Mama come back as a ghost – or that I had gone back to the old days myself in some slip of time. I stared at her and she stared back and then she said in a very unghost-like voice with an accent which at first I could not place: 'Who are *you,* and why are you here?'

I thought, Well, I can ask *you* the same question, but Martha's training won and I said: 'I am so sorry – I came for a walk. My mother used to live here.' She continued to look at me with some suspicion. I must have given her a bad shock. 'My name is Meta Moore,' I said.

'Oh, then . . . but why are you here alone?'

'I came for a walk,' I said again. 'I'm sorry – do you live here then?' For the first time I realized that I was really trespassing and that I had no right to be there. I should have asked Cousin Rainer.

'Come in and meet my mother,' she said, not asking me for further explanations until we were inside the house.

At the other end of the frontage there was a sort of Pavilion on the ground floor with long windows and we went in through a green door and down a long corridor where another door opened into a large room.

'Mother, this is a child I found wandering – she says she's a Moore,' said the green-gowned lady to a smooth-faced woman in her mid-sixties who was sitting in a big chair by an iron grate where a small fire was burning. The room was painted white and gold but the gold had tarnished and there was a closed-in smell to the room.

'I am sorry, ma'am,' I said again. 'I was walking near the lake. I didn't know anyone lived here.'

'We are Mr Moore's tenants,' said the younger lady and I realized she was referring to Cousin Rainer. 'If you are who you say you are you will know him.'

'You mean my cousin Rainer?'

She seemed satisfied, but I was a little ill at ease. They seemed quite well disposed towards me, but I felt an undercurrent of interest from the younger lady almost as though my arrival were not *quite* unexpected.

'This is my mother, Mrs Logan,' she said and I bobbed a curtsey in my best manner.

'You will stay for a cup of tea, my dear?' said the older lady then, and she tinkled a little bell by her side. 'I'm afraid I can't get up very easily,' she said, 'but my daughter will do the honours.'

'Oh, but I must not put you to any trouble, ma'am,' I said. 'I was not going to stay long – I just wanted to look at the house.'

'You've never been here before then?' asked Miss Logan.

I explained that the house had been shut up for a long time, that I had been born here. We were having a conversation of sorts when a stumpy-looking maid arrived with a tea-tray and a plate of thick bread and butter. I was trying to place their accents, when Miss Logan said, 'Take a cup to my mother, will you!' I realized suddenly that she was Irish.

'We only live in this little end of the house, dear,' said Mrs Logan as we sipped the cups of pale liquid. 'You are the South Pavilion's first visitor,' said Miss Logan and under cover of my teacup I took a good look at her. It seems strange to me now that I did not have any special feeling about her then. I suppose I thought I would never see them again.

Miss Logan was of medium height with dark brown hair which she wore piled high in a sort of coronet. She had dark brown eyes, an aquiline nose and rather pale skin. I thought she had a beautiful mouth – the lips were not full but seemed sculpted. She was wearing long jet earrings and when she drank her tea she crooked her little finger round the cup and I saw a ring with a green stone. I decided to apologize for my trespass once more.

'I did not know there was anyone here apart from a caretaker,' I said. 'I'm very sorry if I startled you. I ought to be getting back now. My aunt begins to fret if I am out too long.'

'I'm afraid we have no carriage,' said the older lady, 'so we cannot have you driven back.' Her pale blue eyes were constantly on her daughter. Miss Logan was sitting now like an oriental Buddha, her back straight against a big oak chair. She seemed sad. I made movements preparatory to leaving. 'Lavinia will see you out, my dear,' said Mrs Logan. 'You must come again one day,' she added.

As Miss Logan and I went back through the door of the 'pavilion' I was wishing in my heart that no one was living at Rooks Nest.

'You will find it easier to walk down the *carriage* road,' said Miss Logan, pointing to the sweep of a sandy lane which went underneath the old Coach Road on its parapet. She had obviously realized that I had climbed over the wall not knowing there was quite a simple way into Rooks Nest. 'Goodbye – I am sure we shall meet again,' she said, and I was off, wishing I could have another look at the lake.

'I should love to come again,' I called. I hoped she did not realize that I meant I wanted to see the house rather than its tenants. I walked down the sandy drive which led me to an ordinary-looking lodge, half-way down the Turnpike Road, which I had never even noticed before.

I don't know why I said nothing to Martha or my aunt about my adventure when I got back. Perhaps I was just growing up and wanted to keep the incident to myself, or perhaps I felt they would scold me. For whatever reason, when a few weeks later there arrived our new teacher of French and German I managed to hide my amazement from the others. I had of course met her before.

If my aunt and cousin had taken me a little more into their confidence I should have known that Rainer had found a tenant and a teacher all in one, though it had taken some while. When we came down to the schoolroom on that Monday morning in July just before the school finished for the summer, Aunt announced the arrival of an accomplished lady who would instruct us in our French and German conversation. This lady, said my aunt, had had many connections with 'abroad' and was an accomplished linguist and traveller. Then she went out and returned with the new teacher. It was of course Miss Logan and the tiny smile at the corner of her mouth told me that she recognized me and I knew also that she had said nothing of my rambles.

We were all introduced. 'And this is my niece,' said Aunt

Juby. 'Perhaps you would like a chat with the girls before you give them some holiday tasks? I am afraid we are sadly deficient in our knowledge of the European languages. However,' she said, turning to us girls, 'Miss Logan will, I am sure, remedy this deficiency.' She smiled and went out and we all tried to look knowledgeable and interested. I wondered whether Miss Logan had ever taught before and whether she had to work because they were poor. There had been no mention of a Mr Logan, so I assumed he was dead. I wished Rainer and my aunt had told me a little more, but obviously Aunt thought, no doubt wisely, that it was better for me not to know any more than my fellow pupils about the ins and outs of the school's affairs – just as I was not acquainted with my father's affairs and such things as tenancies and mortgages and debts.

We did not have time for many lessons before the summer break began but enough for me to know that the learning of foreign languages was going to be a delight to me. It was not easy of course and many of the girls found the effort not worth the result, but for me French and German represented Papa and a different sort of life. Foreign words gave wings to my imagination and Miss Logan knew plenty of them.

My cousin Rainer had been glad to install the Logans in a wing of Rooks Nest. Miss Logan was to return there daily in a governess cart driven by Sam Hirst, as her widowed mother could not spare her to live at the school. I had not seen Rainer much since the previous year when he had advised the reading of Carlyle, and thought he too must be in that mysterious 'abroad'. I still looked forward to asking him to explain Carlyle to me.

Barbara was odd about our new teacher. One early autumn day she had come out to join me in the stone garden. I had gone there to be by myself and was a little annoyed that she had disturbed my solitude. Barbara had a passion for knitting and her needles were busy even now as she spoke. She had been taken away to Buxton for a few weeks by her grandparents and had returned somewhat less impassive than usual.

'Do you like Miss Logan?' she began, clacking away with her needles as though she were about eighty.

'She seems sad somehow,' I replied without thinking.

'Do you think she has a gentleman friend?' pursued Barbara.

'Why – no! Has she?' Barbara's mother was the only person I

knew who had a gentleman friend, but we were not supposed to know about that.

'If your papa came back, he could marry her and then you could all go back to that house you're always going on about,' went on Barbara.

'Why – I live *here*, Barbara,' I said, startled. 'Papa lives abroad. How could he marry her? He was married to Mama – and anyway he doesn't know her.'

'I expect she would like to marry. She could marry your cousin, I suppose,' Barbara went on in a strange voice. 'I hear her mama is very ill. It's a pity Miss Logan has to work, isn't it? When I'm grown up I shall not work, I shall be a lady with all the money Papa is going to leave me.'

'I think it must be very good to earn your living,' I said sternly. What serious planning went on behind those round pebble eyes of Barbara's . . .

That term, the first full term of Lavinia Logan's teaching career at Hartsedge, started just after my fourteenth birthday. I was hoping that I would hear from Papa on that day and had promised myself in a superstitious way that if I worked as hard as possible I should be rewarded with a letter from him. I also hoped to impress Miss Logan. In her black silk pelisse and green dress, Miss Lavinia Logan impressed the inhabitants of Hartsedge and its village of Lightholme, though they were suspicious of 'foreigners' in general and Lavinia was undoubtedly one of those. The older girls at the Hall – Viola and Matilda and the irrepressible Frances – discussed her toilette, her hair, and her waist measurements in tones of fervent adulation. Yet I do not think she was a conventional beauty and I suspect the girls thought they themselves would be even more beautiful one day, for I detected a certain pity mingled with their admiration of her coolness, her dress sense, her faint cologne ('Kölnisches Wasser, Frances'), and her undoubted travels, she and her mother having followed the late Mr Logan in his business ventures abroad. For she had never married – and this was a matter for pity. I thought she belonged to somewhere a little more exotic than Belfast, which she assured us was her undoubted birthplace. She spoke of Baden Baden and Spa and Paris as though they were awaiting her return. Perhaps they were? I thought of her principally as the person lucky enough to be living at my beloved Rooks Nest. Until a certain winter's day in Christmas week. We were dressing the Christmas tree, for we were to give a little concert of Christmas songs around it for parents of girls at the school and some of my aunt's friends. That same day I saw my Cousin Rainer again.

Jemima was describing York Minster to us as we threaded the green and silver and gold baubles and hung them on the pine branches. I had been out gathering holly from the field near the garden. Sam Hirst, now a lad of sixteen, had helped me. As we were cutting the prickly holly and twining ivy from the house wall around it, his brother, who was bringing in some eggs from the farm, shouted: 'Haven't thee got any mistletoe, Sam? Shall I bring thee some?' He laughed raucously, like a braying donkey I thought. Sam blushed and bent over the ivy.

'Perhaps we should have some mistletoe?' I suggested.

'Aye, happen – but it's all lasses in't hall,' he said in a muffled voice. Light suddenly dawned. Mistletoe was for kissing under. Some ancient fertility rite, I thought, thinking of something I'd read in one of my father's books. I looked rather haughtily at him, not connecting John Hirst's suggestion with myself.

When I returned to the schoolroom, Jemima was still describing the Minster. She made me want to go there. Sholey Church on its ridge was an elegant tiny church but too familiar, and I longed to enter a high arching cathedral filled with honey-coloured light. Miss Logan was standing at the fire pretending to direct operations but with an air of ennui.

'I prefer Cologne Cathedral,' she said.

'Oh, Miss Logan, do tell us – when did you go?'

'Is it a Protestant Cathedral?' someone else asked rather maliciously.

Lavinia Logan described the German Christmas ceremonies as we went on with our tree-decorating. Her Irish accent was always emphasized when she spoke at any length. She told us about the biscuits iced into star-shapes, the Christ child in his crib, the pointed Gothic houses and the cobbled streets.

'You must teach us a German song. Oh please do,' clamoured Louisa, and Jemima took it up.

'I can't sing. Maybe I'll give you the words and Miss Jewesbury can look up the music.'

Thus it was that in the gathering dusk in the glow of the schoolroom fire with the candles experimentally lit on the tree and the scent of pine needles and burning wax, Lavinia Logan dictated to us the words of *Stille Nacht*.

The excitement of Christmas was upon us all but I do not think it accounted for the sudden feeling I had when I looked up at her and found her looking at me and yet, somehow, beyond me. It suddenly seemed as though I was now focusing on her for the first time, in the same way as Rooks Nest had suddenly become 'real' to me the first time I met her. Then she turned her profile to the window and I thought: 'I will make her look at me again.' She was sad. She was a mystery. She was exciting. She was suddenly the embodiment of my dreams – I don't know why – who knows why things happen? I only know that the idea of her entered into my heart and soul and made the next two years of my adolescence – so ordinary on the surface – extraordinary and ecstatic, and tortured. I realized that I had met no one like her before. It was not just the external appearance of my teacher – it was as though her presence revealed things to me of which I had formerly been unaware, and tuned up my feelings.

Later that evening I felt wrapped in a cloud, floating above the daily doings of the Hall. I hardly registered that my aunt was talking to someone in the entrance passage as I dreamily wrote out once more the words of the carol. Some of the other girls were also doing their tasks for the morrow. The schoolroom candles had been lit and Lavinia was long gone. I was thinking of going up to bed to savour the strangeness of my feelings when Martha came in and said Mr Rainer would just like to shake my hand. He had come on business and Augusta had invited him for a glass of Madeira in her study. Even the arrival of my pleasantly astringent cousin was hardly able to rouse me from my cocoon but I went along and was rewarded with his mentioning, in an elaborately casual tone, that Miss and Mrs Logan had both made my acquaintance. Oh dear, I should have to explain my walk to Augusta! But fortunately Aunt seemed too preoccupied to notice and I quickly turned the conversation to my new passion for French.

'Oh yes, our Miss Logan is a most accomplished woman,' he said. 'I am glad you are learning under her guidance.'

'Oh, she is wonderful!' I said, and my aunt looked up, a little surprised. I wanted to say how beautiful I thought her but it was not the place or the time, though I could think of no one but my cousin Rainer who might understand my new feelings.

The next day we gave our concert and managed to sing *Stille Nacht* quite tolerably. Aunt played the piano and Matilda sang something from Mendelssohn's Elijah. All I did was watch Miss Logan, who did not sing.

Rainer clapped long and loud and smiled at me, and I realized that I had not asked him about Papa.

I missed not having lessons that Christmas holiday and once took the excuse of visiting Martha's mother in order to gaze over to Rooks Nest. I would have to wait for an invitation to go there again, I knew. It was strange to think that *she* was there in *my* Rooks Nest; as though the present and the past had collided. I yearned for a sight of her, for I was already constructing fantastic futures about her as well as a fantastic past. On the other hand I should have liked to wander in the grounds and stand by the lake alone, the better to savour my feelings without her actual presence. It was puzzling. The contrast was brought home to me sharply later during that holiday when I was reading some of Papa's old books. I had already discovered Byron and for many months afterwards – when I had committed his lyrics to memory – I would think of Miss Logan as the object of his beautiful love-songs. When I read : 'She walks in beauty like the night', it was of her I thought and would see her wandering by the lake or leaning sorrowfully over a garden urn. And when Shelley had entered my firmament in a book I found hidden under the others with Papa's name on the flyleaf, I would obscurely feel that his 'desire of the moth for a star' was what I felt myself. These poets had the effect of deepening my love; it seemed that they had written especially for me. I was delighted and amazed. The other girls liked some of the Byron I used to declaim. I think Matilda and Frances saw Byron as writing about *them,* whereas now I imagined I *was* Byron!

Miss Logan did not herself read much poetry. I sounded her out on her reading many times when she taught a small group of us who had decided to continue with learning German. I remember the others teased me about my poetry. In the end, I stopped trying to convey how the 'visionary gleam' meant for me the memories thrown up by my private magic lantern : the baubles on the Christmas tree from long ago ; another snowy Christmas I remembered ; the smell of the leaves burning behind the old wall of the orchard – and even my collections of bookmarkers and dolls' furniture and leaves, abandoned now. They had all held some magic for me. Some German poems worked upon me in the same way and made me write my own verses. I did not show them to anyone.

One day during the spring after my first feelings for her had made themselves known to me, she said: 'We shall learn the *Lorelei*, girls.' Matilda was given the tune and I had to read the words. Miss Logan told us to take down the translation. As I looked up, being the first to finish, I found her looking at me. Was she the mermaid combing her glistening hair, luring me to death on hidden rocks and reefs? Where could we go on these wings of song?

'I do not know why I am so sad,' she repeated, in German, and I thought she was speaking the truth. I was quite happy to invent a passionate lost life for her in that Europe which she seemed to miss so much.

Mr Robertson, our music master, found me highly receptive to what he called European music, chiefly the work of Liszt. But I despaired of ever playing it and would ask him to play to us. Aunt did not mind so long as our minds were being improved. Liszt's 'Dreams of Love' were mine. I luxuriated in them. They seemed to express even more than could any words, the feelings I had about Lavinia. A little of the same strand of emotion was attached to my reveries over Papa's postcards of Garda and Baden, of the Finstaërrhorn in the rosy light of dawn. It made me shiver. Somehow all the exciting things seemed to come from abroad. Perhaps there was a gap between excitement and truth? Then I would feel disloyal to my old loves and long to stride off on the moor. Perhaps my dreams were not only the heady intoxicated raptures over the mystery of Lavinia but dreams of another life which would 'transcend' (I found the word in a book of essays) my puny self.

Many months must have passed as I lived through these moods and grew up a little. I still had not been vouchsafed another sight of Rooks Nest until one day Lavinia said after the Friday lesson: 'Would you like to come over and see Mama? She's always saying you must come again to see us. Would you care to come tomorrow to tea, with Barbara?' I was overjoyed and so excited that I could not at first reply, though the enforced accompaniment by Barbara was not ideal. I decided that Lavinia was so kind that she was trying to do Barbara a good turn. Aunt Juby could not object to us both paying a visit to Rooks Nest surely?

'That would be wonderful, I'd love to come to Rooks Nest,' I answered politely.

She looked at me quite searchingly, I thought.

I felt so much older on my second visit to Rooks Nest. Yet the house was the same – just as the village and the town never seemed to change. The old cobbler still sat in his hut near the village general stores; the lamplighter still went round at dusk in the town and the town gas lights could be seen winking away down in the valley. The skies were the same; the village people were the same, yet I was not the same. I realized that all my Dream Queens had merged with and into Lavinia Logan.

Lavinia had said: 'I believe the place means a good deal to you?' She was pulling on her long gloves at the schoolroom door as she spoke. I had gathered up the books for her. These moments were precious to me.

'To see you,' I answered boldly, 'at Rooks Nest – oh, of course it means everything to me.' She looked at me with a slight smile before she went out.

I asked Aunt's permission naturally but of course Miss Logan had already asked her and we were to go together, Barbara and I, on the Saturday.

Later that day, I was dreaming by the window when Barbara came in. There was a big moon waxing behind the late spring blossoms and the soft scent of the first May trees. I had been imagining all those men, those European dandies, who must have courted Lavinia and who had wished to serve her, sacrifice for her, and protect her as I did, and I did not answer Barbara at first.

'Did you know Miss Logan has asked me to tea along with you?'

'Yes,' I replied. 'We are going tomorrow.'

'You're sweet on her, aren't you, Meta?' said Barbara after a pause, fiddling with the window blind. I looked round at Barbara. I wanted to say 'I *love* her' but the sight of Barbara's rather solid ugly face stopped me. It would sully my feelings to speak of them to *her*. 'Yes, she does deserve it doesn't she?' said Barbara enigmatically.

I wondered whether Lavinia Logan had ever felt for anyone what I felt for her. I imagined her lying in the refurbished skiff on the lake or lingering in the conservatory, framed by magnolias and gardenias. On the Saturday, when Barbara and I arrived in the back yard of Rooks Nest, Lavinia was at first nowhere to be seen. The lilac was even more profuse than the year before. Great swags of heavy purple and mauve, massy, growing everywhere. Then the Logans' maid appeared.

'Ye're to come this way,' she said dourly.

'I hope they'll give us a good tea,' said Barbara, who often thought of food. My mind was not on tea. *Why* had Lavinia invited Barbara too? Was it just to emphasize that this was a visit of two pupils to their mistress's home? But it was not Lavinia's home – it was my home and would have belonged to me if Papa had not gone away and lost money!

How neglected the house and gardens really were. I had not noticed it so much before, but now as I walked across the cobbled courtyard with Barbara, as well as the turrety lilac I saw the rotten wood and the paint blisters and the moss on the walls and the ivy. It was like the palace of the Sleeping Beauty! But it could all be put right, surely, if Cousin Rainer patched it up and painted and restored? Then I thought, What does it matter? I am coming to see Lavinia, not the house.

'Will you own all this one day?' Barbara was asking.

'Oh, no, I shouldn't think so,' I replied. 'I believe Papa has leased it to his cousin.'

'Oh.' Barbara was dismissive. Then: 'But if your papa dies won't your cousin give it back to you?'

'Don't talk of my papa dying, Barbara. Anyway, you need lots and lots of money to keep up a place like this.' I hadn't ever hoped really to get it back.

'I know,' replied Barbara complacently. 'Some day, when my papa dies, I shall be rich, you see. And I'd like a grand house, but one full of servants – and *clean*, everything tidy.'

'Look,' I said. We had come round on to the dilapidated terrace and Lavinia was standing at its other end, leaning against the door of the South Wing. I wanted to run to her as she stood there motionless as a statue. She always had that quality of stillness, and her every movement was frugal. She stood by the empty urns placed at their regular intervals on the flagstones, the moss and weeds growing on and between the flags themselves. The long windows were shuttered. She looked as though she were posing for her picture by the camera obscura. She was very beautiful. The spell was broken in seconds yet I can still see her standing there in that place of half desolation and the light is on her face and I stare and stare.

49

Barbara stumped along in front of me in her neat grey cloak and fat boots. As we both reached the Pavilion door Lavinia turned aside and opened it. It was as though she had been expecting someone but not us, and she had decided to make the best of it.

'Not quite four o'clock,' she said. 'Still a *morning* call, though Mother has ordered tea for you.'

'Good afternoon,' said Barbara politely.

I was surprised she didn't curtsey to her! As we took off our cloaks and smoothed our hair, I ventured: 'I hope your mama is well – it is so kind of her to ask me – to ask us, to come along.'

Lavinia said in an offhand way: 'Oh, it was my idea. Though Mother is always pleased to have company.

'We must not tire her, she is easily exhausted,' she added as the drawing-room door was opened by the same maid. 'Maybe you and Barbara might like to look round the garden and grounds after tea?'

'Would you come too?' I asked.

Lavinia dropped her eyes and picked an imaginary mote off her dark green dress. 'You could probably show *me* round,' she replied.

Mrs Logan was seated in the high-backed chair surrounded by cushions; her plump ankles were revealed as her feet rested on a stool. Although it was late spring there had been a fire in the hearth and the grey ashes were still stirring. Why, she is really ill, I thought. It must be tedious for Lavinia to have to attend and cheer her when she is already tired from her work at the Hall.

The old lady smiled and seemed pleased to see us but every time she took a breath, her lungs seemed to bubble and her face was as grey as the ashes in the fire.

'Eat up, girls,' she said in a whisper. 'My daughter has ordered tea for you. Such clever young ladies – she tells me about you all – and Miss Meta I've met before. I get weary,' she added, 'but my daughter is very good to me.' Then she fell silent. I wondered if she were going to die. Then Miss Logan would be an orphan like me. Barbara was quiet but, unusually for her, most assiduous in helping to refill teacups and hand round scones. I could not take my eyes off Lavinia who seemed nervous and quiet, but I made an effort and said: 'Miss Logan has taught us such a lot,' to the old lady. She seemed so much older this time than last. She imprisoned my hand between her two thin ones and squeezed it from time to time. Her cap was a little askew and a few white hairs had escaped from it, making a wispy frill. How sad and unpleasant it was to be old and ill.

Barbara was plying Lavinia with tea. 'I think we should like a walk, Mother,' said the latter finally as the old lady seemed to be dropping off. The glowering maid came in then and said she would stay with her. 'Meta, you can show us all the treasures, I am sure,' added Lavinia and Barbara gave an unpleasant snigger.

'You go out for air, my dear, out for air,' said Mrs Logan, waking up.

'Thank you so much for the tea,' I said, gently pulling on my hand. We all three went out into the gardens. 'Is she very ill?' I asked.

'Yes, it's her heart. She's all alone in the world except for me – we never see our rich relations.'

'Oh, I'm sorry.'

'No need,' said Lavinia, thinking perhaps she had gone too far. 'I try to be a good nurse,' she added, 'but I'm not suited to it. Barbara would be a good nurse – you have to be strong and silent.'

'It must be so hard to nurse somebody you love,' I said. 'I used to imagine that I should go out like Miss Nightingale and tend the wounded, but I am not very practical.'

'No you are not,' said Barbara.

'Used you to play with dolls when you were a child?' asked Lavinia. She did not seem at all like her slightly disdainful school self.

'She used to imagine they were infants,' Barbara put in.

'Oh, a long time ago and it was only to make up stories,' I said, 'not to nurse them.'

'I'm afraid I never liked weans,' said Lavinia firmly.

'Women lose their looks from having children,' said Barbara. 'Or they die!'

'But then *I* should be the one against babies,' I said, 'since my mama died having me – or after.'

'That is a risk every married woman takes,' said Lavinia.

We were walking slowly across the terrace. I had never heard Miss Logan speak personally. They were perhaps not the kind of words you could say at Hartsedge, neither Augusta nor Martha being presently married. But of course, neither was Lavinia. That was strange.

'Wouldn't it be fine to go abroad, Miss Logan?' I said, changing the subject. 'To the South – like Goethe and Byron – to Italy and the Mediterranean, and hear music in a gondola ... and explore ruins...'

Barbara laughed. 'There's plenty ruined for you here,' she said shortly, gesturing to the decrepit outhouses and the neglected gardens.

'Oh, I used to think it must have been the most beautiful place on earth when I was little,' I said. 'Don't you like it, Miss Logan?'

For answer Lavinia shrugged her shawl round her elegant shoulders. I did wish that Barbara were not there. Lavinia was the chatelaine of this deserted castle and I could be her page but who could Barbara be? As we walked along I felt that Lavinia seemed to suit the place now. *She* looked sad and the place looked sad. I said aloud: 'It's sad,' and she looked at me enquiringly. 'I mean this place – deserted, except for you.'

Lavinia turned her marble profile away and said: 'Come, we shall take a little walk to the summerhouse. You may take an arm each, girls, if you wish, and pilot me there.' I slipped my arm through her rather rounder one. Her sleeves smelt of chypre and camphor mixed, and I felt almost faint with longing to hold her gloved hand. Did she know how much it meant to me to be near her? Barbara grabbed her other arm and plodded along just holding on to her elbow. She was quiet now.

'Tell me about your cousin, our landlord, Mr Rainer Moore,' commanded Lavinia.

'Oh, he is the son of my papa's cousin. Have you not met him more often than I?' I replied.

Lavinia said nothing and Barbara came to life again on her other side. 'He is rich,' she stated.

'Oh no, not so very,' I said, surprised. 'He travels a good deal and he is a great reader like Papa.'

'Did you ever meet him abroad, Miss Logan?' asked Barbara.

'I met him through a family friend, Mr Wolstenholme,' said Lavinia carefully. 'I know him a little now of course as he is our landlord, but I thought Meta might enlighten me a little further as to his character.'

'He is kind, I think,' I said. 'But not ordinary.'

'He has never married, I believe?'

'Oh, no, I don't think so.' I thought, if I did not love her so much, I should think this a peculiar conversation indeed! But she was strange too – and exciting. I wondered what Barbara really thought behind her spotty face and thick nose. But I must not have ignoble thoughts about Barbara. If I loved Miss Logan I must be glad that others did too, for her sake. I believed Barbara was also fascinated by her in her own way, in spite of her own pudding-faced phlegmatic constitution. And it was moving, I thought, to think of others *having loved her.* Perhaps she was sad that she was not young any more and worried about her poor mama. All those years abroad! I wished she would acquaint me with more of her life. If only I could paint her standing against those lilacs with their shadow on her face. But what I said aloud was: 'Do let us look at the lilacs, they are so beautiful here. See – every bush is of a slightly different colour. Which do you like best? – the pale or the dark mauve or that pinky purple – and the white too – they're like castles . . .'

'Oh Meta, stop; you are making my head ache,' said Barbara.

Lavinia smiled. 'Ah! the scent is not so heady as the gardenias I used to grow abroad – that *was* a flower.'

'Lilacs are not English either,' I said. I slipped my arm out of hers and ran through the grass and pulled down some of the branches to sniff the blossom. 'It is better when it's been raining, with the raindrops still on it . . . In a book I read it said the word is Persian – is that not charming?'

'Do stop her, Miss Logan. She is an "enthusiast",' said Barbara who had also not entirely wasted her education.

When I looked up from the lilacs, Lavinia was looking at me. It was a long steady gaze. Perhaps *she* was sorry for *me*?

'Meta was just as much in raptures over the heather on the moors,' said Barbara. 'She will always make something out of nothing.'

'It is not nothing,' I replied. 'There is too much of everything everywhere – flowers and places and houses – and names and books. Why should I not feel for it? How else can I understand it?'

'What is she talking about, Miss Logan?' asked Barbara. Lavinia seemed to shake her head.

'This – is such a little place in the world,' I went on. 'I expect there are grander houses and better flowers somewhere.' I wanted Lavinia to listen me. 'Everywhere there are flowers and ruins and people and thousands and thousands of things going on – people in houses and other countries, other languages. How can I get to know any of it unless I try to feel for it all? And one day it will all have changed, all be gone. It's not just beautiful; it's all terrifying. If I were dead it would all go on – like it all did when my mother died.' I had forgotten that Barbara was there. 'But it all ended for her then, didn't it? How little time there is to learn so much.'

Lavinia turned away and walked across towards the lake and the summerhouse on our right. 'Did you know there is a sunken garden here?' she said. 'I think it must have been a water garden once.'

'With lilies and fountains?' I didn't know, Martha never told me about that.

'Oh, I expect they had everything once,' said Barbara.

We stopped our walk for a moment to look around. The lake lay a little shrunken, in the distance. The grass round it was higher than when I'd seen it before, making the lake look like a secret pool. We came up to the summerhouse. Behind the summerhouse was the grotto, now partially hidden by the willows but there was a high irregular piece of rock poking out of them. A trickle of water dripped over it into the lake.

'It's hollow inside,' my teacher said as she saw me looking at it.

'The grotto? I was told there was once a proper one. There are pieces of mica and glass embedded there – Martha told me – and they used to put gas-candles to illuminate it at night,' I told her. 'I think they had statues too.'

'Nothing there now,' said Lavinia. 'And the fountain in the garden doesn't work either!'

'Nothing works here,' grumbled Barbara. 'It's just a ruin. But think, Miss Logan, if anyone rich were to buy it and set it up again! It could be very elegant – water-lilies and conifers and fruit trees and a gravel drive.'

I had never seen Barbara so animated. 'It wouldn't be the same,' I said. 'I like the statues and the dogs' graves and the little lake as they are. I don't know, but the past here seems more important than the present.'

'Well of course it would for you, Meta,' said Lavinia quite kindly and I thrilled to the fact that she knew about me and my parents, took some interest in me, as I did – and how much more! – in her. Yet I felt that Lavinia was not just the present to me, she did connect a little with my past now that she was living here. I was almost jealous of her own private past and of her present – envious too perhaps. If only Barbara were not there!

We came up to the little summerhouse that was built like a miniature pagoda. Behind it the garden stretched to a hedge, beyond which was an ordinary field. I could still scarcely believe that an ordinary field belonging to some farmer could be so near to Rooks Nest, for the house had for so long been a special place to me that it hardly belonged to the ordinary world of hedges and lanes. Surrounding the summerhouse was a rose tree, just beginning to climb out of its winter sleep.

'Look, there are going to be red roses,' I said. I couldn't seem to be able to stop myself from talking though talking was the last thing I wished to do. 'Think of all the years,' I said, 'when nobody came here, the tree was blossoming – as though people didn't matter.'

'Such a tangle,' replied Lavinia. 'It will have to be pruned.' She went into the summerhouse, blew at the dust and seated herself on a broad plank-like seat which skirted the walls. I walked through the grass to the straggly hedge, moved by a complicated mixture of emotions. It seemed that my feelings for Lavinia were held up and constrained both by her and by Barbara's presence. I wondered how long they would have to wait before I could properly express them. Would they grow like this straggly hedge, still valiantly blooming? There might even be wild roses too, among the hawthorn. The wild flowers came and went and no one pruned them – milkmaids and cuckoo pint and cowslips and daisies. Lavinia was saying that she preferred yellow roses. Barbara was standing by her, not risking her grey skirt on the seat. The summerhouse was covered in ivy and I was suddenly sure that Mama had sat there, perhaps sewing, before I was born.

Paradoxically, the thought brought with it a sudden wish to see my father. Augusta's uneasy explanation as to his enforced stay abroad was beginning to satisfy me no longer. Of *course* he could come to see me if he really wanted to. I knew Augusta was uneasy and discomfited about it. I must speak to Cousin Rainer. I wasn't a child any more though I was still regarded as one by my aunt and surely could be told where he was and what he was doing. I had even wondered whether he was not in prison somewhere! It was some months since I had received one of his postcards and ten years since I had actually seen him. All I retained was the memory of a memory: a brown-haired elegant man with a cane and a big overcoat. I had sat on his lap and he smelt of tobacco.

Lavinia's father was dead and her mother probably not long for this world. She would be alone, like me. But I didn't feel really alone. I was surrounded with people – the girls and Augusta and Martha. I wished I could comfort Lavinia.

At least I had all the postcards from Papa. The last one had been of the Rhineland, the river, two sailing boats, and crags and castles in the far distance with nearer trees painted in great detail in lovely glossy greens and browns and a woman in a red dress and white cap, and a little boy, walking towards a church with a thin spire and blue slate roof. Perhaps Papa would remarry and that was why he didn't want to return home? I wondered if Mrs and Miss Logan had ever visited that part of Germany. It was very fashionable now to take the journey down the Rhine. How dull it must be for Lavinia to find herself here in this neglected old house after the glamorous places she had lived in.

'Dreaming as usual, Meta?' called Lavinia.

'I was thinking how these gardens could be made beautiful,' I half-lied. 'I'd like to plant some flowers here for you.'

'All that needs money, doesn't it, Miss Logan?' said Barbara sharply.

'Money – and time,' she answered.

'I'd dig a flowerbed if I could come here – I'm sure I'd have *time,*' I replied.

'Oh, it would take years to clear the terraces and trim back the shrubberies.'

'Well you could have a winter garden in the conservatories,' I persisted, 'and plant red and blue flowers in the urns.'

'My papa has a large fern conservatory,' said Barbara. 'He has five gardeners working all the time. They get the plants from Cheshire.'

'Well you could make a start with just ordinary plants – lupins and pinks and hollyhocks and Sweet Williams, and lavender and honeysuckle round the Pavilion door.'

'I'm afraid all we shall run to will be a portable grotto and an orchid in a Wardian case,' said Lavinia.

'When I'm rich,' said Barbara again, in that maddeningly complacent way she had, as though there was no question of its coming to pass, 'I shall have a house with everything.' She spoke loudly and with emphasis. 'Not mouldy old grottos or common flowers, but flowerbeds bedded out like Papa's in a geometric garden, and an orchid house and pines and a clock garden and a moss house and an iron fountain and laurel shrubberies.'

I shuddered but Lavinia looked at her curiously. 'Oh well,' I said, 'we can always dream.'

'I'm not dreaming,' said Barbara.

'We must send some cottage flowers to your mother, Miss Logan,' I said after a heavy silence. 'If she is ill, flowers will help to cheer her.'

Lavinia was now looking away to the lake. When she had her head turned like that, her profile was very fine. She was still pale though. Perhaps she was tired. 'Don't trouble,' she replied, turning to me again. 'Mother is not overfond of flowers if she is confined to her room. They are said to sap a patient's strength.'

'Martha says long hair saps your strength,' I ventured. 'She is always imploring me to cut mine. But how could it take your strength – it still grows whether you cut it or not!'

'Many things are mysterious – you are always questioning beliefs, Meta.' Lavinia reverted to her schoolmistress tones. She was a little superstitious herself, I thought. 'My mother feels that statues on pedestals are irreligious – perhaps she is right,' she went on, softening a little. 'Perhaps she is right.'

'Well you have one here called HOPE – so that is a good thing to have,' I said.

'I expect that is just what Mrs Logan means,' said Barbara. Lavinia looked searchingly at her but thought it wiser to ignore the remark.

'Come now girls – I must return you to Hartsedge.' Perhaps she had had enough of our attempts at conversation. After all, we were an ill-assorted company.

As we were taken back in the governess cart by Taylor, who was their caretaker and odd-job man, I didn't notice the jolting and discomfort because I was looking at the sky and also wondering if I had talked too much. Barbara was silent. The clouds were like the sails of galleons on the horizon and overhead there were shredded ones like mackerel scales with trailing wispy tails. The sky was that faint green hue which often changes at dusk to violet. Midsummer would soon be with us.

57

I went to bed early to think over the day. So much seemed to have happened and yet nothing had. If only Barbara had not been there looking sly and sarcastic, I could have spoken to Lavinia of all that was in my heart instead of going into rhapsodies over flowers. Was there never to be any connection between my innner and outer lives? But a cold worm of suspicion turned at the bottom of my young heart – that Lavinia did not really care for me any more than for anyone else and that my thoughts and feelings were as alien to her as they were to Barbara and that these feelings of mine and my desires were perhaps better locked up. For what did I know of that wide world which beckoned? Only the poets and musicians seemed to know, and Miss Logan did not seem to care for the same ones as I, though she was so clever. I puzzled over it all and wished I were a little girl again when everything was simpler.

It was about two months later that I was called out of my drawing lesson. Mr Rainer Moore had ridden over from the town and I was asked to see him and my Aunt Augusta in the parlour.

It was a heavy sultry morning, the sort of morning when you feel that the mists will soon be dispelled and the sun will blaze forth, but they never are and the sun stays behind grey cotton-wool. Augusta was seated at the parlour window in her Jacobean chair and Rainer was standing looking at nothing since the garden was shrouded in a mist. He had a piece of paper in his hand and an envelope was lying on the table between them. I was glad to see Rainer. I hoped he thought I had grown up and was no longer a little girl in boots, now that I was fifteen. Augusta turned and said quietly: 'Come in, Meta, and sit down.'

'What is it, Aunt?' I shook hands with my father's cousin. I did not think a curtsey was appropriate.

'I'm afraid there is bad news, my dear ... you must prepare yourself.' Immediately, I knew: it was my father – he was dead.

'Oh, is it Papa?' I cried.

'I'm afraid so.'

Rainer took my hand and led me to a little low chair. 'I fear, Meta, a letter has just come from your father's solicitors in Germany to the solicitor in Halifax, Mr Widdop.'

'You don't have to tell me. He is dead.'

'Yes, he is dead, God rest his soul,' said Augusta.

I looked at Rainer. I did not want their pity. 'Tell me,' I said. I had never really known Papa and all I could think of was that I was sorry for him, not me. What sort of difference could it make that I would never see him again since I never saw him anyway?

'Widdop wrote to me yesterday. His letter explains. Your papa was at Baden where he was taking the waters. He died suddenly – not quite unexpectedly according to Widdop here.' I was glad of Rainer's matter-of-fact tones.

'Was he . . . alone when he died?' I asked, surprised to hear my own voice.

'Well, yes – a friend found he had died in his sleep. There was a letter for you among his papers. Here it is.' It almost made up for his dying, I thought – a letter for me. He cared about me.

'Apparently my dear, he was thinking of returning to see you (at *last* I thought), but fate ordained otherwise,' said Augusta. Rainer looked as though he wished the whole business were over. 'Go and read the letter,' said Augusta, 'you needn't go to any more classes today, my dear, if you don't want.' Surely I should feel *something*?

'I'm sorry,' said Rainer shortly. 'I'll talk it over with you when you feel ready. Read the letter. No one has opened it. It is only for you.'

'Will everything be different?' I said. 'I mean – should I not go to the funeral? How long ago did he die?' I had intended to go to see Papa as soon as I was sixteen and now I couldn't.

'He died three weeks ago, Meta . . . I'm afraid I wasn't told in time for the funeral. Widdop will talk over business matters with you and with Rainer,' said Augusta awkwardly.

'I am the executor of your father's will,' said Rainer, after a glance at me to see how I was taking all this.

'It will be taken care of. There's nothing you can do. I'm sorry, my dear,' said Augusta again and she did look sorry. I thought she had been weeping and I knew I had not yet shed a tear. Was it what they called a 'blessed release' or was it 'cut down untimely'? I didn't expect he had left me any money. Rainer handed over a thin envelope to me.

'This is from Papa to me?' I asked stupidly.

'Yes. As you can see, it is sealed. All the rest can wait. Go and read it.'

'Thank you for being so kind,' I said. I would go to Martha and talk to her when I had read the letter.

'I shall call for you to go in to Halifax to discuss the . . . business side,' said Rainer. 'Next week some time.'

I looked at the wafer-thin envelope and felt it between my thumb and forefinger. Papa had touched it. It just said 'Margaret from her father', and it had been dated earlier in the year. He had expected something then? What had I been doing when he wrote it? What had he thought of all the letters I had written to him over the years? His cards had never made much allusion to them. But I recognized his handwriting – curly and large with complicated capital letters.

'His things will be sent on,' added Rainer.

I was burning to ask: 'And who will have Rooks Nest?' but could not bring myself to do so. It would seem heartless. Doubtless all would be cleared up by this Mr Widdop.

'Shall I have to wear mourning, Aunt?' I asked with my hand on the sneck of the parlour door.

'I think bands will do, my dear. Your father would not have wished for you to mourn grievously for him – I do know that.'

'He was not a man who appreciated formalities,' added Rainer.

I went up to my bedroom, the little room at the corner near the twisty staircase. I sat on my bed for quite a while before I dared to open the letter. I could hear the voices of the girls out at recreation in the garden. I didn't know whether I felt quite up to reading it. Papa was really a stranger, a mystery. Would his letter make me feel closer to him just when we could never be close? His dying too was an event I must take on trust. If I had never known, what sort of difference would it have made?

I took a breath, bent my head to the seal and opened the thin covering. My hands were trembling, so perhaps in spite of myself I was affected. Inside were two large pieces of paper covered in the curly writing I knew so well. The first page was headed DONNERSTAG in printed letters. Perhaps the hotel had them for every day of the week?

BADEN *April 185-*
My Dearest Child
As you are reading this you will know that I am no more.
I shall have failed to go on living, Margaret, but try not to blame me. Many a time have I wished to pack my bags and hie me back to England, to Yorkshire, and to you. You will

ask: 'And what kept him from coming?' You would be right to ask. Debts, my dear, unhappy associations, hopes always that things would improve. I always thought of you, but if the truth be told I was ashamed of not being able to offer you what Augusta could. I often turn over your letters and those from your aunt. Some time ago my cousin's son, Mr Rainer Moore, came to see me. He told me what a pretty child you were, what those Yorkshiremen call a grand lass – and that you had inherited my love of books and music. A dangerous inheritance, Margaret! Things cannot be appreciated without the money which buys the time to savour them and the education to form the taste. I stand guilty in my own eyes that I cannot hand over to you the sum which I am sure you deserve, to enable you one day to marry well. Yet perhaps it is a blessing, for no one will marry you for your money. Folks thought that was the reason I had married your Mama. In the event I received nothing but Rooks Nest. Enough of that. Perhaps I should not speak of it to you?

Your Aunt Augusta Jewesbury is owed everything by me, Margaret. In undertaking to bring you up she has my eternal gratitude and she knows I thank her from the bottom of my heart. She was so fond of your dear Mama. I loved your Mama, Margaret. And your Mama died. That was when my life began to go wrong. I am an artist, not a speculator, and I made mistakes. If your Mama had not died she would not have let me make them. Do not grieve for me, my child – only forgive me, even though I may not deserve it. I have worked at many things since leaving fair Albion. I have a little talent for painting and strumming, none whatever for business. I could live as the English say 'On the Continent' but not in England as a gentleman among my own people.

I could give you advice but doubt whether I feel up to it. Life is worth the living, dearest Margaret, and my greatest joy is that I shall leave you on earth to do the living for me. Love always – but try to keep your head. I hear you have a good one. The thought of you causes me pain as well as joy. Keep at your studies and other languages, dearest child; they may well one day afford you a living or will adorn a position in society already attained.

I have all your early letters here under my hand. How could I have replied to them in any other way than sending you a pretty picture if I could not return and look after you? But what's past is past. As for the future, when you read this I shall not have one. You will, and I wish for God's blessing upon it. I shall leave a prayer with a candle for you as my friends do here. I can for the present send you only my love. I will remain as long as I live your unworthy but loving father who loved your Mama and will never forget her who gave you life.

Your devoted,
Jonas Moore

There was another thin sheet of paper.

Post-Scriptum. It has been hard to write this. My doctor says I must not travel. My lungs and heart are affected. Should you pass by the house where you were born, bury a thought for me there. I often see it in my dreams with its flowers and fruit and your Mama sitting in the little summerhouse by the lake.

I shall have my seal forwarded to you. For the rest I'm afraid there will be nothing. Augusta has some of my books for you – those that were not sold.

I fervently hope that your heart and head will beat in time together. Keep this little letter, my dear. I loved you when you were a baby. Never forget that. There were many wrongs I should have righted but it was not to be. The world may think your father was a fool, Margaret. Believe me, I meant well, and do not abjure any of my beliefs. My *only* regret is that perhaps mistakenly I did not come to you. Now it is too late – I feel it in my bones. I thank our Creator that you are a girl and will not have to fight the world as well as yourself. Be patient, kind, and loving as was your dear Mama. Farewell – JM.

I read the letter over and over, a little puzzled, a little exalted, very sad for him and for me and yet even then a little critical. It was the last reaction I had expected and I could not think from whence it came. He had loved me. That much was clear to me. If only I could have seen him again just once. Perhaps at the bottom of his heart he blamed me for Mama's death? Why had he died? Was it the decline or a heart attack – or worse? Could he have taken his life? He did not appear to have believed he would ever return to England. He did not sound like a grown-up person, a father, but I understood him. *I* would have made his life worth living if he had ever come for me. Then when I read the letter again I saw it was full of pathos and I could not quite distinguish my pity for him from his pity for himself. Perhaps he had just been improvident? I went down to Martha, having put the letter in my private drawer. I didn't cry. It did not yet seem quite the time for tears. Perhaps they would come later.

I read the letter over many times in the next few days and decided to go to Sholey Church as an act of piety the next Sunday. I was not then a regular churchgoer because I did not wish to go there just out of habit and convention. I took religion very seriously and had serious doubts which I voiced to no one. Not everyone made great professions of Sunday faith and of course we were rather isolated and away from the currents of Evangelicalism, except for Martha and her kind who were what we called Sunday Saints. I had read some books of Papa's from the last century and found my doubts confirmed. Anyway the services of the church did affect me – but they did not seem to connect with the real mysteries of life. I would go and pray for Papa nevertheless.

I walked there on the Sunday. I should like to have believed that the Rector knew the truth about life and death, but liked it better when I was alone in the church. It was very beautiful, quite plain and unrestored. The Rector was more worried about making people believe than in finding out the truth. I had held my tongue in his divinity lessons.

Martha had received the news of my father's death very quietly and looked anxiously at me. 'I'm that sorry,' she said. She had been kind and spared time to talk to me about the 'master'. I'm afraid that her memories had become fossilized after all this time as she always remembered the same things about Papa and Mama.

I believed that Martha thought that I was off to pray for the souls of the dead. According to her they had already either gone up or gone down and praying wouldn't alter that. I think she suspected that Papa might not be in heaven.

'Go and make a good prayer for yourself, love,' she said. 'He wanted you to be a lady – that I do know – and perhaps you could pray for guidance like.'

I thought about this when I was in church. I was there ostensibly for Papa, but was it not in truth to set my own mind at rest? I wasn't going to be a 'lady' – that much I did know, in spite of Augusta's efforts. Ladies didn't work – and I would have to work for Augusta or for someone. I tried to gather all my thoughts together as I sat in church but they kept flying off so I repeated the bits from the burial service and that did me good. There was nothing like the power of language to assuage. But my head ached rather after it all. Why had life treated Papa so badly? And why did You take away Mama, I thought. But it was childish to think those sorts of thoughts. Nothing was simple. I saw my own life stretching out before me. I tried to pray to God for understanding. But if He had made the world different there would have been no need of it. I knew my thoughts were blasphemous and it seemed wrong to be sitting in church thinking them. I wondered whether Papa had lost *his* faith or if he had ever had one. At least he lit candles like his Catholic friends. He had written that. I thought that God was more likely to be out in the winds over the moor than in this building men had created. Was there no one I could talk to about this, I was thinking as I came out of the dark church into the sunshine. Certainly not Lavinia who, incongruously, went to the Presbyterian church whenever her mother was well enough.

About this time I began to write a journal. In it I wrote some of my thoughts about Papa's death. Writing helped me to sort out my thoughts. I realized that I had used the idea of Papa as a sort of dream and this had cut me off from my true feelings about him which were probably rather angry. But Papa had asked me to forgive him, so I would. I knew that he had never known me, just as *I* would never now know *him,* except retrospectively.

I felt that I ought to have 'orphan' inscribed on my forehead in black letters so that then everyone would know and I should know they knew and would not have to endure questions and condolences. I hated people feeling sorry for me. Barbara though did not pity me. 'I never thought your papa would come back, Meta,' she said.

People said that her papa was now a rich man, and maybe her mama – according to Martha, whom I heard gossiping with Ellen – would be sorry for her precipitate dash abroad. I felt that Barbara did not love her mama and I knew she worshipped her papa, but that she did not see much of him. He preferred to send her presents. I hadn't wanted presents from mine, just his presence.

Cousin Rainer was to come to take me to see Mr Widdop, the solicitor, to 'settle my affairs', but I knew there would not be much to settle. He had not asked me what the letter from Papa had said, for which I was grateful. He treated me very circumspectly. I believe everyone expected me to break down hysterically.

As we sat sewing in the parlour the night before my visit to the solicitor, Barbara said something strange. The others were laughing at some sally from Frances Green, who was to leave us at the end of the summer term.

'I wonder if Miss Logan ever met your papa in Germany, Meta?' She had mentioned something like that before, but I had not taken much notice.

'I can ask her,' I replied drily.

'Oh, no, Meta! You see, I think she is a *little* like my mama.' Anything less like Barbara's vulgar parrot-dressed mama than my idol I could not imagine and said so tactfully. Yet I could imagine Lavinia as the object of men's desire – not to put too fine a point on the word – and said so.

'Oh *love* – pooh!' said Barbara.

I was sure Papa had had a faiblesse for beautiful women. And how lonely he must have been with Mama lying in her grave at Scarborough. I already knew from my reading that gentlemen did not conduct themselves in these matters in the same way as ladies – that was another reason along with my religious doubts for my dislike of our English society. But surely 'Amor Vincit Omnia' and pure love could also express itself in fond embraces? That is what I thought then.

Curiously enough I also had a memory of some emotion that had flitted over Cousin Rainer's distinguished features when there had been talk of Mama. I had thought for an instant then that as a young boy he might have worshipped my mother. But I was not going to gossip about that with Barbara, who saw 'love' as a game to play, and if possible win. If she thought she was going to shock me with her hints about Lavinia and my father, she was going to be disappointed. I remember writing in my journal after this conversation that I wished I had been born a male.

I tried to use all my intelligence, such as it was, the next day when my father's affairs were explained to me. Rainer had looked at me rather anxiously. All I said was: 'Well, I expected I should have to earn my living, so it is no surprise.' Perhaps that made me an honorary man. Certainly not a lady! He explained to me that his father was mortgagee to Rooks Nest and that he had himself taken on tenants to help pay off my father's debts to his father. Rainer would have to try and find a purchaser for the estate, but he assured me there was no hurry. I hoped he was not short of money himself. I believed not, as his own father was an astute businessman. I was determined to take it all in and to thank Rainer for all he had done.

'No, you must thank your aunt,' he said and smiled at me.

'When I am eighteen I shall find work,' I said.

A few days later Rainer and I both went to see Mr Widdop in his mahogany office.

'Your aunt is your guardian. There is no need to worry, the school is doing well,' Widdop said. He seemed to find it comical that a young lass should be brought to discuss business. Rainer had explained that I ought to be clear about things and that my father would have wished it.

'I take it that your father does not wish to buy Rooks Nest – um – the property himself?' Mr Widdop had asked Rainer at one point.

'No, it is too big.'

'And you yourself?' the lawyer pressed him.

'I am not long enough here at present to afford it, Widdop,' replied Rainer.

I wondered whether my cousin would ever marry. He was still quite young but I had never heard of any sentimental attachment in connection with him. The face of Lavinia came into my mind and I thought: *He* could marry Miss Logan and they could live at Rooks Nest.

'The present tenants will stay on for the moment then,' Widdop was saying.

'I see no objection. The money will all go into the Jonas fund,' replied my cousin.

I decided to be bold and ask just one question. 'Did my papa leave *many* debts?' I ventured, looking at my cousin rather than at the solicitor.

Rainer hesitated and Widdop answered for him. 'Enough to have swallowed up the estate, Miss,' he said shortly, as though it were none of my business.

Augusta had insisted that I attend this meeting rather than herself, for as the sister of the manager of a big new bank she thought it the duty of women too to acquaint themselves with money matters. I had seen that Widdop, a florid, bespectacled man in middle age, thought my presence there not only amusing but irregular.

The result of our talk at Mr Widdop's was that I remained at the Hall; that as a minor I could not be responsible for any debts incurred by my father, and that Rainer's father had somehow commuted them by reason of taking the house which had been my father's only property. I thought of Barbara, only a month or two before, saying how it could be improved and made valuable. Whoever bought it from Rainer and his father would doubtless have a good investment.

As Rainer put me into his carriage to return to the Hall he said: 'I will send you all the details, Meta. If you were a boy it would be your duty to know all the facts.' *He* was not the sort of man who thought women must not worry their heads about affairs of money, I was grateful to see.

'I thank you for all I am sure you have done for Papa,' I said. 'I shall try to earn some money soon. Aunt Augusta has spared me so much.'

'There is nothing to worry about now, Meta,' he said quietly.

'I only wish that Rooks Nest did not have to go out of the family,' I said.

'Perhaps when you are old enough to marry, your husband might buy it if it's not yet sold,' he replied. I believe I blushed. I couldn't connect the house with money and husbands, though I saw well enough that that was the only way for a girl to lay her hands on money, unless through inheritance and that didn't seem to have been a solution for me.

'I shall take a post as governess or companion,' I said.

'They are ill-paid and women are often exploited,' he replied. 'Better stay and work at the school. I know your aunt intends to leave it to you one day.'

I could not tell him of my childish feeling that Rooks Nest was *mine*. It did now seem childish and was certainly out of the question. Teaching French and handwriting and deportment was not going to bring me a fortune. I saw now why Papa had wanted me to forgive him. The idea of marrying for money disgusted me. It was the sort of thing Barbara would do, I thought.

I had to learn to give up my dreams with good grace and to be grateful that Lavinia was still allowed to live in the little Pavilion Wing of the house. Lavinia was soon to be bereaved herself. She started the new autumn term after the summer holiday looking, I thought, thinner and more unhappy. Effie, the stumpy maid, was to go on living with her, and as Mr and Mrs Taylor, the caretakers, were now in residence at the lodge it was thought enough for propriety. I tried to be a help to Lavinia when we heard her mother had died; I so wanted to comfort her. Although she was almost old enough to be my own mother I wanted to support her in her grief the way I wished my mama had been able to comfort me in childhood. It was strange, and all the wrong way round.

The death of my father seemed to have unlocked my tongue a little where Barbara was concerned. We used to sit in the little room next to the schoolroom now and do our preparation for the next day's lessons, for we were now the older girls. Frances and Viola and Matilda had all left. Matilda had even found a husband who had fallen in love with her voice. Julia and Jemima were still with us but Julia preferred to study in her own room and Jemima spent long hours embroidering her trousseau. I wished I could say more to Barbara about my feelings for Lavinia, but instinct told me to refrain. Beautiful, sad, lonely Lavinia. Barbara knew I loved her. We never spoke of Rooks Nest any more either. What Barbara would discuss were the items of Lavinia's wardrobe – curious, because she seemed to have no interest in clothes for herself beyond remaining always neat and tidy, unlike me. Lavinia's earrings and brooches, rings, fichus, hairpins, gowns and stockings, shawls, shoes and boots, were itemized by Barbara and criticized, admired or deplored. I thought only of Lavinia's hands, white and soft, and her delicate ears and her lips and long neck. I continued to place her in some 'abroad' of the mind. I was beginning to break through the web of the Hall, almost daily snipping a thread and reaching through to some dazzling new world of feeling and images and words. I did try to put the words down in my Journal. Barbara never wrote a journal, for Barbara hardly ever wrote anything, not even many letters to her separated parents.

How did I ever manage to convince my aunt that I needed extra conversation lessons with Miss Logan and that these could take place if I accompanied her in the gig in which Sam Hirst drove her back to Rooks Nest every afternoon? Sam could bring me back, I said. Lavinia did not seem to find it an inconvenience – at least she did not oppose the idea, so on Tuesdays and Thursdays after the end of lessons I would step up by Lavinia's side and share the hard wooden seat as we lurched along together. These extra 'lessons' have all merged in my memory though they must have lasted for about nine months. If it were fine weather I would sometimes let Sam return without me and I would walk back alone through the village thinking of the next time. So it was that our relationship began to change after her mother's death. I may have forgotten our precise conversations but the texture of those times I have never forgotten, not the background of the hours we spent together – early spring dusks, later spring evenings heavy with chestnut blossom. How often they would return to me later. Although I did not know exactly for what I yearned when I was with her, there was little I left unexpressed in words, French and German words which would have sounded strange to a native I am sure. Yet at the same time – up to and beyond my sixteenth birthday – as I sat and worshipped and watched her and read to her, I was changing. From a need to console, protect and serve I began to realize slowly that I was not prepared in the end to sacrifice myself on her altar. It was a painful realization. From a youthful idol she turned into an icon, something to carry round with me which made a marvel out of the everyday and made my life worth living.

Boredom had never touched me, for there had always been the next sight of Lavinia to look forward to. As long as I found her a mystery, her magic worked on me. When she stood near me and I smelled that faint scent of chypre which lingered in her dress I would dream of holding her white hands. And one day I did hold them as I sat at her feet on a little stool in the old conservatory where she went to sew if it were warm enough whilst her maid Effie cooked her food. I was sorting her silks for her, preparatory to leaving. Sam Hirst was that day having a bite of bread and butter in the kitchen and soon I should have to go. As I handed her a skein of green silk she imprisoned my hand in hers for a moment and I looked up at her. She didn't say anything and I bent my head and kissed her hand before she drew it away once more. The touch of her hand over mine and the moment when I brushed my lips over her white knuckles – such tiny gestures, but I relived and pondered them for months.

One winter evening on her leaving the Hall, she let me kiss her goodbye and the stars that night had never been so silver. The deep cold snows made an adventure out of her arrivals and departures. I was not allowed to travel to Rooks Nest in the gig then. I think Aunt would have been quite happy for Lavinia to stay those nights at the Hall and I prayed she would, but she never did. If only she would stay just one night and I could see her standing on the landing in the candlelight wearing her nightgown and with her long hair down her back.

The icon went on being carried round by me, wherever I was – in the garden, at the fireside, on the moor, in the town – a living accompaniment to all my day-dreams. The glowing green summer full of birdsong, the drone of the bees in the ling on a moorland walk where we went 'botanizing', the shadows of leaves under the trees in Cow Lane, the deep red peonies announcing the arrival of summer, the scent from the roses like velvet incense when summer came, the chrysanthemums burning with their bitter perfume in the Hall garden in autumn – all were counterpoints to my imaginings, as though she were part of it all.

And yet inexorably and by the faintest shifts of my mental barometer I began, unconsciously at first, to judge her. I wanted to think she was perfect – I had thought she was – but it began to hurt me to acknowledge that she could not truly share my raptures and rhapsodies. I see now how tedious I must have been but she bore them well on the whole and I think she even welcomed some of them. But that little part of my mind which I had begun to reserve for myself, that part I could not share with anyone, slowly grew larger as I began to develop other parts of myself, even to criticize my old self. It did not stop my loving her but in the end I think it made her colder towards me. There were trivial things about her which I sought to excuse privately to myself but for which I would never have criticized her to a stranger. The way she would not change the fashion of dressing her hair, and would never wear a brown mantle – which would have suited her. And although she was always polite to Sam Hirst she would talk to me as though he were not there. She had her little fetishes – would write only with a certain quill and in a certain violet ink which I thought at first elegant then a little affected. She would never drink tea and eat bread and butter together at the same meal, claiming it made one fat to do so. She would brew a special herbal concoction to which she ascribed magical powers of rejuvenation for she had a fear of putting on weight. She evinced, too, a refusal ever to have her likeness taken. I believe she had a deep horror of growing old and losing her looks, and who could blame her, raised as we all were to believe a woman was valuable only as the object of masculine interest, which waned with a thickening waist-line? She would never divulge her age to any of us, though Louisa, a new girl, often tried to catch her unawares with trick questions about certain happenings at certain dates. 'Of course Miss Logan, you were born long after Waterloo?' she said once to her and Lavinia said: 'Of course.'

I noticed that Lavinia did not seem to like Julia. Only much later did I wonder whether it was because Julia was Jewish. Lavinia had been brought up a Presbyterian – a rather strict sect and one which I had thought would have approved of Jews since much of that sect's faith seemed to be based on the Old Testament, but no, for some reason she seemed to think that the richer Jews had no right to be taking money in our cities. It was a common prejudice of course. It disturbed me that Lavinia should share it, for I myself had feelings only of enthusiasm for people different from ourselves.

She always took care, however, to appear deferential to my aunt and grateful for her employment. Truly she did not much enjoy instructing her pupils. I felt she was holding herself in reserve for some event, some person whom she might enjoy having at her beck and call and that person was evidently not going to be myself. Yet I could not really envisage her in the married state. She was too fastidious and not a person to share herself with anyone. That revelation came to me suddenly on my sixteenth birthday when she quite politely refused to eat a piece of the birthday cake Martha had baked for me. I was hurt even though she had said rich fruit cakes upset her digestion.

I knew that she was not an innocent woman. To us girls she

used to give hints of her past life: casual references to trips up the Rhine when her mama had not been present; masculine names dropped casually into the conversation; under-elaborated incidents which brought a reminiscent sharpening of the pupils of her eyes before she clammed up a little obviously. I do not know whether she dropped these titbits especially before me or that I noticed them more. Was she testing my discretion, or trying to sharpen my curiosity, or warning me off? She gave the impression of not acting instinctively but of planning her remarks – at least that is what I began to feel as time went on. More explicitly she would warn me off men and their bad ways, yet still with an air of mystery.

'You are very naïve, Meta,' she would often say to me. I agreed that I was, that a long absorption in books was no substitute for living. I felt I only knew a more sophisticated world through reading about it, and it was true that I should probably flounder in it if I met it in reality. I realized that we did not mean the same thing by sophistication. Sometimes I noticed that she would rather enjoy showing up any gaps in my knowledge, especially if Barbara were with us. I knew even then that I was more attractive than Barbara but I could be touched on more tender spots than Barbara seemed to possess. Barbara anyway was more interested in mathematics and had no desire to explore the mysteries of Goethe or Lamartine. I did not hold it against Lavinia if my mistakes were pointed out rather cuttingly, for I was cross enough with myself and quite willing to admit to ignorance. But how had it come about that this woman whose hands I had held not many months before could treat me so badly? The treatment had its effect. I decided there were things which Lavinia would never know – I would keep them to myself. I should be pleased if she seemed to favour Barbara or Louisa, for if they became fond of her she would have friends other than myself, I reasoned, since I was determined one day to leave Hartsedge to find work I could do. Yes, she did make me suffer, but a small part of my mind had already prepared myself to do without her. In my seventeenth year this part of myself grew and grew.

So I was not wrecked by my love for Lavinia. It turned out that like all romantics I was tougher than I knew. As I grew little by little away from her in my last year at the Hall, I wondered whether in spite of my feelings that she was not 'marriageable' she might in fact marry someone like my cousin Rainer who might give her security and make her happy in a way I could not. I resolved to throw them into each other's company, which was not easy since we hardly saw Rainer. I began to resign myself to not thinking of her continually, and believed I was emerging from a sweet madness and becoming sane again. Even so, I was not prepared for the surprise and pain I felt when one afternoon Lavinia asked Barbara to accompany her home in the dog-cart, even though it had been some months since my 'conversation lessons' had ceased. I was used to covering up any emotional shocks and I casually went to the kitchen and had a comfortable chat with Martha in order not to see them departing in the gig.

I realized that Lavinia would demand total devotion and if I were to grow up I should not be able to give it to her. The failure was mine. I did not quite know where it had all gone wrong. Later I felt that I had come through a fire I had lit myself and that the poems and the music and the lilac and the snow were on the one side with me still, whilst Lavinia was on some other shore, still loved and still strange but not quite the same person with whom I had fallen in love, so long ago. I determined to be as independent as possible within the confines of my wretched sex, but my breaking away was not to cancel out all my old feelings. In the meantime, let Barbara go and discuss mushroom houses and interior decoration!

Yet it is still the sight of Lavinia at Rooks Nest which remains with me: Lavinia in the garden with the smoke from the valley rising in the distance; Lavinia standing in her dark green mantle among the purple crocuses on the lawn, she and the fragile flowers both so heart-breakingly beautiful. The wider world was calling me and it was by chance, through Julia, that I approached the next stage of my life.

Three

MONTPELIER CRESCENT

'Did you know that old Stott is planning to buy the Nest?' Rainer's words lay in the air and almost took solid form to my stunned imagination. We were sitting out in the garden on a hot summer afternoon, yet my blood really did run cold and a deep shiver ran down my back.

It was a Sunday and Aunt Juby had invited Lavinia to a dainty tea in order to discuss my future.

'Don't look so upset, Meta. I heard only yesterday that there had been an offer, when I saw Widdop in town.'

I had still said nothing but was looking mutely at him, the picture of misery I suppose.

'He is Stott of Stott's worsted you know,' he went on, as though that made it any better.

'Yes, Barbara is always telling us how rich she will be one day,' I managed finally in a choked voice. My Rooks Nest! The thought of Barbara and her father ensconced there made me feel sick.

'Barbara seemed very attached to Miss Logan when I last saw them,' my cousin went on, as though he had noticed my reactions.

I made a mighty effort and gathered myself together. I would try to think about Lavinia instead.

'Who? – Barbara? – well of course – (here was my chance) – Miss Logan is so terribly attractive is she not, and such a lonely person.'

'Ah, yes, life is not easy for ladies who are unattached,' replied Rainer. Perhaps he knew I had planned for him to fall in love with Lavinia, marry her and live at the Nest!

'Is Mr Stott divorced from his wife, do you know?' he asked after a silence. Aunt Juby, whom we had thought asleep, opened her eyes at this and said mildly: 'Meta would not know about that, Rainer.'

My heart sank again. There was so much I was not supposed to know about, yet my cousin was unconventional enough to discuss such a thing with a girl. Girls were usually expected to be ignorant. I was not.

'They do not live together,' I said coolly. 'But I am not sure if they are actually divorced. That would be quite unusual.'

Aunt sighed.

'Oh Rainer – why don't *you* live at Rooks Nest?' I burst out.

'My dear girl, I couldn't keep up that great place. You forget – I'm not rich like Barbara's father.' He smiled. 'Come now, don't look so unhappy. Let's talk about your future – about your plans.' He looked at Augusta who had given another sigh.

As soon as I was eighteen I intended to go away, take a post as governess. A possibility had arisen of my finding work with a Jewish family in Harrogate, some cousins of Julia's parents. I had already spoken to Rainer about it and he had broached the subject with my aunt. She was a little reluctant to let me go away so young but had agreed to talk it over with Lavinia who had experience in these matters. Rainer had promised me a 'character' reference.

His startling news made it suddenly imperative that I go away, away from Hartsedge and all its memories, to cut myself off from all my day-dreams.

'You are not of age yet,' he went on. 'And Augusta agrees with me that we should want to be sure you would be happy with the Angersteins in Harrogate. I think it might be good for you – though we shall miss you, you know.'

'Do you think I shall be able to bear being a governess then?'

'Oh, I expect so. You have plenty of energy, and you wouldn't admit to *not* bearing it, would you?'

I saw he knew me quite well, better than Aunt Juby in fact. That lady added: 'You will have to be very determined, especially if there is a little boy. Boys are not always as tractable as girls.'

'Well, it will be a different *milieu,*' I answered, choosing the French word to impress Rainer. Aunt had shut her eyes again and pulled a large-brimmed straw hat over her face. 'Many of my own friends are Jewish,' said Rainer, lighting a cigar. 'They give an élan to the town and to intellectual life. Mind you, I don't know about the ones in Harrogate. They may not be quite so public-spirited – more concerned with making money.'

'Julia is quite exotic,' I said in reply.

' Where is Barbara?' he asked, I thought to change the subject.

'Oh, somewhere in the garden I expect. I don't see much of her nowadays.' It was true. Barbara seemed to pursue a life of her own now, though she still stayed at the Hall after term had ended if her father was not at home in his ugly mansion in the town, aptly named The Folly.

'I expect Miss Logan will arrive soon,' I said, to get off the subject of Barbara once more. 'I had better go in and tidy myself up a bit before she arrives.'

I wanted to get away by myself to think over the news about Rooks Nest. I wondered if Barbara knew about her father's plans – she must do, surely, yet she had said nothing to me about it. I wondered if she had told Lavinia. The two of them *were* very thick nowadays. That had almost stopped hurting. Perhaps I had loved Rooks Nest more than Lavinia?

As I went indoors to the cool house I heard Martha singing in the kitchen. She only did it when we were not there. I did not want to disturb her so I crept quietly up the stairs. How Martha would miss me if I went away!

Suddenly I had the idea of going up to my 'ramparts' again. It had been years since I had climbed the little stone staircase to the roof, and over ten years since my first visit there. Then I had been a child. Now, I was not a 'lady' – I would never be a lady – but a young woman, about to try to be independent. Yet my cousin and my aunt and my teacher would be discussing my future as though I were still a baby or a fragile parcel they were going to entrust to the Royal Mail.

I squeezed myself up the staircase. Oh, it was hot up there. Perhaps I was just a child again, escaping from the 'grown-ups'? One part of me still wished I could 'play out' with Sam Hirst! But Sam was even now probably courting some girl from the village. I sighed as I saw the whole thing being set in motion again – marriages and babies and life going on as usual. Well, my life was not going to go on as usual. I was going to get away.

The stairs were much smaller than I remembered and the trap-door when I reached it only just big enough to allow me through. It had probably been intended for little chimney-sweep boys in the old days. I did get through it at some cost to my elbows and stockings, and came out into the burning glare of the afternoon sun. Sounds were faint up there and yet I heard two wood pigeons coo from a tree in the garden. By straining my eyes I could just pick out the elm trees of Rooks Nest from this vantage point. Rooks Nest! Was I going to have a good cry up here about it all? It was sad – but perhaps it made me angry rather than sorry that Barbara might live there if her father bought it. I had a lump in my throat.

I leaned against the chimney stack which seemed to have shrunk in height and looked out again across the fields of home. There was a heat haze over the distant hill and I could only just pick out our church at Sholey. But the fields were green, for we had had much rain that year and those in shadow looked lush. How I loved the place, so safe and small and familiar. Was I mad to feel I must go away? I was filled with inchoate longing which the wood pigeons seemed to echo. All here was peaceful but I could at present go no further in one direction if I stayed. I was sure my destiny lay elsewhere, perhaps in the bosom of that Jewish family or in some other family, or in London or in some Continental watering-place where I should find my dreams of a different life coming true. I thought of Papa and I thought again of Rooks Nest. If I had had the money I would have bought it myself. But I would never have any money, and did I want to live alone there, reliving some lost childhood? Last year I would have liked to have lived there with my beautiful Lavinia but now even she seemed to be becoming lost to me. No, the dreams about the Nest had been only dreams. Some rich magnate, if not Barbara's father, would eventually buy it and the most I could expect would be to go there as the governess!

I felt the objective truth of my own orphan state up there on the leads of Hartsedge Hall for the first time, really felt it, knew it, and knew I was alone in all that mattered to me. Here I was, wanting to leave the Hall, the only real home I had ever known – the *only* home. Did Aunt think me ungrateful? I hoped not, for that was untrue. The best way I could repay the debt of my upbringing would be to show her and my cousin that I was not going to be a dependent relative all my life, a poor relation, a burden.

I made my way down the stairs back to my bedroom and washed my hands and face, feeling sad but a little exalted and a little giddy from the heat on the roof. I heard the sounds of Lavinia's arrival downstairs. I thought, one day I would return to the Hall, wiser, older, more experienced. I wouldn't be saying 'Goodbye' for ever would I? – I would return to the village now and again. Poor Lavinia was stuck here in all her beauty with only the smoky town to visit for a change. If only I were a man and could range the wide world like Cousin Rainer had done. Yet even Rainer came back here. What possible attractions could there be for him? Perhaps he did like Miss Logan and they would marry each other and both blossom, although the probability did not seem great. And even Barbara who might one day be an heiress was, I suppose, still confined to the proper bounds of behaviour appropriate to the sex we both shared. Well, my world would be in Harrogate. My childhood could never be taken from me, would always be there if I ever tired of escape. I wanted to see what the wider world was really like. I must chance my luck, for so far I *had* been lucky, lucky and loved – perhaps more than I deserved. Had anyone ever loved the unlovable Barbara? Yet maybe someone would. If only she were not so shut-in and scheming. 'Martha is only a servant' she had once said to me when I had been extolling Martha's virtues to her. I had often felt like strangling her, to be truthful. She was horrid – yet it was perhaps not all her own fault that she was so? And now it seemed that she was turning her attentions to Lavinia Logan. Surely Lavinia could not really like her? I gave her credit for more taste. I wondered what they talked about.

'You will go away and you will forget me,' Lavinia had said to me not long before. 'I *shall* go away – I must – but I shall never forget you,' I had said. It had been our only 'real' conversation for months and I thought of it now as I came down the front stairs and into the garden. What did the mind behind those pebble-brown eyes think about me? I had thought I had understood her but I suppose I had understood only myself – and that not too well . . .

For a few moments I had succeeded in banishing the thought of Barbara's father and Rooks Nest but it all came back to me when I came upon the group in the garden. My aunt was still sitting in her cane chair but the others were strolling round the lawn, Barbara a few paces behind like an inquisitive dog. Barbara and her father at Rooks Nest! The very stones would revolt! Just for a moment I stayed in the porch alone, quiet, looking at them all before going up to Aunt Juby. I think it was at that moment that as I stood there musing, letting the blessed sun infuse my bones with warmth and seeing the garden and the people as though they were on a frieze, frozen for a few seconds in time, that I really said 'Goodbye' to my childhood. Soon I would have to discuss my future but I knew it was already decided. I would get my way.

* * *

The conversation at tea was at first rather desultory. Martha had laid one of Aunt's best lacy cloths on the oak table and the best silver tea-service was displayed on the sideboard. I had placed flowers everywhere – white and red roses. I thought we looked very fine. I looked round at our guests as Martha served us. Martha was continually looking at me, I knew. I also knew she was thinking of the purpose of this little party. I was going to leave them, and she didn't want me to go. I knew too that Martha's ideas of the good life were not mine and never could be. Yet I knew too that she would always love me, whatever I did, and I did not want to cause her pain. She expected me to behave better than girls of her own class. We still had our long chats in the kitchen when we talked about life, or at least I did, and Martha both warned me off 'men' and at the same time made it plain she expected me to marry. On the other hand she had said I was 'daft' to worry that I had not been born poor, guilty that I didn't have to go and work in a mill. 'You didn't make the world, lass,' she would say. 'You've no cause to worry over your luck. Anyroad, none of us has it easy – not even your high-born ladies.' I knew she was thinking of my mother. 'Aye, men are sent to try lasses,' she would go on sombrely. I supposed she thought the 'lasses' would get to heaven easier, they had so much to put up with!

I looked at Lavinia, refusing food as usual, and at Rainer, being polite to everyone, even including Martha who was for ever coming up and filling his cup with her good strong tea. 'Martha and her family are guardians of the past,' I remembered he had once said to me. 'The past was rough and poor but was dignified . . .' And I had said 'Don't you believe in "progress", Cousin?' I received only a smile and a shrug for an answer. Rainer was apparently enjoying Martha's tea-cakes and telling her so when she was near him. I saw Barbara looking rather scornful though I noticed she ate as much as ever, had not yet emulated Miss Logan in her frugal appetite.

I wondered whether Rainer had known about the love I had felt for Lavinia Logan and if he had, whether he had understood it. Only the other day when we had first discussed my going away he had said, 'You are so young – it's a pity . . .'

He had looked at me rather closely, making me feel uneasy. 'What is a pity, Rainer?' I had enquired. 'Never mind, it doesn't signify,' he had said. 'I expect you were thinking it was a pity I had not been born a boy.' He had laughed and replied, 'No, not that, I do assure you.'

I looked at Barbara to whom life seemed to be a matter of being comfortable – more than that, getting the best of everything, having a social position she thought was hers by right. I supposed Barbara and I were both, in our different ways, ambitious. Well now perhaps she would achieve her ambitions, or at least one of them. She saw me looking at her and a smile crept over her stolid features. Yes, she must have known about her father's plans, I decided.

I looked at Aunt Juby as she sipped her special pot of China tea which she had offered Lavinia too. I thought, she is thinking about me one day taking over her school – it is an investment for my future. She wants to say something to Lavinia about my prospects but she doesn't quite know how to begin. Perhaps I could say something about how it would be wiser for me to start my teaching somewhere else than Hartsedge – people would be sceptical of a teacher who had only just finished as a pupil in the same school.

I turned my attention to Rainer and saw he was looking at me as I had been studying the other guests and Aunt. *He* knew I must uproot myself to grow; *he* knew I did not want riches or fame, only to feel that I had not wasted my life, that I had given myself a chance.

When we had all eaten something and passed our teacups over to be filled more than once, Martha went out and brought in one of her special cakes. The conversation was turned by my cousin to the subject of the Angerstein family. No, Lavinia had not heard of them but she supposed they were very rich.

'They are impresarios – they combine the merchandising of the spring waters in Harrogate with the running of an hotel.'

'But who goes to Harrogate?' asked Barbara rudely. 'I thought everyone went to Spa nowadays.'

'Oh,' replied Rainer, 'there are plenty of people who are tired of Buxton or cannot make the journey abroad.'

'I expect there are the *nouveaux riches*,' I could not help adding. 'Manufacturers who send their wives and children to take the waters.'

'Indeed?' said Barbara frostily.

83

I changed the subject. 'Julia says that many of her family are musical – she is such a clever girl.'

'Jewish girls often marry young,' offered Lavinia.

'Women cannot make their way very easily without money or a husband,' answered Barbara with one of her secret smiles.

I do not rightly know why the whole idea of marriage gave me such disagreeable sensations but it did.

'One may become more materially comfortable, but one loses one's freedom,' I said in answer to Barbara.

Aunt must have felt that we were perhaps being a little disrespectful to Miss Logan as an unmarried lady so tried to change the subject, though Lavinia herself had introduced it. I was just about to say that women were all slaves in this Christian country but thought better of it.

'It was too hot to walk about,' said Aunt in a quiet voice. 'You young people seemed to be enjoying the exercise though!' I smiled, thinking that Juby considered Rainer and Lavinia to be young.

'Miss Logan brought her parasol so she should not spoil her complexion,' said Barbara to no one in particular.

'I should have brought you in straight away,' murmured Aunt in some distress.

'No, no – I had a pleasant walk round the garden,' replied Lavinia. 'The sun here is hardly as powerful as it is abroad. I have known days when I could not go out.'

'So you prefer England then?' enquired Rainer, looking at her with a rather enigmatic expression.

'It depends,' she replied diplomatically.

I did wish Barbara was not there. We should never get on to the subject of my future prowess as a governess which was the reason for the party. Still we could hardly have sent Barbara to take her tea in the kitchen.

That young lady was obviously determined to say nothing about her father's plans, except by innuendo, and we were all avoiding the subject. I cast another pebble into the pool of conversational waters.

'It is so much cooler now one's hair is up, is it not?' I asked her, looking at her long nose and high brow – her face had been a little improved by her putting her hair up. It took some of the emphasis from her nose and one saw the dark eyes.

'It is certainly cooler,' she replied, absentmindedly taking another piece of cake which Rainer offered her. 'Of course, you, Meta, do not care too much about your appearance,' she went on. 'But I think your hair is improved.'

'Thank you,' I replied with a slight bow. It was true I had become less careless of my appearance whatever Barbara said and had stopped trying to imitate Lavinia's hair style. Now I looped my hair round my face.

'Oh, girls all begin to take more care as they grow older,' said Aunt comfortably.

I decided to plunge. 'I shall have to look more responsible,' I said with a laugh, 'if I am to be a governess.'

Rainer took up my cue. 'Do you think my cousin will be suited to teaching, Miss Logan?' he enquired, looking at her with what I could see was assumed earnestness but with a smile not far from his lips.

'Well, of course – being a governess in a family is rather different from a school,' she said after a pause. 'I don't think I should like to teach in a family myself, but then young people are more adaptable.'

'Oh you could teach anywhere, Miss Logan,' I said. 'You have taught me so much.'

Rainer looked at me now rather meditatively. 'You have a certain talent, Meta,' he said. 'I'm sure Miss Logan would not wish to cast her pearls before those who are incapable of learning or not already – ' he paused ' – enthusiastic.'

'It is true that Meta has talent,' replied that lady. 'I always knew she would spread her wings. And she would probably appreciate a certain – ' she paused ' – *foreignness* in the family.'

Aunt was listening intently to this estimate of my abilities. Martha came in and Aunt gestured to her to carry away the fluted china cups and draw the blinds down over the mullions. Lavinia sat there at our table like a mermaid in the half-light in her green silk and chypre. 'What do you think then?' asked Aunt.

'Oh I think she is ready to go,' said Lavinia with a full look at me.

Barbara, her face averted, assumed a sort of amused sneer.

'And I think she will do as she wishes,' added Lavinia.

I had the feeling that perhaps Lavinia did not now approve of me and did not really care what I did, but I could not object. It was *my* idea to find a post. Not quite truthfully, I said: 'Of course, Aunt, if you objected I would not go.'

Rainer leaned back. 'Unlike most men I believe that girls –
young ladies rather – should learn to be a little more independent,' he pronounced. 'Like your teacher, Meta.' He bowed to
Lavinia. She looked at him from under her eyelashes.

'Work does give a little freedom,' I ventured.

Aunt again looked a little disturbed.

'Now Meta, learning how to use freedom is a – well, it is a
great responsibility for me – I want to feel assured that you will
be safe and happy. I hear that Miss Logan thinks you are compe-
tent for the work, but we are concerned too for your future.'

I could not bear it when they talked of me as though I were a
child. 'You know I want to see if I can get on in the world,' I
said, after thinking of a tactful way of putting it. 'I know it is unusual for *ladies,* but I am not one.'

'I don't see why anyone should choose anything so disagreeable as work with children,' remarked Barbara unexpectedly,
looking at Lavinia. 'Miss Logan, of course, has made an art out
of necessity,' she added and Lavinia bowed her head prettily.

Aunt obviously thought we were being too personal again.
'Well, Miss Logan seems to agree that she and your cousin might
write a written reference for the Angersteins, so we can then
finally accept for you, dear,' she said, turning to me.

'Thank you, Aunt,' I said, and smiled at her. I was uneasily
aware that there were things that were not being said because of
the presence of Barbara and Lavinia : the fact that I had no
money and depended upon Augusta and that she hoped one day
to leave the school to me if I did not marry. We turned to more
general topics and after tea we went into the stone garden again
which was cooler now. Rainer lit another cigar and Lavinia put
up her parasol and walked round the garden with Augusta. The
hedges at the bottom of the garden were full of wild roses, and
even violets, and under the bowl of the sky the distant brown
hills were wavering in the heat, merging into the moors.

Barbara was sitting hunched up on the old riding block and
seemed lost in thought. I hesitated for a moment near her, but
then turned away. I picked a few flowers for Rainer to take to his
widowed mother who was on a visit to him in the town.

Later, both Barbara and I joined my aunt who was sitting in
the stone garden. My aunt was still wearing her chip straw hat
and Barbara had on a large sun-bonnet. She was doing some fine
needlework. I lifted my face to the sun again.

'She will take the sun, won't she, Mrs Jewesbury?' said Barbara after a glance at me.

'It would be wiser to put on your bonnet,' said my aunt peaceably. Now that everything seemed settled about my future, she appeared calm.

'The northern sun is hardly strong enough to burn, Barbara,' I replied, looking at her through half-open eyes. Barbara had, like Lavinia, a rooted distaste for sunlight.

'Miss Logan puts cucumber cream on her face to avoid freckles,' said Barbara. 'And she washes her hands in honey and rose-water to keep them white.'

'Meta used to have freckles,' said Aunt, 'but they seem to have disappeared.' It was true – my original pale face had changed into a much darker version of itself. All this fussing over looks, how tedious it was. What could they matter? Yet they did matter – or else I should not have fallen into a passion for Lavinia! – I realized suddenly.

'Your face is your fortune,' said Barbara sententiously.

Maybe she guessed the drift of my thoughts. 'You don't need to look like a fashion plate to be a governess,' I replied.

'I shouldn't care to work for Jews,' she went on, as though she were determined to annoy me.

Just then Lavinia came up saying she would soon leave us and return to the Nest. 'I have to get back to let Effie go to church,' she said.

Aunt decided to go inside, while Rainer took the flowers I had gathered and accompanied Miss Logan to her carriage.

'So Meta is to seek her fortune,' said Barbara to me after a pause.

I ignored the remark. I longed to ask her about her father and Rooks Nest, but I was determined not to and so we sat in silence.

One day, a month or two before I went away, Julia came back for an afternoon and Rainer took me and Barbara and Julia out on to the moor. I had never succeeded in persuading Lavinia to venture on these moors – she was a town person through and through. I was in ecstasies once we were out 'on the top', though Barbara seemed to think the expedition a waste of time and refused to look at the view. Julia and my cousin kept up a long conversation about paintings and I felt my ignorance. I should have preferred to be alone, listening to the curlews, and so I was unusually silent. I felt uncivilized and uninformed and wondered whether I would be a fit governess for Julia's relatives in Harrogate. Then I forgot all this in the pleasure of the great lonely sweep of hills and wished I could write a poem about the set-apartness of it. There was a grand smell of fresh air and sun and I began to feel scoured of all my futile preoccupations. Perhaps the only thing to do was to go with Nature and cease striving to understand the world. Julia was discussing the architecture of Gothic cathedrals now. She was very well-informed and seemed to appreciate York Minster, even though her faith forbade her to worship in it. She was a very clever girl and I wished I had got to know her better. She was to go to Germany where some of her relatives were still living. I knew she intended to paint there. When we all returned that evening (we had gone down into Denholme and there taken Rainer's carriage home) Julia said to me: 'I like your cousin, Meta. He is very cultured for an Englishman.'

'I expect he has more time than businessmen,' I replied. 'I believe he was once going into the Church – but he didn't.'

'What *does* he do for a living?' asked Barbara, who had been listening.

'I'm not sure. I believe he corresponds for some financial newspaper – and goes abroad too in that connection.'

'He must have a private income then,' said Barbara sagely. 'And of course he owns *property*, doesn't he?'

I remembered that Barbara too had once said that my cousin would be a good match for Miss Logan. I had not got very far in my match-making. I wondered why he had never married and realized that I did not know him very well. For all I knew he might have a string of mistresses in London. I supposed, when I tried to think about it, that he was quite attractive, with his fair thick hair and slim form and workmanlike hands. He would have made a curious parson!

Julia's family replied to my aunt not long after this. I could be taken on for six months and then if both sides found the arrangement satisfactory I could stay on as long as I was needed. Julia's father's cousin, Mr Angerstein, was the businessman, the entrepreneur who had moved to Harrogate to establish, among other projects, the sulphur waters there. There were also, I gathered, plans afoot for the erection of new Winter Gardens where meals and concerts could be offered to the people who flocked to the town for their health. He was also thinking of buying another hotel.

So it turned out that I was to be taken on in Harrogate in September. In the last few weeks of my time at Hartsedge Hall I said goodbye to everyone as though I were off to the Americas and not going only thirty miles away to a little spa town. I was busy too, sorting books and working out a scheme of instruction as soon as I knew more about my future pupils. Word came from Angerstein père. There were two little girls, Fanny and Zillah, and a boy, Rufus, who was sharing his sisters' lessons for the time being. There had been a governess, but she had had to return to stay with her mother, a clergyman's widow.

'I expect they want to be little English children,' I remarked to Aunt as I packed my books and small possessions. 'Otherwise they would not want a clergyman's daughter – she would hardly approve of their religion. Perhaps that was the trouble,' I added, perusing Mr Angerstein's letter. 'Well, there is nothing here about my teaching religion, just arithmetic and globes and history and composition, spelling and reading.'

'I hope you will not neglect your own religious duties,' said Augusta mildly. I hoped that I would be able to escape regular Sunday worship. Perhaps I could pretend to go, and then take a walk instead. I said nothing.

Lavinia was very cool when I said farewell to her the day before I left. She would not be there when I left the next morning, for I was to leave early. It was a brief goodbye. Until the very last moment I was uncertain whether to take Lear's *Book of Nonsense* in my trunk, or *Tanglewood Tales* – or even *Uncle Tom's Cabin*. I wanted to read to the children and I was thinking about this when I went to the door to say goodbye to her, hearing Sam Hirst and the gig making noises in the yard. She put out her hand and I shook it. I did not kiss her, though I suppose I could have done – it was permissible – and once I would have taken the chance. But I felt sadly unmoved.

'I wish you well, Meta,' she said.

'I hope you will find happiness, Miss Logan,' I replied. She looked at me, smiling slightly. Then she turned and went away in the gig and the last I saw of her was a straight-backed figure sitting alone in the gig as the cloud of dust was stirred and then settled behind her. Later that night I went out to look at the Hall by moonlight and the picture of it remained with me in the months to come, and often came unbidden before sleep, the rose window silver in the light of the moon and the finials topping the gables like little moonlit gods.

The farewell to Martha was different. Martha was moved and trying not to show it and I believe she went straight back to her kitchen to wipe away a few tears. When Rainer came in his carriage in the morning there was only my aunt out at the porch to wave me goodbye, but I saw Barbara's thick figure at the schoolroom window. She raised her hand stiffly and then turned away. I looked back at the Hall, standing more solid now than in the moonlight when I had imprinted it on my memory, but I did not feel anything but a desire to be off.

Rainer did not speak till we were on the Bradford road. The offer of his carriage had diminished my worries about trains and gigs and I was grateful, for Harrogate lay a good day's journey to the north of us and we intended to break our journey in Bradford and take luncheon there.

I had made only short journeys before in our own neighbourhood, so I was looking forward to getting beyond Bradford on the Wharfedale road when everything would be new to me. I believe I saw more novelties on that journey and on my first day in Harrogate than I had had seen in all the past years of my life. The journey itself was interesting and the prospect exciting as well as strange. You learn such a lot on a journey and I had a delightful companion in my cousin who kept up a lively stream of conversation once we had both eaten at the Great Northern Hotel and had a glass of Burgundy with our meal. I wished in a way that the journey would never end. It was pleasant being treated as an equal at last. Over luncheon we discussed the Jewish religion, about which he seemed to be tolerably well informed, and the trade in sulphur well water. I could almost believe that I was on the Grand Tour. The waitress, who was a pretty girl with brown hair and bright blue eyes, called me Madame.

'They think you are my wife,' said Rainer, laughing.

For the first time I realized I was alone with an attractive man. But he was my cousin and I too was amused, though I suppose at eighteen I was not too young to be married. He told me about 'Young' Angerstein, Julia's uncle.

'He wants to provide a more "Continental" atmosphere for the *nouveaux riches*,' said Rainer. 'The cures of water to date have been rather rough and ready. The town has just woken up to the fact we are in the nineteenth century and that people, other than the nobility, have money to spare. I believe they would like to make it more like Buxton, although there is no Duke to back them.'

I was aware that I knew little of the town where I was going to live. I had imagined it as something like Baden where Papa had stayed. Still, this was Yorkshire and I must not weave romantic dreams around it. Rainer seemed to guess what I was thinking for he said, once we were on the last leg of my journey: 'The family will be foreign in a way, but this is still Yorkshire – it is not like going to Spa or Vichy.' I thought of Barbara's remark. 'I wish I could go abroad,' I said.

'Perhaps this will be the first step on the way,' he replied. 'I expect the Angersteins go to Germany – perhaps to the Rhine on vacation.'

'They would hardly take their children and their governess,' I replied.

'Strange how all you romantics aspire to abroad,' he added, and I was pleased that he had given me a name. 'There *was* Wordsworth apostrophizing the homely daffodil but Keats had to have his Rome and Shelley his Italy . . .'

'And Byron his travels everywhere,' I agreed.

'Oh, Byron – he is not a good example for the virtuous, is he? What about nearer home and the poetry of our moors?'

'It is the *Drang nach Süden*,' I said solemnly, as he was taking me seriously. 'I do love our moors, but there is this impulse to go south.'

'Like your papa,' he said, looking at me as though he hoped we could converse rationally about Papa at last.

'It is easier for young men,' I said. 'Even a businessman travels.'

I was quite sorry when our journey ended at dusk, for before we got to Harrogate I had seen the drystone walls and the farms and had thought how wild it would be in winter up there and I loved it all. Then we had got down into the valley again.

'Harrogate is become very genteel,' he said. 'There is a difference between that and true gentility, as I expect you know – but your new family will not be genteel. That doesn't mean you won't have to be on your best behaviour of course.'

I laughed. 'I like Julia,' I said. 'If her family are like her it will be all right. She is so lively and doesn't mind showing her feelings – not that a governess should have any, I know. I shall not presume.'

'Don't wear your heart on your sleeve, Meta,' he said seriously. There was a short silence before he added : 'Julia is a very fine young woman.'

There were now only a few miles to go and the scenery was softer and greener. Dusk had not yet fallen. It was one of those September evenings when everything is golden and quiet with the suspicion of garden fires smoking away in the distance.

'I expect there will be some concerts,' he said. 'And you might go if you save any money, or they might even take you. It depends whether they accept you as a member of the family. I don't think they are socially sure enough yet to consider you with your family background as a "servant", so you might be lucky. I shall deposit you on the Angerstein doorstep,' he went on. 'I shall not queer your pitch by introducing myself. But do write to your aunt, Meta. She will worry until she knows you are settled.'

'Of course I will,' I replied. I thought he was going to say something else, but he did not and now that the town was approaching I began to be more excited. I did say, though, what I had rehearsed already.

'Miss Logan will be lonely. I do not mean that I was any company for her but she is alone at Rooks Nest save for that gloomy maid Effie and the caretaking couple. I thought perhaps you could persuade my aunt to have her over – for dinner maybe – and you might take her to whatever is going on in Halifax.'

'Meta, do not try to arrange other people's lives for them, my dear,' was his reply and I was silent with mortification. 'I worry more about you than your Miss Logan,' he said, mollifying me.

'I don't think anyone should worry about me,' I replied. He was treating me as a child again.

'Well, if you will promise to do nothing rash I will promise to keep an eye on Lavinia Logan,' he said. I assented. 'I wish we *could* have sent you to a lyceum abroad,' he said, after a pause. 'There are very few places for girls to study. In America I gather there are colleges for women starting up. Still, I am sure your accomplishments will pass muster.'

'Provided I don't have to teach fine needlework.'

'You must read systematically in your leisure hours,' he then said. 'If you wish, I will compose a reading list for you to enliven your free time – if you have any.'

'Please do,' I said, gratified. 'You should have been a school-master, Cousin.'

'I am supposed to be above such things,' he said with a smile.

The light was beginning to fade now from the hills and the gas lamps of the town were being lit as we slowed our pace. The house which we finally drew up at was in a crescent of new residences on the right of the main road into the town. The road sloped down in grey cobbles and there were cobbles too outside Montpelier Crescent, and little lamps in front of the houses. Without more ado my trunk and my bags were got down for me and Rainer pulled on a large bell rope. It was a tall house with an imposing flight of steps and before I knew what was happening a maid had arrived at the door.

'I shall not stay,' said Rainer to me. 'This is Miss Moore,' he said to the maid who had red cheeks and a red apron over a brown holland dress. 'Please tell your mistress she has arrived.' Then as the maid departed and my trunks were taken in by a white-haired odd-job man, Rainer bowed to me and said: 'Don't forget now. Good luck! Remember, if anything is wrong you write to me, and I shall come and rescue you.' Then he was gone before I could take it in.

Suddenly I was in the marble entrance hall and the maid was back.

'Step this way, Miss, they're expecting you. Come down to the salon when you're ready.'

I followed her upstairs, up a vast staircase with a window in coloured glass let into the wall of the entresol where the curtains had not yet been drawn. There was a smell of cigar smoke everywhere, and the rooms on the first floor had velvet curtains across their doors. It was the first Jewish house I had ever been in and it was warm and opulent-looking.

I was taken by the maid who said: 'I'm Emma, Miss', into a room at the top of the house. This was to be mine. Hurriedly I combed my hair and discovered a wash-stand behind a false door, where I damped my face and hands and tried to slow the beating of my heart. Then, after finding a looking-glass hanging on the wall near my bed and checking that I looked reasonably rational, I went downstairs. The elderly maid was waiting in the hall. She was sitting on an oak settle but got up and took me

93

through the hall to the furthest door at the back of the house. This must be the salon. It was in fact a drawing room and was rather grand with tall windows and a decorated cornice. A small fat man got up from a low chair and I saw that a dark-haired lady was seated behind him in another comfortable-looking chair.

'Miss Moore, Mr Angerstein,' said the maid and departed.

'Well, well, there we are, there we are!' He stood for a moment peering at me. He had a round face with a long nose and tightly curled grey hair. 'Esther my dear, – Miss Moore,' he said. The lady smiled but did not get up so I thought I had better drop a curtsey which I did . . .

'You'll be hungry – did you come alone? There's a bite of supper for you in the back dining room,' he said, 'time for formalities later.' He had a slight foreign inflection but it was a strong voice which emphasized each syllable clearly. His wife then spoke. She seemed a little ill at ease. I thought she looked rather like Julia but the relationship was on the side of *Mr* Angerstein to Julia's mother.

So these were my new employers. I think I managed to acquit myself creditably in a short conversation about carriages and journeys and Julia, and then I was allowed to go and eat something before retiring to my bed. The children were said to be already in theirs. It was only when I crept thankfully up to my bed and saw four black eyes peeping round a door on the floor below mine followed by a hasty slamming of the door, that I realized that my arrival had not gone unremarked by at least two of my new charges.

It was all as different as possible from the Hall. To begin with there was always the sound of voices discussing or arguing and a good deal of laughter, whereas we had all been rather quiet at my aunt's house. Breakfast was taken in the children's schoolroom and of course there was no bacon and eggs but some cold beef and pickles with a sharp and pleasant taste once you got used to them. I was expected to eat this meal with the children and for that I was thankful.

On my first morning, I rose when Emma, the maid I had seen the night before, led in a little girl with a mop of black hair like a wire brush, deposited her on a chair and said: 'This is Zillah, Miss.'

'Hello, Zillah,' I said.

She looked at me in round-eyed silence. She could not be more than five years old and must be the youngest child. Emma brought in some coffee and I was surprised to see the child drink it and dip her oat bread into it with every appearance of enjoyment.

'Where is your brother Rufus?' I asked.

'He is in bed I should think,' said the little girl. I now saw how like her father she was. 'He likes bed because he is lazy,' she said.

'Oh no I'm not – here I am . . .' A boy bounded into the room and I found myself looking at the same black eyes I had seen the night before.

'And where is your other sister?' I asked him.

'She is talking to Papa – she's coming.'

I wondered whether I was expected to fetch them from their bedchambers. 'Do you have a nursery-maid?' I asked.

'Of course not, we are not babies,' said Rufus, helping himself to a large amount of porridge.

The door opened quietly and a miniature Julia came in, curtseyed to me and solemnly took her place at table. 'You will not say "grace" like Miss Haythornthwaite, will you?' she asked. The former governess I presumed.

'No I shall not,' I said.

They all seemed to have good appetites and we munched away. I asked them the usual questions which adults ask children. 'How old are *you*?' asked Rufus and I remembered how I had once asked Martha why children could not ask grown-ups their age.

'You know she is a little bit older than her teeth,' said Fanny, smiling. She was a beautiful child and I wondered whether her mind was as exceptional as her looks.

After breakfast when their papa came into the schoolroom they did not seem to stand in any awe of him. He explained that the children's books were ready for my inspection and that I might then plan some lessons by interrogating the children as to their knowledge of various matters. 'Then I think you should take them for a walk to the town at eleven o'clock. Rufus and Fanny will show you the short-cut and you may bring them to lunch with their mama at one o'clock.' He took out his watch. 'I must be off. Fanny, look after your new teacher. Rufus, take care of your Mutterle – excuse my wife, Miss Moore – she is shy.' And with that he was off. The children waved him goodbye from the window. He was decidedly unconventional!

No wonder Mama, or Mutterle as he called her, was a little shy. I imagined she could not get in a word to stem his flow. But the children obviously adored him.

I had seen almost nothing of the town the night before and was eager for a walk. So were the children. They submitted to Emma's coming in and brushing their hair and reminding them that their father believed in shining shoes, then after a short inspection of their books and a dictation to the two eldest we were off. I decided to use my afternoon for the preparation of some lessons. I could always read to them until I got the feel of their capabilities and the lacunae of their knowledge. Little Zillah was hardly out of the nursery, but she said she could read, so I believed her until it should be proved otherwise. Soon we were out and down the steps of the stone house, Rufus leading. The sound of horses on the cobblestones was loud and the whole town appeared in a bustle and was more extensive than I had thought it. Fanny and Rufus answered my questions as well as they could while Rufus appeared to be an expert on sulphur wells and other kinds of wells of which I had had no idea.

Harrogate at that time was a prosperous little town. As we came down the road into the centre, many carriages could be seen congregating round a circular building with long windows let into the side and mock Corinthian pillars on its jutting stone flanks. The building was topped by a dome crested by a piece of wrought iron work. 'That's the Royal Pump Room,' said Rufus. 'It's over the sulphur well. Papa doesn't own that of course.' I saw that most of the people were middle-aged or elderly.

'The people come here to retire,' said Fanny. 'Papa wants younger people to come – but he says they've all gone to the seaside.' The children seemed remarkably well-informed and I guessed I should not have too much difficulty in interesting them in lessons if I could make the acquisition of knowledge interesting. Little Zillah was silent. She had not yet been initiated into the mysteries of Papa's business.

'The best wells are on the Stray,' said Rufus. 'And there's another pump room which Papa is managing.'

'That's on the Stray is it?' I asked.

'No, it's the Sweet Spa. The Tewitt Well is on the Stray,' replied Rufus as though I should have known that. I felt I ought to have prepared myself better.

'And there are the baths near the Town Hall,' said Fanny. 'Papa says they used to get into tubs like coffins, but the new pools are nice. You could go there.'

'Should I need to swim?' I asked. I could not swim of course.

Fanny laughed and said no, of course not. She went on to tell me of the things that used to go on in the town in the 'olden days'. Apparently Mr Angerstein wanted to bring back a theatre and a restaurant and a dance hall. Rufus was more interested in the racecourse. They chattered away as we came down to the domed building. The weather was nippy and I hoped that Zillah would not take cold in her thin pelisse. Perhaps I should have consulted someone about their outdoor wear? What a responsibility they were going to be.

'It's much colder on the Stray,' said Fanny, noticing that I was feeling a little cold. 'Mama says that Harrogate will kill you if it doesn't cure you,' she added. I said I hoped not but that perhaps we might walk to the Stray, of which I had heard so much, another day.

'There's an old man there who Papa says is set to live for ever,' went on Fanny. 'He looks after the Sweet Spa and so they call it John's well because he's called John.'

'Are there gardens there?' I asked. I was not very interested in sulphur wells and supposed the children were because of their papa, who seemed to be intent on bringing up his children to understand business.

'Of course,' said Rufus. 'The Valley Gardens. Papa says there are eighty different wells up there – all sorts of waters.'

I looked around me as we circled the Royal Pump Room. The people, besides being rather old, looked comfortable rather than elegant and I was a little disappointed. The women looked like manufacturers' wives or widows or unmarried daughters; some of them were going into the building. On our way back I saw a large hotel with HYDRO inscribed on a large board in front of a new pavement. I wondered what Mr Angerstein was planning for his hotels. I had noticed a great many as we had come down into the town and wondered which he owned.

'Papa is going to have concerts – somewhere,' said Fanny.

'In the Winter Gardens, silly,' said Rufus.

That sounded more elegant so I let Rufus acquaint me with more information as we walked along. My head was quite buzzing with words I had never heard before – Sulphate of Magnesium and Chalybeate and Calcium Sulphate. Governess had indeed been turned into pupil!

Rufus loved the imparting of knowledge, a tendency which must have been encouraged by his father. Fanny did not talk quite as much but seemed to brighten up when Rufus spoke of the plans for a music club. Apart from taking the waters, the folk must have something to do apart from gossiping and dozing and music seemed a very good idea to me. As we wound our way back to the crescent for luncheon, which I was to take with the children and their mother, we passed a few younger couples out promenading and probably flirting. They were not all old then, thank goodness. It would be a trial indeed to have the company only of the very young or the aged.

'Why didn't you want to be a companion instead of a governess?' Fanny was asking.

We all seemed to be on a very democratic footing and I hoped it was not going to mean that I would have no authority over them when I needed it. Really I found the children quite a tonic and hoped this beginning was not going to be untypical of our life together. Little Zillah held my hand for all the world as though I had known her all her life. They must be used to meeting new people and yet they must also have had a good deal of intercourse with their parents.

Later, I found this to be true. Both Mr and Mrs Angerstein were devoted parents and always spent an hour or two in their children's company after tea, even seeming rather reluctant to let them go to bed. It was all very unlike the rather stiff and formal atmosphere I had imagined I might have to get used to. Esther Angerstein seemed less socially assured than her husband. Perhaps she had come to a wealthy life rather late. He was full of ebullience and after tea on my first day there, when I had been told to take a few hours to myself (which I occupied in revising my plans for lessons), he could be heard romping with his children in what would have been regarded as a rather 'common' way in the circles in which I had been brought up. I thought it was delightful, though I found out later he sometimes overexcited the children. Little Zillah seemed to be his favourite whilst Rufus was the apple of his mother's eye. Fanny fell more to me as time went on. She was open and friendly but there were times when I saw her deep in thought with a faraway look on her face. I did not want to breach her confidence, remembering well how I had liked to have secrets when I was a child. Perhaps one day we could share our thoughts.

The talk was all of the winter season when Mr Angerstein and his business associates were to launch their new plans on the town. I heard it in the salon and in the dining room, for sometimes I would be allowed to dine with the husband and wife. I wondered who really ran the house, for I had met only Emma and a cook and the old handyman, and there were two young maids of all work who came daily. I was to discover that the 'housekeeper', who also aided her master with accounts and correspondence, was a Miss Hertz. She was a niece of Mrs Angerstein and was at present away on holiday. My predecessor as governess, Miss Haythornwaite, was referred to with some amusement. I guessed she must have found the children a handful and perhaps considered them too indulged. Rufus was sometimes very boisterous and noisy, but he was essentially good-hearted and I do not think she could have been ill-treated. I might find out more from Julia but she was presently abroad, lucky miss. I discovered that both the little girls were exceptionally musical and this seemed to be taken as a matter of course by their papa. Their mama, too, accepted these gifts as only to be expected.

'My father's family,' she told me one day when I think she was feeling that she could know me better without risking a governess's criticism of her lack of education, 'are all very musical.'

I discovered that her lack of self confidence was because of her early upbringing. She had been born to a poor family of German immigrants who had only in her brother's generation made good in the worsted merchants' business in Bradford. She loved her children but was inclined to indulge them as marvellous creatures of her husband's as though, except for musical talents, she had had nothing to do with any of it.

I found too that Rufus was easily bored and that his papa was hoping to send him to a boarding school. He had not wanted to send him away young. 'The English are barbarians,' said Mr Angerstein. 'They send their boys away to school to learn bad habits. I would rather keep my eye on my boy till he is a little older.' Rufus was mercurial, old for his age and well-informed as I had seen on our first day together. I supposed he was to follow his papa in the chalybeate business or the hotel trade. Many business associates visited my employer every day or left messages, and Mrs Angerstein would often disappear to the kitchens to acquaint the cook with some delicacy. She loved to cook herself and I heard her sometimes singing in her own kitchens. Cook, Mrs Robinson, didn't seem to mind. 'They're foreign, love,' she said to me once, as though that explained everything.

My first few weeks passed so quickly that I had hardly spared a thought for my aunt and Martha, although the sight of some of the ladies in the town in their furs and well-cut costumes had made me think more than once of Lavinia. I was not to return for Christmas (it was not of course a festival for my Harrogate family) but I did not mind. Apparently I could take a few weeks' holiday if I wished in the summer. That seemed a long way away. I managed a long letter eventually to my aunt and Martha and received two myself in reply, one from Augusta and one, surprisingly, from Barbara. Augusta's letter was like herself, a little absent-minded. There was not much news : Martha said to tell me that Sam Hirst was to marry in the spring and that her mother was well but rheumaticky and that she, Martha, hoped I was wrapping up well in that place which she had heard was the coldest in the whole of Yorkshire. Augusta for her part recommended a good book for beginning on English history since I had told her my two oldest charges were forward for their age. In all *these* matters Augusta was precise.

Barbara's letter was more of a shock. She had been to a concert with 'Vinny' which they had not much enjoyed and 'Vinny' had been a little indisposed after it. It took me a minute or two to realize that she was talking of Lavinia. But the lady was now better, though Barbara thought she should take a holiday. She had apparently recovered enough to accompany my cousin Mr Moore to a hospital benefit. Mr Moore had had a ticket and Miss Jewesbury had suggested it would make a little treat for Vinny. Barbara had not been invited and was clearly annoyed, though with whom was not clear. Her papa was not well and this had necessitated her staying over with him at The Folly, his house on the other side of the town. He was a little recovered now but she was hoping that she might invite Vinny to stay for a week or two with them at the end of October. 'The house is very well appointed and I have ordered him a new cook,' she continued. I found all this faintly disturbing. Barbara made no mention, however, of Rooks Nest, for which I was thankful. I had not heard from my cousin, and Aunt had said he was now abroad again. I wondered whether he had succumbed to Lavinia's charms and I felt instinctively that this would not please Barbara. Her letter was on thick embossed paper and written in her peculiar large backward-sloping hand. I replied to it when I had replied to my aunt. I didn't think Barbara would be interested in the details of my new life so did not say much about it to her except that I was well and happy and very busy and learning as much as I hoped my charges were. Then I wrote to Lavinia expressing my concern at her indisposition. I found this letter difficult and sighed over it many times. How I should have once leapt at the chance of addressing her! I hoped, but did not say, that she did not find Barbara's ministrations too tedious. I wondered whether Rainer had seen more of her than one visit to the theatre. His comings and goings had always been mysterious to me. In the end I contented myself with hoping that she was feeling recovered from her illness – I fear I repeated myself – and that she would have a pleasant rest and repose at Barbara's father's.

I was thinking about this letter as Fanny and I were sitting in the schoolroom one November day. Rufus had gone out with his papa, who believed that boys should learn how their fathers spent their time at work. Zillah was being measured for a new coat. Her aunt, Mrs Angerstein's sister Leah, was a fine tailoress and the family were proud that their children were dressed in the latest fashions, secretly conjured through Aunt Leah's clever fingers. Fanny, who had been patiently drawing a copy of one of Bewick's birds and arranging her water-colours preparatory to painting it, had been for some minutes regarding me for she said: 'Am I allowed, Miss Moore, to ask a penny for your thoughts?'

'If you tell me yours,' I replied, coming out of my brown study.

Fanny licked her paintbrush meditatively. 'I was thinking that rose madder – which I think I shall use for the bird's front feathers – reminds me of an Irish girl, like those Irish girls Mama used to know in Leeds.' I laughed and saw the point. 'She had blue eyes and dark hair and a rose-red dress,' continued Fanny. 'Now yours.'

'Strangely enough I was thinking of an Irish lady I used to know,' I replied.

'Did she have blue eyes and black hair?'

'No. She was my teacher and she had – has brown hair and brown eyes and never wears red dresses.'

Fanny digested this. 'Who do you think Green Bice is?' she then asked, squinting at the paint-box.

'Miss Bice?' I said. 'A not very pleasant lady with hobbledy shoes.'

'That is what I think,' said Fanny seriously. 'Miss Haythornwaite thought it was wrong to make up stories.'

'Oh dear, did she? Whyever was that?'

'She said stories were lies,' replied Fanny. 'Wasn't she stupid?'

I thought I had better defend my predecessor so I replied that from one point of view imaginary people were not true in fact, though they might be fun to imagine.

'Was Topsy true?' asked Fanny. We had begun on *Uncle Tom's Cabin* that week which I read to them upstairs before they went to bed.

'I expect there were lots of Topsies,' I answered.

'I should like to write stories or play the violin,' Fanny went on. 'But Zillah has more music than I have – Mama says so – I expect I shall write stories.'

'I shall correct your spelling,' I said. Fanny's spelling was none too correct.

I did not have to teach the children much practical music – their mama took care of that and I was relieved. I still loved listening to music but had more or less given up the attempt to play it. I discouraged myself when I heard the imperfect harmonies my fingers called out of the pianoforte. The children had as yet had no dancing lessons either. My time was fully occupied with geography and history and written compositions, not to mention mathematics. I had sufficient knowledge for the girls but Rufus bid fair to become a good mathematician and I was glad that he would go to school the next year when my knowledge would have been exhausted by him. He was only a year older than Fanny, who was nine, but his interest in numbers and equations far outstripped hers, though Fanny worked much harder. She had told me one day at another of our afternoon lessons that her mama had had another little boy who came after her but before Zillah, but that he had died of the scarlet fever.

I tried to act in a grown-up way now that I was a governess. Studying agreed with my own inclinations but I suppose I was a rather earnest girl in any case and it was good for me that my charges paradoxically kept me young. I wanted of course to live a more exciting life, yearned to fall in love with someone again, but I think I gave the impression of serious-mindedness which must have pleased my employers who did not know the other side of my character!

The weeks passed very pleasantly and I was enjoying my tasks, still novel enough to keep my enthusiasm on the boil, when one evening their father called me to his study.

'Don't look so worried, Miss Moore,' he began. 'It is only a request that you might perhaps begin a little French with my elder daughter. They have German as you know – my wife's family still speak it – but we thought that perhaps a small amount of conversation in the French language would be an adornment to Fanny. I believe you are proficient in it?'

'Yes of course, Mr Angerstein. I'd like to teach them French.'

He was diving about in a mass of papers and I recognized a letter from my aunt, for her spidery script was unmistakable. 'Will you need the purchase of books?'

'I think to begin with we could manage without,' I replied.

Thus it was that French was added to my duties. It did seem a language remote from Harrogate, though I suppose that fifty years before the spa towns would have resounded with it. I did wish that Harrogate was a little more aristocratic. I began my French instruction soon after, and what with that and all my other tasks and the walks on which I accompanied the children, my time was well taken up. Those were happy days, especially with Fanny who was, as I had thought, an apt pupil. Happy days indeed. Uneventful but safe and calm. Sometimes I wondered whether life would have anything more in store for me than the instruction of children and the pleasant but unexciting days we passed.

As autumn drew into winter I felt I had been with the Angersteins half my life. Harrogate itself seemed to come to life a little when the Winter Gardens opened. They were to be heated by pipes from the bathing establishment close by. It was truly a very cold town and I wrapped up well on Martha's instructions when I took the children for windy walks on the Stray. There were no flowers now in its gardens but I observed a great deal of digging and pruning going on.

It was on one of our walks returning from the Stray that I suddenly stopped and caught my breath. We had turned the corner to begin the long wind uphill to home and tea round the nursery fire when across the road I saw a woman in a long green over-skirt whisking round the corner away from us, and for a moment I thought it was Lavinia. Then she was gone. My imagination must be playing me tricks. Usually I slept well although I always rose with a fading dream in my head, but that morning I had woken knowing that I had dreamt of home. Even as we were plodding across the grassy slopes of the Stray the dream had been a little with me in remembered wisps. What more likely than I should think I saw Rooks Nest's present tenant? It was odd, for during my *waking* life at that time I rarely thought of home and the Hall and my schooldays. I had heard nothing further from Barbara, and my cousin Rainer had not written to me.

That day was a Friday and we had to be back before sunset. The family, though not excessively orthodox, liked to assemble together each Friday evening for the beginning of the Sabbath, as Rainer had told me they would. The special candles would be lit and I should be allowed to go in to another room with a fire and my book whilst they ate their unleavened bread. No more work was done after that by Mr Angerstein or his wife, and the maids would tidy the house and lay the fires for the morrow. The children would go to bed at their usual time and after that my time would be my own. None of the other servants were themselves Jewish, except the as yet unseen Miss Naomi Hertz, who helped Mr Angerstein with his accounts. The next day, Saturday, the family would go in the morning to worship in a private house of one of the other Jewish families, the nearest synagogue being in Leeds. I wondered what they did there and how they felt; they always came back happy. Rufus was already learning Hebrew with an old Rabbi who lived not far away. On Sundays I was given time to go to church if I wished. I'm afraid I didn't always go. The parish church at that time was rather Puseyiteish. That did not worry me. I always enjoyed ritual and 'bells and smells' and it mattered little to me how we so-called Christians worshipped, but I preferred to seize the opportunity to go for a solitary walk. The family were kind; I was content with my life as far as it went, but I did miss being alone – and the children hardly ever left me alone. An hour or two by myself, even in the rain, gave me peace of mind and enabled me to sort out my thoughts.

The strange momentary idea that I had seen Lavinia had unnerved me a little. The Sunday after that walk on the Stray I kept thinking that she could be in Harrogate. And I realized that I did not want to see her. Why? I tried to reason with myself as I went on my short walk, wishing that I could walk away further, perhaps to the brown hills in the distance. I was never free long enough to go anywhere where there were no people. The moors, even here, were not far away – but I had no excuse for tramping them. It would probably be considered quite odd enough that I walked to the boundaries of the town alone.

Why though did I still feel uneasy about Lavinia? She had never given me any encouragement when I was her pupil, had she? I had felt strongly for her. I would never recant and pretend I hadn't. She had not changed in the past year; I had. Did I really mind Barbara becoming her constant companion, if that was what Lavinia wanted? 'Vinny' indeed! Barbara had written that letter to make me feel jealous and I did not. I remembered my feelings but I could not feel them in my heart. Did all love end like that? Or was it not love I had felt? Had I ever really expected Rainer to take Lavinia over and court her? No. I had felt easy about it because I knew at the bottom of my heart that he would never love her. She might flirt a little with him; it must be a dreary life for her teaching at the Hall. Drearier than mine? But I was young – that was the difference. I might occasionally feel *ennui*, yet I was full of hope that one day I should lead the sort of life I wanted among the sort of people with whom I knew I would feel at home. Teaching the Angersteins' children was not going to suffice me for ever. They would grow up. In seven years Fanny would be a young lady. Seven years! I should be twenty-five then and what would I have done – what could I do with my life? I was so absorbed in these thoughts that I bumped into a gas-lamp and was forced to laugh at my own self-absorption which made a lady and gentleman passing me on the pavement stare at me in surprise. Had I really imagined that Harrogate would hold the key to a life of glamour and sophistication? The Angersteins were a good and happy family but I did not belong there. Where *did* I belong? Was the best I could expect the founding of such a family myself? I rebelled against the idea.

I don't think any of my thoughts were apparent on my face when I returned to Montpelier Crescent. Sunday was the day for an English dinner which we ate at lunch-time and the conversation was shared by the children and any friends invited to the meal. The talk that day was all of the Winter Gardens and of the new season after Christmas. A violinist and a pianist had to be hired to play there. A Mr Rosen had written pleading prior engagements with the management of Scarborough Spa with whom we were rivals. There was talk of more ambitious concerts and of a new tea-room to be established in the Winter Gardens.

'Don't tell me coffee would be more suitable, my dear,' said Angerstein to his wife. 'I know it would. But we have to cater to English tastes. Like the roast beef.' He pronged a large slice on his fork.

'Well, Jacob, I'm sure you will manage it all perfectly,' replied his wife.

'Is Moses Hirsch coming this afternoon then?' Esther Angerstein was used to impromptu meetings and gatherings in her own drawing room and never complained.

'I was wondering,' said her husband, mopping up his gravy with a large piece of bread, 'whether you might not mention to your Uncle Eli, about the music, Liebling. What news about Eli's son Benjie? He plays well doesn't he? And you were saying some time ago that he won't join Eli in the business.'

'Oh – Benjamin? I don't know, Jacob, would he be reliable? Leah was telling me he wants to go back to Germany – to Leipzig – he says he has friends there at the Conservatory. I could write to Eli if you wish.'

'Yes, do that – better from you as a member of the family. Tell Eli that if Benjamin wants a try-out he could come and play here if we can't get Rosen, and Isaacson is busy with his Elijahs . . .'

'I had better put it tactfully,' replied his wife. 'Papa always says musicians are touchy, and you don't want him to think he's second-best, an understudy.'

'No, I see. Just write, my dear, and I shall make my own enquiries.'

I thought all these musicians seemed to have Jewish names. The talk passed to the Schillerverein and the Liedertafel in Bradford and the possibility of the aforementioned Moses Hirsch establishing something similar here in Harrogate. I wondered how many Yorkshire people would be interested in a German poet or in poetry at all, but of course quite a number of the folk

who took their cures here would be Jewish too, from the manu-
facturing cities. I wished I had some talent in a musical direction.
If I could have been a great singer or played the violin I might
have the sort of life I dreamed of. Even to play in a pantomime
would be one way of escaping the life of an impecunious non-
lady. There must be something I could do. Then Mr Angerstein
turned politely to me.

'I was wondering, Miss Moore, if you had time – you know a
little German – could you copy some words of songs for me? It
would be a great help.'

'Of course, sir,' I murmured.

'Oh Jacob, she is so busy – when Miss Hertz returns?' His
wife rarely tried to alter any of his arrangements but she must
have thought he might be imposing on me.

'No, really, Mrs Angerstein,' I said, 'I should like to do it. I
love the German language and would be pleased to improve my
knowledge of it.' She smiled at me – it was obviously a way to
her heart. From that day she would speak to me a little in
German. It did not sound like the German Lavinia had taught me
but it gave my mind occupation. I thought I might try perhaps
to translate into passable English some of the songs and poems
Jacob Angerstein wanted copied.

The whole Winter Gardens project sounded romantic. I wondered how many similar projects his fertile brain had begun in
his business life. Some must have been successful or we should
not be sitting having coffee in Montpelier Crescent with its
drawing room carpeted in rich thick wool and curtained in
wine-coloured velvet.

It must have been a week or two later when we were all yawn-
ing at breakfast and I was wondering whether the whole world
was reduced to sleepy children and faintly dissatisfied gover-
nesses that I overheard a conversation between my employers.
The schoolroom was next to Mrs Angerstein's sewing room and
I heard her call her husband in. As they always left doors open I
heard her say: 'Benjamin cannot come. How provoking for
you, Jacob. But wait – I cannot read Eli's writing very well – he
says that Benjamin has a gifted friend who plays both piano and
violin and is looking for engagements. You might like to see
him.'

'Oh if Eli says so. His Benjamin is getting big ideas,' said
Jacob. 'The concerts cannot begin until the New Year. I am busy

107

with the Baths committee today. Tell your Eli to tell the young man to write.'

Oh good, I thought, we are really going to have concerts and perhaps I shall be allowed to take Fanny to one or two.

I began to look forward to a visit to the Winter Gardens.

The post had also brought a letter for me and I read it while the children were doing their morning sums, Zillah getting ink all over her face as well as her fingers. It was from my cousin Rainer. He was sorry that I should not be home for Christmas and knew that Augusta was sorry too but looked forward to seeing me in the spring or summer. Meanwhile there was a possibility of his coming over to Harrogate in February on a visit. He did not say why he had not written before, but then *I* had not yet written to him. He assumed that not hearing from me meant I was well and happy. He hoped so. His next paragraph was more interesting.

I don't know if you have heard from that peculiar school-friend of yours but I am told by your aunt that her father *is* about to make a definite offer to buy Rooks Nest from me. This in confidence. I have heard nothing yet. I thought you would be interested. Apparently the man has been very ill and your little friend has whispered that some money or property will be settled on her in the event of his demise before she comes of age. Your aunt spoke to me in quite a tizzy last week for she had a message from Miss Logan to say that she would be staying at the Folly with Barbara and her father, and would not be at the school on the Monday morning. We wondered whether Mr Stott had decided to take on a housekeeper! But no, Miss Logan arrived as prim as ever on the Tuesday bearing a message from Miss Stott to the effect that she would now be devoting her time to her father and would pass round and collect her things from the Hall when it was convenient! It would seem that Miss Logan is to continue at Rooks Nest and I have heard nothing yet from Widdop of the amount Stott is offering for the Nest. Stott cannot surely last much longer. He has diabetes. Such are the excitements of our quiet life here. Since I returned, that has been the only news, if you exempt the turning over of Jem Whiteley's barrow in the market by an irate rival, or the overflow of the town drain by reason of inclement weather. I should of course be glad to hear from you, but I expect you are drinking life to the full in the Athens of the north or should it be the Pompei of the north (all those baths).

This letter made me laugh and also intrigued me. I wondered why Barbara was again entertaining Lavinia at her father's and wondered also why she had not left the Hall earlier. Perhaps she had just been able to prevail upon her papa to lay his money out in the way she had always wanted. But would he really buy Rooks Nest, and what would happen to Lavinia? I felt uneasy.

I was not long to remain in ignorance for I received by the next day's post another letter, this time from my aunt. A definite offer had been received by Mr Widdop from Mr Joseph Stott for the purchase of Rooks Nest by him, from Cousin Rainer's father for the sum of ten thousand pounds. Aunt added: 'Of course, he will leave it to Barbara – she being his only child – in the event of his death. We are all agog.'

I was reading this letter in the schoolroom whilst the children busied themselves trying to produce copperplate handwriting. Fanny heard my sharp intake of breath as I read, and looked up at me. I could not bear to sit still. I wanted to speak – to say to someone, No, no! This is not possible, Rooks Nest to go to Barbara in the end. Perhaps her father might remarry? I had thought that before, or even that he might have his sights on Lavinia. But if he were really ill – and if he died and 'of course he will leave it to Barbara on his death' – my aunt's words . . . the awfulness of all this came upon me. I wanted to shout, then cry. My Rooks Nest – and Barbara. All she had said, a long time ago, about renovating it, and how pleasant it would be to be rich . . . Her father was rich and her father might soon die – and she would live there, change it. My Rooks Nest. I paced up and down once or twice and then tried to collect myself.

'What is it, Miss Moore?' asked Fanny. 'Is your letter bad news?'

I put it under my book and tried to calm myself and smile. There was nothing I could say and, if I could, no one to say it to. But I would write to my aunt and to my cousin immediately that evening. They too, though, would scarcely be aware of all the house meant to me. Then I thought of Lavinia. It was her temporary home. What would happen to her? But why should I care so much that it was *Barbara* who might come into the property? Perhaps I was being unreasonable. Was it not better than the property going to a stranger? I wanted the place to be resurrected, did I not? I didn't want it to moulder away into a complete ruin, which it surely would if no one lived in the main wings.

I remembered that dream I used to have as a child and which I had not had now for some time. The house changing before my eyes, the stones tumbling down, the crash of the pediment into the lake and then the fading away of the garden till it was once more just a meadow as though it had never been . . . I shuddered and took up my book and stopped the children writing. I would begin telling them a story instead and then ask them to finish it.

'Must stories have happy endings?' asked the intelligent Fanny.

'Stories can have the endings you want, since you write them,' I replied.

'Papa says we are always to look on the bright side,' said Rufus.

I gathered in their efforts and said I would correct the syntax and spelling by tomorrow. I wondered what they had made of my beginning – a boy in a magic house in a magic wood which a bad fairy had made vanish at the touch of a wand. Then we all read from *Little Arthur's History of England* before going out for our 'constitutional'.

There were people coming in and out of the long low building called the Winter Garden and I wondered how long it would be before Mr Angerstein had fixed his concerts and cups of tea.

'There will be palm trees in tubs,' said Rufus as we passed.

'Do you think they will have a conjuror?' asked little Zillah, 'like the one at my friend Rose's party?'

'No, I don't think the grown-ups will have a conjuror,' I replied, though I would not have put anything past the children's father in his zeal for bringing amusement to the visitors.

Before Christmas my mistress's nephew arrived on a visit. I gathered that he was the musical one who could not be prevailed upon to perform on the pianoforte in Papa Angerstein's projected Winter Garden Musical Afternoons. It was a dull rainy cold day at the beginning of December and I had still had no reply to my anguished letters to my aunt and cousin about Rooks Nest. I assumed Rainer was away and Aunt too busy – or that there was no news. I had decided not to think about it but to try and live in the present, and goodness knows there was enough to keep me occupied. I had not written to Barbara.

Benjamin Hertz was the kindest, jolliest young man I had ever met. The house rang with his laughter and the children were in a continual state of merriment. He was not tall and rather tubby in figure with a black beard, black eyes and a deep voice. I could not imagine that he was a musician and that he was to go and study abroad – he seemed so ordinary, except that he had an excess of life about him. I was of course mostly upstairs with the children but I was introduced to him and there was no affectation in the smile he gave me or in his firm handclasp. In how many houses would a governess be treated as a human being? I thought. There was no green baize door about Number 17 Montpelier Crescent and family life was not sealed away from me or from the servants.

'Where is my cousin Hertz?' was the first thing I heard Benjamin say, referring I supposed to the housekeeper and secretary who had still not put in an appearance.

'Father needed her in Leeds,' replied my mistress. 'So Jacob is struggling on alone. Now Benjie, why can't we persuade you to come and play for us?'

'No, no, Essie, aunt of mine,' replied Benjie. 'I must learn and improve before I inflict myself on your citizenry. My friend Daniel will be far better at pleasing the ladies than I would.'

'I'm sure his playing can't be better than yours,' said his aunt.

'He has a fine talent,' said Benjie, 'and he needs the money.'

'Well, if he doesn't suit, perhaps you would come to us next year,' sighed Esther Angerstein. 'When are we to meet him?'

They passed through into the drawing room and I went up to my room. Cousin Benjie was to entertain the children after tea so I should be free. Sometimes I did not look forward to solitude when there was engaging company downstairs. It took me some little time to become reabsorbed in my book and as soon as I was, there would be the children again. I was uncomfortably aware that I was *not* a member of the family, even if I were treated as one.

Next morning Benjie had gone out with my employer and the children and I were once again sitting in the schoolroom. Zillah was allowed to play with her toys when she had done her lesson, and she was on the floor in front of the fire with her little dolls which she was putting through their paces.

'You are a genius doll,' I heard her say, and wondered whether she had heard the expression from her mama, used perhaps to describe Cousin Benjie.

'If I finish this calculation before half past eleven,' said Rufus looking up, 'can I play dominoes? Benjie has taught me a new game.'

'If you finish it before half past eleven you will be a genius,' I replied, laughing.

We had various games in the schoolroom which the children could play when they had worked well – solitaire and snakes and ladders and suchlike. Fanny had her scrap albums which she loved to fill and Rufus had a kite for outdoors and a whole range of tops which he would colour in brilliant chalks. But now he felt he was getting too old for these childish games and was agitating for a pair of ice-skates.

'Papa might build an artificial ice rink,' he said. There seemed no limit to his papa's ideas.

'Just get on with your sums and I'll see about the dominoes,' I said, dreading the walk in such cold dank weather. I need not have worried. Cousin Benjie arrived home shortly after eleven and came up to see the children.

'Play for us, oh please play for us on the piano,' begged Fanny.

'When your teacher says you can come to listen,' he said, a big smile on his sociable face. I said I thought that to hear his playing might be a part of the children's education and felt I was speaking like some forty-year-old duenna.

'I'm sure it would be part of *mine*,' I added hastily. 'I hardly ever hear the music I love.'

'And what might that be?' he asked, taking Zillah on his knee.

I was afraid of appearing too full of *Schwärmerei* to this doubtless critical young man. I knew that most young women liked the sweeter parts of Mendelssohn and Meyerbeer. 'I like the music of Franz Liszt,' I replied.

'Ho ho – she wants to give me something difficult, Kinderle,' he laughed. He was so self-assured and yet he could not have been more than twenty-four. 'I shall play something for your Miss and then something for Fanny,' he said, leading the way down to the drawing room where stood the family piano. We all trooped after him and I hoped I was not going to be blamed for not taking the children outdoors. But when he began to play quite simply and naturally, after twirling round the piano stool to the correct height, I was astounded. He really was a genius. The piano, quite a good one, had never sounded like this when Fanny or her mother played! He went straight into music I had never heard before; great swathes of sound, arpeggios, storms and then a quiet dreamy passage. The tubby little man was transformed into a maestro. The children's mother had crept in too and we all sat entranced. Fanny was particularly quiet and Zillah sat very still just as overcome as the rest of us. When he had finished he said: 'Now something for Fanny,' and began a Chopin Nocturne.

'Ach – it's no wonder you want to go to Leipzig,' said Mrs Angerstein.

The music brought back memories to me, arousing the same feelings I had had before. I couldn't believe that such sounds could come from this prosaic-looking, jolly little man.

'But *Daniel* – he will play his violin *and* the pianoforte,' said Benjie as he turned towards his audience. '*I* must perfect my technique – *he* plays from the soul.'

'You are too modest,' said his aunt.

I wondered about this friend Daniel and when he would come, for Benjie was to go away in a day or two and the house would be dull without him.

The music had made me a little unsatisfied again, made me want a life of my own. The Angersteins and their friends and family had music, money and freedom. I wished I were one of them or that I had inherited some gift to lift me above the generality of people.

'Esther – my aunt – played well before her marriage,' said Benjie once to me and I nearly replied:

'If *you* marry, since you are a man no one will say that to *you*.'

Benjie went away soon after and we heard that the Winter Gardens were to be extended but would be ready by February for the new season.

It was a dank November Sunday. I was out walking alone, as was my Sunday habit. As a matter of fact I was thinking about the cheerful Benjie and hoping he had arrived safely in Germany. I wondered whether perhaps there would be a cup of tea at the Winter Gardens and whether I might venture in there. Surely an unaccompanied female would not be turned away from a hot drink? But of course it was only eleven o'clock and I thought I remembered Mr Angerstein saying that on Sundays they would open in the afternoon only. There may have been some trouble with the Sabbatarians. I crept round the big Royal Baths building and saw the little arch which linked it with the new Winter Gardens building standing alongside with its long windows and glassed-in roof. There seemed to be no one around so I walked to the entrance at the back, feeling rather like a burglar. What if a large bewhiskered major-domo should suddenly appear and ask me my business? I would just peep in; the idea of a 'winter garden' appealed to me, seeming a contradiction in terms, something un-English, exotic. I looked through the keyhole and saw the inner door opening into a vestibule. There were a few cloaks hanging up. I supposed this must be the staff entrance. I really should have waited to be invited into the building by the family and so I stood irresolutely, trying to pretend I was just passing by. Then I heard a faint scratchy noise as though music were being played far away. I looked round again and then gently turned the knob of the door. At least I should not be cold inside if I did penetrate the interior. Perhaps I could pretend I thought it was a Non-Conformist place of worship? The door opened quite easily and I got myself round it and shut it behind me. It did remind me of a church, a Catholic church in Halifax which once, greatly daring, I had entered when I had wandered off from some visit to the woolmarkets with Aunt. There was a glass-panelled door hung with net curtains and I peered through it at the side. Disappointed, I saw it gave on to a corridor which probably ran the length of the building at the back. Perhaps if I could walk down it I might find the public entrance and the doors into the big room, which Fanny said was like a ballroom, and where the famous potted palms were to go. Very quietly I opened the glass door and then tiptoed down a long corridor which smelt like the harmonium room at Sholey Church, varnish and dust in equal parts. At the end of the corridor a door stood open and as I saw it I heard the music again. It was somebody playing the violin. I peered round the door. The enormous room was empty but at the far end on a little dais there was a piano and by the piano stood a young man with his back to me. There was a greeny-grey dim light everywhere, I suppose from the grey sky which was seeping its colour through the glass roof. The potted palms were not yet in place but huddled at the side of

114

the room like refugees from the Crimea or somewhere sunny. I
saw that large mirrors had been fixed in place against some of the
wall panels and this multiplied the distant sight of the young
violinist. I knew he was young because his hair flopped over his
collar and he was thin. He was playing a Paganini air. I stayed by
the door, intending to slip back as soon as he finished, but suddenly he put down his bow and turned and shouted across the
expanse of floor: 'Don't lurk – come and listen.' He must have
seen me in the mirror. I felt silly, not wanting to cross all that
long, long floor. But I couldn't stand there saying nothing so I
shouted, louder than I had intended:
'I'm going – I'm sorry. I *was* listening.'
He leapt down from the little platform at the end and swung
all the way down the room towards me. 'Please excuse me,' I
said as he came up.
'Don't you know it's rude to eavesdrop?' I said nothing. He
looked rather fierce. Then he laughed. 'I'm only practising,
Madame.'
The Madame was added either to display politeness or as a
subtle tease on my youth. I was sure it must be Benjie's friend
but I did not want to claim any knowledge of him, or the Angersteins would get to hear of it. So I said: 'I am very sorry to have
eavesdropped – I must go.'
'Come back when the place is ready for my performance,' he
said and strode away again.
I beat a retreat. Somehow I retraced my steps to the outer door
and walked back to Montpelier Crescent rather ashamed of
myself, yet excited. It had been an adventure, something out of
the ordinary. He had looked and sounded out of the ordinary too
with his wavy dark brown hair and rather mellow voice. Not at
all like Benjie Hertz.
I said nothing to anyone when I returned but from then on
kept my ears alert for any further mention of the Winter Gardens
and the concerts there. It was not for some time that there was
development in this direction and by then I was smarting from a
letter I had received with Barbara's early Christmas greetings. It
was terse but to the point. Her papa was still alive although
weak, but had been able to buy Rooks Nest from my cousin.
'I believe your papa had mortgaged it to your cousins,' she
added gratuitously. 'I am glad to say that the deeds will soon be
with Papa and I intend to reside there myself one day. Do not

worry on Vinny's account. She will accompany me. I shall always be pleased to give her a home.' The effrontery of it! I was greatly hurt. Rainer had not yet written to me with any further details and Aunt had written a hasty note to me saying she knew of no further developments. What disturbed me more than anything was that Barbara had obviously laid these plans long ago. And Barbara's plans would succeed because Barbara was going to be rich. The power of money – that it should settle the fate of Rooks Nest! Yet it had been money that had enabled Mama and Papa to live there in the first place. How could Barbara appreciate the house and the lake as I did? It was all so unfair. I was determined not to show Barbara any of my reactions in my reply however, and wrote only to say I was glad that Lavinia was not going to be deprived of a home. I wondered how Lavinia could put up with Barbara. And yet she had never said anything against her – I had assumed that she had as little opinion of her as I did and I was proved wrong. That was all.

I had felt that nobody but me could appreciate that place: it was my spiritual possession – but of course someone else might feel for it too. There was no law against new tenants or owners not succumbing to its charm. Still, I kept imagining the house lying there as the snow fell, for we were having an early snow that year.

The snow was still falling when the family celebrated what they called Hannukah, just before Christmas. There was a large, many-branched candelabrum in the dining room and each evening (the festival lasted eight days) one candle was lit. Fanny told me it was the feast of the lights to commemorate something that happened nearly two thousand years ago when the Temple at Jerusalem was rededicated. I felt so ignorant of Jewish history, and even of their faith, and was ashamed at my lack of knowledge. When the candle was lit each evening, the children were given sweetmeats made by their mother. I was invited to join in the singing and the candles and the games, and I thought it was very like the Christian Christmas, except that Rufus and his father wore their little synagogue caps and the candles were lit with more solemnity than the lighting of the Christian Christmas tree, which had always seemed to me a very pagan idea. But this ritual was mystical, even if it celebrated a particular historical fact and a faith I did not share. Fanny told me that their 'Bible', the Talmud, told of the miraculous replenishment of oil which went on burning for eight days in the Temple, and that reminded me of the loaves and fishes story. I don't think I wanted to believe the Jewish miracles any more than the Christian ones, but it was a beautiful ceremony in the candlelight and I felt it a privilege to be allowed to join in. I remembered dressing the Christmas tree, it seemed so long since, when Lavinia Logan had captured my heart. What was she doing now? But I cast away, rather disloyally, this old self which had worshipped at her shrine and thought of the lean, dark face with its crown of wavy hair that belonged to that violinist.

Yet the lighting of the candles seemed to link us all together, as though that Harrogate drawing room and the dining room were linked with the whole history of the human race and I was one little insignificant part of it all. On the eighth day, when all the candles were lit, they held the Manorah up high and Mr Angerstein said some solemn words in Hebrew. I felt that thrill go through me with which hearing other languages always affected me and I loved their Jewishness. I thought, the violinist was also Jewish and would have partaken of such ceremonies throughout *his* childhood.

I passed a quiet Christmas, going alone to the old Parish Church on Christmas Eve to hear the wassailing and the shouts of the merry crowds of children and to glimpse the lighted rooms of other houses with their Christian trees and candles. I felt a little lonely, and thought of the Hall. The Angersteins tried to make me feel they wanted me to celebrate Christ's birth if I wished, yet it felt strange to be amongst people who had no cause to celebrate it. It was not, to be truthful, a religious deprivation I was feeling, but a social one. However, I had cast in my lot with the others and must make the best of it.

After Christmas I was to look forward to a visit from my cousin Rainer and I hoped that the Winter Garden concerts would be in full swing so that he could take me there. I might, who knows, have another glimpse of the young violinist. But Rainer was not to come until February and the days dragged with that awful Epiphany feeling – spring far away and the best part of winter, with its cutting winds and drenching rains, to get through. The rains however turned again to snow at the end of January.

On one snowy January afternoon I was in the schoolroom with Fanny and Zillah. Rufus had gone out to a Hebrew lesson and we were making an effort to clear cupboards and put aside old toys and books for the local orphanage. The night before, Mr Angerstein had said things were going well at the Winter Gardens and I was wondering whether snow would be an obstacle to the new season of concerts. Nothing had been said about Benjie's friend and I thought either I must have been mistaken in the young man or he had not been invited to the house. I was dividing my attention between looking vaguely out of the window and sewing some lace back on Fanny's dress, for although I was a poor needlewoman I did not mind that sort of occupation. The air had that peculiar stillness given by fallen snow and there was a bluish tinge to the sky which perhaps meant more snow was to fall that afternoon. Marks of footfalls were already a dirty sepia in the crisp white and there were one or two people trudging through it; a woman in a long shawl with a droop to her figure and the lamplighter in the distance with his long pole. Soon it would be twilight, my favourite time of day, and yet the saddest time. From the other side of the crescent I then saw emerge a slight figure carrying a violin in a case. It was the Winter Garden Man I was sure! 'Daniel?' Perhaps he was on his way at last to take tea with his cousin's family. I turned away. I hoped that he would not recognize me if he did come – trespassing was not the sort of thing a governess should have been doing. The bell rang and I heard the maid open the door downstairs. I had no opportunity to check whether the visitor was indeed my violinist for I heard the little bell go in the hall for tea, which meant that Mrs Angerstein was entertaining. I must not appear curious or the children would think me rude, so I bent to my task and rang the bell myself for bread so that Fanny and her sister could toast 'tea-cakes' at the schoolroom fire. I drew the curtains and we were very cosy. I heard Rufus come in and then be detained by his mother for he did not come upstairs. After tea I read from *The Book of Nonsense* and we heard nothing further of the visitor till about six o'clock when I heard the front door close again. I stood at the window and drew the curtain back just a little – and, yes, I was sure that it was he. His shoes would be soaking unless he had been wearing galoshes, but he darted down the steps and skipped along the thickly blanketed pavement on the frosty rim of the snow, and was then out of my sight.

Not till later that week did I hear that Benjie's friend had indeed visited and that 'Papa' was getting together some other players for his February season. Then finally a letter from Rainer arrived, couched in his usual amused style. He was coming in the second week of February. He added only as a postscript that Rooks Nest had been sold.

Four

DANIEL

When he stood in the Angersteins' drawing room making pleasant conversation to the lady of the house, Rainer looked older than I remembered. Older and yet fairer. It must have been the contrast with all the lively dark faces I had grown used to. When I came in in my fur tippet, he smiled and gave me a hearty shake of the hand. It was afternoon; we were to go to a Tea Concert at the Winter Gardens, and I was excited. For a moment I could not get my bearings with my cousin. So much seemed to have happened since that afternoon in September when he had left me on the doorstep like a safely delivered parcel. This time he had brought a parcel of Martha's home-cooked goodies and a pot of jam, together with a letter from Augusta. The cakes and jam were ceremoniously removed by Emma to the kitchen.

Soon, Rainer and I were outside and I could look forward to a whole four hours of leisure. His carriage was waiting and I was driven in some style round the Crescent and down the hill and to the glass-roofed Winter Gardens. I felt it was not quite the mode for a governess and I said so. He looked at me as if to say: 'Stop acting a part, Meta.' I knew he thought that, although he didn't actually say it.

I had determined not to let him think I regarded myself as a poor relation and not to mention Barbara until he did, and here was I sounding bitter. It would not do. Nothing must mar my enjoyment. Perhaps Daniel, whose surname I had now discovered was Reiss, would be billed. I had not been able to get anything out of Mr Angerstein about the programme, he was far too busy. The Gardens were a success and he was on that cloud of entrepreneurial bliss which I suppose successful businessmen must feel.

'Tea first,' said Rainer, 'and then conversation.'

I discovered the music was to be played whilst the bathchair occupants sat and munched and the younger visitors chatted. It was not a 'concert' in my estimation. I supposed that during the evening subscription concerts which Mr Angerstein was planning for the next season, there would be no conversation from the audience. No wonder Benjie had declined the offer of providing afternoon 'entertainment'.

For a time there was no music in the large hall; just tables, covered in white linen and sparkling cutlery, in front of each party of visitors. There must have been fifty tables at least with wide spaces between to allow the waitresses to move with their laden trays; along the sides there were other tables and armchairs. The palms were set at intervals and there were gas mantles in trios hanging at intervals from the ceiling and looking like large white bells. The floor covering was of a pale green. We were at the end nearest the dais, but at the other end the crowd was denser. It was all really rather splendid and most un-English, I thought. Rainer lost no time in ordering a plentiful supply of scones, jam, tea-cakes and muffins to be served with the imposing teapot of electroplated silver accompanied by milk and sugar. I was expected to pour and when I had done so he sat back and said: 'Well, tell me all!'

I found there was plenty to say once I was launched on my narrative, but I did not mention Rooks Nest nor did I speak of Lavinia. Neither did I say I hoped that Daniel, the violinist, would be playing for us. Rainer was always easy to talk to and he did not laugh at me, but enquired very seriously about my state of mind and whether I was happy. I had exhausted the characters of the children; my feelings about Jewish life; my great good luck in finding a family where I was not treated as a social inferior, and was about to drink my tea, for my throat was quite tired with unaccustomed chat, when he said:

'Are we to mention Rooks Nest or are we not?'

I started a little but managed to cover up my reaction by saying as coolly as I could manage: 'I suppose it's better that *someone* lives there.' I tried to change the subject, tried to give the impression of a sadder and wiser girl who knew that dreams do not last, but I don't think I hoodwinked him for a moment. For the first time since I had known my cousin I felt a little self-conscious and this annoyed me. I saw myself only too well as the disappointed young heiress who had been cheated out of her inheritance, but it was all nonsense. I had never expected Rooks Nest to be mine strictly as a piece of property. The trouble was that it *was* mine – by all rights of interest, and of love, and of the past. What was hurting me was that it was going to be Barbara of all people who would live there when her papa died, as he probably would very soon. And some of my old feelings for Lavinia came back to me, with old unreal plans I had had for living with her in the old house in some strange alliance. It had never been a possible future. But why not, if it was going to be possible for Barbara?

Rainer returned to the attack – he seemed determined to discuss the place. 'Why do *you* not live there, Cousin?' I said finally, stung a little.

'But I am not married, Meta, and it is not a place for a bachelor.'

'What about Barbara then?' I said.

'She is a young woman and will have a fine place to bring a husband . . . unless . . .' he paused.

'Well of course,' I said. 'If she *marries* the place will not be hers, will it? Didn't that happen to Mama?' I had suddenly realized why there had been such peculiar relations between my mama's family and my papa's. Rainer was silent so I went on impulsively: 'Was it Mama's? And then when she married, Papa inherited it? So the property was from Mama's family – was that why they were so angry?'

'It's the law, Meta,' Rainer said gently. 'It is a little more complicated than you imagine, but the property was not entailed – your mama brought it to your papa, yes . . .'

'But why did they give it to her, when they knew she was going to marry and that her family would lose it?' I was by this time quite interested. I had never seen matters in this light before.

He looked round and said: 'Do you think I might light a cigar?'

'Please Rainer,' I replied, 'do light your cigar but tell me about Rooks Nest.'

He began, biting on his cigar. 'Whoever married your mother would get the property – it was her portion of her father's wealth. Your grandfather, your mother's father, was ill. He thought the world of your mother. So he left it to her with the proviso your grandmother should live there when your mama married. He died before your mother married your father. As soon as her father died, your mother married. It was much opposed by your grandmother. She refused to live with your parents and went off to Bath with a small competence her husband had left to her. Your mother begged her to stay but she would not. The old lady thought your papa had married for money and she didn't like him. Your mother was the younger of two daughters – the other, your Aunt Sophia, had married a rich man when she was only seventeen. Your mother was of age and could marry without her mother's consent. You know most of the rest.'

'But when Mama died, why did Papa not stay on? Why did he sell it to your father?' I asked. All this family history was fascinating but I felt I should have known it years ago.

'He didn't sell it, Meta. He wasn't a fortune-hunter either. He went abroad in a very depressed state of mind, leaving you to Augusta. He invested in some business affairs, more than one I'm afraid. They failed. He mortgaged the house to my father to give himself an income. In the end – I don't know whether I ought to tell you all this – it's rather depressing . . .' He paused and crossed his elegant legs and looked away a moment to the little platform where the musicians were to play.

'Oh, please tell me it all now,' I said.

'Well – he got into more debt – it was cheaper to live abroad – he felt he'd let you down. He finally gave up the house to my father – the upkeep would have been tremendous if he'd lived there – and lived on the proceeds that remained after paying his original debts. My father asked me to oversee the place. I couldn't find tenants so we put in caretakers . . .'

'But you found Miss Logan and her mother.'

'Yes, but that was only for the wing. Nobody else could afford it. There was a textile slump – things have only been picking up in the last few years . . .'

'So the property was your father's after that?'

'No. Father saw it as a millstone. He mortgaged half of it himself, the rest I was to rent out and use for income.'

'So that Mr Widdop will be glad he's found a purchaser?'

'Widdop is only a man of law, Meta; he and I are relieved that at last the whole place will be removed from our books. The buyer – Mr Stott – will pay off the mortgages and the whole thing will pass out of our control.'

'So we should be glad about Barbara! If Papa hadn't got into debt though, it would have been his to leave to me?' I thought how sordid it all was. My lovely Rooks Nest – just a piece of property sold to the highest bidder.

'I know you've always been fond of it . . .' he was beginning, but I interrupted him.

'That's all over now. It's going to be Barbara's – or her husband's, if she ever marries. I suppose she lost a mother and gained a fortune,' I added cynically. Then I asked, as he looked at me meditatively, 'Is my aunt – Sophia you said – still alive?' I didn't know I had any relatives left on Mama's side.

'I believe she lives in London,' replied Rainer. 'But she won't want anything to do with you. They all turned against your mother when she married. They didn't approve at all of her choice.'

'Poor Mama,' I said.

My initial agitation had changed to a mixture of sorrow and of wanting to be rid of the whole thing. It had obsessed me in childhood and now I knew the facts they seemed far from romantic. It was even more obvious that I had been lucky to be adopted by Augusta and that I must cast off all this history *now*.

'You feel cheated then, of your inheritance?' asked Rainer after a pause.

I determined to appear grown up and grave, so I steadily added water to the teapot, though my hand betrayed me by trembling a little. What I really felt was still an unreasoning anger against Barbara and that was a childish and silly reaction, and one I could not afford to allow my cousin to see. 'No – it just makes me feel I must do something for myself, that I must make my own way. And what is there for me but governessing?'

He seemed to divine my thoughts for he said: 'You are young, Meta, and will marry, I am sure, when you are tired of working for others.'

'No – no, what sort of an answer was that for Mama? It's ignoble, is it not, to marry for money, to slip the yoke of work?' But as I said it I thought how I had been feeling recently, how in spite of the happy position I had found in Harrogate, I found it hard to envisage that I should be a governess either there or elsewhere for ever. How would I ever be able to burst my way out of the cocoon of service to others and have a life of my own? But what sort of life did I want? I was happy with the Angersteins. They had money, and freedom, I thought again – whereas I had nothing which did not depend on them. I didn't want to be stuck in my childhood, no, and Rooks Nest *was* my childhood as well as Hartsedge Hall. I was not disappointed so much as restless. Talking to Rainer was making me feel more restless. There was safety of a kind in Harrogate.

'I should not have told you all this, it will make you dissatisfied,' said Rainer, pouring himself another cup of tea. We could hear the musicians tuning up behind the scenes.

'I am glad you have,' I replied. 'I ought to have known of it long ago. People think girls should be spared sordid financial details as though they are soft little things who cannot bear reality.'

'Oh, I've never thought of you like that,' said my cousin. 'But I think you have some revolutionary ideas.' I wondered what I had said that seemed so revolutionary. He answered my question. 'You said it was wrong to marry for money, Meta, but in *my* mother's generation it was regarded as the safest thing to do. It's only all this new thinking that has made it seem "ignoble" – your words, Meta. Love doesn't last, my dear, and money does on the whole.'

I was horrified. 'You can't believe that, Cousin. Why, if my mama had lived do you think she would have stopped loving Papa? And you told me yourself they married for love! And Papa's money didn't last.'

'I am doing my duty as your only male relative,' he said.

I could not be angry with him for I was not sure how much he believed his own advice. Perhaps he had had bitter experience himself? We had no more time for conversation for suddenly the murmurs of talk faded and the focus of attention was now the platform at the end of the Gardens, where stood a piano and a music stand. They were going to play at last. I was tired of all the talking and all the unhappiness of the past which had seemed almost tangibly present as we spoke and was glad to be back again in my present self sitting with my kind and attentive cousin in Harrogate Winter Gardens waiting for 'my' violinist, Mr Daniel Reiss, to appear.

'The violinist is a friend of the Angersteins' nephew,' I murmured. But it was not as a violinist that Mr Reiss was to appear first today. He came out suddenly from behind a distant palm tree with an elderly man and a golden-haired lady. Daniel Reiss sat down at the piano where the elderly man sat beside him to turn the music pages. Then the man got up again and advanced to the edge of the platform.

'We are fortunate in this our first season to have secured the services of Madame Frescobaldi,' he was heard to say and the golden-haired lady who was wearing a plum-coloured crinoline came forward on to the platform. Daniel must be about to accompany her then. I had never heard of her and was disappointed. She started on some French songs which the scattered audience clapped politely before returning to its tea. The pianist seemed detached from it all, though he clapped her too when she took her bow. I have never liked sopranos very much and Madame Frescobaldi was no exception, though she must have had a powerful voice and nerves of steel to have sung to this mixed audience, among whom I am sure there were a few music lovers but who were there mostly for the lack of something better to do. The large room was getting quite warm and I hoped that it would soon be Daniel Reiss's turn.

The elderly man thanked his audience for their appreciation and announced that Monsieur Reiss (I wondered why he had to be French), a young pianist of exceptional talent, would play a selection from some composers of the day. He left it at that. Rainer grimaced and said: 'They could produce a programme.'

I could not at first concentrate very well upon what was played but I did recognize the first two pieces as they were from my beloved Mendelssohn's Songs Without Words. His playing was very different from Benjie's – dreamier but quite as technically proficient, I thought. I looked across to my cousin but he was absorbed in the music. The applause was moderate. I clapped loudly and was rewarded by the next piece which was Liszt and a very different kettle of fish. Oh how he plunged and swam and breasted the notes and shook the piano – not gentle at all now. Such music! I had not heard the piece before but was entranced. All my sad thoughts of Rooks Nest and Mama and Papa seemed to float away on it and I knew that it was expressing the things I felt and that I did not need to explain myself so long as I could hear music like this every day of my life. When the last note finally died away there was great applause. 'It's because it sounds difficult,' whispered Rainer.

'But he is very good,' I replied, though at the bottom of my heart I knew that the music, even when played by an indifferent pianist, would have made an impact the first time I heard it.

There was something else too. The sight of that young man was not quite separate from the music he played. The music was not exactly an expression of himself but it made one think of the person who was playing it. He stood up and came out to the front of the platform and took a bow. The audience clapped again but the murmur of their voices soon rose once more. I looked at him again. I could see his features very distinctly at this distance and I recognized his wavy hair and saw that his eyes were very dark. 'He plays the violin too,' I remarked to Rainer, for there was to be an interval.

'I expect that they'll institute a more formal sort of music season one day,' said Rainer. 'This is not fair on the players but the management *will* do as they do at Scarborough and have the music as background. The audience in the afternoon don't really want a proper recital – they want a pleasant backcloth to their chats.'

'Do you know Scarborough well then?'

'Tolerably,' he said. 'It's pleasant in the Pavilion when they play in the evening, but the company is getting just as stupid as it is here. Soon there'll be decent music only in the towns – they say that Bradford is to go in for a proper concert season.'

'Mrs Angerstein's nephew would not play here,' I replied. 'He went off to Leipzig. But this young man is a friend of his and needed the money. *Is* he good?' I wanted Rainer to say he was.

'Too good for the Winter Gardens,' he replied. 'Now Meta, are we to stay for the interval or take a stroll? I gather I can deliver you back at seven o'clock.'

'Oh, don't let's go! We might miss the next bit. I'm sure he's going to play his violin.'

I was not disappointed. After about twenty minutes he came on to the platform again, his violin tucked under his arm.

'Our gifted young musician will now play an air of Paganini's,' announced the elderly man. There was silence for a moment, for the violinist's appearance surprised all but me who knew he was also the pianist. And when he took his bow and waited for a long moment before he began to play all eyes were upon his slight yet wiry figure. The music began and all eyes were still upon him. I did not want to share the sight of him with others. I closed my eyes and tried to concentrate on the sounds which he plaited in the air. The melody was haunting, the playing I thought perfect. The music immediately brought back the old feelings I had had for Lavinia Logan and those emotions in recollection were no longer exciting but sad. I forgot how, latterly, she had been cold to me and how all my passion had become dissipated. Paradoxically, although the music aroused the sadness it stood also by itself and when I opened my eyes I was full of gratitude to the player for he had seemed to reveal himself as well as interpreting the music. And how handsome he was – and young. He had that air of vulnerability which I had once thought I had seen in Lavinia. He was admirable. I felt protective towards him and excited. *I* had met him before all these people – the young violinist of my Sunday adventure. If only I could get to know him better so that he would acknowledge *my* presence. I was so absorbed in my thoughts that for a moment the music faded away. Then it returned in full force and this time it was not reminding me of the past but beckoning me again into the mind of the man who was expressing it. If I could feel as I was feeling I was *not* alone, for Paganini had felt it and so it seemed did Daniel Reiss. I knew that I must separate the art from the feeling but I was too weak to do it. The music showered on me in a sensual cataract. When it stopped and I clapped – and others around were also applauding wildly – Rainer was looking at me. I did not want to show any undue interest in Daniel Reiss, so I hugged the idea of him as though it were a secret, and resolved to speak only of the music. All the things we had been saying seemed trivial compared with that. But I couldn't help looking exalted, I suppose, for my cousin said as we were walking away from the Winter Gardens : 'You are glad you came then?'

'I am very glad,' I replied. 'I hope you enjoyed it too. I thought he – the music was wonderful.'

'Yes it was very good. I expect it is just the sort of music you like, Meta.'

'Oh – '

He added quickly : 'There's nothing wrong in that, it is music for youth I think. And was marvellously played.'

He must have noticed my absorption for I fear I was indifferent company on the way back. He deposited me at Montpelier Crescent with a wry smile. 'Look after yourself, Meta.'

'Thank you for the lovely afternoon,' I said. 'Please let me know about what happens at Rooks Nest, will you?' I added, although at that moment I felt a hundred years away from my old feelings for the place. He said he would and I went in and up to my room with half an hour to spare before it was time for me to put Fanny to bed. I spent the time sitting on my bed in my room, turning over the sight of Daniel Reiss in my mind and hearing in my head the air he had played. Now, whenever I hear that tune I see the small narrow room at the top of the Angersteins' house and the cupboard door and the brown rug at my feet – those objects themselves have taken on a nostalgic sheen and bring back to me the pure excitement of my nineteen years.

In Papa's small library of books left with my aunt at the Hall, I had once found a French volume, a small unregarded book, with Papa's signature in it and the date '1833 : Paris' on the fly-leaf. I had scanned it eagerly, for it was called *De l'Amour*. The first time I read it, it was too advanced for my French but a year or two later I understood it better. It spoke of love; love which began with admiration, aroused hope and then proceeded to add ideas of perfection to the image of the beloved. Beauty was also very important too, I read, or the imagined beauty which is of course in the eye of the beholder. I derived one image from my reading of this book, the image of a crystal which forms almost imperceptibly, perhaps taking an hour, or days, or it might be weeks. But once this crystalline polyp is there, there comes a day, an hour, a moment, when it takes a strange glitter and lights up all the corners of the imagination and can only be dislodged when its light fades, not at the will of its possessor. Then the possessor's mind recovers only slowly as it peers out from its new darkness. I too thought that this was love. But – I was disappointed that women were always the *objects* of the crystal glow, though they were allowed in return some feelings aroused by the lover.

Some people called the feeling 'infatuation', especially if it happened to some young untried hearts longing to give love. The object might be unsuitable, indeed usually was; and very often unworthy – yet who is to say what is fitting or sensible?

After my afternoon in the Winter Gardens with Rainer I remembered that little book and I thought continually of Daniel Reiss. Perhaps the new information about my parents had shifted my perspective of life, or perhaps I was tired of the old Meta and needed a new object of desire. I know only that my new feelings irradiated my days and I was content for a few weeks only to dream of him, to gather information about him and to look forward to every tedious walk with Fanny and Zillah with new enthusiasm, in case – just by chance – he might cross my path. I did think then that it was a little like the time I had loved Lavinia – I was not entirely without self-knowledge – but Lavinia seemed now like a dress rehearsal for this new object of passion.

His music had begun in me this yearning, this sadness; if music be the food of love, play on, Daniel Reiss! – I thought. I centred my thoughts on him not on myself, although I was aware that the pleasure was all mine. It was not a self-conscious decision, it seemed to have found me rather than I found it. I did not see myself as the recipient of anything from Daniel Reiss – how could I, since I did not know him? But I became, after a time, more determined to make sure he did know me. I could reach him through Benjie, I thought – and one day he would be sure to be invited to the house.

In truth, all I was certain of in the absolute uncertainty of ever being anything to Daniel Reiss, was that I could truly love him if I were ever given the chance! All the operations of my intelligence were weak and feeble compared with the certainty of the truth of my feelings. What his music *was,* was the truth of my feelings. And he was 'in' the music the way I was 'in' my feelings. No words were needed and yet I knew that words were all I had to say what I felt, feeble as they were. If only *I* could create music or play it to him. If only *I* could write poetry to read to him which would express my feelings better than I could in the words of every day. I wrote sad lyrical stuff at night in my room which I would have been ashamed of anyone finding, but the writing seemed to assuage me a little. Yet I did not know him at all!

I was 'one of the family' to the extent that even if there *had* been a green baize door behind which the servants lived, I would not have been there, so I used the advantages of my position to listen for any more crumbs I could gather from the lips of Mr Angerstein. Surely one day he would mention the violinist? I did not want to mention him myself, although I should love to have let drop his name just to hear it resound in the air, so I bided my time. And spring came and the Afternoon Teas were pronounced a success and would continue through the summer. I took to leading the direction of our walks round to the Winter Gardens but never saw Daniel Reiss again until one day in April. I thought I saw the whisk of a coat-tail at the side door of the building, and went round on purpose on our way back to have another look. If he had been playing at two he would be out at about four for a short break, I reasoned and I was right! I saw him emerge so I halted the children to allow me to adjust the lace of my boot and risked a long look at him as he brushed by me.

Of course he would not remember me. Why should he? Even if he had seen me, which I doubted, it would need my presence at more than a few sessions rehearsing in the Winter Gardens for him to know my face.

Yet strangely enough the depression which these thoughts brought was to be succeeded very quickly by elation. It was Mrs Angerstein who told me as we prepared to go out the next day, which was a Saturday, that Benjie's friend was to dine with the family on the Sunday evening. If I cared to join them they would be pleased for the governess to forsake her lonely bedroom and come down after dinner when a few others of her husband's friends were to foregather. She did not see my elation, I think, for I said quickly, to absorb my reaction, how pleased I would be to meet a friend of Benjie's. It was true that we had often discussed her nephew Benjie. This was by far the best way of my getting to know 'Benjie's friend'. For him to see me in a family setting might stop me from showing too much interest in him. Yet I wanted to be my old free impetuous self.

How I looked forward to the Sunday! I decided to wear my best lavender dress which I had brought with me but so far found no occasion to display. What *had* come over me, who up till now had spurned the artifice of dress as a means of attraction? Nobody would know why I had made an effort however, and I might as well look my best; there were few opportunities for even a well-treated children's governess to shine in Harrogate.

Miss Hertz was to return on the same day to take up the duties which she had abandoned in favour of her other uncle's wool business and I looked forward to meeting her too, imagining her to be the sort of woman a Daniel Reiss would admire.

I was not normally a shy person and it was with only a little trepidation that I went down to the drawing room that Sunday evening, having tucked up Fanny in bed. 'Promise me that you'll send Naomi up to say good-night,' Fanny had said as I lowered the blinds in her room. I presumed this Miss Hertz was a favourite with her and so I promised.

On entering the room I was at first hidden from the guest of honour by the plump form of the elder Mrs Angerstein who was visiting her son. She was a snappy-eyed, deep-voiced version of her granddaughter Fanny and was volubly amusing the company. I decided to be useful and offered to take round some Süssigkeiten made that morning by Esther. The latter seemed a little wary of her mother-in-law and stood by the fire with a young man, a dark-haired, slim young man. I saw at first only the back of his head but as I advanced with a dish of glutinous and delicious sweetmeats I got him to turn and take one. Then Mrs Angerstein moved away to talk to a small, thin young woman, not an imposing lady at all, who I guessed must be Miss Naomi Hertz. She had fierce and furry eyebrows and a nice smile. Would Daniel Reiss say: 'Have I not met you before?', or would it be a flirtatious 'So we meet again'? It was neither. He took a sweet in an offhand way, licked his finger and said: 'You did not come to listen to me again. Why?'

I threw any idea of caution away as I replied: 'I saw you on Thursday when I was out walking with the children but you did not see me.' He said nothing and I handed him another sugary morsel. 'And I did come to listen to your music a few weeks ago,' I added.

'And what did you think of it, Mademoiselle?'

What could I say? 'Wonderful' or 'I thought you were splendid'? Instead I said, 'My appreciation would be useless, for you might think it presumptuous of an ignorant person to tell you.'

He looked at me, considering how to reply to this. Was he not going to express surprise that I was here in the drawing room of his friend's aunt? No he was not, and so I said after a pause before turning to continue my peregrinations with the sweet-dish, 'I have met your friend Benjie. I am the children's governess here and he visited his aunt last autumn. He told us what a magnificent musician you were.' He bowed slightly as though it were only his due. 'Of course,' I said, emboldened, 'he is a very good pianist too, is he not?'

I could not have said anything better. To praise someone else put Daniel Reiss on his mettle but I saw at once that he was not going to be ungenerous. 'He is a Wunderkind,' he said. 'But tell me – why have I not seen you before? I came to the Angersteins' last Christmas.'

'I know,' I said. 'It was snowing. I was up in the nursery.' Let him work that out for himself. 'I am glad to meet you again,' I added. 'But now I must go and do my duty. Perhaps you could tell me if that is Miss Hertz?' I looked over to the thin young lady who was in serious conversation with my employer. There were about twenty people in the large room, enough for my entrance not to have been remarked and I did not want to draw attention to myself by chatting too long with Mr Reiss, though I longed with all my heart to have him all to myself. The promise in his dark eyes was even more overpowering than before. Everyone must think him very handsome indeed, I was sure. I moved away though, for I had enough to think about for the moment and I must give Fanny's message to Miss Hertz.

I felt more shy with her than with Daniel Reiss for she was not much older than myself but so very clever – as they were always saying. Mrs Angerstein saw me then and came up in her modest way piloting the young lady. 'Everyone is enjoying your Süssigkeiten,' I said for I knew that one thing she was not modest about was her cooking.

'Ach, Miss Moore, I would like Naomi to talk to you,' she replied with a smile and I found myself with the young lady in a window embrasure that looked over the back of the crescent. She smiled pleasantly and shook hands with me in a very continental manner. She was a fragile-looking little creature and I felt like some northern interloper even though I am not tall myself. I gave her Fanny's message and she promised to go up and say goodnight to her. 'I shall be glad to be back,' she said. 'My uncle will be getting himself in such a muddle you know – I mean his accounts and things. He is so good with the ideas, but Esther has just been telling me they want me to come back before he decides to entrust his bank account to Rufus.' We laughed. The two Yorkshire maids were coming round with trays of wine, and Naomi Hertz said: 'Do you think we shall have some music? The family is so good at giving parties, don't you think?'

'They are indeed,' I answered, 'and there is the friend of Mrs Angerstein's nephew to play for us. Do you know him?'

'I know of him,' she replied but said no more and we began to speak of the children of the house, and of education. She was remarkably well-informed, I thought. She was beginning to tell me of the school she had gone to in London, in Harley Street, for apparently her own family were settled in the north of London, and I was wondering how old she was, when I saw that Daniel had sat down at the piano. Mr Angerstein clapped for silence and announced there was to be a little recital of songs with the accompaniment of the professional pianist present who had abandoned his violin but would be happy to play if the friends would like to sing some old favourites. I thought this was a decidedly peculiar way of using the talents of Mr Reiss but the company, who all seemed to be Jewish and all enamoured of music, murmured their approbation. 'I shall go and see Fanny,' whispered my new friend to me. 'I cannot sing.' And she melted away. I sat down in the shadows as far as possible away from my employer in case he conscripted me to sing too, and sat and awaited the music.

Without more ado Daniel began to play. I do not know what he played at first; everyone else seemed to be familiar with it. He played for them to sing and sing they did, in German – and sometimes in an unfamiliar language which I supposed must be Hebrew. Then there were requests for Liszt, for Mendelssohn which he smilingly denied them. I was entranced. I wondered at their all knowing the words but I suppose it was as if a good old Yorkshire party had launched into The Hallelujah Chorus, tackled with equal enthusiasm. At last Mr Angerstein was requested that he ask his wife to sing. I looked round for her but I believe she must have hidden in the cook's quarters, expecting the request. I wished I knew some of the words of the songs myself – they had seemed familiar and I resolved to ask to borrow some of the books which I had seen in my employer's study, books of young German writers I thought. These people were as German as the Germans, I felt, although they were mostly Jewish. The German culture was part of their wandering heritage. I had nothing to contribute. I wished I had said something sensible to Daniel Reiss when I had had that rare opportunity to speak to him. He played with a true accompanist's skill but I wished he would play for us as Benjie had done. Mrs Angerstein came back but prettily declined to sing, promising perhaps another time, so her husband decided to remind his party of the delights of the Winter Gardens. 'More of our young musician, friends, if you buy my season tickets – then perhaps you may have the Winterreise as well as your Songs without Words!'

I wondered if Daniel could sing too – he seemed to have all musical talents.

Wine was brought round once more and little groups of people clustered together. I found myself alone again and thought I had better make an effort to say something to someone. If he had played Liszt or Mendelssohn I should have had at least something sensible to say about the music. I did not want to hang around looking foolish. Then I saw that Miss Naomi Hertz had appeared again and was talking to Daniel, her head on one side and a slight smile on her face. I squeezed round to them and wished I had another tray of sweetmeats.

'Well, did you enjoy the sing-song?' she asked.

'I thought everyone showed unusual talent,' I replied.

'Did you not wish our visitor had played real music?' she said.

'I do wish I could hear him play again as he played when my cousin took me to an afternoon recital,' I replied diplomatically. 'I think I know some of the poems they were singing . . .'

'And you would rather they had been said than sung,' Daniel put in.

Before I could answer, Naomi said: 'Meta is a literary girl, she has told me. I expect she would prefer to keep her poems apart from her music.'

'Well no, not quite,' I said. 'But there are poems – like Mendelssohn's On Wings of Song – which are better as songs than as poems, and others which meld together.' I thought of the romantic poems I had read with Lavinia and how they had the same effect as music.

'I shall be playing some early pieces of Liszt,' said Daniel, allowing his glass to become refilled.

'I shall come if I possibly can,' I replied, at which point some other guests joined us and Daniel turned rather wearily, I thought, to them and I was left again with Naomi.

'Did you see Fanny?' I asked.

'Oh yes. She is a sweet little girl. She could hear the singing and she said "There is Papa conducting again."'

I laughed. 'I am not quite sure of my musical tastes,' I said. 'Do you think he will put Chopin on his programme?'

'I shall ask him,' replied Naomi.

I was so exhausted from the meeting with Daniel, all confused with the company and the songs and trying to talk sensibly to Naomi, that I went up to my room soon after, but I stayed at my window to see Daniel leave and wondered if I was ever going to be able to see him apart from a crowd of musical guests. Perhaps Naomi Hertz would accompany me on my free afternoon to hear him – but no, she said she didn't like singing! I could hardly believe it and decided that her taste was too refined for a Musical Evening, that was all.

* * *

Amazingly I was soon to be given another chance to meet Daniel Reiss, once more through the Angersteins. A walk to one of the sulphur wells some miles away was to be arranged for another Sunday in April. I was told they were called the 'Old Wells' and that we should all be expected to taste the magical waters. By the time the visit was arranged, my six months' probation had passed and I had been offered permanent employment with the family. Naomi Hertz was not living with us at Montpelier Crescent but lodging with an old lady near the Stray and accompanying Jacob Angerstein to his various places of business every day, returning to sort out his accounts when she was not wanted elsewhere.

The outing to the Old Wells was arranged because Jacob wished to prospect the likelihood of a new source of income. There was much punning by Naomi on the 'source' of his income and it was Naomi too who suggested I might accompany them. She seemed to have taken a liking to me. Mrs Angerstein was not enamoured of 'walks', being a town person through and through, but she said the children would enjoy it and it might even do them good. The family had better try out the waters first if they were going to be exploited and sold commercially.

At the last moment Mr Angerstein, who had happened to see Daniel the day before, said he had invited him along too, so quite a large party was to set off from Harrogate for the wells, first in the carriage and then a longish walk over the moor.

It was one of those deceptive spring days which promise summer but are then betrayed by cold winds a day or two afterwards. I privately wondered how much interest Daniel Reiss had in sulphur wells and decided he had thought he had better humour his patron. As it was early closing day there was no concert at the Winter Gardens.

Our carriage picked him up at the crossroads on the Turnpike road near his lodging but to my disappointment he sat on the top with the coachman. Still it was nice to feel his invisible presence. I was always telling myself that I did not really know him at all and that I must beware of my impetuosity, but I could not deny that the very thought of him changed my world. As the rest of us sat together in the carriage, the children were being amused by their indefatigable papa, so I chatted with Naomi. In fact she was the one who first brought up the subject of our extra passenger.

'I am sure that ladies are quite silly about him,' she said. 'They think he is a sort of Paganini I suppose. Do you think Paganini had any time for women? I don't.'

I would like to have said what a very beautiful young man he was and asked her true opinion as to his musical talents but I thought I had better be discreet; I had suffered in the past from telling Barbara even the smallest parts of my feelings for Lavinia and felt I must be wary. Naomi was no Barbara, but I thought I would keep my thoughts to myself.

'I believe he finds Harrogate too genteel,' she said, for she had had the opportunity to meet him once or twice on business at the Winter Gardens with her uncle.

'Why does he play here then?' I asked. 'His friend Benjie wouldn't.'

At the mention of Benjie I thought she coloured up a little. 'He needs the money,' she replied, 'his parents are dead.' Like mine, I thought.

We descended from the carriage in a welter of skirts and children and saw before us the moors all around and a rocky path strewn with boulders. Daniel was down from his perch and helping us out. He had nice manners, I noted. The touch of his hand as he set me on the ground was firm and a small thrill went through me. But he was helping the others just the same as he was me. The sky over the great expanse of the moor was almost the blue of May and I was filled with that happiness which a young person possesses at the proximity of the person who is perhaps just on the point of being loved but without the anguish of that love yet being told.

'We can't go down that way, Papa, can we?' asked Fanny, pointing to the rock-strewn path. A tiny stream was flowing nearby and I almost imagined I heard larks singing.

'The path is not too bad,' said her father. 'Come now, if the ladies can manage it, I'm sure our friend Daniel will carry you, Fanny, if you think it is too much for you.'

But Fanny said: 'All right, Papa – but Rufus must not try to trip me up.'

Her brother was already off, jumping over boulders. I wondered again why girls were usually expected to dislike walking. Fanny herself had said or implied she didn't much fancy it. I loved walking, myself.

'This is the old Roman Road,' said Mr Angerstein as we tramped along in single file. The stone was of millstone grit and it made me remember home, for that was the colour of the stone which filled our delfs there.

'Can we go to the river later?' asked Rufus, running back to us and then on again.

I was walking next to Daniel, who was whistling. 'All this trouble for some muddy water,' he said to me, and sounded rather like a sulky child himself.

'Don't forget that muddy water may bring someone a fortune,' I replied.

The going was quite heavy but I enjoyed it. It had been months since I had walked beyond the confines of the town. That morning I had received a letter and I wanted to think about its contents, but having the object of my desires so near me had put it out of my head.

We came out on to a more level piece of land and in the distance a drystone wall announced the intake of some farm, perhaps the one where the well had existed for generations.

Naomi was in deep discussion with her uncle and I could not see Daniel without turning round so I concentrated on the landscape, and gradually the sensation of freshness in the air and the sun mildly shining on the brown moor and the grey walls, made me feel very tranquil; too tranquil to want to think about Rainer's letter which had told me of the death of Barbara's father and the decision by Barbara to have Rooks Nest renovated for her own occupation. She was now twenty-one, a little older than me, and so she could do what she wished with her own money. It all seemed so far away from the place I was walking in now with the knowledge that the most beautiful young man in the world, I thought, was walking just behind me. The sun and the air went on increasing my sense of happiness. Just for one day perhaps I could drink to the full from the heady wine of his company. I had seen him only five times so far. Each one was engraved on my inner vision: the time in the Winter Gardens when he was rehearsing; the time in the snow, all unknown to him; the concert; the glimpse in the street when again he had not seen me; and finally the party where I had perhaps shown myself in the worst possible light as a flirtatious chatterbox, purely out of nervousness. And now here he was, and here was my happiness I was sure, even if he took no notice of me. I was as

certain of my feelings for him as I could be of anything. Now I
felt it was in the lap of the gods. I wanted, and did not want, in a
curious way, to get to know him – as if I knew of him all that
mattered, and was reserving a fuller knowledge because I could
never feel more strongly. Would he be interested in me? Why
should he be? I felt partly in another world because he was
there, and even more in *this* world too with a soaring sensation
in my throat as though I were one of the larks which would soon
be on the moor in the spring sunshine. I wanted to sing too and
wished I could. The children had broken away from us now that
the path was broader and in the distance I could see a little white
house and a rocky crag. Daniel came up to my side.

'Are we at journey's end?' he said.

'Are you tired?' I asked.

'No, just a little bored.'

'Pretend it's a magic well, then,' I said.

'What do you mean – a wishing well?'

'Perhaps,' I replied, wishing it were, for I knew what my wish
would be.

He was walking beside me now and I could look up at him.
Although I knew he was poor I thought he looked very elegant
in his black frock-coat which was cut in an old-fashioned way.
He was not a tall man and yet he carried himself well. I noticed
that his black curls were escaping from his rather battered top
hat.

For the first time I saw him looking at me as though I were a
person who might hold some interest for him. I don't think he
had really thought much about me before in spite of our previous meetings. Somehow I knew I must not make an effort to
appear interesting to him – what would have been the good of
that? He might as well know me as I really was. When he smiled
at me I felt relieved of a burden. Here I was, and here he was –
and let the fates take me in hand. We were now approaching the
little vale where stood the white house. The children ran down
the path and their father turned and said: 'See, all of you – a
most natural spot for the culmination of a walk ... Look, it is
quite sheltered and there are already a few others here partaking
of the waters.' Indeed there seemed to be a family party there –
father, mother and three little girls. There were no horses to be
seen, so like ourselves they must have walked.

As we approached the white cottage I saw that there was a

paved forecourt in front, and in the middle, standing by a rather tumbledown wall, what looked like a stone hut – almost but not quite a grotto – enclosing a gushing spring. A man in check trousers and a squashed cap was standing by the well with an iron cup in his hand.

'Do we all have to use the same implement?' murmured Daniel.

There was a little stone bench on which the lady and gentleman sat whilst their children gambolled around. The man in the check trousers raised his cap as he saw new customers and Fanny and Rufus eyed the three little girls.

'Sweet spring watter,' shouted the proprietor as we came up. Mr Angerstein seemed to be asking to see the owner, thinking that this check-trousered one was possibly a servant.

'There's only the missus. Mr Stead don't come nobbut Saturday for the takings,' said the man. 'You'll be wanting a cure for the rheumatics or for the wasting disease,' he said, eyeing me and Naomi. I wanted to giggle – I hoped I did not look in need of a cure.

'The waters are good for all manner of ailments, I know,' said Mr Angerstein, 'but my companions have come only for a refreshing drink.' It did not look very refreshing and the cup was rusty. I saw another on a long chain inside the stone surround.

'Ugh,' said Daniel. 'If it's anything like the taste down in the town, I shall be grateful to be spared.'

Naomi said she would taste the water and Mr Angerstein looked gratified. Naomi, ever full of foresight, had brought along a brass picnic set in her large reticule and there was a mug for each of us.

'I'll wait my turn,' I said. 'I think I can oversee the children from this crag.'

'You disappoint me – I expected you would rush to the cool spring and make your wish,' said Daniel.

'I will if you will,' I replied. 'I would rather drink from the moorland spring – it might taste of peat but not of sulphur.' We took care to keep our voices low in case Mr Angerstein was hurt by our rejection of his plan that we should all drink and pronounce.

'Oh well then,' said Daniel, 'I shall just wet my lips.'

We looked into the stone hut where the water was gushing up

from a hole in the ground like blood from a never-staunched wound, for it had a slight rusty tinge. Naomi had her cup filled and prepared to do her duty.

'Come now, Uncle, you first,' she said.

I thought my employer, a connoisseur of the waters, made a slight grimace as he sipped the strange liquid.

'"Ambrosia", he is going to say,' said Daniel.

'Delightful,' he said instead. 'This could be a place of pilgrimage, I believe, like Mother Shipton at Knaresborough.'

'Oh aye, there's mysteerious properties like,' said the old man.

Daniel had his mug only half filled and so did I. I wished, as I drank the unpleasant, flat, smoky, red-grey water, but not aloud.

'Have you wished yet?' Daniel asked me. He was holding his nose behind my employer's back. 'We only need a lime tree,' he said, 'and the romance will be complete.'

'*In einem kühlen Grunde,*' quoted Naomi, bravely sipping away.

'Yes I have,' I replied to Daniel's question. 'Now you must make one, Mr Reiss,' I said.

'Miss Moore,' he bowed, and I couldn't resist looking at him. He must be awfully bored with the trip. 'Now I have made a wish – that the audience will be completely silent next time I play a Chopin Ballade,' he said.

'If you like I will come and keep them in order,' I said, and he smiled at me. I turned and went up the path to the little crag which was no more than an outcrop of dark grey stone with a little wall around. My employer was deep in conversation with the old man and Naomi was still standing holding her mug of water.

'Can we have some?' shouted Rufus.

'Just two sips,' said their father. Perhaps he was not too sure of its life-giving properties!

I found Daniel was following me when I reached the top of the boulder and leaned against the wall. He leapt up beside me.

'Do you like walking?' he enquired.

'Oh, I should love to walk and walk over this moor and the next and find myself back on my home ground,' I replied. 'But girls can't go on solitary walks – it's better *alone* on the moors really.'

'Shall I go away if you wish to commune with Nature?' he said, looking at me in an amused way.

'Oh no, don't go,' I replied hastily. 'This is a different kind of walk. I like being sociable too.'

'When are you going to visit the Gardens again? Don't you like my music?'

'Oh Mr Reiss, I do like your music, almost more than anything in the world,' I said, and spoke truthfully.

He dropped his bantering tone. 'Why, I do believe you are serious,' he said in a surprised tone. 'All the ladies adore their romantic music of course – it's a matter of fashion and fashion pays for your bread and butter.'

'You play differently from Benjie,' I ventured after a pause. I had been afraid of making myself look foolish because I knew the extent of my ignorance in matters musical and my taste had been developed only from hearing our music master at the Hall play the classical composers, and sometimes the newer ones, for me. 'I used to love Liszt,' I said. 'I still do, but I think my heart is more touched by Chopin. I know he is popular among women but I heard there are pieces not so often played...'

Daniel seemed interested and pensively chewed a long grass he had plucked from the edge of the path. 'What is this difference you say there is between my playing and Benjie Hertz's? Mind, of course, he is a friend of mine!'

'Oh I wasn't going to say anything that detracts from his merits,' I said. 'He seems to me to be a master of technique – but I understand so little about these things. Of course I didn't hear him play anything you did. It seemed to me you played from the heart as well – not of course that I'm not sure your "technique" is just as good.'

'I hope it is,' he said meditatively. 'But the aim of art is to conceal art, and that may be a point in my favour. Yet when you say I play from the heart it may be you think I am sentimental, but I am not. Like the ladies who play oh so expressively that a few wrong notes don't matter...'

'I didn't mean you played wrong notes – I meant that something arises from the music that *is* the music but which seems to connect with my thoughts. It is no good analysing it – there aren't any words for it.' I was thinking: Just as there are no true words for love, it is pure feeling and like some music ... but words were all I had.

'You *are* a strange girl,' he replied. 'Of course all women swoon over the music but they would really like to swoon over the player.'

'Now you are flattering yourself,' I replied with my heart in my mouth. Was all I had a general sharing with womankind in a sort of *Schwärmerei*? Music was not that – because I knew that poetry wasn't either. Yet Daniel Reiss must be very sure of himself to dare to say that women swooned over him. I was not sure that I liked this but I could see that he had not intended me to think that he might consider *me* one of the swooners. He was considering me as a *serious* girl I could see. I determined not to appear too earnest.

'When are you coming to hear that Chopin?' he asked as we walked to the edge of the boulder and waved to Fanny who was running around with the three other little girls. Naomi was in deep conversation once more with her uncle.

'I should like to come next week,' I said, 'if I am allowed a little time away from my charges. Perhaps you could educate my taste and play some Schubert as well. By the way, which instrument do you really favour – the violin or the piano? It is unusual to be so proficient with both.'

'My father put me on to the fiddle when I was only four,' he said, 'but the best music of our day is for the piano I think. Though your opinion of me might rise if I told you that I shall never be as good as Benjie. No – don't protest, it's true.'

'When Benjie played to us at Montpelier Crescent,' I said, 'it was like reading Wordsworth – or perhaps Shakespeare – I had to understand the thought or the language first. But when you played – ' I stopped.

'No – please tell me, this is interesting,' he said.

I was frightened of boring him, and did I really want to share this part of me with anyone? 'I just felt it was like the time I first read poetry. It was like an escape from the world, I suppose, yet I knew that it was speaking a language I understood.'

'Ah, the feeling was in you – as I said.'

'No, not just that. It corresponded to something I knew – yes – but some poets teach one more.'

'Are you always wanting to learn something?' he enquired, laughing.

'Yes, it is true, but I like to say what I feel,' I said. 'There always seems to be some difficulty though.' He looked at me searchingly as I spoke. How simple it could be, I thought, to escape from the world through Daniel Reiss – but of course I could not say anything of the sort. Yet perhaps our whole conversation had been about something other than music. 'Naomi is serious too,' I said, to change the subject.

'Naomi Hertz is serious about her cousin Benjie,' he replied. 'And she is a clever woman, I think.'

The children were now hallooing us and I thought we had better go down to them.

'You should read the German poets,' said Daniel, as we descended. 'Now *they* are even better than your Byron or Shelley, I think.'

'Tell me what to read,' I said. 'There are books at the Angersteins' but I don't know where to start.'

'Then start with Heine,' he said. 'And I'll guarantee you'll think it was written for you.'

We had no more time to pursue this subject, but as we walked back to the carriage he and Naomi were bandying quotations and Daniel was singing them out loud in a pleasing tenor voice. It was a merry, if rather tired, party who piled into the carriage. Zillah sat on my knee and this time Daniel condescended to come inside for it was getting a little windy. I saw him looking at me once or twice when I glanced out of the window. Mr Angerstein was trying to write in his notebook and Naomi was talking to Rufus in a very earnest way about spring water and concessions. Before Daniel had to descend to walk back to his lodging, he took up my hand which was lying on Zillah's lap and for one small precious moment seemed to press it lightly as he whispered: 'I shall expect you in the audience. Angerstein will tell you when the programme turns to Chopin, and he will not wish to obstruct your musical education.' Then he said a louder farewell to all and bounded away. I was in a rapture, yet I could not believe that my jejeune comments about music had done anything to arouse his interest in me. Perhaps he did not find me ugly, and after all he was a young man who obviously liked women. So, I had plenty to think about when I finally got the children off to bed after thanking their papa for such a pleasant day.

It was a few days later when, pausing in the Hall passage to collect the letters the maid had placed on the table, Naomi handed me a programme which they had just had printed for the visitors to the Winter Gardens.

'I think you will find the list of musical items interesting,' she said with a slight smile. I thanked her and went into the schoolroom where there was a warm fire and on the table a little pile of the books I had borrowed from Mr Angerstein's study. I had got into the habit of reading whenever Fanny and Zillah were writing their exercises or compositions. I could not be blamed for consecrating a little time to myself for I did work quite hard with the children. I had started with Heine and a German dictionary. Why had Lavinia not read us more of this? But there was the *Lorelei* and it had brought her back so clearly. Where was she now? I was soon to know, for hard on the letter about Barbara's purchase of the Hall I was to hear from Barbara herself.

You will be glad to know that I have now taken Vinny under my wing and she is furnishing a new home at Rooks Nest. Your aunt may possibly have told you – Vinny is to reside permanently at the Nest with me. But we are soon to be off on a long tour abroad whilst the alterations and refurbishing take place. I have great plans for the gardens and for the decoration of the interior. We may be some time abroad and in London. It was kind of you to write when Papa died. Lavinia too sends her affectionate wishes to you. I'm afraid Mrs Jewesbury may require you back when she loses her French teacher for a space, but I have told her it would be better to let you stay in Harrogate longer. Vinny knows someone who may oblige for the time being.

Yours, B. Stott.

Now that I was further away from Barbara, and from Lavinia too, I was better able to analyse more coolly my erstwhile schoolfriend and her newfound companion. Reading between the lines I saw that Barbara had indeed detached Lavinia from her source of income and was obviously rich enough to keep them both; that my aunt would be upset but would not have liked advice from Barbara; and that it was unlikely Aunt would call upon me to return. I should not have put it past Barbara to have suggested it in the first place. I'm sure Barbara would have liked me back to survey her new realm and to show me the power of money. What Lavinia thought of all this, apart from joining in good wishes to me, was beyond my powers of imagination to conceive. Would she welcome being an adjunct of Barbara? I had no idea. The whole affair seemed fishy to me and I was longing to get on with my own concerns, to renew my acquaintance with Daniel and to allow myself once more the luxury of loving.

What sort of man was he, this Daniel, about whom I was busily weaving so many dreams and hopes? Had I any real idea, apart from what my intuition told me? I tried to discover from Naomi what she knew of him without arousing her suspicion that my interest might be extra-musical, so to speak. Naomi was shrewd but I was older now and was not going to unburden my packed feelings to anyone. I shuddered to think of the use to which even a few of my avowals might have been put by Barbara, remembering our conversations about Lavinia's frills and furbelows and Barbara's strange obsessive interest in her and in money. Was it unthinkable that my feelings for Daniel Reiss could ever 'come to' anything? Why, only the other evening the family had been discussing a friend's son who had 'married out', and I had no intention of marriage – not in the abstract way. What a less than abstract pair of handsome dark eyes and an elegant figure allied with a clear and amusing mind might do, I could of course imagine.

Naomi implied that Daniel was highly talented but could not resist saying that he was not as good as Benjie. This did not surprise me after what Daniel himself had told me about Naomi and I puzzled over her so-called aversion to singing. Surely if she were at all musical she would like to listen to songs. Why then had she beaten a retreat on the day of the party? I gathered, although she did not say so in so many words, that Daniel was a bit of a *coureur de femmes* and that he had had a few love affairs. Like Benjie though she thought he would never marry 'out'. I wondered whether she was warning me off but I had spoken of him only in connection with music. I knew that if I could get Naomi to talk of Benjie I would pick up some unregarded crumbs about his friend.

'Daniel is not serious, not like Benjie . . . of course they both have characters of great magnetism but Benjie is an outgoing personality whereas Daniel – well you never know what he is *really* thinking. Benjie is very kind, he is a very virtuous man. Daniel is not unkind but his looks give him an unfair advantage, for he is of course very handsome, I can see that ... Both of them put their music first, but that is natural with men who are talented.'

They both had a long way to go but she was sure that one day the world would resound with praises for Benjie's genius and so on. I gathered that Daniel was regarded as something of an opportunist. His family, unlike Benjie's, were not rich. Benjie was very fond of his family ... She had never met Daniel's father or mother when they were alive but they had lived in Leeds and were tailors. Daniel reminded her of the hero in one of those rather naughty novels by a French writer – could it be Stendhal? She was quick and intelligent and her judgment was sound, influenced though it might be by her partiality for Benjie.

We talked of other things too when Naomi came up now and then to the schoolroom for tea and muffins before going home. She was secretary, bookkeeper and accountant all in one to her uncle and was happy to snatch an occasional opportunity for a rest. I did not mind discussing my thoughts about life in general with Naomi – she was an education in herself. She was a person who always took you seriously and made you ashamed of your more frivolous feelings. We spoke of time and death and nature and of the new discoveries and writings of the great of our day. She would sometimes bring the *Westminster Review* for me to borrow and we would talk about religion. It was refreshing to see Christianity in a new light. I did wish I could have this sort of talk with Daniel but it was not possible.

I made arrangements to go to the concert on the first Thursday in May. Naomi could not accompany me then but I determined to be a 'new woman' and to go alone, shocking as this might be. As I was known to be at the Angersteins', it would pass, and perhaps one day I could take Fanny there too.

So it happened that I sat with a tray of tea and buns before me in the crowded Winter Gardens one afternoon in early May with the new summer sun bouncing through the glass roof and a feeling in my heart that I was for one afternoon able to give myself up entirely to pleasure. All the conniving was forgotten, together with the last-minute fear that Fanny had a cold and that I might have to stay with her. Here I was alone and expectant, waiting for the blessed sight of Daniel Reiss. Yes, there he was on the platform at the piano looking slight and abstracted.

The Angersteins had seemed to think it was all right for me to go alone, for I would be advertising that I worked for them and supported their schemes for the town – almost a family affair. I knew there was to be some Chopin but I assumed it would be some of the more anodyne passages, and perhaps one or two of Mendelssohn's 'Songs Without Words'. But I was not prepared for the item which Daniel played just before the interval. I had never heard it before and doubted anyone present had, apart from the pianist. I had taken a place as near the dais as I dared and several people had looked at me strangely at first, wondering what I was doing unchaperoned, perhaps waiting for my father or brother? However, I was free to listen and savour the sight of Daniel who came after the singer and first of all played a short piece for the violin which was politely applauded. He followed it on the pianoforte with a valse of Chopin's, as I had thought he would, and a pleasant Mendelssohn melody. I thought that he actually looked at me as he finished this but I was not sure, for he moved to the front of the little platform and announced a recently discovered sonata by Schubert. I had thought Schubert the composer of cheerful songs of the kind the Angersteins sang at their Musical Evenings, but this was quite different. Daniel played only part of a whole sonata and people talked and rustled and tinkled their teacups throughout but I was enchanted. I had never heard anything like this before, not even from Liszt or Chopin. It was a sad and noble movement – not a piece to play in a place like the Winter Gardens. It needed an old castle on a dying autumn day, but even as I struggled not to cast it into a background of romance I could not help but realize that I was touched in a part of my being which was not just me, Meta Moore, but a member of the human race and proud to be one. It was insistent and tragic, tragic in its implications, but not easy music and as far as possible removed from that Schubert I had vaguely known through Mr Robertson and Matilda's songs.

The piano was an old one, not the splendid new one which was to be bought from the profits (Mr Angerstein had told me), but something came through to me, not because it was this beautiful young man playing but something of the man who had written it, I think. When the notes finally died away and Daniel bowed and disappeared, I was too moved to clap and just sat in a daze. Suddenly as the buzz of conversation re-awoke in the long room, I heard a voice in my ear and there was the pianist, leaning over my tray and saying: 'Are you not drinking your tea? I thought that was what people came here for.'

I looked up and Daniel was already pulling out a chair for himself next to me, ignoring the stares of neighbouring tea-drinkers. 'What?' I said rather rudely. And then: 'Oh, do sit with me – of course – I was dreaming – it was the music – it was – I can't find the words...' He sat down, smiled at me and took a bun. I poured him a cup of tea with trembling hands and strove to appear unmoved. He looked at me solemnly.

'The piece you just played,' I said, still thinking of that rather than the fact that he had come to sit by me. 'It was better music – better than anything I've ever heard. I didn't know Schubert wrote like that. But it was too good for here.'

'You are right,' he said. 'So you liked that best?'

'Oh yes. It made me feel as though I were alone and was looking down on the whole world – it isn't music you can talk about, is it?'

'I played it for you. I saw you come in and I thought: Let me surprise Miss Moore and show her I can be serious.'

'If only everyone else had kept quiet,' I said. 'I suppose it makes you angry too?'

'Yes, but when I play I try to forget everything else. I concentrate on doing my best with the notes. I'm not satisfied with my Schubert yet. I heard a great pianist play it last year and of course it's not popular – they are only now discovering all Schubert left for us.'

'I should like to hear the rest of the sonata,' I said. 'Was it written at the end of his life?'

'Poor devil, he was only thirty-one when he died,' replied Daniel. 'It was Benjie who introduced this sonata to me. I'm glad it pleased you.'

I couldn't help looking at him surreptitiously whenever he turned his head away. I had never been quite so close to him before and it unnerved me a little. The music had both uplifted and saddened me but it was the sort of sadness you need to be alone to savour and I said as much to Daniel. I was careful not to spill my enthusiasm all over him. It was not the place or time – teatime in a Winter Garden in Harrogate!

'I am grateful it moved you,' said Daniel seriously. 'You must not look so sad though. Do they work you very hard at Mont-pelier Crescent? I know they do with Naomi.'

'Oh no, it is a pleasant post,' I said. 'The children are kind and good and I am very lucky . . .'

'*But?*' he continued. 'Tell me what you were going to say and I'll eat another teacake if I may. People don't realize how tiring performing is, you know – they think it's done with the brain not the hands.'

'Oh, I'm sorry,' I said. 'Please let me pour you more tea. I shall have to go soon.'

He looked at me again. 'What were you going to say – about your work?'

'Just that I sometimes wonder if that is all of life,' I said. 'But your music shows me it isn't.' I felt very daring and yet he was so easy to talk to. I could tell that he did not find me unattractive, but it was his mind I wanted to understand – it would be so easy to fascinate him with my eccentricities which were only the froth on the top of the wave.

'Have you no one at home, then?' he asked. 'Naomi told me you were an orphan – '

'I have a very kind aunt,' I replied. 'And I am not really an orphan for I never knew my parents. I was brought up by my aunt.'

'And it is she who keeps the school?' He must have been quite busy asking questions about me! 'Oh, do not be annoyed. I am too curious, I suppose. I wondered if there was anyone you had at home to discuss music with?'

'There is my cousin,' I said. 'He brought me here in February when you played. He is a very cultivated man and I am always afraid of appearing stupid when he discusses such things as music or painting. I feel a little more at home with literature.'

'Ah, then you must teach me some *English* poetry,' replied Daniel. He stood up. 'I shall have to go now for I must accompany the singer once more. Do come again, won't you, and I shall try to present you with some more Schubert.' I got up confusedly and we shook hands, and I felt I was the cynosure of all eyes because the pianist had been talking to me. (I don't suppose other people were even looking in my direction!) I did not want to get up and go back to Montpelier Crescent at all. I should like to have stayed there for ever. The music and the man had run together again. I struggled to separate them but I could not. When I did reach home eventually I felt quite exalted and dreamy, but putting Zillah to bed and brushing Fanny's hair and preparing her bedtime beverage brought me back to earth. Even so I was not hungry myself, only thirsty. I admonished myself: I must study Schubert and try to improve my musical knowledge so that Daniel Reiss does not take me for a fool or a hysterical young person . . .

I was, even so, surprised when a few days later I received a letter in a hand I did not recognize.

Dear Miss Moore,
I think you had better learn a little more about the composer you so rightly admired the other day. If your employer will permit I shall call on you all with a short concert for the delectation of the infants in your charge. [What a curious style I thought and then realized he must be trying hard to convey a message and be witty about it.] Perhaps if you would care to add a little musical education to your syllabus it could be arranged. In the meantime I hope you will approve of the suggestion I am making to the respected Angerstein père that he should allow a little visit from me to discuss my forthcoming programme and acquaint him and you with its contents. I fear if not I shall be asked to play for another Musical Evening. Yours in anticipation, Daniel Reiss.

How extraordinary!
It was as we were having tea together with their mama on the same day as this missive arrived that Mrs Angerstein said to her children: 'Benjie's friend would like to play to you next week – would you like that?'

'Oh, yes Mama,' said Fanny. 'Miss Moore has told us and so has Naomi, of the concert he gave you. *I* should like it very much.'

'Will he play for me too?' asked Zillah.

'I'm sure he will, dear,' said their mama and I said nothing.

'How was it, Meta, when you went to the Gardens?' enquired Mrs Angerstein of me. 'Did you hear the Ballades?'

'Oh something much better,' I replied, trying not to sound too eager. 'We heard some music of Schubert that I did not know.'

'I believe Mr Reiss went to London last year to the Crystal Palace concerts with Benjie. My brother tells me they are discovering Schubert's "lost" music everywhere.' She seemed well-informed. 'Perhaps you could give the children a little talk on Vienna and the composers?' she said shyly. She was always rather tentative with me – perhaps she thought it would be an imposition. 'I should have to visit the Mechanics Library,' I said. 'Or if there is not one here, perhaps I could ask Mr Angerstein for his ticket to the Literary and Philosophical one.'

'Of course, my dear,' said she. 'Jacob has little time to make use of his membership. I am sure he would allow you to go in his place and take out whatever volumes would be of use.'

This was a bonus indeed. How clever of Daniel to organize a perfectly proper meeting at the house of my employers. My life was so circumscribed that a visit to the library and an opportunity to talk further with him represented the height of my ambition then!

I did go to the quiet gloomy building the next day and managed to find a few scores of the music I wanted to hear played, and a book or two as well. I busied myself trying to learn as much as I could in the short hours when the children did not need me. Fanny tried to play some of the music on the piano in the drawing room and performed tolerably well.

'Do you like it?' I enquired of her solemn little face as it bent over the music.

'It is not difficult, I think,' she replied. 'But I think it needs something I do not quite understand: Herr Ludwig told me that great music is simple but it is not *really* easy to play. He said it is the simplicity of genius.' Herr Ludwig had been her piano teacher but was now ailing and so her lessons had been terminated.

'Fanny,' I said, inspiration reaching me. 'Why don't you ask your mama and papa if Mr Reiss could teach you the pianoforte? He is very good and I'm sure he would be pleased to do that!' I did not add that I was sure he would welcome an additional income.

'Oh, what a good idea,' said Fanny. 'You always have such good ideas, Miss Moore.' I blushed to think of my duplicity but saw no harm in the suggestion.

Daniel came a few days later to play for us in the afternoon and to see the children's father in the evening. In the meantime I had replied to him suggesting that he offer himself as piano teacher to Fanny. I said I was sure that Fanny needed a good teacher and that I would speak to her mother. I did so on the morning of the day of his visit. It had been quite easy to convey how I thought Fanny needed more musical stimulus that we could give her and Mrs Angerstein thought it a good idea so long as the rest of her studies would not suffer. 'I shall speak to Papa tonight about it,' she said. She often called her husband Papa, in an effort to sound English.

'As Mr Reiss is coming to play for us this afternoon,' I said, 'perhaps you might mention it to him, then.'

'Yes, of course. I am grateful, Meta, that you care for Fanny's musical education. I hear from the children that you told them a story about Vienna and the musical circle there.'

'It was all in the books,' I replied. 'I learnt as much myself.' And yet not for one moment did that good woman suspect that my recently enkindled interest in Schubert had one cause that was not strictly musical. Naomi was coming round that afternoon and she was harder to put off the scent so I resolved to be particularly cool and circumspect in my dealings with Daniel.

It was hard though. As soon as he was introduced by the parlour-maid to us all in the drawing room (not the schoolroom, for Esther Angerstein had insisted we must do the honours correctly), I felt my throat go dry at the reality of his presence. Rufus had of course been introduced to him previously but Fanny, bless her, was overcome with excitement, for she was going to hear a 'real' pianist.

We all sat down at the back of the large room which was bathed in the light sunshine coming through the long windows. Daniel was not at all abashed and smiled at us all. 'How very kind of you,' he murmured to Mrs Angerstein. 'Perhaps, if you permit, you would listen to a little selection of pieces and tell your husband if you approve.' He had no 'façons' as the French say but was free and easy and charming. I wondered if Naomi was wishing it was Benjie playing rather than Daniel, for she looked a little sad.

Daniel gave a brief bow to Mrs Angerstein and then addressed himself to Fanny, but I believed he was talking to me too. 'You may know these little pieces as songs,' he began. 'But the great Maître Liszt, whom I believe your cousin Benjie has met – the great Liszt has transcribed them for the pianoforte. Miss Hertz' – he bowed to Naomi – 'will recognize most of them as the settings for poems by Heine and Goethe.'

Naomi cheered up visibly at the mention of Benjie. Without

more ado Daniel sat down at the piano and the concert began. Zillah sat at my knee to begin with, but as the music commenced she unconsciously crept nearer the piano at the other end of the room, and no one stopped her. I gave myself up to delectation.

'Ah-"Gretchen!"' said Mrs Angerstein when he began to play.

At the end of each perfect little whole he waited for a moment and then began the next. Even Rufus was still and I believe he recognized some of the titles as I had told them the stories of the verses which were set to Schubert's music. Liszt's transcriptions were of course something rather more sophisticated. Daniel turned round after playing The Wanderer and I thought the concert was finished. Mrs Angerstein was sitting happily and Fanny whispered to me: 'He makes it sound so easy – this music is harder than the ones I was trying to play.' I wished he would play a song and sing it too to us.

'For a last little piece,' he said, 'here's one which might send you to sleep, Zillah. It's not set to Heine's words but don't be disappointed – you will all have heard it I'm sure. Schubert was little appreciated as a *great* composer outside Vienna till Liszt put his songs to the keyboard in a grander manner. Now all England is beginning to listen.' Fanny nodded sagely and Daniel announced: 'Ständchen.'

'Oh, the Serenade,' said Naomi. 'Benjie sang it,' she added, blushing.

And Daniel began to play and then to sing. I was astonished. He had read my mind. It was what I had wanted above all.

The music was that divine song which has since become so popular with the audiences of our land, but at that time I had never heard it and words cannot describe adequately the effect it had on me, a strange mixture of feelings. The music compelled, was almost mesmeric in its sad power; it seemed to hesitate and yet be inevitable; it was staccato yet curiously muffled in sadness. And the way he sang it! I imagined some wandering minstrel at the castle of his love telling her to come out to join him in the moonlight, for although Daniel sang it in German I understood most of the words. Yet the words were not the most important – it was the air, perfect, urgent, and his voice that sang. I did not want it ever to end. It was quite simply the most beautiful music I had ever heard. And when the voice died away in the last long minor cadence we were all silent. I had bowed my head, for tears had sprung to my eyes and I did not know why. Mrs Angerstein began to clap and the others followed suit.

'That is a very sorry song,' said Zillah, breaking the spell.

Daniel remained at the piano and then turned and bowed. 'How beautiful,' I whispered to Naomi to cover my feelings with a meaningless phrase.

'You must certainly play that at the Gardens,' said the lady of the house.

'But not sing it, no,' replied Daniel. 'I thought you would not mind hearing my voice in the sanctity of the drawing room, but it is not for a wider audience.' And he looked at me – I am sure he did, for a long moment. It had been a love song, but I didn't know whether he had any idea of its effect on me.

'Mama, Mama, please can I learn the pianoforte from Mr Reiss?' begged Fanny.

'If Mr Reiss has time, I'm sure we could ask Papa,' replied Esther.

Zillah had gone up to the piano and suddenly we heard the air picked out by that childish hand, the air of the Serenade. Faultless.

'Does the little one play too?' asked Daniel in astonishment.

'She can play anything,' said Fanny proudly, not at all jealous that her sister had this gift.

'My brother was the same,' said Esther Angerstein. 'And now, Mr Reiss, may I offer you some refreshment and you can tell us what Benjie is doing before my husband returns to discuss his business with you.'

I made as if to take the children back up to the schoolroom but: 'No, Meta,' said my mistress. 'You and Naomi must stay and Emma can give the children their tea.'

She went out quietly with the children who saluted the pianist gravely as they departed. Naomi and I were left with Daniel for a moment.

'And what does the governess think?' asked Daniel.

Naomi looked at him curiously, but I replied: 'I enjoyed it all – but especially the last song. Liszt is all very well but the finest music is sometimes the simplest.'

'Why did you not take up singing?' asked Naomi. 'Benjie always told me you had a fine tenor voice.'

'I know my limitations,' replied Daniel, throwing himself back on a low sofa and contemplating her with a smile.

'If only there was some way of keeping the sound,' I said. 'I must learn to play that song – the words must be in one of the books I got from the library.'

'So you took my advice?' he asked.

'Yes, I have been learning in order to tell my pupils what I did not know till last week. I hope you *will* give Fanny lessons.'

'The other little girl is gifted, I think,' he replied.

'Yes, but Fanny is very hard-working and can only profit.'

There was a short silence. Naomi was looking faintly amused.

'I shall play the Schubert transcriptions when they have had their fill of Mendelssohn and Madame Frescobaldi at the Gardens,' he said. 'Will you come again to listen?'

'Of course,' I replied. 'If my work allows.' But, I thought: If he comes to teach the children I shall see him every week.

'Are you reading all the German poets then, Meta?' asked Naomi.

'All I can borrow. They are not so easy. I wish my German were better.'

'Mr Reiss will have to teach you too,' said Naomi rather tartly. I suppose she must have seen from my face that I found Daniel clearly the best thing that had happened to me in Harrogate.

'Read the Rellstab aloud – the poem Schubert set for his Serenade,' said Daniel.

'Oh you will not like my accent.'

'Never mind, I should like to hear your German.'

Naomi got up and moved to the window. 'Read it, Meta,' she said with a backward look at Daniel. I took the book with some hesitation. I had not read the poem before.

'It is really a poem for a man to read,' I said. 'All the best love poems are for men to say.'

'Never mind,' said Daniel.

It was easier to read it in another language for it was not a poem for a well-brought-up girl to read aloud with a member of the opposite sex in the room. Well, I thought, perhaps I am not a well-brought-up girl.

But as I read, curiously it was as though I were back in the old place reading to Lavinia and a stab of something like anguish echoed in my heart at the words. 'Do you hear the nightingales sing? They are crying to you, with their sweet plaints. They

159

beg favour for me. They know the heart's yearning and the pain of love; with their silver tones they touch every tender heart. Let your heart too be moved – hear me my love! Trembling I wait for you; come: make me happy!'

'Not bad,' said Daniel.

'It's not like the music,' I said. *'That* is not about nightingales – it says what the words only *try* to say.'

'They are always about nightingales,' remarked Naomi.

'Yes,' I said lightly. 'But I would rather be able to sing.'

The song went echoing through me that evening when Daniel was closeted with Mr Angerstein. I was told by Naomi before she left that Fanny would get her way and would soon receive instruction from Daniel.

'He certainly knows how to arouse feelings,' she said enigmatically as she took her leave and I went up to the schoolroom. Would it be more prudent if I did not acknowledge these feelings? I asked myself again and again. But I knew I was caught – not by music alone but by Daniel Reiss who surely must know how he made me feel. Or did he perhaps intend to acknowledge that he himself had just a little feeling for me too? I was all at sea in these new emotions and swore I would do and say nothing more but leave the outcome to whatever fate was lying in store for me. But I turned and turned my head on the pillow that night as though I had drunk some powerful potion that had turned my veins to fire.

It was amazing that Mrs Angerstein did not express any disapproval when she heard that Daniel had asked me to read words which were certainly unsuitable for a young unmarried female to utter when an unmarried man was present. I guessed at first that she probably thought I had not understood the German, but later I wondered. It was something Naomi said a few days later.

'Auntie is very fond of Benjie,' she remarked.

I had been sitting at the nursery table and Naomi had just popped in to collect some papers for her uncle.

'It is a pity you are not a man,' I said. 'I expect Rufus will take all your work over when you marry.' It was an unspoken admission in the Angerstein household that Naomi wanted to marry her cousin.

'I don't know whether I shall ever marry,' she replied.

'But surely you and Benjie – ' I stopped, confused. It was then she said: 'Auntie is very fond of Benjie.'

'She is not the only person to be fond of him?' I enquired teasingly, for by this time Naomi and I were quite friendly.

'Oh, they want me to marry him – and I – well, you know I am very fond of him too. But Benjie wants to travel and live abroad – not that his wife would have to mind *that* – but I like the work I do for Uncle.' She was silent for a moment and then said: 'Auntie thought Daniel Reiss was flirting with me the other day. She thought it would show me what a shallow young man he was compared with Benjie.'

I did not know what to say – for perhaps Daniel *had* been thinking of Naomi, not me?

'He was not flirting with *me*,' continued Naomi, looking at me with her direct shrewd gaze.

'Was he not?' I said.

'Do you know, Meta, it is true what Auntie says. Benjie is a deeper person than his friend.'

'I don't suppose Mr *Reiss*,' I said, enunciating the words clearly, 'is thinking of marriage every time he flirts with a young lady.'

'Well of course not,' said Naomi. 'I can see he is very attractive, but he will never marry "out".'

I pretended that such considerations were not my affair for I could not bear that anyone should know of the deep feelings he aroused in me and I still did not think they were really connected with a future married state.

Just then Fanny and Zillah came in. They had been playing in the garden at the back, overseen by the cook, and I had allowed them a twenty-minute break before our next lesson.

'I must go,' said Naomi.

'I thought Benjie was a very *good* man,' I said to her as a parting shot. Then we went down, the children and I, to the drawing room where I was to hear them practise their scales.

'Mama says she may ask Papa to buy a little piano specially for us,' said Fanny.

Zillah went up to the piano and I asked idly: 'Can you play the air of the Ständchen that Mr Reiss played the other day, Zillah?'

'Of course I can,' said Zillah, whose musical memory was phenomenal for a child who was even now only six years old.

And she went straight to the piano and played it by ear. It was a great treat for me and I promised Zillah I would obtain the music for her.

'It will be written as a song,' said Fanny.

'I shall try to get the transcription. I am sure there must be easy ones,' I replied. 'For you, Fanny. Zillah would find it too hard – it is easier for her to play without music, but of course she must learn the clefs.'

That afternoon I spent teaching them from a little book I had, *Musicians of Olden Days,* but it was sorry, faded stuff and I preferred to set them small tasks of putting words to music themselves, once they had mastered the staves and keys.

'I can do this better on the piano,' grumbled Zillah.

How was I ever going to see Daniel Reiss again without the presence of Naomi or the children or the rest of the Winter Gardens audience? I was fortunate in that ours was not a conventional family, and *I* was not a young heiress whose every move was watched. I could in fact sometimes be alone and, even that rarity, alone with a young man. But how to contrive it? If Daniel wanted to see me I felt that he would soon find some means and I was frightened of giving too much away about my feelings for him, feelings which I found it harder and harder to deny as the days went by.

Fate was to intervene in the shape of an invitation to a reception at the Winter Gardens from Mr Angerstein himself. Naomi and I were to go as companions to his wife – since he would be too much occupied with administration – to a reception the town was giving to a few notables and a baronet or two. I was touched and pleased that he should think the lowly governess worthy of an invitation, but as he said, Esther would like me there and we would be accompanied by Esther's brothers who had also been invited. I was lukewarm about the invitation until I realized that some of the musicians would also be on hand and perhaps Daniel among them. I imagined a large party at some ball in the country and the dancing there would be, and the talks under the chandeliers or the stars. Of course Harrogate would not be like that in reality, but if Daniel were there it would seem like it. I had, as yet, no acquaintance with balls or country houses nor was I likely ever to have any, so that my day-dreams had transposed the Winter Gardens into the Conservatory at Rooks Nest. I realized with a pang that it was a few weeks since I had thought of the old house. What was Barbara doing now? Where was Lavinia? If only, I thought, I could take Daniel Reiss to Rooks Nest one day and see him in a place I had always loved. But Rooks Nest was not mine and Daniel might not be considering me in any light other than that of a young girl with whom he could exchange teasing banalities. If only I could tell him how I felt – how I loved to think of his face, his hands, his voice.

The day after receiving the invitation to the ceremony, I heard that there would be some music, and my diligent, though innocent seeming, enquiry told me that – yes – *he* would be there. The day after that, I was out on a walk with the children and trying to persuade Rufus not to buy some very suspicious-looking humbugs at the 'spice shop' when I heard a voice in my ear. I turned, and there was my heart's desire waiting at the shop entrance! He raised his battered hat and said: 'I thought it was you. Always surrounded by children, Meta. Are you invited to the "Grande Réception"?' He pronounced the words with irony but oh how overjoyed I was!

'Yes. I am to accompany Mrs Angerstein and Naomi. Are you to play?

'If you come I shan't play,' he replied half-mockingly.

But I did not mind the mocking tone. 'Oh, please, please come,' I replied. He looked faintly surprised at my enthusiasm but I was too happy to feel embarrassed.

'May I walk along with you?' he added.

The children came sidling up, Rufus with a bag of humbugs which he offered to Daniel.

'I shall keep one to eat in my dismal lodging,' said Daniel solemnly. 'Do you ever take a holiday?' he murmured.

'You mean – away from here? I am to go home in a month or two,' I said. It was true, the family were to go to the coast, to Scarborough, when the 'season' was over here and I had been told that very morning that I could have a few weeks away. Somehow the news had not excited me.

'Then we must meet at the reception,' he said.

'Will you be back in September?' I asked him. 'Do you intend to stay as resident musician?'

'Concerts every week until something else turns up,' he replied. 'But I too may be given a holiday. I like the green ribbon on your bonnet, Meta.'

This surprised me so much I did not know what to say.

'*Grün, grün,*' he said. 'Remember the song?'

'But I have no lute strings,' I murmured, remembering. He smiled and touched Fanny on the shoulder as he said: 'Goodbye, then, till next week – wear a green ribbon, do!'

I missed him all the way back to Montpelier Crescent.

The rooms were all decorated with swags of greenery and flowers in window-boxes and the evening sun was gilding the windows as we entered the buildings housing the Winter Gardens. I thought: 'Now it is a summer garden.' It should be filled with young people and dancing, not with these respectable greybeards and their stout ladies. Naomi and I were flanking Mrs Angerstein who seemed a little overcome. Behind us marched her two brothers, Abe and Michael, come to appreciate the wonders of their brother-in-law's activities. They were both neat, merry-faced men who had arrived that afternoon when we were all in a bustle of clothes and flowers and ribbons. We had been driven ceremoniously there by Abe in a handsome carriage and now that we were actually in the Gardens I hoped that we should not be disappointed. The music was to be provided by a small orchestra as a background and I did not think much attention would be paid to it. We were relieved of our cloaks and bonnets and gloves and joined a long tail of overdressed dignitaries and their wives who were to be presented to the Mayor and to the Trustees of the town's Spa. There was no sign of Mr Angerstein as I looked around. Nobody took any notice of us so we chatted amongst ourselves. I was wearing a green ribbon in my coiffure which, for once, seemed as though it would not disgrace me by falling down.

There was that polite murmur of conversation which always accompanies a public event, with a few sudden high-pitched trills and giggles from the ladies and a rumble from the men.

'Papa says we are to sit at table number eleven,' murmured Esther to me. 'Abe will go and find it whilst we wait to shake hands. Oh I do hope Jacob is somewhere about ... He is so excited on these occasions.'

I smiled and looked ahead and shuffled along with the rest in my evening slippers. Naomi was looking rather grim: she did not enjoy ceremony. At last we were led to the welcoming party and a few gracious words were spoken to us all before we went off to find our table.

'Is there to be dancing?' asked Michael.

'What are you thinking of?' laughed his sister, cheering up.

'A barn dance perhaps?' he replied.

I was listening keenly to what they said for it had occurred to me already that perhaps there might be a celebratory waltz or two. But most of the company seemed past the age of waltzes. Just then Mr Angerstein appeared as if by magic.

'Ach, Jacob!' exclaimed his wife, really delighted to see him.

'I am just off to meet Sir Moses Finkelstein and the Lord Mayor of Leeds,' said her husband, bestowing an absent-minded kiss on his wife's forehead. 'Now, Naomi,' he added as he was about to bustle away again, 'when you have had the ices and champagne you can go in to the small salon. They've con-sented to a tiny amount of dancing – apparently Sir Moses likes to dance! And you too, Miss Moore,' he went on kindly. 'There are sure to be a few cavaliers for you.' Then he was off again. What energy! But – dancing! dancing! Perhaps Daniel would play for us. I was full of excitement, as though my happiness de-pended on a dance – if he were there and if he asked me. Now perhaps I should at last know whether all my feelings were truly reciprocated. I had never been to a dance, though Mr Robertson had taught us some of the steps, since he played for the As-semblies in Halifax. Of course it wasn't really the dance I cared about – I was honest enough to admit that. But what young girl cares more for the dance than the partner? Unless of course she is a good dancer and can show off her skills – which I certainly was not. The ices came and people moved around between tables chatting to friends. Michael popped the champagne cork and I was offered a glass. They were treating me so well, as though I were really now a member of the family. Then we heard a distant strain of music from the adjoining room.

'Come girls,' said Michael. 'Onkel Michael will pilot you to the scene of debauchery.'

'Really, Michael!' complained Esther Angerstein, but she seemed quite content to stay chatting with her other brother, who was like her in face and figure.

'Do you want to dance?' asked Naomi. 'I hate dancing, but I suppose we must.'

'I can't dance,' I answered truthfully. 'But I should like to hear the music.'

We both rose and rather self-consciously patted our hair and smoothed our dresses. Naomi was wearing a beautiful gold velvet crinoline whereas I had on my best green silk which I had had made in Lightholme when I was seventeen, having chosen the colour myself to be like Lavinia's. I had hardly ever worn it but I hooped it up and followed Naomi. It was obviously an afterthought, this dancing, and not a formal affair. Jacob Angerstein always followed the whim of the moment – that was why he made people enjoy themselves.

When we finally pushed through the tables and the clusters of chattering groups of people and arrived in the 'Little Salon', there were already a few couples essaying a stately dance. I looked eagerly up to the dais where the musicians were seated. Would Daniel be there? If he were, he would not be able to ask me to dance. The room was not very brilliantly lit, unlike the one from which we had just come. A tall man with grey curls was moving round the room wearing an expression of bliss, with a lady, a rather stout one, on his arm. That must be Sir Moses. I did not recognize anyone else. Then a man in pince-nez and a high collar approached Naomi and asked if she were Miss Hertz, the daughter of his old friend Isaac. And would she like a stroll round the salon if Miss – looking at me – would like to accompany them? I was about to accede to the request, for it was a little improper perhaps to be there without a chaperone. Naomi laughed and said: 'Of course' – Papa's friend and she would like a chat. And Meta – she introduced me – would doubtless walk with them. But she was too late, for just as I was resigning myself to another family chat, there was a hand on my shoulder. And there he was, and there without more ado than a smile at Naomi and a bow to her escort, there was *I* standing looking up at Daniel Reiss.

'Ah well, then,' said Naomi's papa's friend. 'We shall watch you take the floor for I'm afraid my rheumatism forbids anything but a slow walk.'

Naomi looked quite thankful and said: 'Let us see you dance, Meta. I am here to keep an eye on you, remember.' But she smiled as she said it and turned away with the gentleman.

'They are quite right,' said Daniel. 'I was about to ask you to dance with me – if you don't object, of course.'

'How could I object?' I replied, but I was quite tremulous at the thought of his taking my arm for he never had, even on the walk to the sulphur wells, though he *had* touched my hand, and there was more to waltzing than arm-taking.

'Don't look so scared,' he said. 'I shan't break you,' he said.

'I can't dance,' I said.

'Never mind – I can show you. Just follow me.'

Thank goodness it was not one of those old formation dances which I had never been able to learn. Before I knew what was happening I was held in the arms of Daniel Reiss and a strange and yet comfortable feeling it was. He was just the right height for me so that I did not have to stretch my neck up and away; neither did I have to regard his shirt buttons for he was not above the common height. I just wished I did not have to move around and that I could just be held in his warm embrace for no other reason but that I wanted to be. There were not many couples dancing – most were standing round the room watching. I didn't mind if they were watching me. I was so perfectly happy.

'That's better,' he said. 'I don't want to hold a croquet mallet, but a girl.' I laughed and he squeezed my hand.

As I have said, the room was not well-lit and the shadows cast by the gas brackets were more like candles. His face was half in shadow. At last I was alone with him – even if only for the time it took for an Austrian waltz to be played.

I felt as though I had known him all my life after the initial strangeness of finding one of his hands clasped in mine. I knew that the waltz was still regarded as a rather risqué dance, especially for young girls, and that it was only because of the less close supervision these Jewish people permitted that I found myself in his arms. But I cared nothing for respectability and I had no 'reputation' to lose as far as I could see. I was just swept along on the delicious tide of music.

'I could write a better tune than this,' he said as we turned a corner.

'I did not know you were a composer as well as a performer,' I said.

'Yes, that's what I am – I have to play to live, but I prefer to invent my own music.' He laughed. 'Don't look so serious. I suppose like most women you have elevated ideas of the artist!'

'Oh, my ideas about you are elevated,' I replied. I thought: I love you, I love you and what can possibly happen to me? All my ideas and thoughts are swept away when I'm here close to you.

'After this we shall sit out and I shall get you an ice-cream and we shall talk. *Would* you talk to me – not of sulphur wells, or even of music? I know you are a great chatterbox.'

'I am honoured you have noticed,' I replied. Indeed I was really surprised. Perhaps he had been feeling something for me if he had bothered to judge my character.

'I expect we should argue if we discussed music,' he went on.

'Oh, I would not argue with you. I should want you to teach me. I am very ignorant, going only by what moves me – in music,' I added.

'That is the best way to begin,' he said. 'The listener doesn't have to worry about technique. We can study it of course – but after all, music is for pleasure.'

I wished the waltz were slower for I should like just to have walked up and down on his arm – and I could not really concentrate on the music. All my body seemed to be centred on our points of contact where his hand held mine and his other hand on my waist. But I was so happy.

'You are smiling,' he said.

'Yes – I am happy.'

It was true. I had not felt this kind of happiness for a long time. It was like running in the wind when I was a child, but there was nothing childish about it.

'We shall sit now and you will tell me all about yourself,' he ordered. The music had come to a final whirl and he lifted me half up from the floor and I laughed.

Everything, the wavering light and the proximity of Daniel and the music and the certain knowledge that I should have him to myself for a quarter of an hour at least, combined to make me feel I was in another world from that of my ordinary self. Perhaps the glass of champagne I had drunk in the other room had helped too.

'You are not giddy, are you?' he said. 'Your cheeks are pale.'

Excitement now always made me pale rather than rosy, so I reassured him. 'But I should like to sit down,' I said.

For so long my life seemed to have been, however pleasant and busy, so static and a little dull except for the looking forward to seeing this man, that I felt a new era had opened for me. His touch was magic – I felt like the Sleeping Beauty who awoke at last when the Prince kissed her. And mingled with the longing to be even closer to him and the feelings of excitement, was the knowledge that at least he had chosen to dance with me and wanted to know me better, even if this were just the usual way young men, I gathered, were supposed to behave. He piloted me to a small anteroom off the Little Salon, waving to Naomi on the way with that insouciant assurance he seemed to have. We sat at a little table; there were a few other couples and a sprinkling of elderly ladies who looked at us, I thought, with envy.

'Now I know you are a very *serious* girl, but there is more I want to know,' he began when he had ordered ices for us both. 'I would buy us a bottle of champagne, but alas, I am not rich,' he added.

'I don't need champagne,' I replied. I wanted to say: 'Your company is all the champagne I need.' And I also wanted to say: 'This is the tenth time we have met,' for I knew the litany of my seeing him off by heart. It seemed years ago since I had stumbled on him rehearsing in this very building, and seen him walking away in the snow that winter evening later.

'At least we don't have to drink the tonic water,' he said. 'I believe they are touting it around instead of champagne.'

'Do you wish sometimes you were not in England?' I said. 'All this stuffiness and respectability. You could play anywhere – like Benjie.'

'I shall not stay here for ever,' he replied, and I must have looked sad for he took his cue and said: 'I had the idea you were not English yourself Meta – but of course I know you are not of my race.'

'Oh, I am English,' I said. 'Only the English are "romantic" about "abroad" are they not?'

'I think *you* would do better abroad somehow.'

'Why, in what way?'

'Well – you appreciate poetry I know, and you want to travel. You mentioned it on our walk to the well, I believe.'

'Yes – I did want to,' I replied and I told him about Papa and my childhood and Daniel listened and then spoke of his ambitions – to go to Vienna or Leipzig or Paris and have a life of dash and fame.

But all the time we were speaking I could tell that he did find me attractive, it was there in the way he looked at me. I wished I knew about the women I was sure he must have loved – or they had loved him – for how could anyone not have loved him with his deep, dark eyes and slight look of disdain, which perhaps covered other feelings? But I knew I was not going to be what is called 'courted', in common parlance. Daniel was unconventional; his way of life was not ordinary and I wished I were a great lady or an actress or something different from myself – a twenty-year-old ingénue – for that is what I thought he would think me.

Then he said: 'I have not met many young English Christian girls you know – it is unusual.' He paused and, as I said nothing, he said: 'There is something about you. I feel I know you very well – I am not flirting with you, you know.'

'I am not flirting with you either,' I said.

'You must beware, dear little girl, remember what happened to Red Riding Hood.'

'I am not Red Riding Hood,' I said quite calmly. 'I am the Sleeping Beauty.' Then I added: 'Only in name of course, I would not like you to think me vain!'

'Why should you not be vain?' he said. 'I know the Angersteins like you – they told me so. I was very politely warned off you. Oh, they didn't mean any harm – they seem to have an exaggerated idea of my reputation.'

'They are kind,' I said. 'I should not wish to embarrass them – and my duties keep me in their home. I am lucky I suppose, for most girls live at home with a papa and a mama. I have to make my own way. I do not complain, but I often feel – ' I laughed, and parodied my feelings ' – I am "meant for higher things", but I don't know what. I would like to be like you and write music or play it. And all I do is appreciate it – and you.' I stopped. I had been carried away, and yet all I had said was true. It was just that one should never, never say such things.

'London would suit you better,' he said.

'Oh, if only I had a fortune, or a large circle of friends, or was older.'

'We are talking dangerously,' he said. I looked at him and a shiver went down my back. 'There are people and milieux in London where feeling is not denied,' he said, looking at me with a slight smile.

What a long way we had come in a short conversation. I remembered it had taken me two years to speak to Lavinia like this. Men were decidedly lucky. And all I knew was that I had recognized a mutual attraction which seemed at first separate from my yearning for him, and was perhaps not the same thing at all and yet I felt it was, for me at any rate.

Then he took my hand : 'May I ask you if you have some village swain to whom you have plighted an eternal troth?' he asked ironically.

What could I lose by being open with him? 'I used to play with the farm boys,' I said. 'Till my aunt stopped it – and I used to be very fond of my teacher.'

'Was he a handsome man, the teacher?'

'No, she was a beautiful woman!'

He laughed and then took my hand and I wished he would kiss it. I think he would have done but he did not want to embarrass me. I felt once again, when he took my hand for that one tiny moment, that I would do anything to stay with him for ever. How artless I was – I tried to tell myself to be sensible but it was of no use. I was what Martha would have called a rash lass.

'I should like to know if I could see you sometime away from here – when you go home? I could ride across the moors to see you, couldn't I?'

'If you can ride,' I said. 'I shall be home in the summer – I told you – when the family go to Scarborough. But we can see each other here, can't we?'

He laughed. I looked at his brown hand lying on the table and remembered Lavinia's white hands. I knew I wanted to have what they called a love-affair with this man. I wanted to be a 'fallen woman'. But all I said was : 'Take me back to Mrs Angerstein. I think she may be wondering where I am.'

This seemed to redouble his ardour. 'I shall ask her for a dance,' he said. 'And when she refuses I shall ask you once more – and then you will go home with them. Look, here is the intelligent Miss Hertz.'

Naomi was suddenly at our table and Daniel rose and said : 'I was just saying to Meta, we must go and pay my respects to the family.'

'Are you enjoying yourself, Mr Reiss?' was all she said and looked at me, rather worriedly this time.

'I have taught Miss Moore the waltz,' he replied, deciding to use my formal appellation to show he could play at that game too.

We got up and made our way back to the large room where there were now fewer people. Mr Angerstein had joined his wife, and the uncles had broached another bottle of champagne.

'Ah Meta,' said Esther. 'We thought you must be dancing – have you enjoyed it, my dear? Mr Reiss...' she smiled a little warily at him. Daniel bowed and said:

'Would Mr Angerstein permit me to invite his wife to a dance with me?'

Esther smiled prettily. I could see she must have been a very attractive young girl once. 'Oh, my dancing days are over,' she said. 'Jacob has to stay a little longer to oversee the departure of Sir Moses, but why don't you dance with Naomi?' I saw a look pass between Naomi and her aunt, but Naomi said:

'I do not like dancing – '

'Oh please dance with me!' cried Daniel.

'Thank you – I shall sit with Uncle Michael and he will tell me about double-entry book-keeping,' replied Naomi.

'Then perhaps I may have one last dance with Miss Moore?' said Daniel.

I affected a nonchalance for the benefit of the others. 'Should you not be playing the fiddle?' I asked. 'I would rather listen to that.'

'I'm afraid my music is not danceable,' he replied. 'May I ask you formally for one more dance?'

I got up and said 'Thank you,' and to the others I said: 'Will you be here when I return?'

'We shall wait for you, Cinderella,' said Naomi. She seemed amused again now.

Thus it was that I contrived once more to find myself in his arms. This time we said nothing at all and I gave myself up to the delicious languor shot through with arrows of bliss which the nearness of his skin and his breath and his hands aroused in me.

'Do not forget, Meta – I shall come to see you when you go on holiday. I may be going to London later.'

These two statements filled me with contradictory sensations of joy and woe. 'But I shall see you before then?' I murmured. 'We don't expect the family to go away before July.'

'Yes, of course. I wanted only to make a little tryst with you for the summer.'

Oh, Daniel, don't go, don't go, I wanted to say. Why should social arrangements prevent our meeting and holding hands?

'I am in earnest,' he said and it must have been a great tedium for a man who had obviously conducted affairs in more sophisticated surroundings to find himself forced to make necessary arrangements just to see a young lady. 'Come here,' he said suddenly, just as the dance was ending, and before I knew what was happening he had swept me through a door into one of those long corridors I had seen before. It was dark and I felt his hand grip mine. Then he held me close to him and kissed my forehead, brushing his lips over it like the flight of a moth over silk. I did not struggle or do any of the things well-brought-up girls are supposed to do. I clutched him and kissed him back and then he tore himself away and we were back in the ballroom.

I went over and over every second of the evening when I returned home with the family for I was far too excited to sleep. The whole world seemed to have undergone a transformation in the twinkling of an eye. I tried to appear unmoved and decorous in the carriage as we returned and I wished Mrs Angerstein a polite good-night after thanking her heartily for the evening. I hoped I had not acted impolitely in her eyes in dancing twice with Daniel and I did not think she had noticed anything but Daniel's own insistence that I dance with him. Naomi was another matter and she had bid me a quiet good-night when we dropped her at her door.

The future seemed now to beckon to me in a sort of glory. For so long I had mooned over Daniel and for so long thought he had no particular feelings for me. And now? Would he ever call them 'love'? I wanted to say 'I love you,' and I would say it, but I intended to savour that night for as long as possible whatever happened in the future.

What happened first of all was the arrival of a note from him; just a simple little note which was waiting amongst my other post two days later; and a talk with Naomi who, I thought, had perhaps been deputed to urge moderation on me – or perhaps she did it out of kindness, for I knew she was not jealous of me, all her own thoughts being with the absent Benjie.

Daniel's note said: 'Dear Sleeping Beauty – Thank you for the dance you led an impecunious prince. I shall expect to see you chez Angerstein or in my audience very soon. And I remember the bal des couloirs too, DR.'

I suppose he had to be fairly circumspect in case my employers inadvertently read my post. Naomi was more direct. She came up to the schoolroom the next day when the children were down in the kitchen helping the cook make a birthday cake for Rufus. I

173

knew what she was going to say and knew she would have said more if she had known even half my turbulent emotions. 'You are fond of Mr Reiss?' she began.

I looked up from the papers I was correcting and resolved to be calm. It was no good trying to explain to Naomi that I did not care if Daniel's intentions were what they called 'not strictly honourable' because I knew that mine were not either. And in any case I was sure that he 'loved' me, whatever I should discover that word to mean. 'Yes – I like him,' I replied, putting down my pen.

'I noticed he was doing quite a lot of wooing,' she said drily. 'I hope he did not embarrass you.'

'Oh, I am not easily embarrassed,' I replied as coolly as I could.

Naomi would obviously not believe that I would ever instigate what she called wooing. And after all it was quite true – Daniel had been doing more than the permitted amount of wooing. 'I wouldn't like you to be hurt,' she said, sitting down at the table with me.

'But how can he hurt me if I don't mind?' I asked reasonably.

'If he engaged your affections,' she said.

I was not worried about my affections being engaged, as they already had been for quite some time. I said nothing though, and she went on: 'You are not an actress, Meta, or a light woman – does he know the difference?'

'But I have hardly seen him alone,' I replied, which was true. All I cared about was whether he loved me. Actresses did not come into it, and anyway what was wrong with actresses?

'You know what I mean. I am not saying you have encouraged him – but Meta, even if you did come to . . . like him more than you do . . . he would never marry you. Apart from . . . our religion . . . I don't say it's impossible, but I don't think he is a marrying man.'

'No, I suppose he's not,' I said.

'You know you have to be careful of your reputation – it is all we women have.'

'I know, more's the pity,' I said and looked at her. 'Naomi, please do not worry about me. I know it is because you are a kind person and think I might be hurt, but perhaps I am not a marrying girl either. Is it wrong to enjoy a young man's company?'

'No, of course not, but he is such a handsome man – and he is a little . . . unsteady I believe.'

'Not like Benjie,' I said, and she blushed. 'If you think I have not behaved well to the Angersteins,' I said, 'I should be sorry, for I would hate to think they thought that. But Naomi, are men and women never to get to know each other without this idea of marriage? Is there nothing between that and being a loose woman?'

'The family have said nothing,' she replied. 'And you have done nothing improper. I only don't want you to suffer, Meta, for you have such a face for suffering.'

I was astonished and said: 'What do you mean?'

'It is just that we women *do* suffer, Meta, especially in a society as unenlightened as ours. One doesn't speak of these things of course, but you might find you had . . . feelings which were dangerous – and be led to do things which would not do you any good.'

'And what about men?' I asked, glad to lead the conversation from the particular to the general. 'Are they not also endowed with feelings? Why should *they* be allowed the expression of them and women be confined to simpering and waiting for them to declare themselves?' I had not known the extent of my thoughts on this subject until I spoke.

'Women are not supposed to feel *first*,' she replied.

'But that is all nonsense,' I explained. 'I would not do anything here in Harrogate to harm the family, or my own reputation. Why should I, though, have to curb and restrain even my feelings about other things – like music or poetry –?'

'Stop, Meta! You are an enthusiast, you are just like one of my teachers in London – and *she* was ruined by a man who she thought loved her. Now all she can think of is the Woman Question. I am sure things will change. I did not mean to imply you had done anything improper – I just wanted to warn you that men like Daniel Reiss are a trap. I'm afraid if you really want to change things you have to remain untouched and rational.'

'Like you?' I enquired. 'Oh, I am sorry Naomi, I know that's not fair. And believe me, I envy you your future happiness with Benjie. But perhaps there are different ways of arranging these things. You need not worry – I shall conduct myself with the utmost propriety.' And, I thought, once given a moment's freedom I shall behave as all lovers behave, throwing caution to the winds. 'I hardly go out much,' I said. 'And if I see a young man here in the house there can be no objection, surely, even though I am only the governess?'

'No, Meta, that is all right – perhaps I should not have said anything.'

'I'm not cross, Naomi,' I said. 'I know you have my interests at heart – and I too have yours. When will Benjie return?'

'I don't know – that is the trouble. Sometimes, Meta, I get so tired of waiting. But I know now we shall marry – he is such a good man.' And she went on to speak of the virtues of Benjie Hertz and I listened and thought my own thoughts and wondered why I had not been chosen to be the intended of a paragon like that.

There was to be another concert of piano music the next week, I learned, at which the soprano I had heard with Rainer was expected to sing. I hoped I should be able to go, and decided that in order to show my goodwill I would ask Naomi to accompany me. She was not uninterested in music as I had thought that first evening when Daniel played for the Angersteins, but she admired what Benjie admired and that was Beethoven. She was prepared to admit Schubert however. I was even disposed to find the singing interesting, in spite of the lady singer. If only *Daniel* would sing the Serenade.

'I'll come with you, Meta,' she said. 'We could take Fanny too, if her mama approves.'

When we asked Fanny if she would like to go she was very pleased and her father thought it a good idea and one adding to her general education.

'Will it be Mr Reiss playing?' she asked immediately. She had not forgotten her mother's promise that Daniel should come to teach them. I decided it would be a good opportunity to mention the subject again.

'Why – of course – I had forgotten,' exclaimed her mama. It had been a good chance too for me to see whether I could introduce his name without constraint. 'I shall write to him,' she said. 'What about Thursdays? He doesn't play at the Gardens then, does he?'

Daniel wrote again to me when he received the invitation from Mrs Angerstein. 'Liebes Metalein – I am to thank you I believe, for the formal invitation to the Angerstein foyer as professeur de piano. I look forward to next week when I shall appear in professorial guise. But before then *please* come to my concert. I have written a little piece which is not completely unconnected with our dancing. Your devoted DR.'

It was June now and I was looking ahead to my holiday in July as well as the more imminent visits of Daniel to the house. The day of the concert I received a letter from my aunt. I gathered through her rather unconnected paragraphs, disconnected one from the other because she was continually interrupted, that Rooks Nest was undergoing extensive repairs now that Barbara and Lavinia had gone abroad. Before they had gone, friends had been invited there to see the first alterations. A large room had first been painted and decorated, apparently as Lavinia's boudoir.

We were all invited to see it and pass judgment and I must say it was very fine. Barbara is quite grown up – you would hardly recognize her. Lavinia *had* consented to finish the term with us as I was without a teacher of languages but we have found an elderly man who knew your papa and it seems to be a success. Miss Logan is delighted with her new life and does not seem surprised to be the recipient of Barbara's generosity. I cannot make it out for I always thought she favoured you, not Barbara. Still we should be glad the old place will come alive again, though Martha does not agree with me, I know. Martha sends her love and is counting the days till your holiday. Will they let you have the whole summer? I do hope so. Rainer says Mr Widdop has received a letter from your Aunt Sophia! He will acquaint you with the contents later. He is off abroad again. His poor mother says she never sees him and is thinking of retiring to Buxton. I hope you are hearing some good music. Your loving Aunt Augusta.
P.S. No I have not had another attack of rheumatism – you are not to worry. Martha looks after me well and has persuaded me to take a holiday in the summer with Caroline Walker. I should go away *only* if you were not at home. A.J.

I wondered about this Aunt Sophia, Mama's sister, from whom I had never heard a word in my whole life, but I was more concerned to think about the coming concert.

At last Fanny and I and Naomi were sitting amongst the potted palms. Fanny was behaving very well and was drinking a mug of milk with her finger crooked in imitation of the grown-up ladies around us.

'They can't play anything serious in this atmosphere, surely?' remarked Naomi.

'No, I agree. It's not fair – I wish Mr Angerstein would hurry up with his proper concerts. It would be better to have them in the evening.'

'What are they going to play?' asked Fanny.

'I don't know, dear – it's usually announced just beforehand.' I wondered whether it would be the violin, the piano or even the voice this time. It was neither exactly. The fat man came on the platform and announced a new piece to be played by a little orchestra whose services they had been lucky to acquire. Perhaps Daniel was ill? But surely we would have known if that were the case? A tall old man came on with a cello and then two string players – a violin and a viola – and then bounding on the dais came, thank goodness, Daniel! He made for the piano. 'A valse,' announced the fat man, 'composed in honour of the Winter Gardens by Mr Daniel Reiss.' Daniel got up again and bowed. So this was the piece he wanted me to hear – but when had he written it? I composed my features for listening and they began to play, the tinkle of teacups always in the background. Then I realized that the tinkle was also in the music and that Daniel had invented a clever way of incorporating the Winter Gardens. Naomi was laughing and Fanny looked rather puzzled. 'He is imitating the ladies at their tea,' I whispered. Then the music changed and the viola player took up the tune with the others softly plucking their strings and Daniel sounding strange chords in muffled bass notes on the piano. The tune was very easy to listen to – it reminded me of a ballroom at a castle, beginning very softly and then rising to a crescendo and then dying away again. I wondered whether it was a memory of our waltz together for it seemed that he was looking at me occasionally. Or did I imagine it? The 'Winter Garden Waltz' I thought.

When the music's last chord died away there was a silence and then clapping began, and a few hurrahs from the elderly 'sparks' present. This was going to be a popular piece of music and no mistake.

'He has done it!' said Naomi under cover of the clapping. 'It is a success, it is going to make his fortune,' she whispered. Was it true? Was that it? I seemed slower than Naomi to grasp what it was all about. 'My uncle will be able to have it as the special air for his seasons,' she went on.

Daniel was getting up and bowing and the other players bowed too.

'That was written by Mr Reiss!' exclaimed Fanny. '*Will* it make him famous, Miss Moore?'

'I am sure it will,' I said.

'If Zillah were here she would be able to go home and play it,' said Fanny. 'I shall ask him if I can learn it for my first lesson.'

'It will not be published yet,' said Naomi.

Then as the salon settled down to a general chatter and more cups of tea and cake were brought in the interval between the last item and the next, I saw Daniel coming towards us. When he sat down all eyes were upon him and there were whispers of: 'That's the composer with Angerstein's little girl,' and a few heads craned round.

'You are going to be famous,' I said.

'Did you like it?' he asked, after saluting Naomi and smiling at little Fanny.

'Splendid!' said Naomi. 'That will make your name – be careful to whom you sell the copyrights.'

He sat down and I didn't know what to say. 'Well?' he said again. Then he lowered his voice a little. 'The inspiration was our dance.' And then, turning to Naomi, he added: 'I wrote it to commemorate our last week's festivities.'

'I liked the piano bit,' ventured Fanny. Still I had said nothing.

'Shall I call it "Meta's Dance"?' he continued.

'When did you manage to write it?' I managed to say. I was confused, not quite believing what I thought he wanted me to believe, that it was a love song and that he had written it for me and because of me.

'I wrote it last week, stayed up to write all the parts, got my old pals from Bradford to rehearse it – and there you are – ' He was excited. So was I. He turned to me again. Naomi was trying to attract the attention of the waitress to bring us another pot of tea. 'May I dedicate it to you – just between ourselves. I shall hope to make a little money with it from your employer, of course – but it *was* for you, you know.'

'When can I hear it again?' I said. I was being so stupid, tears were not far away. Nobody had ever written a piece of music for me before. It seemed, though, to make public our private feelings – or mine, anyway.

'Didn't you like it?' he was persisting.

'Daniel – I – it was lovely . . . I don't know what to say,' I managed.

'Then I shall bring a copy to Fanny's lesson on Tuesday.' And he was off. 'Sorry I can't stay for the cup that cheers – I have to accompany Madame Frescobaldi.' He was gone.

'Well,' said Naomi. 'He is an extraordinary young man, Meta, I must say.'

I spent the rest of the week helping Mrs Angerstein sort out the children's clothes for the summer and waiting to see Daniel when he came for Fanny's piano lesson.

'It seems a pity Fanny will only just begin with him and then we shall be away,' said Esther. 'Still, I expect he can get her started.'

Not for the first time I wished it were myself about to have a piano lesson from him. News of the 'Winter Gardens Waltz' had spread round the household although of course no one knew that he had written it for me. Three days before her lesson Fanny came up to the schoolroom with a parcel. 'Papa says Mr Reiss has sent his new music for me to learn – it's the piano part, Miss Moore. Papa says everyone is humming it!'

'May I see it, Fanny?' I took the music down to the piano with the girls and together we tried to make out the spidery squiggles. 'He will have to have it printed,' I said. 'And of course the air is in the string instruments.' I saw then an envelope enclosed with the music and addressed to me. I pocketed it quickly. Why couldn't he write to me and put his letter in the post – it would have been embarrassing if Mrs Angerstein had opened it!

Dearest Meta,

Did I give you a shock at the Gardens? I thought you looked a little upset. Of course I should have played it to you first if I could have seen you, but I thought it would be a surprise – it is for you. The music came all unbidden and I wrote it easily in a style I have not attempted before. I should be touched if you would regard it as yours, whatever anyone else thinks.

Yours ever, DR.

The incongruity of the situation was beginning to get on my nerves a little. Here was I being written to, music being written for me, and yet I had no chance to speak to Daniel except at times I could not choose. I *must* contrive to see him away from the family and away from Harrogate or I should go mad with the continual waiting and anticipation. I felt obscurely that I was uneasily poised between one life and another. I should be away for almost the whole of July and August and already there was an atmosphere of unrest at the prospect of change for the children and for myself. Fanny told me that they were to go first to Scarborough where their old nurse lived in retirement and then to Leeds to stay with Grandmama.

'I wish you could come too, Miss Moore,' she said over and over. I would miss them, I knew, but I could not pretend that a change was not needed for myself, too.

I must see Daniel to arrange how and where I could meet him at Lightholme or in Halifax. An idea was already forming in my brain which first of all I thought was impossible, but when I thought over what Aunt had said about Barbara and Lavinia being away I realized it might be possible. I should ask Daniel to meet me at Rooks Nest! That was what I would do. I did not look beyond this – I only knew that I must see him.

I replied to Aunt Juby's letter of the week before, saying how I was looking forward to returning home. It was true – I *was* looking forward to it, but it all seemed unreal. I asked whether Cousin Rainer would be there and also what message Widdop had had from my unknown Aunt Sophia. That bit of information was puzzling me.

But in the midst of all these plans and preparations which were going to take me another three weeks or so, I was even more anxious to think about Daniel. He had written music for me – did this mean he loved me in the way I loved him? Did he even have any idea of my feelings for him? There was just that little grain of uncertainty about everything which tormented me and I did not know what I could do about it without appearing foolish or precipitate or forward. I decided to write to him, since our meetings were so peculiarly irregular; I must let him know what I felt; there was no other way. What else could I do? He had sung me a serenade; he had made me read it to him; he had danced with me and paid a sort of court to me and kissed me; and we seemed to have advanced years of intimacy in our last two meetings. Yet – I was at sea. I almost would prefer not to see him again until I should be a little more my own mistress, but then the thought that he might be at the door would set me off in another delicious turmoil of anguish and excitement. Was my love requited? I could not, of course, ask him that, but there were things I could say. I knew in my bones that he desired me – I could not mistake that and the feeling was reciprocated. But it was not the only or even the principal emotion I had for him. That was something different, almost painful. I tried each night to rearrange his features in my head before I went to sleep. I caressed his every pore in my imagination and yet he eluded me. I could no longer live for ever in dreams. I must wake up and act.

My Dear Daniel [I wrote. I should like to have written 'Dearest Daniel' but I dared not]

My mind is in a confusion. On the surface I am calm and busy with the children and I go about my daily tasks as I have always done, perhaps even more efficiently because I am happy. I am happy because I am thinking of you and am almost persuaded that I have not misunderstood all you have said to me. So I can say it to you, as I must if I am not to go mad with a strange mixture of joy and terror. Yet I am still frightened that if I write to you like this you will mistake it for the ravings of some hysterical miss. When you sang the 'Serenade' I thought you might be saying to me what I want to say to you – but women are not allowed to say such things. When we were together at the Winter Gardens party I felt I was right and that I need not any longer hide my true feelings for you. Yet I become gloomy and I don't know why and wonder whether I am not deluding myself. I am soon to go away on my long holiday and as I told you I shall be at home in Lightholme. For almost two months my time will be my own. I am not closely supervised at Hartsedge Hall and I am able occasionally to walk out to friends or ramble around the village. Yet even to tell you this fills me with trepidation as though I were mistaking your intentions. Rather I should wish to invite you to visit at my home, but this you might not want to do and I can see that it would be to act as though things were a little more ordinary than they or we are. I write to ask that, as your plans are so subject to alteration with all your appointments and your concerts, you write to *me* when I am at home so that I can meet you. Perhaps in a place where I know we might remain quietly together without interruption.

You said you were going to London. Do you know the date? If I see you here at the Angersteins' on Tuesday please do not refer to this but know that I am most deeply touched that you should have written the 'Winter Gardens Waltz'. It is that which has emboldened me to propose that we meet in the summer, though I know that every 'right-thinking' person would consider me forward and unwomanly.

The house where I was born is situated in its own grounds which adjoin the village of Lightholme. It is now occupied by two of my acquaintances who happen to be abroad. I know there are walks there where we might meet and talk. I hope this suggestion will please you. If you wish, of course, you may still visit me at Hartsedge Hall but that may perhaps not be as private. Please let me know whether you think this a good idea. I am longing to talk to you, dear Daniel, away from all the intrusive duties and people and inconveniences of my present state. Tell me you do not think me wrong to do so. I am aware that I do not act with the circumspectness required of females. Forgive me – write to me and cheer me up. I loved your music.

Your friend, Meta.

I puzzled long over this letter, not wanting to appear coy yet seeing no other way to advance matters.

My mind was set at rest by a letter which crossed with mine and arrived the day before his lesson with Fanny.

'My darling Meta – I must see you away from this pestilential spa. You must tell me where to see you in the summer for I think of you continually. Your presence will bless my days. Your DR.'

When I had written and posted my letter before receiving his, I felt I had burned my boats, and became calmer. I could not see that there was anything wrong in proposing to see him in Lightholme, and yet of course, it was wrong to encourage a man (I had been told), wrong to take the initiative, wrong to admit even a little of my feelings and wrong to appear that I had things I could not say to him in company. But I had given him an opportunity to see me at Hartsedge Hall. Naomi and others would say that if he were 'honourable' he would see me only at my aunt's. That would mean he was a suitor, intended to marry me, and nothing worried me more than to think I might give him the impression I expected this. Was it that I did not expect him to treat me as a future wife? I wondered whether I should be expected to make myself over into a marriageable quantity, even though I was sure that this was not in his mind. Was nothing else allowable then to respectable women? Such a little thing – to meet a beloved person in order to advance our mutual knowledge of each other and yet it was liable to the grossest misinterpretation. I shuddered and yet I was rebel enough to know that there was no other way for me, that I should have to play according to his concepts of honour which I was sure were not of the world of the conventionally respectable. I was amazed at myself too for it was unheard of for a girl to encourage a love-affair openly. But I was prepared to wait years for Daniel if he really wanted me. I felt there was nothing else for me, and although I tried, I could not help myself. Perhaps he would prefer to visit me at home, but it seemed unlikely after what Naomi had said about Jewish ideas of marriage. And why should he marry me? That was not the sort of thing I felt happened to girls like me. I recalled people I had read about – Mary Shelley and her mother and the ladies Lord Byron loved. There was no precedent for me in all that. I was not living in the fashion of fifty years before. For that you had to be older and richer than I was.

Sometimes my blood ran cold at what I had done. Then I would console myself with his letter. When he came to teach Fanny, perhaps I could see him. By then he would have received my letter.

I knew that he had some feeling for me but I did not quite know what sort of feeling it was. He couldn't possibly be as besotted with me as I was with him – I never expected that. I had to take my courage in both hands and dare to reveal some of what I felt about him; feelings which had grown and grown ever since our first accidental meeting in the Winter Gardens when he was rehearsing his music. Now there was no stopping it. What should I do when he came to teach Fanny? Should I wait and say something to him, or sit in the room with him, or stay upstairs and expect a message from Fanny? He wanted to know where to see me in summer – I had already told him that in my letter. All I could do would be to tell him how to get there, and now that Lightholme boasted a railway that should not be too difficult. I must admit that in my imagination I had seen him riding up the long lane to the house and tethering his horse to a tree, but the reality was going to be more mundane. We should have to fix on a date and a time when I could walk to the old mansion and perhaps that would have to be done by letter. Aunt had never supervised my post and I knew that I could receive letters without too much difficulty. Yet this all seemed so tedious and practical. All I had to do was give him my address at Hartsedge!

When he came to the house the next day I was busy in the schoolroom with Zillah who was doing pothooks – her little fingers were nimbler on the piano than with a pen between her fingers. Emma came up to fetch Fanny who was excited. I could hardly ask the child to take a note for me – it seemed too clandestine. I should hope to catch him on his way out. Then I hit on an idea. 'Tell Mr Reiss I have a book for him which I should like to give him when he leaves,' I said. In the book I should put the directions. He might think it odd that I did not send them by post but such was my impatience to settle the matter that I could not bear to wait. I wrote rapidly whilst Zillah wrote her copperplate with much sighing and groaning.

> Thank you for your letter. It seems we agree. I shall be at Hartsedge Hall from the 19th – that is if we ever get the children's luggage organized in time – and I suggest that you let me know when you could meet me. If you prefer I can be at Rooks Nest on the day you choose rather than meet you at the new railway station. Go down the Turnpike Road from the station entrance, turning right until you come to an old lodge which is uninhabited. Go down the sandy lane which is under the parapet of the old Coach Road and leads into the grounds.

Then I thought: this way someone might see him and ask him his business, so I tore up my note and began again. I thanked him for his letter and gave him instructions to follow the old Coach

Road which led earlier off the Turnpike down to the high wall and to climb over it where I would await him. That way we could go to the lake and the summerhouse without the danger of prying eyes. 'Write to me at Hartsedge Hall, Sholey, nr Halifax.' I clipped the note in a paper with his name and put it in the book about Vienna I had been reading. It was one of the books from the Angerstein study. I felt ridiculously conspiratorial. What if Daniel would prefer to make a formal visit to my aunt? I opened up the note again and added: 'You are, of course, welcome at my home – it is your own choice.'

The music could be heard only very faintly from the drawing room and I sat waiting for the half hour to finish. I did not expect him to linger afterwards – Mrs Angerstein was out. But when the half hour was up and Fanny had still not returned, I could not forbear to creep down to the first landing, hoping that the servants had done their day's work and would not be in the way with their dusters and brooms. Then I saw the door open and Fanny come skipping out. Daniel followed her. Had she told him of the book? He looked upwards and I summoned up courage and came down the stairs.

'Go up to the schoolroom, Fanny. I have the book for Mr Reiss,' I said, as I slowly descended. He remained at the foot of the stairs. Emma would be there any moment to let him out. I held out the book for him, saying quietly: 'Here is the book you wanted and you will find something for you inside.'

'Oh, Meta,' he said, looking up at me. 'I thank you for your sweet letter. Did you get mine?'

'I see we are of one accord,' I replied. 'I have written it all for you . . .'

'Then I may come once you are at home?'

'Either to the Hall or – to the Nest – it is all here.' I kept looking nervously towards the kitchen in case a servant should appear. Suddenly he came up to where I was standing on the stairs, took the book, then bent and kissed my hand in an extravagant gesture.

'You are an angel,' he said. 'And an angel should be seen in Paradise.'

'Then come to Rooks Nest,' I whispered.

For answer he took my hand again, just as I heard the door to the basement open.

'Write to me – please write to me?' I murmured. 'Daniel?'

He brushed my fingers again with his lips and looked at me for what seemed a long moment before releasing my hand and tucking the book under his arm. I fled up the stairs as Emma came to see him out of the door. My heart was beating wildly. It was the first time I had acted towards him in a less than conventional way, the first time I had taken the initiative except in my letters. I saw him turn down the crescent as I watched from the schoolroom window and he was walking with a light springy step, not turning round or hesitating. Fanny would be waiting to tell me all she had learned so I returned to the children, my own heart lighter than it had been since the concert.

There was no time for another music lesson for Fanny, for Mr Angerstein, in his usual impetuous way, had decided the family would go immediately to the coast since the weather was so good. There was only time for some frantic packing, with the excited children already out of their routine and talking of nothing but the sea. I had time to write to Aunt to tell her of my impending arrival and to pack my few necessities, leaving most of my books and winter garments at the Crescent. I had no time even to say a proper goodbye to Naomi. I was off! I was on my way home!

As Rainer was abroad, I was to make my own way home and I looked forward to the journey. I should be conveyed to Harrogate Station by carriage and thence to Bradford. There I was to take a train to Lightholme where my aunt would send the fly – the same little cart Lavinia had used. The day came. Farewells were spoken. The children made me promise to return in September. All I remember noticing on my journey were the urchins in the street who were parading their St James's Day grottoes and begging for 'a penny for the grotto' from passers by. It reminded me of Lavinia and the Rooks Nest grotto so long ago.

Five

WESTMINSTER SQUARE

It was a hot day and I was lucky to find a porter. Several people stared at me, a young woman travelling alone, but I took no notice. It was indeed not my return home I was thinking about but my meeting sooner or later with Daniel. I prayed that nothing would go amiss and that he would be waiting for me, on the day we decided, at Rooks Nest, that place of my dreams and my delight, which was getting nearer even as I bumped along in the omnibus and then the train. When would he come to see me? That was all I could think of as the governess cart clip-clopped up the lane to the Hall.

Here were all the old fields, green in the summer sun; the leafy lanes, and in the distance browner hills, and the plumes of smoke from the town in the valley smudging the sky over by Hippercliffe. And Aunt and Martha would be eagerly waiting for me. How would they find me? How should *I* find *them* after what seemed an eternity? My first stay away from them, almost a year ... What a pity that Rainer would not be there – or perhaps I did not want his hooded eyes, that yet missed nothing, scrutinizing me?

If only I could speak to someone of my love for Daniel – but there was no one who would not worry about me if they knew. To go all that way away – and it seemed a long way – to return with mind and heart and body irradiated with the idea of a beloved person! There over the fields and down the lanes beyond was Rooks Nest, which I also loved. I saw the line of trees marking its parkland even as I thought of it and then Sam turned the dog-cart and we went up the hill towards Sholey to the Hall.

Sam had grown very taciturn. I knew he was now wed, though he was only twenty-two. Did he ever remember our childish games? Now we were going down our lane, and there was the Hall spread out, dark-stoned and gabled, the porch door open and Martha at the window of the parlour.

We drew up and the porch was suddenly filled with both my aunt and Martha. Martha was beaming. Aunt stood a little stiffly and I alighted, embraced and was embraced. 'You've grown, love,' Martha said and Aunt looked both relieved and happy to see me.

'Meta, we thought you'd take longer, dear. How pleasant this is!' She was smiling. 'Sam will bring in your boxes and Martha'll take them up to your old room.'

I was inside and sniffing at the roses which filled all the vases on tables everywhere. 'And I've baked you a nice tea,' said Martha, still eyeing me as though I had come not from Harrogate but from the moon.

Later that evening as I sat at the open window of my little room at the top of the house I was wondering how I could ever show them I loved them and still carry on loving Daniel? I had to see Daniel and yet – would it be breaking the trust of those who loved me? There was nothing else for it. I had to try my wings now that I had savoured a little independence. I wished he would come to see me here in my home and yet I could not imagine how it would be if he did. I went down to give Aunt the little book I had found for her at the secondhand bookshop and to present Martha with the scarf Fanny had knitted for her. I had plenty to tell them, but of that which filled my mind there was nothing I could say.

The next day Aunt Juby called me into the parlour where she was busy with her accounts. 'I can help you now,' I said and gave her a packet containing the money I had been able to save during the year.

'Why, Meta – no!' she said. 'I shall not take this. It's your money, my dear, you have earned it – and besides – '

'I want to help you,' I said, with some embarrassment for we had never discussed her finances before.

'We are doing very well – the school has even made a sizeable profit this year,' she said quietly. 'And I told you your mother's sister Sophia had written to Widdop?'

'Yes.' What had that to do with my finances?

'She wants to see you in London,' said Aunt shortly. 'Of course it is up to you whether you go or not – I can't imagine what she wants with you . . .'

'You mean she wants me to go to see her in *London*?'

'Yes, she invites you to write to her and arrange a visit. She must have changed. I met her only twice before her marriage and she was a giddy girl then – '

'Perhaps she has a guilty conscience?' I said.

'I don't know. She must have enquired about you from

Widdop. You must write to her, Meta, and decide for yourself.'

If I could go to London, I could be with Daniel – that was all I could think of – but, how to arrange it? Aunt was vague enough, but would my comings and goings be monitored? Could I perhaps arrange to stay with this Aunt Sophia – the address was in Belgravia – and fix the date for my departure earlier than Aunt Juby would expect me back? I suddenly discovered in myself a terrible talent for dissimulation, and I felt guilty and yet excited that I might, if I were careful, have a day or two in London with Daniel Reiss.

'See what you think, my dear,' said Aunt, handing me a letter written on thick white paper.

'Has she plans for employing me?' I remarked as I took it. 'Does she have children?'

'Grandchildren – she was married so young and she must be almost fifty now. Don't feel you have to go, Meta – it is a puzzling letter.'

I took it up to my room, more concerned with writing to Daniel and arranging our rendezvous at Rooks Nest than with the reasons for my Aunt Sophia's sudden interest in me.

To Mrs Augusta Jewesbury care of H. Widdop Solicitor,
Park Chambers, Halifax.

Dear Mrs Jewesbury,

Circumstances parted my dear sister's daughter from myself as you are aware. I write not to bewail them but having ascertained that the child is still alive, I write with a proposal. I hope you will forgive this letter which cannot be anything but a surprise to you. I am now a widow and unfortunately deprived of the companionship of my own daughter through marriage and removal to India. I have the charge of my two grandsons aged three and five, whom it was thought the climate out East would not suit.

I have a good staff here. I thought it my duty to enquire if I might see my niece Miss Moore, knowing nothing of her or of her attainments, with a view to perhaps offering her employment in the capacity of nursery governess, should I deem her satisfactory. Naturally I should wish to see her first and to this end write to enquire if she would visit here for a week or two this summer. It was the Dear Lord who after my husband's demise whispered this proposal in my ear. I should not have taken it up knowing the rift between our two families, but much prayer convinced me that I have perhaps a duty to the living. Would you be so kind as to ask your ward to write me a letter so that I may better judge of the possibilities before I extend an invitation to her to stay with me? I must mention that I am almost a permanent sufferer being often confined to my couch and unable to do justice to the high spirits of my two grandsons.

Yours sincerely,
Sophia Grosvenor.

I could hardly contain my anger, that after twenty years of neglect by this lady I should be offered charity – or even worse, a post as governess to my own mama's great nephews. And the mention of the Almighty only added to my angry scorn. But what if it were the only way to go to London and be with Daniel? Would Aunt think it odd if I were to accept? Would she be hurt? Perhaps I could represent my motive as sheer curiosity. I had no intention of finding another post. If I had been unhappy in Harrogate the proposal from my Aunt Sophia might have presented itself as a possibility, but even then not one which my Aunt Juby could possibly feel happy about. What should I do? What could I say to Aunt – and how could I reply to my other unknown aunt with the proper mixture of politeness; an agreement to stay in London for a little time with her, but a hint that I had no intention of taking up her offer?

I sat at the window of my bedroom with the letter in my hand, thinking hard. Suddenly I had plans to make, things to do, things to say which might affect the whole of my future. I could not miss the opportunity of meeting Daniel. And how else could I ever contrive to get to London?

The bees were droning in the honeysuckle which wound along the wall under my sill and the sky was of so deep a blue that I could have imagined I was in Italy. The fragrance of the honeysuckle and the wafts of perfume from the Bourbon roses below and the faraway shout of someone in the lane or the fields induced a languor in me. For a moment I wished I had never fallen in love, never come across this person who was jerking my whole life out of its accustomed tracks. How would I have replied to this peculiar letter if I had no ulterior motive for travel south? I should have said:

Dear Aunt Sophia,

I am indeed grateful for your kind enquiries about me and the invitation to London you offer me. I have however a good post in Harrogate and have no intention of leaving it. In any case your offer that I should become governess to your grandsons does not attract me. I know nothing of the circumstances of any rift you may have engineered with my mama, but I am only too aware of the sacrifices my Aunt Augusta has made on my behalf ever to accept that I should leave her alone and live in London. I have no knowledge of very small children and even less of a grand household such as yours must be. I am truly sorry to hear of your husband's death but this can make no difference to my resolve . . .

This was what I should like to have written.

I moved reluctantly from my window seat under the mullion and went down to Martha. Perhaps I could represent my interest in going to London as a sort of duty owed to my mama? How wicked I was. To what lies would I not stoop to find myself for a few days alone in London! I was sure that I could arrange to spend a week with Aunt Sophia, but to Augusta I should say I was to be away for a fortnight! That would give me a spare week – a free week to be with my love. And if Aunt Juby wouldn't take my money, so much the better. I should need a few guineas in London and was sure I could find somewhere to stay – or perhaps Daniel would already be there . . . I went to my writing-table and quickly wrote to him arranging to meet him four days hence at Rooks Nest. The place had been described to him – I only had to advise him of the date. And if he was unable to come – well, then I could walk alone in Barbara's domain at will.

I went downstairs and out to the village postbox, a walk of about half a mile. The sun was beating down and I lifted up my head to it and prayed to it: 'Forgive me for dissimulation – how else may I, a girl, escape? Forgive me if I hurt Aunt Augusta's feelings. Let me see this other aunt of mine. Let me then go to Daniel – and let it all turn out for the best.' When I returned I went into Martha's cool kitchen. She beamed at me when I entered. I dipped my finger in her cake mixture as I had been

wont to do, and enquired after her mother and sister. But
Martha wanted to talk about Barbara and her fortune, and about
Lavinia. She saw however that this did not particularly please
me for I said only, 'Barbara always said she'd be rich,' and 'It
will be good for Miss Logan not to have to work.' Then I said
with affected indifference: 'Did you hear about the letter from
Mama's sister, Martha?'

'That I did, and I'd never credit it after all these years. And she
not lifting a finger to help us – not that we'd have wanted it.
What a carry-on! Lonely now she is, I expect . . .'

'I agree, Martha,' I said. 'But don't you think I might just go
and see her? It might not be a bad thing to mend the rift, not that
I'd ever want to work for her, but if she's invited me to London
it would be a good opportunity for me to see the metropolis.
And it would let Aunt Juby have a holiday – I'm sure she needs
one but she won't go away with Miss Walker while I'm here for
my holidays.' There was a silence and then Martha looked up.

'Well, if you put it like that, Meta, I suppose it would be
Christian just to go and see her – and it's true your auntie needs a
change of air. But you've only just come home, love!'

'Oh, I know, Martha, and I'm so afraid of sounding disloyal,'
I heard myself sound more and more plausible as I spoke! 'But I
would like to see London and it wouldn't do any harm just to be
polite to her. If there was any question of my hurting Juby's feelings I wouldn't go, but I'm grown up now – and apart from
Cousin Rainer, this lady and her grandchildren are my only
blood relatives. Not that that means anything to me – but perhaps it would be the right thing to do?'

'Perhaps you are right. If you put it like that to your auntie
she'll understand. You can't be blamed for wanting a little holiday yourself. I'd be afeared meself to go down London but
you're different and they're your people when all's said and
done.'

Thus was my duplicity rewarded and I wrote a polite letter to
my Aunt Sophia not at all like the one I had planned.

Dear Aunt Sophia,
    I was surprised to hear from you and am touched you
should wish to see me. I am afraid that I already have a good
post as governess in Harrogate but I should like to see
London. Perhaps one day I should wish to change posts but

not yet. I am eternally grateful to my Aunt Juby for bringing me up and am looking forward one day to helping her with the school she owns up here. If you feel that my journey in these circumstances would be a waste of your time I shall of course understand but I should like to see my dear mama's only sister. I take the opportunity now of commiserating with you over your husband's demise. I could stay a week with you at the beginning of August if that were agreeable to you.

Yours sincerely,
Meta Moore.

All Aunt said when I had talked it over with her – Martha had already put in a word for me – was: 'Rainer will be surprised. He thought you wouldn't want to go.'

'*You* must have a little holiday,' I wheedled, and it was true she did want a change. 'I shall go only if Aunt Sophia's answer is at all agreeable,' I went on, but I thought that lady's curiosity rather than her conversation with the Almighty would prevail upon her to invite me definitively!

I posted this letter too and then relapsed into the old ways – long conversations with Martha about the Angerstein children, and talks with Aunt about my teaching duties. I waited only for the Thursday when I expected to see Daniel, and laid my plan for a visit to Rooks Nest well in advance. Only inclement weather would ruin that plan and fortunately the sun continued to burn high in the heavens above Hartsedge and Lightholme and I felt I was going to be lucky. On the morning of my rendezvous a letter arrived from London – still nothing from Daniel, but I knew he would keep his word. Was I a little disappointed that he had not preferred to see me at the Hall? Perhaps. The London letter was brief – I might like to reconsider the opportunities a post in Westminster Square would give me but in any case Sophia would be pleased to extend the hand of friendship to her dear sister's daughter and may God be with me (as He certainly appeared to be with her). She sounded a puzzling woman, perfectly sincere in her protestations of devotion and curiously unaware of her condescension.

Thursday had dawned blue and gold and the warm air was breathing all over my little room from the open window. I looked out over the hills and wondered whether Daniel had yet set out. I tried to eat my breakfast slowly and then I announced I was going for a walk. 'You should look round the Nest,' said Augusta. 'Since they're away they can't mind and there are probably workmen in the house – but the gardens will be lovely now.'

'Yes, I might look over there,' I replied. I believe Aunt thought I was so wounded over Barbara's ownership that I wanted to avoid the subject. I set off with a small basket, promising to call on one or two people and to be back about teatime. In the basket were two freshly baked rolls and some fruit. I waved goodbye to Martha, closed the wicket gate behind me and set off on my way. I walked slowly till I turned the corner of the lane and then moved swiftly down by the fields and through the cottage lanes and past the village stores and on to the Turnpike and down to the Coach Road. Would he be there before me? Would he come at all? Was it just a figment of my imagination that he loved me? Perhaps he would lose his way or ask someone who knew me – but they wouldn't connect me now with Rooks Nest. If I went straight there along the lane at the bottom of the old Coach Road I should probably arrive before him and could look at the gardens and house. We could go to the summerhouse and talk and I would say: 'I'm to visit London,' and then I should tell him that I could see him there with a little contrivance. If only, though, I didn't have to go to London but was walking to meet the love of my heart to stay for ever in the place of my heart. But I must not think of that – Rooks Nest was Barbara's, and never would be mine to take a lover to. Never would I lie there in the great rooms and fill the house with roses, lead the life I had always wanted to lead, the seasons passing and changing, but my love never changing, with the sound of the rooks in the elms and an eternal summer in our hearts.

I woke myself up from my fantasies when I reached the bottom of the lane and saw the high wall where I had used to stand with Martha and the place where I had walked with Lavinia. I decided to enter it the old way and was still agile enough, in spite of my supposed dignity as a governess on leave, and my long skirts, to scale the wall and jump down on the other side. It was all as I remembered it, but the trees were even greener and I could hear the sound of the brook which fed the lake and disappeared on the other side to the farm. There seemed to be no one about. If a gardener espied me I should say I was a friend of the owners and did not know they were away. I walked carefully down to the lake, a little wary now that I was there in those enchanted grounds. Surely I had given Daniel clear instructions and he would arrive soon? The lake seemed smaller and the grass had been cut. I turned now and saw the house, surrounded by greenery. There was scaffolding at one end but no one in sight. I passed the grave of the dog Puck and remembered Mama again, and I hoped Mama would approve of me – for she had *died* for love, I thought. And I gave another thought to Papa who had asked me to bury a thought of him there. I walked on past the lake and came to a place beyond the grotto I had never explored before, and discovered another rose garden where Barbara's new gardeners had not yet been. The place was a tangle of thorns with great swathes of pink rambling and climbing roses as far as the hedge which bounded the land. Barbara would cut them down one day, but she was not there now to see me bury my face in the blossoms and listen to the bees and lie in the long grass by the hedge and stare at the shining sky. I put my basket on a step and looked around me. The summerhouse was visible at the turn of the path. We could go there.

How long did I wait? My thoughts were such a jumble of the past and the present that I must have fallen into another reverie and it was only the sound of a step on the flags near the grotto that made me look up. At first I thought it was a stranger. In fact, I had almost forgotten why I was there, so strange are the machinations of the imagination, and then I saw that it was him! It was Daniel. He caught sight of me as I stood up to welcome him. I didn't ask if he had found the place without difficulty, or was the train on time. I didn't attempt to speak at all at first. He approached and said: 'Are you surprised? You *look* surprised! Is this your fairy kingdom?' And he came up to me and took me in his arms and all my previous thoughts seemed to flee away, for this was the here and now and I loved him. He kissed me quite softly and then he drew away and looked at me. The very sense of his presence was overpowering, and yet it was strange too for I could not believe in another part of my mind that he was really standing there, framed by rambling roses under that blue sky, as though *he* belonged there, not me.

'We can sit in the summerhouse,' I said finally and took his hand boldly. 'But we must not make a noise for there may be workmen and gardeners around.'

'Are we trespassing then, little Meta?' he enquired.

I told him who it all belonged to now – he knew only what I had said to him before and written to him about my link with the place.

'Thank God you have come and you are really here,' I said as we found the little arbour and the summerhouse and he stood for a moment looking out at the lake and back to the house.

'You were born here then? It's like a piece of paradise – no wonder you love it.'

'Oh, I do love it,' I said. 'Just for a moment I couldn't connect it with the present and with you . . .' He came and sat by me and took my hand. 'I always wanted to be here with someone I loved,' I said and I did not feel at all shy. Suddenly I felt that Rooks Nest was a happy place and I smiled.

'You are smiling, Meta. Usually, you know, you look so sad,' he said and put his arm around me. I was surprised. I had not re-alized that I looked sad. 'I always feel somehow that you *are* sad,' he said after a pause.

'But I am very happy now,' I replied, and it was true. Why should I ever leave the warmth of his encircling arm except to gather flowers for him and return!

I do not remember what we talked about then. What do lovers talk about? I think he teased me and then he was grave and I showed him the other gardens in the distance and he said he would like to see the house. And I was so happy, wanting only to explore his features and hold his hands and feel just for one moment both at peace and excited. Finally I did tell him about my plans for London as the bees wove a dance before us and the fleecy clouds promenaded slowly across the sky and we ate the fruit and the bread. We seemed to become friends too, for what chance had we ever had of becoming friends when everything men and women said to each other, every move they made, every little feeling they might have, was monitored by that vo-racious goddess Public Opinion? I said as much to him and he was silent for a moment. 'Do you want to stay with *me* in London then – after you have visited your aunt and if it were possible?'

'Yes – if you will have me,' I said.

'Meta, darling Meta, look at me. You know that if you come to me you will lose your reputation. *I* care for you, but society will not – and I've already told you I'm not a marrying man.'

'What do I care?' I replied. 'What does anything matter but love? I love you, Daniel. I know it is wrong for girls to *say* it, but can we not just be happy – why must we always be worrying what other people will think?'

'You wouldn't want to hurt your aunt,' he said.

'You mean Aunt Juby. But she wouldn't know. I want to be free, Daniel – free to love you – if you love me ... You wrote things to me I can't forget – tell me I wasn't wrong to think that you – '

'You weren't wrong, Meta. But I can't promise what might happen to us – you are so young and you need a steady love, you will marry one day – or will want to. Do you know what you are asking of life – that I take you and make you my mistress? Of course I love you, you passionate girl, but dare I take away from you what will one day be your "value" in the market place they call the world? If I do that, could I answer for the conse-quences?'

'Oh Daniel, you are talking like a respectable man. *I* am not respectable – no I am not – and I do know what love is, and I will prove it to you,' I replied, feeling disturbed and a little angry.

'I don't want to spoil anything, that is all,' he said. 'You will do as you will and I shall not stop you.'

He began to kiss me again. 'You see – nothing else matters,' I murmured as he finally let me go and I put my hand up to his face and tried to turn it to mine again.

'It is hellishly difficult for me,' he said. 'All you say is true, and yet you see we men have to warn lovely girls that love does not always last. If you had a mama she would warn you against men like me.'

'But the music –! And all you said...'

'I find you madly attractive and madly tempting,' he said. 'I'm only doing my duty and warning you. There is nothing for madly attractive young girls like you but marriage. Anything else reduces them to penury or the streets.'

'What nonsense you are talking, Daniel. I have nothing against marriage in the end, but I am young and want to see the world and love and be free.' As I said it I knew that I should like to be married to him one day and that he would never marry me. Perhaps if I were Jewish he would.

He read my thoughts. 'I only don't want to make you unhappy. You are such a desirable creature. And I couldn't live with you, see you constantly, without wanting your body as well as your heart. I know I have your heart.'

Did I have his? I could not ask. I should know, perhaps, if I 'gave myself' to him, as they said, utterly without fear and of my own volition.

'I *will* see you in London,' he said after a pause.

'Let us walk to the other rose garden near the house,' I replied. I was not disturbed. His speaking so frankly had been honourable, I thought. He was so beautiful. I stole a glance at him as we rose to walk along the path that led away from the summerhouse to the house. If I had been a man I should have had no problems about morality and respectability. And I should not either have had to worry that my love might lead to the birth of a little replica of Daniel. I shivered in the sunny air. How I would like to have that, and never would – unless I cast myself off from respectable society. All society's laws were made because of that, I felt dimly. But I was not going to give Daniel up, so long as he returned my love.

Here we were amongst Papa's roses. Tea roses and Portlands, Chinas and Damasks and ramblers, framing the vista now across the green lawns to the house. There were roses of every shade and scent and some scentless and droopy; others firm and curled, striped even, open, closed, in clusters, singly, in a great rampageous riot. The ground was freshly turned – Barbara's gardeners had been *there,* I could see. There were even little labels and I stooped to read them. 'Félicité et Perpétue' one said and there were others with the names of French ladies and English aristocrats and others simple and white and nameless – Rosa Albas. I remembered that Lavinia had liked yellow roses whereas I had always stuck out for the deep dark red ones. How long ago it seemed.

'Can we go up to the house?' asked Daniel. 'There doesn't seem to be anyone about. I am quite prepared to flout the laws of *property*,' he added. 'I wish *I* had a lot of money,' he went on, looking at the house which stretched out now quite near to us, its glasshouses like flashing eyes full of tears in the sun. 'Then I would install you here and go and play to the world, and make you proud to know me.'

'I am proud,' I said. He was silent. 'Here I feel I am taking you "home",' I said softly. 'More than if you came to the Hall – more than anywhere. I'd have a salon here and great house-parties and we should feed on peaches and sleep between silken sheets and I'd make a music-room where our friends could come to hear you play – and perhaps artists and writers and famous people...'

'Is that all you would want, Meta? Nothing for yourself?'

'Oh, I should hold everyone spellbound with the brilliance of my conversation,' I said laughingly. 'Look, I can show you the "pavilion" where my – my teacher used to live, before my cousin sold the house to Barbara's father.'

'I'm sorry if I spoke roughly, Meta,' he said and took my hand again. 'I know we could be so happy together – I do know – it's because I value you, little one. Now show me your house and we shall peer in like the street urchins in those improving books.'

I laughed and we forgot to look decorous but ran across the lawn and up to the windows of the South Pavilion. They had been cleaned, I could see, and white paint gleamed on the doors. In the distance on the other side of the house we heard a workman singing and we stopped for a moment; but he was probably the only soul there, the others having gone off for their mid-day meal. The caretakers would be round the back. I peered through one of the windows where the blinds were not pulled. Most of them had Venetian blinds now which gave an air once more of occupation to the place – like lidded eyes, shrouded this time and brooding. But just this one window was unshrouded, probably forgotten by a dusting housemaid, and when I had adjusted my sun-blinded vision I saw into the old drawing room where Mrs Logan had used to sit and Effie had stumped around with the tea and buns. The walls were now painted dark green and there was a gilt-framed portrait on the opposite wall. At first I thought Barbara must have acquired aristocratic ancestors, but then I saw whose portrait it was. Daniel, at my side, looked in too.

'Is it your mother's picture?' he asked.

'Why, no! Barbara wouldn't have any portraits of Mama. Besides there weren't any. No, it's Lavinia Logan – they must have had her sit for it quite recently.' The face with its aquiline rather haughty features looked at me and I stared at it. Lavinia was wearing a green velvet dress and looked every inch a duchess. Barbara must have a great deal of money to be able to afford to spend it like this. No one had mentioned a portrait to me.

'She is a very beautiful woman,' said Daniel, 'if she is like her portrait – but she looks a bit stoney, doesn't she?'

The room was high-ceilinged and spacious. A marble fire-place now stood against the wall on our left and on it were placed an ormolu clock and a tall vase containing dried honesty, pale and unsummery. There was a long, low table too against another wall, I remember, and a thick Persian rug in front of it; another rug in front of the fireplace with a tapestry screen standing on it. I saw a side table bearing greenish glassware, a corner cupboard with crockery, and three stiff stand-up chairs. On the opposite side from the fireplace there was a large oval gilt mirror – or perhaps it was framed in real gold, I would have put nothing past Barbara – and the portrait of Lavinia was reflected in it. What opulence – I could not believe it was the room where we had once drunk tea.

'She's short-sighted,' I replied and felt a twinge of disloyalty to my old passion.

'She's not married, is she?' enquired Daniel.

'Oh no. Barbara has taken her over lock, stock and barrel,' I replied. 'I don't think Lavinia is the marrying kind.'

I looked again at the room with its dark green walls and then once more at the dark green velvet of the dress. Barbara had spared no expense ... Seeing it made me say almost automatically: 'I love you, Daniel.'

'I know,' he whispered, and turned again to me. 'But not too much,' he said.

'There is a piano I expect – Barbara will have installed a piano I'm sure. I wish we could get into the house and you could play it,' I went on. 'I loved *her* once,' I said suddenly. 'But not enough. I will love *you* enough.'

'What does the word matter. If it were music there would not be a word – only a feeling.'

'Then like music,' I said and leaned against the window-sill to look at him.

'Women always want the word, in the end,' he said.

'You are too honest. Have *you* ever loved anyone, apart from Schubert?'

'Oh yes, I think so.'

'And was it a possible love – was it returned?'

'No.'

'How could anyone not love you!' I cried. I thought, It is true. I can't make him love me in the way I love him. Whatever he says – I know I love him more.

'I just have more experience,' he said.

'I wish I were a man,' I answered after a pause.

'Then I could not love you,' he said with a half smile. And I thought, in our most vital hopes we are powerless to intervene on our own behalf – if I resisted him and flirted with him he would end up pursuing me – but why should I do that? 'It's not in your nature to resist your feelings,' he said, stroking my hand and almost echoing my own thoughts.

'Let me show you the rest of the house, and the fountain – I expect it is restored – in the sunken garden, and the old stables . . .'

'You are in love with this house too, Meta,' he said and took my arm and we walked back to the other side of the gardens. The sun was now high in the sky and I was happy again. I never wanted to leave him, or for him to go away from me. We had to discuss how we should meet in London for I was still determined, even after all he had said, to be with him there.

'When I arrive at Aunt Sophia's I shall write to your London address to say where I can meet you after my week at Westminster Square is come to an end,' I suggested. 'And then they will probably send me to the station with a footman, for I believe they are very grand. But I can get rid of him, I'm sure, and meet you at the terminus. Then I shall have a few days before Aunt Juby expects my return and no one will be any the wiser.'

'What a schemer you are, Meta. What if you are expected to let your London aunt know of your safe arrival home?'

'Oh I think we could manage something,' I replied. 'I can't see this Aunt Sophia worrying too much about me once she knows I don't want to look after her grandchildren.'

He was silent for quite a long time as we walked down to the lake again. Then he said: 'I want you to be in London with me, Meta – you know that. I've done my best to dissuade you. I feel I have learnt more about you this morning than during all those days in Harrogate.'

'Yes.'

Then we were silent again and stopped worrying about the world and the future and made ourselves a little nest in the long grass where Barbara's mowers had not reached and lay there entwined all afternoon. And no one came to interrupt us. He did not take my virginity away from me then at Rooks Nest, but the way he embraced and caressed me told me that he was the perfect

205

physical accompaniment to myself and I had no doubts, no fear, only a strong desire to become his at whatever cost. I think he knew it too for he drew back from me once as though he were half afraid of me and he said : 'I am your first man, Meta!' Only when the sun's rays were a little slanting and the late afternoon came upon us did we part.

'Why must we ever part ?' was what I wanted him to say, but he did not say it though he held me close.

We had walked back to the old road. Nobody seemed to have seen us ; no one saw us come over the old wall. I had a last look at the lake before jumping down into Daniel's arms. The day was still warm and golden but I would soon be expected back for a meal, and I hadn't visited any of the people I said I would.

'Do you want to come back with me ?' I said.

'No, Meta. They would start to treat me as a suitor, and they would not be pleased – and neither would you.'

'I don't want you to go,' I said and to my horror and surprise I found I was in tears. 'I'm sorry,' I wept. 'I just can't bear to think of being apart – promise you'll write to me.'

'You can be sure I shall be thinking of you,' he said. 'Let me follow you home and then I can sing you a serenade.'

I tried to smile. 'No – you must return to Leeds.'

'I'll write from London,' he said. 'I'm hoping the agent will have something for me there even if it's only the Music Hall.'

'Whatever happens, Daniel,' I said – I felt he was going away to the Americas rather than just to London, 'I shall write from the address I gave you. And if I don't, you must think of something and come to rescue me in case Aunt Sophia is a religious maniac who wants me to be a nun.'

He laughed at this and I laughed too and was happy again. We risked walking back up the Coach Road together. I did not care if I was seen in the company of such a handsome man for it looked as though we had just been for an ordinary walk. But when he had to leave me at the Turnpike Road which went down through the village of Lightholme to the station, my heart was heavy. Only the thought of the planning I had to do to get away to London sooner or later kept me from weeping at his absence. Absence in my case certainly made the heart grow fonder. I hoped it did with Daniel too, though I knew that men were not accounted so sentimental as women and I could not believe that anyone could miss me the way I should miss Daniel Reiss.

Hartsedge seemed homely in a pleasant way after my glimpse into one of Barbara's refurnished and redecorated rooms. I loved Hartsedge and it was not without an inner pang of guilt that I contemplated being disloyal to it and all it stood for, because of my determination to see Daniel in London. I sat in my aunt's comfortable parlour and wrote once again to Aunt Sophia. The parlour had even been changed a little as Aunt could afford it as time went on and the boarders had paid their fees. There were books and a new-fashioned scrap-book scattered on the round table, and Aunt's work-basket and a red vase of blue delphiniums stood on another table. The fire was not lit but there was a low easy-chair before it and I sat there and thought of Daniel, then moved to the davenport in front of the window, reading or pretending to. I would not be able to fix on anything until I heard back from my London aunt. And yet the dear remembered objects in the Hartsedge sitting room seemed to want to pull me back into safety and childhood. I resisted them; I felt I had to express my love for Daniel. It was not the kind of love that could be expressed in a comfortable provincial sitting room with its trays and China vases and its window embrasure looking out over the garden of infancy. It needed, I thought, a grander or a more lowly surround – Rooks Nest, with its curtains of yellow velvet – or an anonymous rooming house in some lost and strange district of London. If I could not be the châtelaine of Rooks Nest and conduct my life in a grand and romantic way, well then I would take my chance on what was exotic or alien. I had told Aunt Sophia I could be away only a week in case my old employers needed me in the north. To Aunt Juby I said I would probably stay a fortnight. I dared only hope that these two ladies did not compare notes. I did not think they would – I gathered no love had been lost between them long ago when they met at my mama's funeral. If only I could tell Aunt Juby that I was not attracted by Aunt Sophia's wealth but needed only to contrive to visit London. I should have been as happy anywhere just to be alone with Daniel. But let Aunt Juby blame me a little for something I was not guilty of. Let her feel I was eager to see my newly found relation. If she knew the truth she would blame me so much more. I was making myself misunderstood on purpose because I *did* feel guilty. Thank goodness Cousin Rainer was not in the north – he would have found me out, I was sure.

That night, after I had seen Daniel at Rooks Nest, I could not sleep. The actual sound of his voice was ringing in my ears when I lay down in my bed. It was strange; there were even strings of words as though my head had registered their echo when he was close to me . . . It was the first time that I had had aural hallucinations. But they had gone in the morning.

The next day and the next, my letters being posted, I could do nothing but wonder where Daniel was. Would I receive a letter from him? I had already received one from Fanny at the seaside. As I sat in the garden, occasionally popping into the kitchen to chat with Martha, I felt restless and wished only to be off.

'Your clothes will not be grand enough for London,' sighed Aunt Juby.

'Sophia only wants to see me as a prospective governess,' I replied.

'Promise me, dear, if you are not happy there – come home . . .'

'It is only for a fortnight,' I replied. 'And she will be in mourning – there will be nowhere grand to visit. If it is unpleasant I shall return here,' I added, thinking that if for some unaccountable reason Daniel were not able to see me, this might be necessary. But I hated deceiving that good woman. Why could I not be free to go where I wanted, with whoever I wanted? I had saved some money. Surely I was not asking much? But I knew I was asking for far, far more than any young woman would be allowed unless she were a lost soul – or perhaps a rich widow. And even what I *was* allowed was a great deal for a respectable girl. Yet I had a sudden realization that life was for the living, that life *was* only the living of it – there was nothing else. I had known it before of course, but it had not struck me so forcibly. *My* life was all I had; life was there only for each individual person. There was no living whole – apart from the turning earth, the sea and sky. Only separate people; separate bodies and minds. We were all like little silver balls on a bagatelle board, I thought, moving alone, sometimes passing each other or bumping into each other. There was perhaps no meaning laid up in heaven. I must march forward and make my own meaning, and love Daniel.

There was no need to be miserable because I knew I loved him *more* than he did me. After all, he *did* love me. With this realization, in the midst of all my longing for him, not knowing what the future might bring, I had made the conscious decision to become his lover, if he wanted me. I cannot pretend that this did not frighten me a little and that I was not disturbed by, and guilty over, the risks I would take and the obloquy which would descend on me if others found me out. I *was* aware and I *did* know the consequences but I resolved to put all that out of my head and to go forward in love to him. I should take a chance, or have nothing. I expect my mama had felt the same about my papa once. And he *had* married her! But what had happened to Mama later was not ordained. *I* was not delicate. *I* was not going to marry in any case, was I?

How I loved Daniel's hands and face and voice and his music. The rest of existence was dross – or life to be endured rather than lived: that is what I felt then. It was not a sudden impulse but the perfect form of the crystal that had formed in me without my willing. I wanted him to need me. I wanted to be a slave to my feelings – just for a little time before I rejoined humanity and did as I was bid. Why should it matter that he was too circumspect to visit me at Hartsedge Hall? Except that *I* would have braved lions to reach *him*! He was being careful for my sake and because he could not pretend that he was going to woo me to the altar. If only morals were different and we could enjoy our love. A happy love, not a doomed one.

I looked out over the gentle swell of our summer lawn and the thought came again that perhaps I no longer cared whether he would ever love me as I imagined I loved him. I would be like a man and move forward to claim experience. The worst that could happen would be that in the end he would reject me. And unless there was someone else he preferred, why should he not take what I wished to give? A little worm murmured even in the midst of my thoughts: Do not be greedy, Meta – receive rather than give, for that is woman's destiny. I told the thought sternly to vanish as I heard Aunt playing the piano in the parlour. She had ascertained my new tastes and was playing Schubert to please me. The music brought all of Daniel back to me and I turned my back on words, my enemies and my friends, and resolved to do what my heart asked, nay commanded.

★   ★   ★

I was there. I was in London. The crowds surged around me at the station; the engines hissed, the noise of porters and escaping steam and the shouts of boot-blacks and sellers of newspapers and servants dinned in my ears. I had my leather bag and Daniel's letter, which had arrived only on the morning of my departure, and already Yorkshire was in the past, vanished in a cloud of steam and vapour, two million miles away in my heart if only two hundred in reality. All had been arranged. My aunt was expecting me within the next hour after my long journey; Daniel was to meet me in a week at this very station and might even write to me again at Westminster Square. It was now evening. I had left Yorkshire in the early morning, having risen at sunrise with the pink and blue of dawn. How could it be the same day? My Aunt Sophia's footman would be there to meet me once I had pushed my way through to the front of the station. The crowd was so vast that no one remarked a young woman alone except for the occasional middle-aged and respectable-looking men whose eyes seemed to linger on my face. I took no notice of them but made my way to the place where Aunt Sophia's carriage would be waiting for me, wishing that I need not go at all and that I might seek out Daniel immediately in his lodgings which were somewhere in the north of the city. But I must fulfil my part of the bargain. And anyway I was curious to see how my aunt lived. After all she was my mother's sister. Would she look like the miniature of Mama?

How dirty and noisy everything was. After a few false turnings I found myself on the station concourse and held up my green umbrella which I had described in my letter to Aunt Sophia. This was the signal for the footman to come forward and take me to the carriage. I stood there on the pavement as carriages and carts passed in endless ranks and then saw a little further away a smart brougham with a man sitting atop. He pointed with his whip in my direction and waved an umbrella at me. I waved mine back – it was quite ridiculous. Surely I could have taken a cab myself! A lugubrious-looking man in livery approached and said: 'Miss Meta Moore? At your service.'

At number 27 Westminster Square, my first impression was of a long dark and gloomy hall. Great shrouded stairs raised themselves above me and I wondered if I had come to either a museum or a morgue. There was a sooty smell – or perhaps one of cats – and it was so dark that it was hard to believe I had just left a summer evening outside. Nothing less like my arrival at Montpelier Crescent in Harrogate could be imagined and I felt quite homesick for my second home with Fanny and the Angersteins, rather than for the Hall. A wiry-looking maid came out of a door to greet me. 'Madam will see you after you have dined,' she announced, and another younger maid came behind her to take my case. I held on to my umbrella and followed them all up some back stairs and to a sitting-room and bedroom, the former plastered in brown and containing a dusty chandelier and a large sofa. The bedroom had a window looking out on the back of the square and I leaned out to ascertain where I was. Fresh air could not enter the room for the windows seemed to be sealed. Oh dear, I should never stand a week of this. But after I had unpacked and reread Daniel's letter and washed my hands and face and followed the older maid to a small salon next to my sitting room where I was offered a tolerable meal of fish and a glass of wine – which surprised me – I felt better.

'Madam will see you now' announced the maid at the end of this repast to which I had done full justice, for I was hungry. I followed her downstairs, upstairs, down a long corridor and came out into a better-lit area and a landing with many large doors leading off it. I must have been heretofore in the housekeeper's quarters, I thought.

A small, gaunt woman in her late forties was sitting on a long Chesterfield in the middle of the room as we entered, while in another chair sat a middle-aged clerical gentleman. I curtseyed. 'This is my niece,' the woman said by way of explanation to the gentleman. He inclined his head but did not rise. I bowed to him and stood there awaiting orders. 'Come in, Margaret,' said the lady. She had a rather hollow voice. 'You must excuse me. I suffer from rheumatism so cannot get up – come here and let us have a look at you.' I advanced somewhat awkwardly. Then I thought, She is Mama's sister after all. Should I kiss her? I thought better of it. She was not ugly or unpleasant, but so very gloomy with rather greasy hair and dark strained eyes. She motioned me to sit and I lowered myself rather abruptly into a vast armchair. The woman, Aunt Sophia, continued to look at me very openly, sighing as she did so. Then she pronounced: 'You are not very like our side of the family.'

'No,' I replied. 'I have been told I look very like Papa. Mama looks so pretty in the miniature I have of her.' She did not reply to this – Papa had obviously not been forgiven. She had a curious habit of turning her eyes heavenwards, and I wondered whether it was the influence of the Reverend Gentleman. I decided to be polite. 'It is most kind of you to invite me to London,' I began.

'I thought you should see us first, my dear, before you decided about the post,' she replied.

'Oh, I see,' I said in a panic. I had better put the matter right straight away. 'I'm afraid I already have a post, Aunt Sophia, as I explained in my letter.'

'That will not last for ever, Margaret.'

'I am contracted to stay with the Angersteins for another year – and, of course, Aunt Juby has probably told you I am to help her with *her* school eventually.'

'Ah, Mrs Jewesbury, yes – well we can discuss that later. Cyril and Eric are with their nurse. You may see them tomorrow.' I made a few perfunctory enquiries about Cyril and Eric and then Sophia began to talk to the clerical gentleman, whose name was Mr Wortlesham, of stock-market shares and early services, ignoring my presence. 'You will be tired,' she said to me quite kindly after some time had elapsed, and rang a bell for the maid.

As I made my escape from that room, I glimpsed beyond one or two half-open doors and saw vast ceilings and shrouded chandeliers, heavy furniture and tables with silver épergnes. The room I had just left had been nondescript. It occurred to me then that the main rooms were not used. The whole atmosphere of the house was strange. Servants glided up and disappeared and no one spoke except to show me to my room. I thought my aunt must be a little mad. Clearly she saw nothing but great generosity on her part in inviting me to become a part of her household. I wondered whether she might even expect me to undertake governess duties immediately with Eric and Cyril. At least that might be better than enduring her conversation for a week. I was uncomfortable, not only at the sight of such obvious wealth, for I knew my late uncle had been a banker, but at the feeling of deadness in the house.

In the morning I felt better. I was not expected to see Sophia till lunch-time and after breakfast I was taken on a conducted tour of the house by a silent relative of the wiry maid. Every room we entered was darkened by drawn curtains but I espied silver, pictures, rugs, carpets, lamps, bibelots, filling each of the rooms in bulky profusion. The silent one said she was Perkins and suddenly added: 'Madam's son-in-law is to inherit,' in case I thought otherwise. It was surely rather a large house for a lady and her two grandchildren. Clearly I had been presented as an object of Madam's charity. I thought of Barbara and how she would revel in a house like this. Did my aunt ever go out, ever entertain? I was taken to luncheon with her in a small dining room which was perhaps a little less gloomy than the rest of the house. Sophia was, I realized, a very self-absorbed woman and really did not notice very much. Her conversation was of the Church and of her dear dead husband. I found that if I gave the appearance of listening and occasionally muttered 'How interesting' or 'How dreadful' or 'I see', she was quite satisfied. We said a prayer at the beginning of the luncheon – the Rev. Wortlesham must surely live in the house – and a prayer at the end, and I was much exercised in attempting to discuss the varieties of religion in Yorkshire. When they heard I worked for a Jewish family, silence fell.

Surely Mama was never like this? I resolved to ask if there were perhaps any daguerrotypes or cabinet photographs which I had never seen of her. Had she lived, she would have been in her mid forties now. But my mama was clearly not approved of even now, though she had been dead these twenty years. In truth I was sorry for my Aunt Sophia. She seemed to take pleasure only in the Church. I wondered whether the late banker had been a religious man and resolved to ask.

But first I was presented with Eric and Cyril. I hoped they had not been told I was to be their governess – they would be upset if I went away. They were in the 'schoolroom', attended by two servants, a Scottish woman of middle age and a young frightened-looking Indian girl who must have accompanied them home from India. They were very little boys, almost babies, and one had not yet been breeched. The elder, Cyril, plucked at my skirts. 'Are you going to take us away, Miss?'

'I am your grandmama's niece,' I replied. 'I live in Yorkshire and look after children older than you. One day if you like you can visit me – but only if you wish.'

'Will Salima come too?'

'Salima would be very welcome,' I replied. 'But before that, I expect you will go to school.'

The Scottish woman had left the room and the Indian girl spoke at last in a soft, hesitant voice. 'I am to return home, madam. I do not know poor little Eric what he will do, his papa wants him to stay with Mrs Thomson.'

'Was that Mrs Thomson?' I enquired. 'The Scots lady?'

'Yes. She was found for Cyril and Eric by their grandmama.' She took the younger boy on her lap and caressed him.

'They should let you stay,' I said. 'They know you from home.'

'Ah, alas, alas, I am to go,' said poor Salima. 'And my little Eric what will he do?'

'*I* shall look after him,' said Cyril.

'Cannot we go into the park?' I said.

'Mrs Thomson, she does not like the park.'

The thought of these children mouldering away in this great gloomy house was terrible. 'I will ask my aunt. They need fresh air,' I said.

'She will be angry – Mrs Thomson.'

'Perhaps I could say she needs a rest?' I went on, resolving to accompany the children outdoors. It was stifling enough for me, so how much more so for children used to sun and light, snatched away from their mama. Truly, life was very sad. But perhaps Mrs Thomson would be a sort of Martha for them?

I betook myself then to my room and wrote to my Aunt Juby and to Martha and to Fanny, for I had a lot to say. Then I wrote to Daniel at the address he had given me, wondering how I was to get through the days until I could see him again. I had been at my Aunt Sophia's only two days and it seemed thirty. I felt I would never get away, but I had made a bargain with myself that I would go through with it, in order to 'earn' time with Daniel. In the middle of the night I woke and thought, what if Daniel cried off at the last moment or was simply not there when I arrived at the station? Thoughts of him were incongruous in the surroundings I found myself in and if my aunt had had any real interest in me, apart from possibly paying her own debt of conscience to my mother, I doubt that I would have got away with it, for I must have appeared preoccupied to say the least. And yet, being young and confronted with this new experience of how the very rich lived, I observed a good deal about my aunt's household. I could not make her out. Except for her religiosity she was an enigma to me. Surely Mama could not possibly have had anything in common with her? Papa had not been rich, but

I was sure he would never have wanted to live in Westminster Square!

I found out a little more the next afternoon when I was summoned to the Presence. For once the Reverend Gentleman was not there and Aunt was alone in her own sitting room, a room crammed to the ceiling with crosses and bibelots and stools and tapestries which to my ignorant eyes all seemed very ugly. She motioned me to sit by her on a stiff, upright chair. 'I hear that you believe the boys need more fresh air,' she said without more ado. Salima must have dared to approach Mrs Thomson, reporting my opinion. I had not yet spoken of it to my aunt for if I showed particular interest in the children she might once again offer me permanent employment with her. I was uncomfortable but I thought I should say something on behalf of Cyril and Eric. After all I did have experience now of small children, and I knew it could hardly be good for them to pine away indoors in summer. I thought of my own happy childhood in Hartsedge and I said: 'I believe they are very fond of their Indian nurse, ma'am. I am sure she would take them for a little walk in the park.' I stared at a large silver épergne as I spoke. It was draped in black feathers and I thought it hideous.

'If *you* came to look after your little great-nephews,' said my aunt, holding a black handkerchief to her mouth, '*you* could give them this fresh air.'

'I am very sorry, ma'am, but as I told you I am already employed in Harrogate and my employers expect me back soon. Your grandchildren are pleasant little boys and I am sorry for them, but I am trained as a governess not a nursery-maid!'

'You would not have to be a nursery-maid I am sure,' said Aunt Sophia, looking at me rather narrowly. 'There is more opportunity here for you to make a good marriage. We ought to speak of these things, since it was your own mother's folly which landed you in this inferior position. There would be no question of your remaining a governess, though you might be useful as an educational guide to the children later and you could accompany me in your own rank as my niece.'

I saw with horror that she was envisaging a sort of post of companion to herself. 'You are very kind, ma'am,' I managed to get out. 'But I like my present post and shall inherit Aunt Augusta's school one day.' I did not quite like to put it so bluntly but it seemed the least brutal way. 'And besides,' I added, 'I am a provincial person. I have not had the opportunity to live a – a *smart* life in London and doubt that it would agree with me...'

'Come now, Margaret, I am willing to wait. My own daughter will be away for years and I am advised that with a little care one might make a lady of you – we will speak frankly as no one is listening. There is no reason why you should suffer from your mother's follies...'

I thought she was being very rude and I wanted to defend Aunt Juby and Papa but I was visited by the sudden irrational fear that I might never escape this great house with its rugs and lamps and silver and pictures and I wanted to fly out of the window. My aunt was so single-minded that I do not believe she had the slightest interest in the sort of person I really was, but I could imagine that she had felt the same about Mama too. I was just an object of her charity who might also prove useful. 'Indeed, Aunt Sophia,' I said, looking at her as she sat in her large ebony chair, the afternoon light, such as it was, hardly entering the dark panelled room and her face, slightly petulant, slightly aloof, framed in her black bonnet, 'I am very grateful indeed to see you and your fine house and your dear little grandchildren, but truly I believe I am called to another task and it would be wrong of me to allow you to entertain false hopes of me. I believe Mama and Papa would have been – indeed I *know* Papa *was* – very grateful that Aunt Juby adopted me. My place is with her,' I went on, feeling uncomfortable even as I said it, knowing that Aunt Juby no longer had first call on my love.

'We don't mention your papa in this house,' she said majestically. At this I was really angry but controlled myself. I thought she was really very rude. 'I shall pray that you will change your mind,' she said finally, indicating that the interview was over by turning her head away and gesturing me to rise. But I was not going to let her get away with insulting my dear papa whatever his deficiencies had been and so I said softly: 'Aunt, tell me about Mama – I mean not about Papa, but before – what was she like? I never knew her and you did. You must have understood her once.'

'Understood her? No, that I never did – your mama was always flighty, Margaret, she had no conception of duty. Why even as a child...' She seemed for a moment to become more animated, but she checked herself. I suddenly knew that she had been jealous of Mama! Perhaps that was why she had said on

216

first seeing me that I did not resemble her. Suddenly I felt sorry for this strange aunt and I put out my hand.

'I am sorry, Aunt. Truly I am sorry. You have been most kind and I know you mean well. I should not have come to raise your hopes. Indeed I think that Eric and Cyril would benefit from a young governess and I am sure that Aunt Juby could find you one.'

She did not take my hand but turned away again and said: 'I shall pray for your poor mama, God rest her soul. For your papa I doubt my prayers would avail. I see you have something in common with Mary – your Mama, for she was very stubborn ... I might have taken you visiting, but perhaps better not unless you change your mind.' I did not say that she could have done something for me long ago if she had had the will – and I was extremely glad she had not. 'Jenkins will take you to the station on Saturday,' she said. 'I may not see you again, but I do ask you to write to me when you have had occasion to think over my offer and pray over it.' She bowed her head and I had the presence of mind to mutter something about taking some time to reply, before I went out.

I spent the rest of my week in that dark house in the vast nursery playing with the little boys, and in the library where I found books I thought must have belonged to her husband, my deceased uncle. Perhaps she thought that more time spent with the boys would win me round; at any rate she made no attempt to forbid me the nursery. I wrote a letter to Rainer. I felt I had better communicate with someone, for I was very angry about the position I was in. Then I realized that I had better not post it or he would think I was about to return home. It was a mercy I had lied to everybody about the length of my stay in Westminster Square for I would have wanted to leave after a week in any case. I had gone through with it only to see Daniel and he seemed as far away as some remote mountain god; I had heard nothing from him. Saturday would be my day of release and if he was not there at the station I should just have to go home to Hartsedge. But why should he not be there?

I wrote to Aunt Juby, instead of Rainer, saying I might be away a few days with Aunt Sophia but should in any case return north at the end of the following week. I went out myself to post it. I had hardly put my nose out of the door since my arrival and sniffed the air with pleasure, even that dusty London air. I didn't think anyone would miss me so I walked round the square, which had an empty shut-in look as though everyone was out of town – which they probably were. There were no ugly noisy streets, no vicious dirty people here. It was a sealed-off mausoleum for the likes of rich people such as Sophia. At one end of the long high terrace which led into the square was a tall dusty-looking church, probably the abode of Aunt's Reverend friend. I wondered where in this great metropolis Daniel was and whether he would ever play his music at some salon in a house like the one I was staying in. Where was the real London? I had but a hazy idea of London and would have liked to walk in it all day. Perhaps sooner or later, after Saturday, I should. After Saturday, I thought, my fate would be sealed. I should become Daniel's 'mistress' and that would be that. If only I could become a young man just for a day or two and wander where I willed and be free to taste and enjoy and discard! Ladies did not walk, even to pillar boxes, and I returned to number 27 where the parlour-maid let me in with a frozen expression of disapproval on her face.

It was the early morning of Saturday. I had breakfasted, kissed Eric and Cyril goodbye and received a message that my aunt would not come down that morning but sent her good wishes for my return journey. Jenkins the footman had been detailed to take me in a cab to the new station at King's Cross and had deposited me on the platform to wait for the train to Leeds. He had wanted to wait with me but I had said with a smile that I should be perfectly safe and that I was to be met at the other end. He had been glad to go off on his own business and I stood with my box, which he had carried for me, looking round everywhere for Daniel. I could not leave my box and did not want a porter as I had no intention of getting into the train. I prayed only that Sophia would not take it upon herself to write to Aunt Juby to announce my departure. I did not think she would. She had not evinced much interest or liking for *her*. I moved myself and my box to the entrance to the Ladies' waiting room and stood outside it where I had told Daniel I would be. What if he did not come and I missed the only train? But of course he would come and I was not going home yet. I had a little money with me and could put up at a hotel. A few people looked at me curiously as I stood there. They were probably thinking I was a governess en route to a post, for well-brought-up ladies never travelled alone, even less now than in Mama's youth when there had been women who travelled alone all over Europe. But they had been the exceptions. Here I was, twenty years old, free and excited and anxious. What sort of figure would I cut if I began to panic as I stood alone at King's Cross station?

Then suddenly I heard a voice: 'Meta!' and turned – and there he was, smiling at me, looking a little nervous.

'Oh Daniel!' I wanted to embrace him immediately, I was *so* glad to see him, but he said quietly:

'I have a cab. Thank goodness I've found you. I was so worried when I got your letter – I thought you would never escape. Are you sure, Meta, that you *want* to miss this train?' I said nothing – only looked at him so he went on: 'I have news for you, too. I've been offered an appointment to play at houses in Chelsea and I *think* I've landed Würtemburg too!'

'I don't want the train,' I said. 'Oh Daniel, how wonderful – but shall I be in the way?' I turned and looked at him and a rush of love and desire enveloped me. This was a real person after the stiff cardboard people at Westminster Square. This was a real man and he was going to be my real lover and I never wanted to leave him. He put down the box and said:

'Oh, my dear, what am I to do with you?'

'You mean you don't want me to come with you,' I exclaimed, horror-struck.

'*Of course I do.*' He put an arm round my waist. 'I just meant . . . the sight of you here . . . it is such a responsibility, my darling. I have missed you – and I have been so busy . . .'

We walked to the cab-rank and he gave the address of a lodging-house he had found that morning in Bloomsbury, having left his old 'diggings' as it would have been awkward to explain the sudden arrival of a wife! The cab passed through the crowded, shabby, noisy streets which were, I thought, the real London I had missed. There were dirty children in the gutters of some of the streets we went through and some men leered at me through the cab window. Then we stopped at a rather faded apartment house off another square.

'They do theatricals,' he whispered. 'You will have to be my "wife" – no other way, only one room free.'

'I can help pay,' I said. 'I've saved some money.'

We dismounted, entered the house and found we were expected and no one seemed to think anything of it. I was free at last. Not a governess, not a child, not someone's niece, just a girl with the man she loved. But we had to sit down and talk a little as we both felt strange. I had come from another world and he had interrupted a busy schedule and we both had the feelings of these ten days of separation to overcome if we were to get back to what we had been to each other at Rooks Nest. How long a time ten days seems when you are twenty. It was as though I had made the tour of the world – and yet nothing was more daring or more unusual than that I should have turned up here with him.

I poured out my Westminster Square adventure and he listened and laughed. I had talked myself out before Daniel sent up for some glasses of porter and two chops. The room was quite large with an iron balcony and a curtain at one end behind which was a bed. I unpacked my ordinary dress and sat at the fireplace. The afternoon sun was coming through the blinds before we had got used to each other again. Something was growing and growing in me and I believe it was the same for him, for after we had talked there was a silence and he said: 'You seem different, Meta. I wish we could go away on a long journey together in Europe. Just be together to get to know each other – it has all been so strange – I can hardly believe it is you.'

'Yes, it is,' I said and threw my arms around him and he kissed me softly and then not softly and I responded with all the ardour of my young body. For so long I had loved him, imagined him, and longed for him, that I was in no way surprised by his own ardour for it matched my own. His caresses and kisses were all part of *him* – they revealed him to me, although I had always seemed to know what he would be like. Everything he did – and all I did too – felt right to me. Tenderness and passion were all one; as long as we were together in that embrace I seemed to be lifted above myself. I think he was a little surprised by my passion for I did not feel only gentle. I felt a sensation of power that compelled me to enact a mystery. I felt equal to him and yet that he was a part of me and I was a part of him. I wanted to annihilate any sensation of remoteness, to make it so that these moments would set a seal on time. He desired me and I desired him – oh how much! – but that was not all. He seemed at times both the man I loved and also a representative of the male sex and also not in complete charge of himself – which of course made me the more ardent. I believe I roused him to feelings which he was surprised to find in himself, for in his eyes I read, as well as delight and pleasure and ecstasy, an air almost of innocence. After those intimacies we could never be the same, I thought! The world covers up these stark needs because they are savage and strange, but they are good, they are natural – they are nothing to be afraid of and women have them as much as men.

We spent the rest of the afternoon and again in the evening drinking from the well of desire, quenching a thirst that seemed to grow with every draught we took to quench it. I thought it was love – but I knew that it was also lust and madness. Together we seemed to be imbibing a potion stronger than either of us, except that as night fell I felt the more tender as he lay with his head on my breast. I felt older and, in a strange way, wiser than he. I was proud when he said: 'Who taught you those arts, Meta?' and I could reply 'No one – it's only that I love you and you make me whole.' But he was not just Daniel or just a man, young and handsome and strong and beautiful. He was also a complicated artist and there were ranges where he trod where I could not follow. I did not mind about this so long as he came back to me after a time away with his own thoughts. I tried not to be greedy and eventually he turned back to me and smiled and the remote look went away and *he* was whole again in my arms. Only later when night had fallen and we went out together for something to eat – for we were hungry! – did he say, his arm round me and my head on his shoulder, and I must have looked the very picture of the submissive bride: 'You love me too much, Meta.'

Whenever I see a blue coverlet and a Chinese screen which has seen better days or a wash-stand with a cracked ewer painted with China roses, and whenever I hear that muffled clatter of wheels from a balcony overlooking a London street, or peel an orange in a certain afternoon light, I think of Daniel. When I hear the sound of pigeons in the eaves of a London garret sleepily susurrating or catch sight of chestnut trees waving outside a window, I feel that calm sense of security and happiness which comes from the knowledge that you have crossed the bridge – there is no more you can do. You are safe for a few days – which seem like eternity – in the arms of a loving man whom you know well enough to adore and with whom life seems to take on an almost mystical depth. You know you can say anything. You know you can surprise and yet be found delightful and that as far as you are concerned you have come home and need not think for some time of a future or of the gritty, grimy world beyond.

I knew that our time together would be short; I knew that nothing can last or stay the same for ever, but for a little time it did and I felt magically irradiated. He was happy, too, at first, I know. After the initial uncertainty and worry that I was doing something he could not be entirely responsible for, he gave himself up to pleasure and also took pleasure in me. I had no regrets. I was living with and in the sensation of eternity. When he was not with me, had gone to a rehearsal or to post a letter, I heard his voice and felt I was near him in spirit. I tried not to demand of him any declaration, tried not to put into words the feelings I had, for I wanted to give and give without introspection and without girlish avowals or importunities. 'You are too good *to* me,' he would say and 'You are too good *for* me.' And even when I knew I 'knew' him as well or better than any woman he had known – and he seemed to have known a goodly number, which made it somehow exciting for me – there was still something mysterious in him for me, something I would never possess. There was something involuntarily strong about him. Perhaps it was to do with his music. There was a piano in the lodging and he drew such melodies from its tinkling tones that the whole house would fall quiet. But often he would sit saying nothing for an hour or two and cover manuscript paper with squiggles – and then toss it away.

I could have lived for ever like this, or at least for several years, but I had only a week and I did not know what I was going to do when I had to return north. Daniel had now been invited to go abroad! What if I decided to go with him and to write to Aunt informing her of my decision to 'run away' for ever, from duty and home and respectability? 'I should have to marry you!' he said and I laughed.

'You don't want to marry anyone, my darling, do you?' I said a little wistfully, for I was not experienced enough to deny myself the hope that one day we might in fact marry, which would make everything miraculously right with the world.

He had said once that my presence would bless his days. I know that his blessed mine. Once or twice, unbidden, the thought of Lavinia Logan would come into my mind. Well, she had prepared me for love but not inoculated me against my finest feelings. It was passion I felt for Daniel Reiss, not adoration only. I lived aeons in that one week, learning more about myself than in all the years of my life to date – yet that childhood and girlhood had led to him. Sometimes even, through a trick of light I would catch a familiar expression or some fleeting presence in Daniel's eyes and not be able to remember whose it was. Then at night in some half dream I would see the portrait of the Jacobean lady that we had at the Hall, the one I had thought as a child to be Mama's portrait. And those eyes, too, reminded me of Lavinia. I turned to Daniel who was not a dream but a separate reality sleeping beside me and I would know once more that however much I loved him, I should never possess him – and ought not to wish to do so. And he desired me as much as I did him, I am sure. He did not want more of me though than he had. I knew this intuitively. He was able to place the exigencies of total absorption into his music and, not for the first time, I wished that I had something to which I could always return when Daniel was busy, something to which I could always be true but which did not interfere with my loving, indeed sent me back refreshed to it like drinking from a deep well. Instead I would sit and read whilst he scribbled.

I tried not to think of a time when we should not be together, and managed to live for three days in that timeless happiness which comes so rarely in life. It reminded me of when I had been a child and some days had been suspended in joy as though I was swinging on stars with no thought for the future. But of course I was no longer a child and Daniel was as aware as I of the fact that at the end of a week I should have to return home. His engagement abroad was still somewhat vague but he had a definite invitation to the concert platform in late August in Baden Würtemburg.

'You will see Benjie,' I said.

After three days my bliss began to be mixed increasingly with an intimation of future sorrow, for when I had to leave him. Hartsedge was only two hundred miles away and Westminster Square only two or three, but they were both in different worlds and I wanted none of them.

'Will you come back to Harrogate after Germany?' I asked him on the Wednesday of my week of happiness. We were sitting at a table in the window before the balcony and the sound of the German organ-grinder below was floating up to us. Daniel waited a moment before replying.

'I don't know yet – it will depend on my getting further engagements. You can see that Germany would be better for me than Mr Angerstein's tea-rooms.'

'Yes, of course,' I replied, thinking how desolate I should feel in Harrogate if he were not there. I seemed to have spent almost all my time when I *was* there thinking about him or planning to meet him. 'It won't make any difference,' I added. 'I shall go on loving you wherever you are.'

'You see, Liebling, I can't promise where I shall be or what I shall be doing. That's why I can't ask you to come with me – and anyway, I don't want to be arrested for corruption of a minor.' I laughed. It was so ridiculous. Yet I did wish – oh *how* I wished! – that I could go with him. That was really impossible unless he asked me to stay with him for ever, and both of us knew he would not do that. 'Do you think that if Benjie goes to live in Germany, Naomi will go with him?' I asked.

'Well if they marry, they will go together. Don't look so sad, Meta – you always said you weren't "respectable".'

'No, I'm not.'

'And anyway,' he persisted, 'you must make a life of your own apart from me.'

'But what can I do apart from governessing? Are women always caught by their feelings?'

'What do you mean? *You* will marry one day, Meta, I know you will. You are the sort of girl who does marry in the end. You will be an ornament to society.' He was teasing me and I took it in good part but it made me sad, for however much I felt myself set apart from the conventions of middle-class society, I knew I was not a strong genius of a woman like the lady who wrote in the *Westminster Review* and of whom Rainer had told me. She lived with a man whom she could not marry but she was accepted in her circle of London literary friends. I wished that I were gifted or rich or somehow able to make my own way – yet wanting to go with Daniel was the opposite of all this and I could not understand myself. I knew that I was not wicked but I knew that I wanted love to last even if it were without benefit of clergy. Daniel pulled me on to his knee. 'You are a good girl, Meta,' he said. 'You ought not to love a scapegrace like me.'

What was the good of wanting to be independent when I was

close to him and wanted nothing more than to go on being close? Perhaps I should have burned my boats there and then and bought a ticket to Ostend.

The next day was sunny and still and we went for a walk in the Regent's Park. Many others had had the same idea and there were crowds of working girls and boys too, larking about round the lake and being shooed away by the keepers. We walked on further where the crush of people was less and found ourselves in a part of the park which was still being built, near a great terrace of grand houses. I wished I belonged either to the grand houses or to the working girls. Was I really a *'femme devergondée'* – a shameless woman? Daniel must have guessed my thoughts for he was rather quiet and when we sat down on a little bench near a pond he said with peculiar constraint: 'Meta – if – if – there should be a result to our love-making, what will you do?'

I looked at him and tried to guess what he would want me to say. 'What would you have me do?' I asked finally.

'I don't know. Somehow I don't feel there will be, but if there were you could always come to me in Germany.'

'If I could come with a baby I could come in any case,' I said slowly. 'It wouldn't make any difference would it – if I were not married to you?'

'I was trying to be "honourable",' he replied with a sigh. 'I'm not ready to be a father – but all girls want babies, don't they? Isn't that what Mother Nature is doing with us?'

'No,' I cried, surprised at the vehemence of my feeling. 'One day I should like to have children and I should always love a child of yours – but I don't want one yet. I've only just begun to grow up, I'm not ready. It would be unfair.'

'Well don't worry about it,' he said as though dismissing it from his mind. But it had already weighed with me and I had taken that risk knowingly because I loved him and wanted him. What had that to do with adding to the human race? I suppressed thoughts of a little Daniel or a little Meta, but he saw I was upset.

A few people were walking at some distance on a path parallel to ours, a few couples dawdling along who had that air of married couples who are used to each other's ways and bored with them. Daniel began to eat an apple – I have never known anyone who was able to secrete apples and oranges on his person so successfully, and eat them in public so fiercely. I was looking vaguely at the promenading couples when suddenly, before my conscious mind registered them, my heart began to beat wildly and my legs felt weak. It was Lavinia and Barbara. Yes, I was sure: the one a slim figure twiddling a parasol and the other walking slightly in front with a purposeful air. I gasped and Daniel said: 'What is it? Have you a stomach ache?' His words were so incongruous that I gasped again.

'There – along the path – ' I pointed in their direction. They would pass us at about fifty yards' distance but need not see us.

'Who is it? Not your aunt?' He looked a little scared.

'No, no. It's Miss Logan – you know, you saw her portrait – and Barbara. I thought they were abroad.'

'Why not go up and say good morning?' he said, tossing his apple core into the grass unconcernedly.

'No – I don't want to see them unless I have to. Barbara would tell Aunt.'

'She looks elegant, the one with the parasol,' he said.

'Yes – she is – so elegant. And she's wearing brown for once.'

'*That* was the person you were fond of?' he asked.

'Oh yes. I wonder where they are staying.' As I spoke they drew a little nearer and the figure in front turned round and took the arm of the figure with the parasol. I knew that Barbara was as short-sighted as Lavinia but I was still worried. I did *not* want Barbara to see me. Somehow she had the faculty of turning wine to water and dousing a cold variety of the latter on my most precious thoughts and feelings. In a way I should have liked her to know that I too was no longer alone, but that was unworthy of me. I looked down at my boots as they reached the point nearest to us. Daniel continued to stare for he reported to me that the younger one looked a little proprietorial. 'And well she might,' I replied, 'seeing as how she has practically bought her, along with Rooks Nest.' I had not said a great deal to him about my early love, trusting that from hints I had dropped he had some idea of what she had meant to me. He had not taken much interest, as men do not in women unless they are interested in them for their own sake.

The sun had disappeared behind a cloud and thankfully I watched Lavinia and Barbara disappear into the distance.

'Are you sure it was your friends?' he asked.

'Yes. I wonder when they go north? Perhaps they are tasting the delights of London out of season.'

I thought I had escaped and my relief was great.

That evening Daniel had to play in some house in Chelsea where he had been introduced by his agent Mr Pinkelstein. 'I wish you could come,' he kept saying. 'I could play the Liszt for you.' But I knew he would play the Liszt for *everyone*, and that I did not mind. He would return to me at midnight and we would reassume our *vie intime* which was always something to look forward to. I never ceased to wonder at what I could arouse in him and I was proud of it. I could have a quiet evening reading the books I had bought on Oxford Street at Mr Bumpus's the day before when we had gone shopping. I still enjoyed my solitude and Daniel's return was always an object of pleasant anticipation.

But this time when he came back he was more talkative than usual. Usually he would flop down in the armchair in silence for five minutes and then shake his hair and flex his wrists and chase me into the bed. This time he said : 'I have an interesting piece of information.'

I thought he was going to say he had been offered work and I braced myself for the news that he would be off in a day or two to Europe, for I lived in dread that even our short week together would be cut short. But no. He continued to look mysterious and motioned me to come and sit on his knee. Then he said : 'I have seen your Fairy Princess again.'

'Who?' I thought at first he was talking about little Fanny Angerstein, I don't know why, and said : 'I thought they were in Scarborough.'

'No, Meta – your magic Rooks Nest lady!'

'You mean – Lavinia Logan?'

'The same, the one you showed me in the park this morning.' That morning seemed a long time ago. I had put Barbara and Lavinia firmly out of my mind. They did not belong to my 'London life', as I considered my snatched clandestine week with my beloved Daniel. 'They were at the concert in Chelsea – at Lady D's – I recognized them because they sat close together and I thought, this is a piece of news for Meta ! I suppose they must have connections with musical life ?'

'Not that I know of. Any connection Barbara has will be with money, though I suppose Miss Logan might know people who live in London and go to concerts.' I fell silent.

'I thought it would interest you,' he said.

'It does – it makes me sorry they could be there listening to you and I could not.'

'You could have come if you'd wanted – as a friend,' he said, turning to detach his velvet evening cravat and slacken his stiff white collar. 'I thought, this is Meta's Miss Logan, and so I had a good look – they don't know *me*. She is a very beautiful woman,' he went on.

'Oh she is,' I replied. 'I think when I was young and unfledged I saw Mama in her,' I mused, trying to make conversation.

'She looked rather bored,' he added.

'Thank goodness I was not there. They would tell my cousin Rainer who thinks I am safely tucked up in Westminster Square – if he thinks at all about me.' But I was sad, not because Daniel found Lavinia handsome but because I was living a life of subterfuge and it did not really suit me, even for a week. 'What about Barbara?' I asked. 'How was *she*?'

'Oh, she's a deep one I should think,' he replied, pulling off his shirt and undergarments all in one. Usually I retrieved them from the floor, but I made no move. I was thinking about the two of them and what they would make of me living a life of sin with the musician they had most likely politely applauded. Soon this bliss was to come to an end and who knew how many beautiful women Daniel would be captivating in foreign capitals, far from me? I could not restrain my tears and he was upset, I could see.

'Don't cry, little Meta – there, come and let me comfort you.' But some brush of a wing of I knew not what – fate? fear? anguish? – seemed to have touched me. It was all Barbara's fault. I could imagine what she would make of my flight to Daniel. Not that she was conventional or even backbiting but I was ashamed that the life I was leading could be the topic of malicious conversation.

'You do love me, darling, don't you?' I said through my tears. I was ashamed to cry but it was also a little delicious to have those warm capable arms around me.

'Of course I love you. I should never have agreed to – all this – if I didn't . . .'

'I wish I were older and sophisticated like Lavinia, and did not show all my feelings,' I whispered.

'They seem to have upset you. But I never spoke to them – and they didn't see you this morning, I'm sure.'

But somehow the bliss of our first few days was spoilt. I felt guilty, not about my love for Daniel or even about the unheard of step I had taken, but some old guilt – as though I would be recalled and punished for my happiness. I had wanted to forget all my old life in these few days but it seemed that one could never escape it and that in the midst of happiness there was a worm in the bud, though what sort of worm and how it would wriggle its way to me I had no idea. He soothed me and I fell asleep, but when I awoke, remembering that I had only one more day with my 'husband' before we must part, I still felt sad. But I wanted Daniel to be a success even if far from me and so I tried not to worry. I thought of them all waiting for me at home on my return from 'Aunt Sophia's' and prayed that lady had not written yet to my aunt. I had told Sophia Grosvenor that Aunt Juby would be away till the next week and we would not expect a letter from her before then. I had my letter of thanks all ready to post once I arrived in Yorkshire. I did not expect she would have concerned herself with my safe arrival.

'You'll be in Harrogate next month,' said Daniel over our breakfast which was brought up by a slatternly maid.

'And when will you come back? Truly, do you think you will stay long abroad?' I tried to be calm and rational but there was a tremor in my voice.

'I just can't tell. I'll write of course – but don't fret, little Meta. Just be a good girl and wait for me. Get them to play the Meta Waltz when you miss me.'

This made me feel worse. I had reckoned on remorse and anxiety before I decided to come away with Daniel, but I had not realized how much *more* I would miss him once I had known the delights of the flesh. It seemed all wrong that we should ever be parted. But I knew that he did not see matters quite in this light. He did love me but he was still able to concentrate on his work in a way I could not. I should leave him and go back to the Angersteins and *he* would be free to roam the whole of Europe. It was not just his genius, it was because he was a man – men couldn't 'fall', could they, nor need they worry over the consequences of their acts? I had reckoned too without my aching heart. I was trapped in love.

I said how bored I would be at home now I had tasted the delights of a different way of life.

'Your cousin will be back soon then?' asked Daniel.

'Oh, yes, I expect so. Though we never know where he is or when he is to return.'

'That will be some compensation – he will talk to you and then you will be happy to go back to Fanny and the family.' *He* seemed quite happy to have arranged my future happiness for me, and I could not resist, in my youthful anguish, asking him whether *he* would miss *me*. 'Of course I shall miss you. There is something quite special about you, Meta – and I know it will be my fault if you ever lose any of that bloom.' He touched my cheek. He looked at me seriously. 'I should not have let you come,' he said. 'A better man would have worried I should leave you sad.'

'Oh, don't talk of virtue,' I replied.

He got up and lit a cigar. 'The extraordinary thing is that, although we have had – that – ' gesturing to our unmade bed ' – it is not that I shall miss. No, it is your loving heart – and that makes me sad that I have let you love me.'

'Oh, Daniel, don't say such things.' We are only just beginning, I wanted to say, and you talk of finding something more important than desire. I knew that I would always desire him and it was an additional burden.

'I didn't mean to sound gloomy, or not to be grateful for what you have so unstintingly poured out on me, but I think that perhaps I underestimated – not your Zärtlichkeit – but your intensity. Do you know that you look different? And I am proud to have made you look different, but you must try not to love anyone too much, my Meta, for you will be unhappy.'

'Do you mean you would like me more worldly – more like Lavinia Logan?' I asked.

'No, I still want you just as you are. But you see I am not entirely dishonourable and it worries me that you should suffer for me.'

I knew then that whatever we were to each other in the future, he would never suffer for me the pangs I could and would suffer for him. He had told me he had loved other women, and that I was different, but he seemed to think I had changed a little during the week from the gay, sweet companion he had first thought me. I knew that I had not, that I had always been intense and romantic and that he had not quite realized the extent of my passion, so full had he been of his own feelings. I tried not to think about it all, but to enjoy our last day before my departure, and I think I succeeded for he preferred me talkative and lively and I made a pretty successful attempt to be what he wanted. But surely we could finally be happy together even without the bonds of matrimony – in spite of the difficulties which our society imposed on the meetings of the unmarried? I could follow him to Germany and he would not stop me, but I felt a common-sensical need to take stock – and even perhaps to let him go 'free' so that I might be a little missed. At the bottom of my heart I knew I still hoped for permanence and I was astonished at the force of my feelings.

Yet I was, even so, wary of showing all I felt; the week spent together had revealed not only Daniel to me but a new aspect of myself and I was not sure I liked all that I saw. When I was alone I was usually happy with myself. I had been in the habit of 'wanting something to happen'. Now that I had spent a momentous week 'on his arm and in his arms' so to speak, I began to feel a vague sense of dissatisfaction. The more I had, the more I wanted – I suppose that is a general human experience. It was the first time I had felt the power of the senses to bind. The romantic way I had regarded him changed subtly to a better-founded and sturdier feeling and our parting would be that much harder. I had stored up a good deal of unhappiness for myself in the very act of achieving happiness. What did he really feel for me? I went by his actions, which showed me a man always hungry for sensual bliss, but able to operate sudden withdrawals of the mind when I knew he was thinking, not of me, or of any woman, but of his music. Even as we sat at our mutual little table in that faded gilt-wallpapered room, even as we ate our chops or engaged in quiet moments of reading or mused at the window, there was one part of him which I could never reach. And I was cross with myself that I should wish to reach it, for I did not want to stop him working or thinking. I saw that a man like Daniel – perhaps any artist – must have long periods alone or uninterrupted by others. I wanted him to have that, I was not jealous of his work. I should have liked to have been able to myself 'withdraw', but as long as he was there I could not. Were all men like this? I did not know any other men so intimately, so could not guess. Daniel was not just a man; he was the man I loved – and a musician. 'I don't want to be your muse,' I said once on our last day together. 'It's a great honour to have a waltz written after me – but I feel useless and passive. You would have

written that music one day somehow.' He looked at me in astonishment. He did not really understand my tortuous reasoning. I
felt that I had to explain myself to him – and even explain himself
to himself; and that was unsatisfactory, for him as well as for
me. Yet all the time, I was thinking: Oh, how I shall miss him
when I am gone, wanting to be together with him always and
yet knowing we *must* have times apart and alone. I wanted to say
'I love you, I love you' constantly to him whereas he said it only
when we made love. I did not quite know how to receive that
love – it almost embarrassed me to see myself as an object, yet I
poured out my love on him. 'You are too generous,' he would
say and I would think 'How can lovers be too generous?' I felt
that even if we were married, I should still go on pouring this
tenderness and passion over him. Was he frightened he would
drown in my love? Did he not want me to love beyond all
bounds?

'Your heart leads you to act with the freedom of a man, Meta,'
he said. 'You ought to be sometimes stiff and cold to people or
you will be hurt.'

'But *you* don't hurt me,' I replied, not quite honestly, knowing that his withdrawals *had* sometimes hurt me, but that I
blamed myself for the feeling. I knew he desired me, found me
precious, for he told me so many times. I wondered though
whether he could ever, with anyone, be as utterly lost in love as I
could be. Sometimes unwillingly almost, I called Lavinia to
mind. What should I have done if my love for *her* had been requited even a little?

If I remained passive and smiled during his love-making he
seemed to like it better. When we went out together on our last
day I made a great effort to be amusing and succeeded in making
him laugh, for then all his attention was caught up in me. I found
it quite easy but at such times I would occasionally wish I could
fall silent and just look at him and think about him wordlessly.
Most people had weeks, months and years to get to know each
other – we had only a week and even that was snatched from the
jaws of impossibility. I cared only for my family, not for myself
as far as my 'reputation' was concerned. It was an unfair world. I
needed time to travel and have adventures and love and desire
people as young men did, but girls were not allowed even to
want this under pain of excommunication from polite society –
if, of course, they were discovered. When I was out with Daniel

in London, I had seen young women waiting to pick up men, and had wondered how they had started off in life. I remembered Peg Clough, a girl in Lightholme, who got pregnant and was abandoned by her young man and shunned by her family.

'If I came away with you,' I said, still turning over in my mind the possibility of an elopement that did not end in a marriage, 'should you still love me for ever I wonder – and should I be able to love you if we were constantly together?'

'Oh, you would always be the same, my darling,' he said and stopped my mouth with a kiss. 'But would you?' I thought, but did not say. It was a new experience for me not to say what was in my head.

Yet when the time came for us to part – for it seemed I could not abandon everything to go away with him: my aunt, the school, the Angersteins, even for a few months – how I yearned towards him and felt the rising tears and horror of parting, making all the world bleak, the world I had thought I could master alone. He looked a little frightened himself.

'It is only for a few months and then I shall surely be back in Harrogate,' he said, as we walked to the great railway station. He carried my bag and I held on to his other arm and again I wished I *had* the courage to stay with him for ever. That little spark of commonsense, though, had saved me from making the gesture. I knew he would miss me; I knew that what we had had was precious and that I would have died rather than miss it. 'I shall miss you – you don't know how much,' he whispered as we stood beside a pillar near the platform, with the world roaring around us and making me feel dizzy. If only he would say 'I want you for ever' and I would cancel my previous resolutions and go away with him and never part from him more . . . But he did not say it. 'Be brave, Meta,' he said. 'I should not have done it, you know – but I am glad I did.' I felt despair as it seemed that our feelings could be summed up as something which was now past. I wanted to go on whatever happened even if he tired of me – I wanted to go on and explore more, love him more.

'Promise to write from Baden, and from Mannheim – ' We had arranged all that the night before. I set such store on letters from him. He saw then that there were tears in my eyes.

'Meta, Meta, thank you. Never forget that you are the most wonderful girl in the world,' he murmured, stroking the velvet lapel of my jacket and holding my hand with his other long, lean, brown hand that seemed part of myself, not a limb that could break away from me and go hurtling across Germany. Parting was not 'sweet sorrow' at all – it was despair, anguish. I saw the railway lines marching into the distance before they turned a corner and disappeared. I wished we were alone and that the crowd would melt away and that Daniel could say his farewells to me from a tall horse and then ride away into the distance. I did not want to do the riding away, so passively, borne off by the growling, hissing engine that even now was being stoked for my return.

I thrust my tears away with a shake of my head. Neither did I wish to behave like a weak woman and yet what else was I?

'I must go,' I said. 'Or I shall never do so.'

It was only with a supreme force of will that I turned away from him. 'Don't wait to see the train leave,' I said. 'It will only make me cry – I shall take out my book and think about you.'

'Oh, my little Meta,' he said and kissed my cheek – 'I shall return. Be happy, as you have made me.' Yes, he did say those things and I turned them over and over in my heart as the gruff and beastly engine bore me with every puff of its dirty smoke further and further away from Daniel Reiss.

'Didn't they feed you up there?' Martha kept saying when I arrived home. It was true – I seemed to have lost weight.

Aunt Juby had been delayed for a day or two and there was, fortunately, no letter lying on her table from Sophia, to accuse me mutely of duplicity. So there was only Martha, and I had determined to give her a long and detailed description of Westminster Square as I sat in the kitchen while she shelled peas and bustled around. 'She were nothing like your mother,' Martha kept saying.

'I'm glad,' I replied. 'I was sorry for her, truth to tell – but wild horses wouldn't drag me to be governess to my aunt's grandsons.'

Martha listened carefully to all I had to say. 'You'll be glad to get back to Harrogate then?' she asked wistfully.

'It's not for two weeks,' I replied. 'I shall help you, Martha – I'm sure there's a lot I could do to be useful.' I felt instinctively that some occupation was necessary to enable me to cast off the shade of Daniel which lingered behind my eyes. If I worked hard for Martha then Aunt would be less likely to notice what I felt was a visible impress upon me of love. He would be crossing the Channel, then He would be in the train, then He would be in the Rhineland – I could not expect a letter for some days even if he wrote straight away.

'That Rainer's back they say,' said Martha. 'I'm surprised you didn't see him in London where he gads about.'

'Oh London is a big place, Martha,' I replied, thankful indeed that it was so. I had even looked about on the station in case there might be someone who knew me, and prayed now that he too had not been in the habit of taking walks in the Regent's Park. I could not tell Martha I had seen Barbara and Miss Logan, so contented myself with asking if anyone knew when they were to return.

'They say they're off again abroad, leastways that's what Bessy Taylor says – her down at the lodge – seeing as how they haven't done all the repairs yet. They were off to some foreign place – Italy was it? Eh, I don't know. You ought to go down and have a look while they're away.'

'I did go, don't you remember – for a walk, before I went to Aunt Sophia's. The gardens were looking lovely – but I think there were workmen there.'

'They say she's having the conservatory – them old glass-houses – done up to grow foreign fruits and all. More money than sense if you ask me,' grumbled Martha who still did not like Barbara and had tolerated Lavinia Logan only for my sake.

I found it quite easy to chat to Martha and was rather surprised that she did not see the guilt written all over my face. Going away with a young man she might understand – but for a lady to come back alone with nothing further planned, no wedding to make everyone forget about any irregularity . . . Well, some folks did that, but not many, and not real ladies – and certainly not her Meta. But I could not bear to worry her and had said nothing to her about my feelings for Daniel, even though she was constantly asking whether there was 'anyone serious-like, in Harrogate?'

The rhythm of the Hall and the old life enveloped me so that I was able, against my will almost, to measure up to it again and be little Meta and Miss Meta and prepare my work for Fanny's next term and write letters and await Aunt Juby's return with equanimity. I had posted the already written letter to Sophia and a return letter came for me before Augusta arrived home. That was good – Sophia did not date her letters so it looked as though I had just left. She begged me to think over her earlier proposition and sent 'affec. regards' from Cyril and Eric. Poor little boys. I hoped Salima had not left them to the tender mercies of the Scottish lady. I wrote them a letter as friendly as I could make it without giving them any impression that I was to undertake their charge, but hoping I might see them one day in the north. It seemed a long time since I had said goodbye to them. Everything in my life now was to be *ante* or *post* my week with Daniel.

Fortunately, I found that Daniel had been right and that I was not to expect a little Daniel. I had somehow known I would not and curiously enough had not worried about it. The wages of sin were not to be drawn on my account this time – at least not in this way. But I shuddered at what could have happened, knowing the risks I had taken.

Only at night could I give myself up to my feelings as I sat at my casement window breathing in the honeysuckled air and thinking of him far away. I went down sometimes to the old piano – my playing would not disturb Martha, who was getting deaf though she denied it. I played airs I had heard him play, as well as I could, but despaired at my stiff fingers and lack of talent.

In the summer the postman always left our mail on the sill and there I found one morning a letter for me in Daniel's almost unfamiliar spiky script. Aunt Juby had been further delayed and I found a letter from her too so was able to bring it to Martha and then disappear to my room with Daniel's note.

Tell me I have not 'ruined' you, sweet angel [he wrote]. Tell me you forgive me even if I have! I am writing in my new lodgings in Baden. I have an audition – violin this time – tomorrow. The company at the spa is all very grand and the gardens are gay with geraniums. Believe it or not, I have seen your Fairy Princess again! The two Englishwomen were eating their dinner last night at the hotel where I had met my sponsor. I recognized them but I do not know if they recognized me from London. Is it not a coincidence? All I need, though, apart from musical engagements is the presence of my little Meta. Heart's darling, I do miss you – but I am a busy old thing as you know. Tell me all you are doing and when you are to return to Harrogate. I thank you for that week of paradise and hope you are not unhappy. Do not worry about me, I have an infinite capacity to employ myself and enjoy it. I hope only that you are well and send you all my love.

Dein ergebener Daniel.

PS. Shall I speak to the ladies? It would be interesting if they mentioned you. I should not of course mention you had been in London, but might say you had attended the Winter Garden concerts in Harrogate.

I read this letter many times and kept it under my mattress where no one would look. But my feelings about Barbara and Lavinia being abroad in the same place as Daniel haunted me. They seemed somehow to muddy up the swift current of my love. I was envious of Barbara – that she could go to Europe and stay there – but that was not quite it. I did not want Daniel mixed up with what I thought was my old life – but that was not quite it either. I wanted Daniel for myself – that was more like it. But I wanted him to be happy and fêted too whatever he was. Why should I feel so miserable that he *was* happy – or seemed so – without me? Was I so possessive that I could not bear him to be living in his own orbit? I wrestled with my conscience, thinking about it all. Nothing could take away our week in London, I know – but when could we ever be together again like that? There we were, poor humans, with only one life – and yet everything conspired to separate lovers and give the beloved presence to those who could not possibly care as I did. Yet *I* had first fallen in love with Daniel, had I not? Would he ever have become aware of me if I had not cast the first glance? This tortured me. Must I, should I, remain passive, wait for my fate. Was it not allowed to women that they meet it half way? I confessed my impatience to myself as I sat at the open window. Why had I not been made like other girls who were content to wait for lovers or suitors. Yet he *did* love me, he *had* loved me. Was I torturing myself needlessly? I tried to read; tried to absorb what Shelley had to say on the subject. But Shelley was a man! I had no one to turn to, no one to whom I could talk. They would all think I was wrong-headed, if not evil. Yet I felt I was right, that my feelings were good, not to be shunned. The only thing that worried me in the worldly sphere was that somehow the Angersteins would get to know of my escapade through

Benjie, for I was not sure that Daniel would keep his counsel when he met his friend.

High above all these sharp stabs of unease and envy – which I recognized full well and accepted as the result of my unconventional conduct – there remained the bright beacon of Daniel. Daniel as I had seen him with so many expressions, in so many moods – his hands, his voice, his appearance of almost involuntary determination.

Aunt Juby returned the next day and I made an effort to talk to her about Westminster Square, and my distaste for Aunt Sophia's way of life. I think she was secretly pleased that I was so little seduced by wealth and worldliness.

'But it is dull for you here, Meta. When shall you return to Harrogate?'

'I am quite happy here, Aunt,' I replied.

'Oh, I do not want you to go away, darling,' she said in unaccustomedly soft tones which made me feel remorseful at my duplicity.

'They are expected back in the first week of September. I await a letter,' I replied.

'Your cousin Rainer has not yet returned then?' she asked as we sat down at the table to the meal I had prepared for her return, sending Martha off for the day, as I thought she had been overworked whilst we had all been away.

'When is the school opening, Aunt?' I asked. Somehow I did not want to discuss Rainer. He of all people would be able to penetrate my façade and I was sure he would guess that I was a changed person.

'We start next week.'

'Then I can do a lot for you before I go.'

'Rainer said he would call round on his return – he has not been?'

'No. I have seen nothing of him all summer. I expect he was enjoying himself in London. Martha said he was back but he hasn't called.'

'He must have gone on to his mama in Derbyshire. He is very devoted to Ada although she is not the easiest of mothers.'

It was pleasant just talking to Aunt and having nothing more momentous to consider than the arrival of the new sheets for the boarders and the tidying of the schoolroom. Only once did Aunt Juby say anything of more consequence as we folded sheets and listed items for the Halifax grocer to bring round in his cart. 'I hope one day to be able to leave you a flourishing school, my dear. By next year I think I shall be able to say we are established. Unless of course you marry before then!'

'Oh Aunt, I am sure I shall not marry,' I managed to get out, in spite of sudden palpitations of the heart and a dry throat. I don't think she noticed my discomfort for she said:

'Time enough – and you could always sell the school one day.'

'When would you like to retire, Aunt Juby?' I enquired, more for the lack of something to say. I was surprised that she hesitated a moment.

'Caroline wants me to go and live with her in her little house in Manchester, but of course it would not be possible.'

'You would like to leave Hartsedge?' I was aghast. I could not imagine Hartsedge without Aunt and my home here.

'I'm not getting any younger,' she said peaceably. 'And it depends of course on the railways.'

I could not think at first what she meant and then of course realized she was talking about her shares.

'That is what I wanted to talk to your cousin about,' she added.

'Oh Aunt, I am such an ungrateful girl. Here you are worrying about railway stock and I still have some guineas wrapped up for you. I was going to ask you again – you wouldn't take them before.' I remembered I had spent one or two of the guineas with Daniel.

'You are not to think of it. Put them in the Yorkshire Bank for your dowry,' she smiled. 'It is a good feeling, is it not? – money one has truly *earned*.'

'It is indeed,' I replied. I was thinking of all the money Barbara had not earned. Aunt must have guessed my thoughts for she said:

'I hear Barbara and Miss Logan are abroad.' My heart threatened once more to turn a somersault.

'Oh yes,' I answered vaguely. 'I believe Martha said something about it.'

'Gadding off all the time – that wouldn't suit me. I'm surprised she doesn't want to supervise the alterations herself.' I was silent. I had a feeling Barbara would not be too long away.

The next day it rained and was more like March than late August. I was sitting doing a bit of plain sewing for my aunt when I heard the sound of horses' hooves on the cobbles outside the parlour window. I glanced up and saw Sam Hirst chatting to my cousin, who had ridden over despite the weather. I heard Aunt greet him and bent back to my sewing. Rainer did not come into the parlour at once so I had plenty of time to rehearse my remarks about London. I turned my thoughts to Westminster Square and assembled a mass of little anecdotes and observations to keep him amused and his sharp blue eyes off my face. When he came in though, he was brisk and friendly and did not ask any awkward questions. We discussed the weather, my Aunt Sophia's religion and when I should return to Harrogate.

After that Martha provided us with an apple-pie and cheese lunch and he teased me saying he thought I might be too grand now for humble Yorkshire folk and food.

'On the contrary,' I replied. 'Home has the best food of all when Martha cooks it.'

It was only when I saw him to the door later that afternoon, when a fine drizzle was still obscuring our nearer hills that he said: 'I'm sorry. I shan't be able to take you to the Angersteins' this time. Will you manage with the train and the omnibus?'

'Yes, of course,' I replied. 'I must learn to look after myself, you know.'

'Look after yourself, Meta, yes. I have some business to do in London again, but I'll come to the Winter Gardens once more, if you'll invite me.'

'Yes, you must come,' I replied and I noticed that he seemed to look at me in a more appraising – or was it a critical – way, as we shook hands; perhaps it was my imagination.

The next day I felt restless. I wrote again to Daniel telling him the date of my arrival in Harrogate and to address his next letter there. I was not sure whether I should hear from him again before I left the Hall. Once more I made an effort to appear the old Meta and went for walks in the woods when the weather cleared and chatted with Aunt's friends in the village who never seemed to have anything more momentous to discuss than the price of ribbons. I tried not to be neglectful of my appearance and submitted to Martha's plans for a new dress for me with good grace. Aunt had come back with the stuff from Halifax, a beautiful cobalt blue which Martha said 'sets off your colouring something grand'.

It was only the day before my return to the Angersteins when everything had been pressed and packed and I had made a selection of my books that two letters bearing foreign stamps arrived for me. One was from Daniel I saw immediately, and the other? I concealed Daniel's and opened the second rather ostentatiously. When Martha came in to 'side the pots' I said: 'Fancy – Barbara and Miss Logan have written to me.'

'Oh aye – I saw you'd two letters.' Her sharp eyes missed nothing, so I let her believe what she had obviously already decided.

Dear Meta,

We are holidaying in Baden and thought to write to you as perhaps you would be so kind as to check with Mrs Taylor at the Lodge that the new brocade has arrived for the salon. Vinny is not sure how long she will want to stay here. It is a most pleasant and salubrious spot. I thought perhaps you would do this little service for us as Mrs Taylor cannot be persuaded to write letters. Our respects to your Aunt. Perhaps we shall see you at Christmas? Please write Hotel Europa.

Yours faithfully,
B. Stott.

This was a piece of cheek which I would have thought had been beyond even Barbara. The postscriptum said: 'Vinny sends her best respects and hopes your German is improving – she rattles away in it herself.'

'They want me to find out if some wallpapering silk has arrived with Mrs Taylor,' I said to Martha.

She shook her head. 'You're not her lap-dog, Meta. Still, no harm in my asking at the Lodge for you and then you can put her mind at rest.'

'Oh, Martha, thank you.' I did not want to go near Rooks Nest again until I went there once more with Daniel. It would seem a desecration, like visiting Olympus when the gods had left.

I read the other letter in the privacy of my room. There were endearments enough and little words we had used and a lively description of his audition (which had been successful) and then I read:

I have seen the Fairy Princess again with the dragon who guards her. I said nothing in the end about knowing you. They talked of their large estate in Yorkshire and I smiled to myself to think I had been there with you. It was at the Casino. The younger and uglier lady does not gamble – the other lady did. She is a handsome woman, your Miss Logan, and I can see she was wasted on little girls. I had the idea my own dead Mütterle looked a little like her and when we were chatting, someone who came up took me for her brother. Was that not strange? Not very complimentary to me as I am a little, or more than a little younger, than the lady – but perhaps the fellow was wanting to compliment *her*! You can see that life is not too bad and I feel the stirrings of some new music – nothing profound but a little something for my violincello – why must Paganini have all the favours?

It was a chatty, kind letter, but it did not satisfy me and I felt in some curious way compromised and uneasy. I resolved to wait till I returned to Harrogate before replying. The other letter I replied to as soon as Martha came up with the intelligence that the 'Browcade' had indeed arrived and they were awaiting further instructions before putting it up. I thanked Barbara for her communication, said I was sorry I had missed them this summer, added I had happened in July to see the improvements in the new garden and assured her that her wall-coverings had indeed arrived and only awaited her presence to be hung. I had sensed a little impatience in Barbara to be gone from Baden. I was sure she was more interested in her new house than in loitering in German spas and had probably only gone there to please Lavinia Logan.

Oh what excitement when I finally returned to the Angersteins' the next week after a rather tedious journey which convinced me of the usefulness of young men in the matter of carrying trunks and parcels. Fanny came hurtling through the door before I was even on the steps and Zillah was jumping up and down with apparent joy. I was pleased and surprised that my advent was so welcome. But it made me heavy-hearted. There I was again for another year, and there was my love far away.

When we were all settled in the schoolroom, Fanny said shyly but with a nervous smile: 'I am glad you are with us again, Miss Moore.'

'Papa said you wouldn't come back,' piped Zillah.

'Oh – why ever not?' I asked.

'He said you'd be married – and that we should have to look for another governess,' went on Zillah implacably, in spite of Fanny's shushing. I was amused but a little thrown.

Did Papa Angerstein think Daniel had his eye on me for a wife? Surely not. He of all people would know the respect due to custom and the impossibility of marrying 'out', even if he had noticed Daniel's interest in me. Of course there was the Waltz – but he hadn't realized it was written for me.

The next visitor was Naomi. Scarcely had I unpacked and greeted the family – Mr Angerstein was absent – before Naomi Hertz tapped gently at the door. I was busy sorting out books but nevertheless was very pleased to see her. Indeed all the old Harrogate life was proving surprisingly attractive. If I had to languish alone it was perhaps better in Harrogate than anywhere, though I dreaded going to the Winter Gardens without Daniel. I could see that Naomi had something to tell me and thankfully that would prevent me from being questioned too closely about myself. We chatted for a time and discussed the summer before she looked away for a moment and then said shyly: 'Benjie and I are to be married!'

'Oh, Naomi – when?'

'In the spring, I think – when he comes back from Leipzig. He is to take up a post in London, it was all arranged during the summer. I'm sorry I didn't write, Meta, but I was all over the place with the family and then with Benjie's. I haven't even *seen* him. He wrote from Germany to my uncle, and then proposed to me by letter! He didn't have the time or the money to come over to us, but this appointment in London means we can get married!' She spoke quietly but with suppressed happiness.

'What sort of work is it in London then? Will he play at concerts?'

'It is something to do with the Academy. He will have to teach, but there will be time for other engagements.'

'You thought he would be away for years. I am so glad, Naomi! I expect you will like to be married!'

'Only to Benjie,' she laughed. 'I didn't say anything before as it was all so uncertain. Auntie is so awfully pleased,' she added shyly.

'And so am I,' I said and we kissed each other heartily. I did wish I could talk to her about Daniel, but I could not. She would not approve, and the contrast between her own good fortune and my longing for something permanent with Daniel would, I knew, disturb her sensitive soul and she would urge me to give up my dream. As though she guessed my thoughts, she said: 'Have you heard from Daniel Reiss? Benjie tells me he also is in Germany.'

'Yes, I did have a letter from him,' I answered truthfully. 'He is in Baden. I think he wants to see Benjie, but it is a long way from Leipzig.' She was silent and I said no more.

That night after putting Fanny and Zillah to bed – Rufus was to go away to school in a week and was now allowed to stay up with his parents – I felt very depressed. I was glad for Naomi. Benjie was a splendid man and I knew she loved him and they would have a wonderful marriage, but I could not help envying her. What if I myself were Jewish – would Daniel want to marry me then? I truly wished he would, but then I thought, if I had been Jewish he would not have stayed in London with me; that was not the way marriages were made, in dingy little apartments in Bloomsbury. I opened my poetry book and sat at the table in my room trying to find something to correspond with my thoughts which might yet cheer me. All I found was *'Ich grolle nicht'* and that made me cry, for sometimes I felt my heart was breaking – not over my love for him but because of his being so far away and the impossibility of our ever having a life together. I wondered whether he would tell Benjie about me. I hoped not, for I could just imagine the indignation Benjie would express, believing that Daniel had seduced me and that I was an innocent young girl whose reputation he had taken away. In spite of feeling desperately miserable I resolved to apprise no one of my feelings – certainly not Naomi, for I wanted to preserve my independence such as it was. The only thing I could not bear was to lose Daniel's love. I should have to make do with it, I thought, for the rest of my life and decline gradually into a spinster lady like Aunt, who always appeared a spinster to me in spite of her long-ago marriage. I reflected that life was easier for widows, who were the only women free from bondage to men. Then I thought, I had put myself voluntarily into this bondage and that there was something wrong with me since I wanted to have my cake and eat it. The state of marriage did not really attract me; it was only to live with Daniel that I yearned and that would be a sort of marriage if he wanted me to stay with him. He was so different from Benjie and yet they were both so gifted. I did not know whose talent was the greater but I felt Benjie was going to be recognized and I wished that Daniel might be given the same opportunities. I remembered his saying to me that he wanted above all to compose and I thought of the Waltz and wondered if they would play it next season at the Winter Gardens. He wanted to write grander music, operas, and what they called 'chamber music'. I hoped he was doing so.

I was a little comforted when I finally went to bed. I would try to bear up, so that no one would suspect anything to Daniel's discredit. Most of the discredit would be mine of course, but I did not regret it. It had been my decision, my own feelings that had led me to act as I had, and perhaps there had even been something 'romantic' about my rash conduct.

During the next few weeks, busy as I was, I found a release in daydreams. I read and reread Daniel's letters and replied to the following one, which also was posted in Baden. He did not comment on Benjie's engagement, although I had mentioned it, but told me a good deal about his music-making and the effect his playing was having on the ladies of Baden. He was to go to Mannheim for a concert, and seemed busy and happy. I tried not to write him letters which might upset him, and confined my longings to my Journal. Although Daniel did proffer to me some words which made me happy and reminded me of our days together, he did not possess the art of letter-writing. I began to feel that I was living on borrowed capital, though I believed my store of devotion would never dwindle. The ache of missing him was not the almost pleasant misery I remembered feeling in the past. My mind itself seemed to ache, heartache, I suppose. I did not feel it was too much to bear, so long as I could look forward to a time when we should be together. Fanny would often notice me staring into space and would come and sit by me, so I always was able to jerk myself into the present and busy myself with all the tasks I had to undertake during the day. Her parents were as kind and cheerful as ever, though Mr Angerstein was even busier, occupying himself now with the refurbishment of a recently purchased hotel. Esther would sometimes sigh and say he need not work so hard, but it was in his blood. He could not bear to rest on his laurels and must be forever extending himself.

My letters were always brought up to me by Emma who sorted them out when the postman delivered, so I did not think that the German postmarks had been noticed by the family except by Fanny who collected stamps. The autumn evenings were not taking away the sparkle of summer. There was something infinitely attuned to my mood in the sunsets which bathed Harrogate in a golden light and cast long lean shadows over the grass of the Stray and gilded the grey stone buildings with an almost supernatural stagey brilliance. As September gave way to October, even the sunsets changed to a mingling of pink and smokey grey, a backdrop to the lacy branches at the back of the Crescent, turning the towers of the big hotel on its hill into a gothic palace. I would often stand watching the sunset, thinking not only of Daniel but of some sadness at the heart of things when each day died to the next. Sometimes I confess I thought that if *I* were in love with Meta Moore, nothing could have stopped me bearing her away into the sunset! But any tears I shed were real, not stage ones, and even occasionally I would awake before dawn and stand at my window in the sleeping house to see the new sun rise in a mild pink and blue sky, fair again as though night had never been. Sunrise and sunset were real enough, but I felt strange when I thought of my own existence.

I had a letter from Aunt at the end of October when the gap between the sunset and sunrise lengthened. Rainer had that week sent me a card from Paris where he was on business and Aunt told me that Rooks Nest was said to be ready and awaiting its owner.

Barbara has written to Bessy Taylor to say that they will be back soon, having toured the Rhine and seen all there is to see. I think she might have written to you again, since she wanted the wallpapering bills, but I expect that as there is nothing she *wants* from you, you will hear nothing. What a beautiful autumn we are having. It will be a splendid Christmas at Rooks Nest, I should imagine. A pity the house has been left so long unoccupied – I had thought they would return before this. We are having a good term, my dear, and I am grateful for the music you sent. With the mild weather we have had no colds as yet. Martha sends her love as usual and says she hopes you have put on a little weight. She was worried you lost it in London. Have you heard from your Aunt Sophia? I believe she wrote to Rainer as your father's cousin – he mentions it in his letters. She wanted to see him in London to try and persuade him to persuade you to come back and help her with the little boys. Has he said anything to you? You must not set your face firmly against it, my dear, it would take you a little more into society if you ever should wish it. But I expect, as you told me, she wants you mainly for a governess.

Poor Aunt Juby, trying to do her duty by everyone and determined not to let me think she was unfair to Sophia. I wrote back a day or two later and put her mind at rest on this score but I was intrigued that Rainer had heard from Sophia as he had not mentioned it in his card from Paris. It all seemed very remote from me. The week at Westminster Square seemed to have happened years ago whilst the week with Daniel was ever present in my mind.

November was approaching fast and the afternoons and evenings lost their autumnal gold hue, though the sunsets were even more beautiful. I was surprised on the first day of the month to have another letter brought in for me in Aunt's writing. She did not write often and I had not yet replied to her previous missive. I hoped nobody was ill – Martha perhaps? The fire had just been lit in the nursery and I sat by it for a moment whilst we waited for the porridge to arrive. Esther breakfasted alone with her husband downstairs in the morning room now that Rufus had gone away to school, and she would do her accounts down there and consult with the cook about shopping and errands. There was time for me to read my aunt's letter and I opened it with some apprehension.

Rainer has just returned from London where he saw Barbara Stott. Apparently she was alone and gave no explanation beyond saying that Miss Logan was to come on later. We were all agog to see whether Barbara comes up north by herself and to know what has happened to Miss Logan. Rainer offered to help her with her trunks and boxes and to accompany her to

Leeds on the train but she told him she was awaiting a letter. She said she would be back in a day or two. Rainer thought you would like to know – I believe he is rather a gossip. I thought at first that he was going to tell me he had decided to marry Miss Logan himself, but I suppose that was stupid. Do you suppose she has found herself a rich husband abroad? He just said to tell you he would be over soon to see you but had to go off straight away to Manchester for something, so expect him perhaps next week. I am rather sorry for Barbara if her friend has abandoned her. It is all most peculiar.

Your loving Aunt Juby.

Fanny's coming in with the maid hardly roused me from my rereading of this letter and I had to make quite an effort to pull myself away and attend to the children. I wondered why Rainer was so insistent that this piece of news should be communicated to me. I had long ago stopped considering him as a husband for Lavinia – but it seemed something was afoot. Barbara alone in that great house without Lavinia? What could have happened to tear Lavinia away from her companion? Surely Barbara would not confide anything to her own disadvantage to my cousin? Somehow I did not feel very much attracted to the idea of his coming over to visit me in Harrogate. The last time, in the Winter Gardens, was clear in my memory, when we had talked about my mama and papa and that very same afternoon I had fallen in love with Daniel. Seeing Rainer in Harrogate was different from seeing him at home and I was aware that I should have to hide my feelings in his presence. I wondered if Daniel had seen Barbara before she left Baden, but was not clear where the women were going after that.

'Will you be here at Hannukah?' Zillah was asking. 'Because I am knitting you a scarf,' she added. 'And if you are to go home for the holiday I shall have to give it you before and so must hurry up.'

'Zillah, presents are supposed to be a surprise,' reproved her sister.

'How kind of you, Zillah,' I said. 'I am not sure – I didn't last year did I?'

'It is purple and green,' said Fanny, of the scarf. 'You might as well know since she has told you of it. Personally I would not have chosen those colours, but Zillah thought otherwise.'

Zillah looked hurt. 'Now you have upset me,' said the little girl coolly.

'I'm sorry,' replied Fanny, humbly, helping herself to toast as the porridge was still not in evidence.

'I love purple and green, my dear,' I said to Zillah. 'Doubtless Fanny would have chosen differently, but I am partial to all colours I think – except brown, which is so dreary.'

'I am making something too,' offered Fanny. 'But do not tell her, Zillah, even though I told her the colour of your knitting.'

'I can keep secrets if necessary,' replied Zillah. 'But it would be no good if she were not here to have her present, would it?'

'You are very commonsensical,' I said to the younger child. Except where her music was concerned, she was a very sensible little girl – and even with her music she went forward with such determination that we all knew she would get her own way.

When I was not talking to the children, I dwelt upon that letter from Aunt Juby, feeling a strange sense of fear and anxiety for which I could not account. I was glad that Barbara did not always get her own way and I was not any longer caught up with Lavinia in the old fashion, but I felt that somehow things were happening to me too, beyond my control, and for the first time since my return to Harrogate that autumn, was *glad* that I was safely ensconced in my employer's family and that my days, dull though they were, were a shield against my anxieties.

The night-time was different. I longed to be back in London – or anywhere with Daniel. I constructed plans to go abroad and teach English, tossed and turned in half-dreams, dreamed again of Rooks Nest and the strange toppling into the water of Barbara's house; and seemed also to be back watching the scene with a lady and gentleman I knew to be my parents, as the house made its soundless descent into the water.

Six

HEARTACHE

Two days after Aunt Juby's letter arrived I was returning from a brisk walk with Fanny. The afternoon was foggy and damp and the cold seemed to numb my mind as well as my body. We had left Zillah with her mother and I had taken the opportunity of turning our steps towards the Winter Gardens for the first time since summer. I might as well see it on a bad day when I could blame my depression on the weather. They were not yet opened for the winter season but a few ragged posters were stuck on the iron pillars of the entrance, tattered and dank. The place was being repainted and a few workmen were busy up ladders scraping off rust. I wondered whether they would ever play my waltz there again. It did not seem possible. I was answering Fanny's polite chatter, my thoughts elsewhere. I had been waiting a week for a letter from Daniel and the sight of the Winter Gardens, unpeopled and shut and dark, had made me feel I should never hear from him again. But the walk probably did us good and warmed us up.

It was a surprise then to see a letter for me, in the now familiar spiky writing with the Palatinate stamp, lying on the hall table.

'May I have the stamp?' Fanny was asking as we went upstairs.

'Later,' I replied. 'Can you amuse Zillah for a moment? I have to go to my room for something.'

Fanny assured me she would go down to tell Emma we were back and would help Zillah with the famous scarf in the schoolroom if her mama were busy.

I ran up to my room, took off my bonnet, unwound my scarf, unpeeled my gloves and tore open the precious envelope.

A moment's reading and my heart seemed to stop. My hands which had been glowing as the result of our walk felt suddenly cold again. I remember now his exact words.

Dearest Meta,

Forgive me, my darling, for not having written for a week or two. I have to write to you now to tell you that something strange has happened. Try to understand. I am in terrible trouble, Meta — I think I am out of my mind.

Why should I burden you? But I must. If I did not, it would inflict worse pain on you, so I have to write. I did not want to – did not intend to – she has woven a spell round me, I think. I have fallen in love with your Fairy Princess – she does not love me – I do not know what will happen. Almost I wrote 'Save me, Meta' – but only forgive and I will write again. I do not forget you. I am not a monster, dear one. I am in a strange state of mind – yet the music is pouring out. Did you know I could not compose in summer? I shall go to Mannheim. I do not know whether I shall see Benjie. Thank you for all your news. Look after yourself. I should not have taken you away. Oh Meta . . .

Daniel.

I sat down with the letter still in my trembling hand. All I could think at first was: But Daniel loved me – he must still love me – or why would he write like this? I love him! I love him! What has happened? I could not sit there for ever – Fanny would be waiting for me. I put the letter under my pillow and went down-stairs, holding on to the banister as though I were going to col-lapse. I must hide my state of mind, must have time to think it over. As I went into the familiar nursery I thought it looked changed and could not at first recognize it. It was as though a curtain was hovering in front of my eyes. But I went in and oc-cupied myself with the children and miraculously they did not notice anything untoward. I set them some copying to do – music for Zillah and some poems for Fanny, and sat at the window, the same window out of which I had glimpsed him in the snow nearly a year ago. I took a book, but I did not read. I was thinking of Lavinia. So that was why she had not returned with Barbara. Curiously I did not blame her, for she knew nothing of my love for Daniel and I hoped he would not tell her. How could I blame her when it was Daniel's changed feelings which had erupted over my happy world? I had missed him, sorrowed for him, found the absence well nigh unbearable, but I had never thought of this – that he would fall in love with some-one else! I did not then, and never did I later, regret that I had gone away with him. But – 'in terrible trouble', and 'out of my mind' – I almost ran up to my room to check that those had indeed been his words. Yet he was writing music – it was 'pour-ing out of him'. I knew that he had been preoccupied in the summer but had not realized in my new-found happiness that he had not been able to compose. How self-centred I had been. The charm of Lavinia Logan had unlocked his mind, his creative powers. *I* had not done that. How well I understood the charm of Lavinia, for had I not covered acres of my Journal years ago with poems to her, inspired by her? What magic did she have that I had not? The irony of the situation was not lost upon me – that I and the man I loved should at different times love the same person. She *was* mysterious, but I had thought her magic had gone now that Barbara had taken her over.

I turned the page and tried to read – it was a volume of Carlyle that I had picked up in Mr Angerstein's library. I remembered Rainer telling me years and years ago to read Carlyle. And I saw not the words of the 'Sage of Chelsea' but the face of Barbara on the page. What must Barbara be feeling now? I was almost sorry for her. I knew instinctively that she loved Lavinia too, but in a different way from me – and that she was more ruthless and would stop at nothing to get her back. The question was, would Lavinia go back? If she returned to England we would all be happy except for Daniel. But how could I be happy again if my lover adored another woman? Lavinia as the object of his passion – the Dark Lady of his musical sonnets? He had written *me* a waltz though, had he not, and as though to echo my thoughts, Fanny looked up and said: 'Shall we go to the new concerts when they begin again, Miss Moore?'

'You mean at the Winter Gardens, dear?' I asked a little unsteadily.

'Of course – and perhaps Benjie will come too and play for Naomi.'

I thought with a stab of envy of the lucky Naomi who had played the game according to the rules and was to get her reward. I must not be bitter. I must be patient. I would resolve to wait. I would reply to Daniel, put aside all thoughts of myself. But was love for another only a love of oneself; the giving was to please oneself, was it not? I put away for a time this question of moral philosophy as too difficult for me in my present frame of mind but I was to return to it.

In my room, when the children were in bed and I had retired pleading a slight headache, I took out the letter again. It *was* true. It was all I thought he had said. I got out my secrétaire, a present

from Aunt for my last birthday, and wrote a long, long letter –
and tore it up and drafted another. What could I say? I would
'forgive' him of course, since he asked me to. But what else? I
had thought we were so happy and that it would be like that for
years, even if we could not be together always – and now it was
not to be. Unless it all passed like a dream for him and he came
back to me. I wrote that I understood his feelings, for I had had
them myself for that lady. I wrote that I had perhaps expected
too much, and that why should I deserve him? All this sounded
too humble but I went on writing regardless. I wrote of love
unrequited and that I should always love him and that I would
try not to be unhappy. Again it sounded as though I were being a
brave little girl but still I went on writing. I wrote that I *knew* he
had loved me and that I had only the happiest remembrances of
him – and that made my letter sound valedictory. I looked up for
a moment, my eyes swimming with unshed tears. I finished the
letter somehow and went to bed and once there I sobbed into my
pillow as though I were eight years old and Martha would soon
come to comfort me.

I dreamed of Daniel's dead mother that night and woke wondering how much older than Daniel Lavinia was. Sixteen, fifteen
years? I wished I had a magic carpet, even if it brought me only
to sights I did not want to see. Were they together? Had he
made love to her? Somehow I did not think that Lavinia would
be so easy to catch. I comforted myself with the thought that
perhaps she had other fish to fry in Baden and that Daniel was an
excuse. I added a postscriptum to my letter: 'Please write and let
me know how you are ... I heard that Barbara Stott had
returned alone and I am anxious for you both. My aunt told me
that Miss Logan was to visit some relatives abroad. Please see
Benjie and then I may have news of you, for he will return soon
to England, Naomi tells me.' Then I sealed the letter and went
down to a breakfast I had no appetite for.

'Miss Moore must still have a headache,' said Fanny, 'for she
has not eaten her porridge, Mama.'

Mrs Angerstein had come into the schoolroom for a moment
just as I was putting out books. 'Oh Meta!' she said with genu-
ine concern. 'Are you well, my dear?'

'It is quite gone,' I replied. 'I was just not hungry.'

The postman brought another letter for me with the second

post. It was from Rainer and I read it when the girls took a quarter of an hour's recess. He proposed to visit me the following week if that were agreeable. If there were no concerts, perhaps we could go to a tea-room. He had some books for me and was sorry that he had been so busy over the summer. He hoped life was not too dull for me in Harrogate and mentioned again my account of Aunt Sophia with which I had amused him.

Never had I felt less like seeing Rainer. I liked to be amusing and relaxed with him and it would be difficult to pull the wool over his eyes. I should have to exert a supreme effort of will to appear as though nothing had happened. I could not refuse to be taken out by him for it was kindly meant, and he of all people was probably the only person to whom I could have unburdened myself, if there existed anyone. He did not mention Rooks Nest or its inhabitants in his letter, so I said nothing about them in my reply.

Naomi came round the next day and I had once more to affect a lack of knowledge about Daniel's movements. I did manage though to insinuate a few enquiries under cover of my polite interest in Benjie and his travels.

'I'm waiting to hear from him, Meta – I can hardly believe he will be back in two or three weeks.'

'You are lucky,' I could not help saying.

'Yes, I know,' said Naomi simply. 'I never expected him to ask for me so soon, you know. I'd quite resigned myself to wait two years at least!'

'It's wonderful that he has found work in London.'

'Yes. Just think – a post at the Academy and time to play too. I shall see my old haunts, though I shall miss Harrogate once I am married.'

'What will Mr Angerstein do without you?'

Indeed that was a problem. Naomi would be leaving the north and taking with her some of the brains of my employer's business dealings. I could see her as an amanuensis to Benjie in the sphere of music as she had been for her uncle in business.

'Don't you sometimes wish you could work for yourself?' I said. 'You are always doing things for other people, Naomi.'

'Oh, I shall have much to do once I am married.'

She coloured slightly. I wanted to say: 'But you are just as clever in your way as Benjie' but of course I could not say it. Naomi would be a superb wife, and doubtless one day a wonderful mother to Benjie's children. There was an ache at the back of my throat.

The Tuesday of the next week, the day of Rainer's visit to me, dawned pale and cold. I wished he were not coming. I had heard nothing further from Daniel and my imagination was keeping me awake at night. During the morning I was busy and managed to carry on my duties as normal. What would Daniel feel if he knew that I was off my food on his account? I had always been renowned for a good appetite, indeed Rainer had used to say I was a good trencherman. Ladies, though, were not supposed to get hungry, so perhaps I could pass off my new-found distaste for food and the rings under my eyes as a fashionable attempt to lose weight. Next I should be having the vapours. I cursed my treacherous body which would not be controlled however much I tried. I felt lethargic, dull. Not sick – that had passed after the night of Daniel's letter. I pinched my cheeks after luncheon on that Tuesday afternoon and rehearsed lists of topics which might interest my cousin, beginning with an attempt to discuss my reading.

He was on time as usual, perfectly groomed in his dove-grey cloak and glossy hat. His clean-shaven face looked pleased to see me. I made a great effort to dispel any suspicions he might have, not only about Lavinia but of course about my own London adventure.

When we were seated in the Spa tea-room he seemed a little less at ease than usual. I put it down to something in my own manner as we began again to discuss Westminster Square. Then I told him about Naomi and Benjie, which was sailing a little nearer the storm, but I had to appear unconcerned.

'Yes, you told me about his music the last time,' said my cousin, sipping his Russian tea with his eyes upon me. 'A pity the Winter Gardens are not yet open. I could have done with a little culture,' he went on.

'I am reading Carlyle,' I burst out. 'Don't you remember you told me to read him when I was only twelve?' I babbled on. Rainer did not seem to think anything amiss and listened politely enough to me. 'I feel such a provincial hoyden,' I said. 'Not that I would have had to know anything about literature – or music – at Aunt Sophia's. I've been trying to improve my German of course...'

'That's good. Did you know – did Augusta tell you – the

lovely Lavinia is still in Würtemburg?'

I looked down at my teacup to try to hide the flush that was creeping over my face and hoping that he might take my confusion for the memory of the *Schwärmerei* I had had for that lady. 'I expect she is flirting with a rich man,' I replied equably and toyed with another Eccles cake.

'Do eat, Meta, you look quite thin.'

'Why don't you like her?' I asked suddenly, perhaps foolishly.

'Why don't *you* like Barbara?' he replied, looking at me again over the top of his teacup.

I shivered suddenly and he said: 'We shall have to buy you a muff, for I believe your hands are quite cold.' I was not thinking really of Barbara but she was a good excuse for another divagatory attempt, I thought.

'*She* doesn't like *me*,' I replied, not looking at him. It was too absurd. It was not Barbara my love had gone to in Mannheim, was it?

He stirred his tea meditatively. The tea-room was now full and a lilac dusk was seeping through the shutters. I thought, How lovely it would be if Daniel were here. 'She was jealous of you,' he said, looking down this time at his saucer as though it held a secret for him.

'Why should she be jealous? She has got what she wants – to have her "Vinny" – Miss Logan – to stay with her, to spend her money on. All that money – there must be a lot – and they say Lavinia dotes on her now.'

'Ha!' he said.

'You say that very melodramatically,' I said rather rudely. But then he laughed.

'You did your best to palm me off with Lavinia Logan, didn't you, Meta?' he said after a pause.

It was my turn to gaze at the teacups. 'I suppose I did. I was so fond of her, you know, and I thought she was a cultured woman. And there aren't many really – come, be honest – in Lightholme are there?'

'Well there's your aunt for one,' he answered and I smiled.

'Why *don't* you like her – Lavinia?' I asked again.

'I suppose for the same reason that Barbara didn't like you,' he replied. This was too deep for me so I hazarded:

'Do you think Lavinia will come back soon, Rainer?' I said,

trying to sound casual so as not to betray the direction of my thoughts.

'I'm not sure. It depends if anyone else could raise the stakes,' he replied.

'Barbara is very rich – it's not her *fault* – aren't you being a little unfair on Lavinia?' I asked. Strange to be undertaking the defence of the woman my darling had begun to love. Daniel, Daniel, I thought. Why didn't you rescue me from all this?

'I don't expect we shall have to wait long,' said Rainer. 'Barbara doesn't seem to think she will miss Christmas at any rate. She's planning a grand luncheon party, except she calls it a "reception", at the Nest. She seems quite sure the prodigal will return – and she wants to show the place off to the rest of the yokels.'

'I love that place,' I said, surprising myself as I said it.

'Yes, I know you do. It was all a pity, a great pity – but there's nothing we can do about it.'

'I used to think – don't be cross – that if you married Miss Logan, you could buy the Nest and then I wouldn't have minded. But – Barbara!'

'I'm not as rich as that young lady,' he replied. 'And anyway I don't love "Miss Logan" as you call her and never could.' He looked suddenly sad and I wondered whether there was some melancholy mystery in his life that none of us knew about.

Poor Daniel, I was thinking, Lavinia won't stay with him if he's not rich.

'Barbara holds the purse-strings,' said Rainer curtly.

'Like a man,' I replied.

'Some men – not all – not your poor papa for one,' he answered.

'I'd rather work for my living,' I said proudly.

'It's always paid for by someone's labour,' he replied. 'Stocks and shares and property – like old Stott, Barbara's father. He worked hard in his youth, I know. Then that girl gets the benefit. I don't mind that, not personally – but think, Meta, of the people who slave all their lives and never have any fun, or even enough to eat. It's a mad world.'

'I didn't know *you* were a Radical,' I said, somewhat surprised.

'Then you know now,' he said curtly.

'*I* work for a living,' I said proudly.

'Yes, Meta, I know you do. And you must tell me more about it – when you are not gadding off to London, I mean.'

I wondered whether he was referring to anything other than Aunt Sophia's. 'You work too,' I said, after a silence.

'Yes, if you can call writing reports work – I suppose it is.'

'You seem depressed,' I hazarded.

'Me, depressed? Oh no, not more than usual anyway. What about you? You look rather peaky, as Martha would say.'

Oh dear – we had got around to me again, just when I was thinking that that hurdle was over and he had even made me – not forget, but hold in abeyance for ten minutes – the sorrow that seemed to envelop me like a thick fog.

'I am "fine" as the Americans say,' I replied. 'I am rather caught up in Naomi's joy as a matter of fact. She is awfully nice, you know, and she seems set for happiness.'

'I haven't met her so I cannot say, but from what you say she seems a good girl and a clever one.'

'Oh she is.'

'Then Benjie is a lucky man.'

'When I talk to her, everything seems simple, yet I don't suppose it is really. She's always loved Benjie and I believe he loves her, and all the family approve – and everything is right for them.' I hoped I had not betrayed anything by my tone of wistfulness for he looked at me sharply.

'Jewish people always stick together. They have to since everyone is against them. They are great ones for families. I suppose that's where Christians got the idea from – except when in the Old Testament they allowed the *men* lots of vices.'

'How nice for them, but what about the women?'

'You know things have never been equal for women,' he replied.

Was he warning me of something, or was it just his normal tone of conversation? 'Well, there were the Amazons,' I essayed, trying to sound light-hearted.

'And Barbara,' he said, with a grimace.

'I wish I were a man,' I went on. 'I've always wished that – to be able to choose, and do what you want – if you are rich enough of course. I do see that there's not much freedom for the operatives, but even so, more for them than for their wives.'

'That's one thing you can't change – being born a woman, little cousin. You will have to make the best of it.'

261

'I never can talk to anyone the way I talk to you,' I said. It was true. He was always willing to take me seriously.

'Then I shall go on regarding myself as an integral part of your education.' He smiled. 'Have you warmed yourself up? We must go, I'm afraid – unless you want more of "the cup that cheers" as your dear father used to say.'

'Oh, did he say that?'

'Yes. *He* was a nice man, Meta, but of course being a man didn't mean he had it easy. So perhaps you should think about that when you get dissatisfied with your lot.'

'I'm not dissatisfied. I mean there are some things I'm glad about, if things were arranged a little differently.'

'Lesson one,' he replied. 'Life is hard. Do you spread your subversive doctrines to your pupils?' he went on.

'Oh no. I think Fanny will be a fighter anyway. And Zillah has her music.'

He helped me put on my cloak and paid the serving woman.

'You must have something, apart from people. You cannot always be giving, you know,' he said.

I was startled. It was what I had thought in the summer. 'I have my books,' I answered rather stiffly.

'Yes, and there are people I don't doubt who are waiting to give you what Naomi has,' he said as we walked along the Parade in the biting wind.

'No, Rainer, I am alone,' I replied, without thinking. Had I come to think that?

'You have changed – a little,' he said as he piloted me across the road where a brewer's dray seemed about to crush me to bits.

'I hope for the better?'

'I don't know,' he replied.

It was only as he bade me goodbye at the Angersteins' door that he said: 'I saw Lavinia and Barbara on Oxford Street in the summer – did I tell you?'

'No,' I said after a pause. 'I hope they were enjoying the air.' He looked at me with a long, rather appraising look, raised his hat and said no more, leaving me to ponder his words.

Oh heavens, I thought, if Rainer had seen me with Daniel in London, what should I do? Then I realized there was nothing I *could* do. If Rainer had wanted to get me into trouble with Aunt he would have done so already. And perhaps he hadn't seen me at all – but it was the way he had said it that made me wonder. What a coincidence if we had all been on Oxford Street together one summer day. Anyway, he would probably have thought I was out for a few hours' respite from Aunt Sophia's. But he would have recognized Daniel I was sure, for he had registered my interest in him that first time in the Winter Gardens. He could not possibly know that Daniel was in love with Lavinia. I thought over what he had said about Lavinia. He certainly seemed to have no fondness for her. The worry over anyone discovering my escapade in the summer did for a moment, but for only a moment, supplant my abject misery over Daniel. The last thing I wanted, even so, in spite of the tears shed into my pillow at night, was sympathy. People feeling sorry for me had always made me ashamed, even when I was a little girl and I fell and bruised my knee, and later when Papa died. I might cuddle up to Martha when the pain was gone but I did not want her, or anyone, feeling sorry for me. Perhaps I'd been brought up to fight my own battles, but whatever the reason, I was proud. Barbara was perhaps more like me than I cared to admit, I realized with surprise. She was proud too. Perhaps she too had feelings she never revealed to anyone.

When I went down to the dining-room that evening after Rainer's visit, I determined to appear cheerful and did actually manage to eat a slice or two of roast beef to keep my strength and spirits up.

'You had a pleasant time with your cousin?' asked Naomi who was eating with us in the evenings when she could be spared from the 'counting house', which was what she called Mr Angerstein's study.

'Very,' I replied. 'He is always amusing, and listens to my chatter.'

'Our families always listen to us,' said Naomi, smiling. 'That is the great virtue of family life I think. They do not ignore us – even if we annoy them.'

'I hope I don't annoy him – if I do, he never says so,' I replied.

'What exactly does he do?' asked Esther.

'I believe he collects information for political and, what is the word – economic? – journals, and he has managed some of his father's business interests. He writes articles too for various newspapers in the north. He once told me he had been destined for the Church. He went to Oxford, you know.'

'Oh, I cannot imagine him as a Christian clergyman,' said Naomi. 'He looks too sceptical.'

'I believe he is a sceptic. He is interested in all intellectual matters, though.'

'Yes, I would imagine he is an intellectual. I believe Benjie met him once in Bradford at some meeting for the foundation of the new philosophical society.'

I saw she could not resist bringing Benjie's name into the conversation. 'I didn't know Benjie was interested in philosophy.'

'Well there are so few people up here who take an active interest in matters of the mind, so they often get together with artists and musicians. I suppose they have something in common.'

Mr Angerstein put in his conversational oar. 'What they have in common is a lack of interest in profit and loss,' he said.

'Oh Uncle, we cannot all be entrepreneurs,' said Naomi, teasing him.

'And, of course,' I said, 'money has to be important hasn't it, or we should all be back on the land – but it is so distasteful – ' I hastily corrected myself in case my employer thought I was criticizing him. 'I mean I do not understand it. So much has happened to this country so quickly, nothing is simple any more. Wasn't it better to have the old order and to forget the machines? What have they brought but misery?'

'But of course, Meta,' said Naomi seriously, 'there has always been misery. Now there is the chance to raise the populace. When they expect something better, then they will make their own efforts to achieve it.'

'I suppose so, but some people seem to have too much money – ' I was thinking of Barbara's father.

'Can you ever have too much?' joked Mr Angerstein.

'It depends upon how you spend it, and whether you are thereby raising everyone to something better. This country needs investment – even in our artists and writers and musicians, or they will all go to America,' said Naomi.

'That is true, Naomi. If I were a young man I should go west.'

'Ah, Jacob, I am glad then that you are not,' interjected Mrs Angerstein. 'I am quite happy here, although of course Uncle Abe is always saying he will emigrate.'

'Your people have always gone where they could find work,' I ventured. It was rare for us to discuss the Jews. I always felt that I must not say anything to hurt their feelings. There was so much prejudice against them because they worked so hard, whether it was making money or playing musical instruments.

'You are very "romantic" about us,' laughed Naomi. 'It has usually been a case of no choice. We have gone where we could. I should like to go to see America though,' she went on. 'Perhaps Benjie will have engagements there when we are married.'

Esther Angerstein smiled. She was so fond of Naomi and absolutely delighted that her marriage with Benjie had been arranged.

We fell to discussing Naomi's plans, and again I began to feel cut off and lonely. I think Naomi sensed my pain, for she would often try to turn the talk back to me.

'How is Daniel Reiss?' asked Jacob suddenly.

I looked fixedly at my plate and strove to appear unaffected. I could not control the sudden lurch of my heart when his name was mentioned. I believe Naomi noticed though the others did not, and she answered: 'Benjie is to see him this week in Mannheim, he tells me. It is a pity you seem to have lost your best Winter Gardens performer for the time being.'

'That was a good tune he composed – the waltz, you know,' said Jacob, sublimely unaware that it had meant anything more than the evocation of 'his' Winter Gardens on a summer evening.

'I shall miss the music,' I said finally, with a great effort.

'Yes – that was good,' said Mr Angerstein.

'Though of course I believe he got rather annoyed when people talked through it,' I added, taking the bull by the horns.

'Alas, perhaps it is better to concentrate on light music,' said Esther. 'Daniel should take a leaf out of Benjie's book and try to find teaching work.'

'He is really a composer, not an executant,' said Naomi. 'Is that not true, Meta, in your opinion?'

'I believe that that is what he wants to do above all. I am sorry that Fanny has lost him for the present as a piano teacher.'

'But perhaps it will not be long and he will come back soon,' added Esther comfortably.

I changed the subject quickly, seeing my chance, and spoke of Zillah's abilities in that direction. Mr Angerstein said he thought it was perhaps not the life for a young lady, playing music all over the place. 'Perhaps I could be her chaperone when she's grown up?' I offered.

'Oh my dear, you will be married by then,' said Esther.

'And so will Zillah, I hope,' said her father.

Naomi looked inscrutable. We went on to talk of Naomi's old school on Harley Street and thence of my aunt's school and from there we went to the subject of the Christmas holiday which they thought I should spend this year at the Hall.

I went up to bed thinking I had not acquitted myself too badly, especially when the talk had been of Daniel. But I felt I was a betrayer. How could it be my 'fault' that I could not say: 'You are speaking of my lover, of the man I have shared a bed with.' They would be horrified. I didn't want to throw their kindness to me back in their faces. I determined that, unless Daniel one day married me, they would never know. But it was hard and I lay awake thinking of the gap between polite society's estimate of our inner lives and of the reality beneath it.

I wondered whether Rainer would have imagined what I had done if he had seen me with Daniel on that summer morning. Would it horrify him as it would horrify most people? If my conduct were ever discovered, however far away in the future, I should still be an outcast. One must dissimulate, dissimulate to live.

Two or three weeks passed and I still had heard nothing from Daniel. Had he even received my letter? I was by turns feverishly impatient, then flat and dull. I could not forget him for one moment. I even noticed that the sight of other young men made me feel a sort of distaste – purely because they were not Daniel. The Winter Gardens were opened again and the usual crowds of bored town worthies and tourist grandees swarmed around its rooms, took tea and sat chattering whilst a new orchestra played – this time 'light' music. My employer was much occupied refurbishing the new hotel he had bought and Naomi and I were despatched to the Gardens to gather our impressions of the reactions of the public to the new music. We took Fanny. She had shot up that year. She was now eleven and like so many Jewish girls was full of precocity allied to a new verve. As we sat at our table at the side and sipped our tea, Fanny said, 'I do wish Mr Reiss would come back – don't you, Miss Moore? I don't like this music.'

'Other people seem to like it well enough,' I replied.

'Oh – public taste!' said the child in the best imitation of her Uncle Abe. 'Perhaps Mr Reiss is just too good for Papa's Gardens,' she went on.

I tried to explain that there were different tastes and that perhaps Yorkshire was not quite ready for all that our new century could offer. 'Schubert would have written to please other people, Fanny, as well as writing for himself and his friends,' I went on.

'Yes, I know, Miss Moore – people have to live.'

Naomi interposed gently with 'You will hear some good music when Benjie returns. I heard from him this morning.' I waited to see if she would mention my dear one. 'He saw Mr Reiss,' she said to Fanny, studiously avoiding looking at me. 'I believe he may come back to England. Benjie said it depended on whether he could get further engagements over there.'

I was once more tossed and turned in a whirlpool of feeling. Would he return with Lavinia? What was happening? Should I write again? I had firmly prevented myself from writing every night since that one letter to him; instead I confided my feelings to my Journal. I was becoming turned in on myself.

Both young and middle-aged men were all around us at the Gardens. One or two came up to our table and greeted Naomi who was well known in the town as Mr Angerstein's amanuensis. I shrank back from them almost visibly. They seemed coarse and crude and annoyed me by their very existence – 'O the difference of man and man'.

'I do hope he comes back,' said Fanny simply. 'He is awfully handsome, don't you think?'

I smiled at Fanny. She would, be like me, a rebel, I thought.

'Don't you think so, Miss Moore?' she repeated.

I should have told her that this was not a proper way for a child to talk, but she was fresh and ingenuous and why should I pretend there was something ill-bred in noticing young men? At least Fanny seemed to be firmly set in the direction of *male* beauty. I didn't think she would have a Lavinia in her life. 'Yes, Fanny,' I said.

'What does your cousin look like? I never saw him when he came to fetch you out,' she went on. 'Does he look like you?'

'Fanny, don't make personal remarks,' said Naomi.

'I am only seeking information,' said Fanny, rather sulkily.

'I believe my cousin looks like his mama and she is not related to me,' I said. 'I look like my papa though, or people say so. I can't remember what he looked like really. I was only five or six when I saw him last.'

267

'Oh I am sorry, Miss Moore!' cried Fanny. 'I did not want to make you sad. It must be hard not to know your papa.'

'I am not sad now about that, Fanny, time heals you know.' I wondered if it did and if one day I should be able to talk about Daniel. Perhaps in forty years when I was old I should think of the follies of my youth? No – I never would!

The next morning was the first of December. It dawned frosty and bright. The leaves had now all gone from the trees. In one of them a crow was perched cawing and croaking outside my bedroom window. I was suddenly filled with a longing to be home, to be able to go down to one of Martha's fires and toast myself, to sit in her kitchen and plan a day to myself, a day of reading and musing and perhaps a short walk over the fields to Wynteredge. I wondered if the snow would come early that year and if I should walk in it in reality and see a sunset over the Nest and sit near the fire after my walk as the shadows gathered and the fire lit the parlour with that red glow I remembered so well. *There* was safety and happiness enough. Why had it all changed? Why should I ever have wanted to leave the comfortable confines of the Hall? My mood was attuned to sad nostalgia as though I were seventy, not almost twenty-one. I was not surprised then to find a letter on my plate in Aunt's spidery hand. I often found that I would receive news from home on those mornings when the Hall had been present to my mind. I slit the envelope open carefully, in some way reluctant to read it and dispel the glow of the fire that had lit my morning thoughts. She would want to know when I planned to return for Christmas.

It was true – she did. But she also mentioned, casually in passing, after a sentence or two about Rainer's visit to me (he had been impressed, it appeared, by my amusing conversation), that Lavinia had returned to Rooks Nest.

Miss Logan has returned from her protracted visit to relatives in Würtemburg they tell me. We have not yet visited but I hear from Bessy Taylor that the two of them have settled down nicely and are 'ever so pleased' with the improvements. There is more talk of this large party Barbara intends to have at Christmas. Apparently we shall all be invited – your cousin may have mentioned it. I shall believe it when we receive an invitation. They say that a large fir tree is to be or-

dered to be planted in a tub in front of the house just for the
season and Miss Logan is to decorate it in the German fashion.
I shall tell you more when I hear. Not much other fresh news –
I fear our lives are sadly dull. Look after yourself. Martha adds
the usual injunctions to keep warm. We shall be ready to
receive you whenever Mr Angerstein will release you and are
looking forward to it since we scarcely saw you in the
summer. Please give my kind regards to your employer's wife
and perhaps you could give the children a few sweetmeats
from me.

One half of me exulted. She was back! Had she left him in Germany? Now he would write to me, I felt sure. I was glad, glad!
But how was I to see him once again if he did not return. Or perhaps he had returned with her and was even now staying at some
remote inn, visiting her clandestinely? No, Barbara would prevent that. It must be that Lavinia had grown tired of him. I knew
so little – not even that she had ever shown any interest in him at
all.

I did not have to wait long, for this was to be the day of letters.
By the second post there was another letter – not from Daniel,
but from Aunt Sophia, offering me twice as much money if I
would leave Harrogate, having given notice of course, to go and
stay as companion to the boys in the holidays. Truly, she was
persistent. There was something almost indecent in her sporadic
attempts to seduce me away. Surely I had not made such a good
impression? I would not go, no, not even if she settled money
on me. But it was a drudgery to explain again. Something must
be troubling that lady's conscience and I suspected it had little to
do directly with me.

Then most unexpectedly another post arrived just when the
children and I had sat down to toast and muffins in the schoolroom. This time – yes – it was – at last – from Daniel! It was
short. Lavinia Logan had returned to England. He had not written before because there was nothing he could say. He had
received my letter. It had touched him. He did not forget me. He
believed Lavinia's return was not strictly connected with himself
and therefore he proposed to return to England too to try and
understand what the situation was. Would I find out for him
what she was doing – for the sake of the love he knew I bore him,
and for the sake of his music. He was to be given a patronage by

the Margrave of Würtemburg if he would stay in Germany to compose. It was his great chance. He was writing feverishly – but he *must* know where she was, what she said of him. He would come to Yorkshire just for a few days, he thought, to see his distant relatives and perhaps to stay with Benjie who was himself to leave in a week or two for London . . .

He did not sound like his old self, he sounded despairing – except for what he said about his music. I did not understand this, but I reflected that perhaps a little sorrow would not hurt him. It might enable him to think more deeply. I seemed to be acting as a judge and jury at the same time. I loved him, wanted him for myself, was actually sorry about Lavinia in a strange way. Yet how could I help but be glad that she was no longer there to cast her spells, whether she knew what she was doing or not. It suited me on the one hand for him to stay in Würtemburg until all this had blown over; on the other hand I wanted to see him. What should I write in reply?

I think I tried in my reply to show him both love and sympathy and not to let any jealous recrimination ruin his idea of me as a 'noble-hearted girl'. But above all, and creeping along almost surreptitiously under my thoughts, was an irrational fear which at first I could not pin-point. I thought it all over again. I tried to be rational. As I deliberated, pushing away images from the summer which might have swayed me one way or the other, it was the picture of Barbara that came to my mind. I did not doubt that Barbara would make short shrift of Daniel, especially if she knew of my connection with him. Would she be pleased to find a rival for Lavinia descending on Rooks Nest? She could hardly dismiss him from her gates, as he would be Lavinia's acquaintance, unless she could prevail upon Lavinia to tell him to go away. Barbara was dangerous. To be crude, though, Lavinia would know which side her bread was buttered and if she had no particular feeling for my darling it would be easy for her to refuse to see him. I felt in my bones that whatever had been the situation between Lavinia and himself, there was little point in his coming to plead his case with her.

If I intimated to Daniel that Barbara, whom I had known from childhood, was a slippery customer, he would perhaps put my remark down to jealousy. What could I say? – Only that he was more likely to cut ice with his Fairy Queen when her attendant was away?

This time I did not write draft after draft of my letter. Instead I thought about it half the night without putting pen to paper. I tried it from all angles; tried to forget that I was personally concerned in the matter, but that, of course, was impossible. Did I or did I not want him to come up to Yorkshire? Yes. What did I think that Barbara could do that I should warn him against trying to see Lavinia at the Hall? Would he in any case take my advice? If he was determined to see Lavinia I might as well write 'Beware of the Bull'. Barbara might in some way wish to revenge herself on anyone who might take 'her' Vinny away from her just at the moment of triumph when the marble halls were all gilded and burnished and she sat back to enjoy her wealth. The trouble was that I had never properly tried to understand Barbara. I had sometimes felt that she was hardly human. But I knew that she was excessively jealous and that she did not let this become apparent. She had grown up. I knew she did not like men. In this she was not like me. How long had she nursed the ambition years ago to detach Lavinia from my passionate partisanship? Had she ever crowed over me? Not in so many words, no – but in every gesture, every plan, a certain ruthlessness spoke through. If I had gone on loving Lavinia in the way I had begun so long ago, what would she have done? I felt I would not have been the victor in that struggle. Had I in some way snatched her victory away from her by going away when I did? It was long since I had seen her; perhaps she had changed. And it was Lavinia who had chosen to live with her. Did Lavinia envisage spending the rest of her life being petted by Barbara? I did not see Lavinia as a woman who only loved women, whatever one meant by love. Lavinia liked, I knew now, power over others – she had never encouraged me until she had seen what I felt for her. *I* had started all that. Who else could I have loved at that time – loved in that exclusive, almost insane way? I had not expected a return, just as for long months I had not expected Daniel to return my love. Even now, when all seemed lost, I was still amazed that he had felt something for me. But that was easier – I was young and not unlovely, I knew. But the only sort of return of love that I cared for – a complete commitment, body and soul – seemed barred to me for some mysterious reason. Was love never requited, or not for long? Must I always be the prime mover? Once more I pulled my thoughts away from myself and dragged them back to Daniel and Lavinia. I would

write as well as I could, as though I were a dispassionate ob-
server.

If only I knew more of the facts of the case. I kept seeing that
gesture of Barbara's in the Park. Lavinia had not seemed to be
out of charge of herself. She had walked along beside Barbara
because it suited her. I ought to write to *her,* not to Daniel. I
wondered whether he had mentioned me at all to her. If he had, I
hoped that Lavinia had kept it to herself. Barbara would love a
spot of blackmail – all in a good cause of course: my own
morals.

In the end I wrote Daniel a short letter stating as simply as
possible what I felt he should do. I told him I knew Lavinia was
back, that I was sorry if it had not worked out, that I loved him
still but was afraid to burden him with that, that Lavinia's friend
(and I begged him to destroy this letter and never repeat it to
anyone) was a strange and powerful personality who would take
it very amiss if he succeeded in detaching Lavinia from her.

You must do as Lavinia asks you, my dear Daniel [I said], if
you are to remain on good terms with her. I believe that she
will, as far as possible, do what she wants. I loved her very
much once as you know, but I know that she takes the only
weapon possible for women if they are not to be destroyed by
love. She is happy to have a pleasant existence and close her
eyes to some of Barbara's importunities. I do not know the
true state of relations between them. I would imagine – and I
say this knowing it will make no difference to you – that she
will never be held long by love unless there is something else
to provide a balance on her own side. Believe me, she is not a
weak person. I think she has had much unhappiness in her life.
But be careful of Barbara Stott. Please do not come and find
yourself rejected, although you know that there is always and
always will be a place for you in my heart. Miss Stott is an
enigma. I do not think that Lavinia will want to tangle with
her and will certainly try to keep different compartments of
her life separate. For the rest, I should love to see you and perhaps I will – with Benjie and Naomi at their wedding perhaps? I care more that you should be able to write your
music. Do not let it feed on loss, my dear Daniel. I believe in
you and am always your – Meta Moore.

I was a little uneasy that I had overwritten or had made myself appear too involved. I kept the letter for a day or two in my secrétaire. How had I got myself into this tangle of emotion? Should I have denied these two occasions in my life when Love had spoken through me and invaded me? Should I have kept it all to myself? I remembered how the love burst out of me when I saw Lavinia by the Christmas tree in the Hall so long ago, and how even more powerful feelings of excitement and desire had engulfed me as I listened to Daniel Reiss's music. Would they ever have met if it had not been for me? Should I have denied movements of my body and soul together and recognized them as nothing but covers for egoism? There was no easy answer to that. Perhaps I was just carrying on in a new generation Mama's and Papa's ill-fated union.

I had plenty of time to reflect on all this, as Fanny and her sister were in bed with heavy colds over the next two or three days and I was left in the nursery to prepare lessons and read. I went up once or twice to the girls' bedroom to read aloud to them, but mostly was left to my own devices. I had not posted my letter to Daniel. Somehow it seemed as though I had signed over the death of his love for me when I wrote coolly of his other concern. Yet I could not bear not to reply; I must keep in touch with him by whatever method I could. It was not over – how could it be? I felt again that my one precipitate decision in the summer which had led to my present misery, must have arisen itself out of something 'wrong' with me. I was a rebel, that I knew, but I had not been wicked by my own lights.

I knew that it was, in a mysterious way beyond conventional standards, 'right' to have done what I did. When I thought of it in the abstract, allowing the consummation of a physical passion for a man to whom I was not and never would be married, my blood ran cold. But why was it wrong, if it were not wrong for men to do this – if not 'right' at least condoned? I saw quite clearly that people who loved too much could be victims, if they allowed themselves to be.

It was the same with religion as with love. I had told no-one and I knew no-one to whom I could unburden myself about my doubts about the truth of Christianity as it had been presented, at least to me. It was another subject beyond the pale. It was not that I did not have religious feelings, nor that I did not want to be 'good' but I disagreed as to what that 'good' was. I could not seem to stop asking myself these questions though continued introspection made me dizzy. Even young men were not permitted to question religion in public, whatever they thought in private. Most people did not concern themselves with questions like this, I knew. And if young men acted on their feelings in matters of love, even they would be censured, were they to claim that they were not 'wrong'. And who was I to question it all? I knew that if I had been a factory girl or a servant I could have given myself up to 'love' and I might have been ruined, but no one would have been surprised. People did not expect girls of that sort to have opinions. They were just slaves of nature. Was I then a slave of nature, but with just that little further spark of understanding which allowed me to rationalize my urges? No, no – I was not! And there *were* women who gave themselves up to love – I had read about them in Papa's library. And there were men who dared, from the highest motives, to question the false morality of conventional religion. I remembered my early reading of Shelley. If Shelley and Byron had finally had to flee England, what deserts were lying in wait for me? My conscience spoke up for me, but I did not want to die for it! *I* was no genius. It was absurd to compare myself with Shelley.

And yet, was it 'God' or the world which had prepared this punishment for me – that I should lose the love of Daniel? Was I just a fool who should have been scheming and cold and cleverly hypocritical if I had wanted Daniel to commit himself to me? But he could not, because of his own religious tradition. All these thoughts and worries and guilts and fears and small rebellions went round and round in my head and got me nowhere. I surprised myself by the force of my feelings. Why should young women, even if they were to be married, have to hold themselves apart and keep their virginity intact in our world? In the solitude of my bedroom I railed against that world, and asked the almighty, if He existed, why He should have made me unable to accept the acknowledged decent standards of behaviour. What if our political life, about which I knew very little, were conducted in the same way? I had never seen myself as a person with radical political interests, but I began to wonder whether, there too, I should find myself an outcast, in my own mind at least. What if I questioned why I, Meta, should have a reasonably comfortable, if hard-working life, and others less gifted live on the fat of the land – or others poorer than I slave their lives away in some terrible mill? But I could not attack everything. Perhaps one day I should be able to think it all out.

I took up my letter to Daniel yet again and added:

> I do not condemn your love, my darling, though I fight against a sad jealousy that these feelings you write of are not for me. Do take care if you return to England. Please tell me if you are to come – I would rather see you here than nowhere. I shall always love you and I shall never, could never, forget our week in Bloomsbury.
>
> Have a care of yourself for my sake. I shall be at Hartsedge Hall for the Christmas season. Perhaps if Benjie is returned also you could come over with them to see me. I promise I shall not make a scene. No one knows of our love. That love on my side is still for you, if you want it. Meta.

I posted it without reading it through again. At least he should know I was faithful to him.

By early December the children were better. Fortunately I had not caught their cold. Naomi was in and out every day. Benjie was soon to arrive in London and would come north when he had been interviewed about his duties at the Academy. They had fixed their wedding for the spring, to give Benjie time to find suitable lodgings for them in London and Mr Angerstein an opportunity to find another general factotum. We were all rather restless. The weather seemed to have reverted to a peculiar version of September – golden mornings but cold evenings. It was arranged that I should go to the Hall the week before Christmas when the Angersteins would be celebrating Hannukah and stay there till Aunt's boarders returned after the holiday.

I had had no further letter from Daniel and knew only from Naomi that Benjie had seen him in Mannheim and that he was talking of returning to England for a time, his concert engagements at the spa and in Mannheim being terminated for the present. I said nothing to Naomi about the real reasons for Daniel's not staying in Würtemburg, and I don't believe that Benjie had been told anything about them either or, if he had, he preserved silence over them to his fiancée. I was awaiting further news of him; Naomi was in a fever of impatience to see Benjie, which she tried to conceal; and all the family were preparing for the holiday and festival. It felt as though the world was holding its breath just before the winter solstice when the earth turns over and starts a New Year after the stillness and then the rush and dazzle of Christmas. I waited in a strange mood of fatalism for news from the person I loved, and tried to escape my torpor by setting the girls a lot of work to do before Rufus arrived back from his new school. Mrs Angerstein was taken up with work for some new Jewish charity and her husband seemed even more preoccupied with his business deals. We were taken to see the hotel he had bought – on a hill in the old part of the town. It was all going to be very sumptuous, and workmen were already there preparing for the opening. Harrogate seemed to be getting back to its old popularity, in spite of its being such a cold place in winter. I kept wondering if Daniel had received my last letter but some instinct told me not to write again. Perhaps he was even now in England. Or had his other offer, which Benjie had told Naomi about, kept him for the time with the Elector of Mannheim? I knew that Naomi would tell me if she heard he was back, and she had said no more.

Then, soon after our visit to the new hotel, on a day which had abandoned a false gold of summer for the crackle of frost and a sky like a goose's wing, Benjie arrived in Leeds. He was to stay with Esther Angerstein's family and come over to see Naomi at Montpelier Crescent. She could not, of course, see him at her lodging in the town! I decided not to go down, unless I was asked, on his first evening visit, for I knew that, however kind they were, I was the governess, did not share their faith and therefore should wait to be asked. I told Naomi I hoped to see him the next day and that I had some work to do in the school-room after I had seen the girls to bed. She understood and said that she was sure her aunt would be delighted for me to join their luncheon party for Benjie on the Thursday. I heard his arrival and imagined Naomi's happy face and I was glad for her. I heard too Benjie's deep baritone and the laughter and later the piano being played. He had seen Daniel not long ago – I was in the same house as someone who had seen Daniel! – was perhaps privy to his secrets. That was enough for the time being. I listened for a moment and then went to bed early where I lay sleepless, feeling wretched.

The next day they entertained Benjie and his family and

Naomi to luncheon. Naomi's own mother and father were to come up north for more celebrations and arrangements later. I felt out of it again, though naturally pleased to see Benjie. I couldn't help wondering as he shook my hand heartily and beamed his usual smile at me, what he would really think if he knew about Daniel and me. Nobody spoke of Daniel at the luncheon and I was glad. That morning I had received a short note, which was even then nestling behind my camisole against my heart, whilst Benjie was telling stories, and Naomi was sitting looking proud, and Esther was smiling, and Jacob Angerstein was for once silent. The note was from Daniel, and it was from London, and it said that he intended to come to Yorkshire! It was obviously not to see me, but to seek an interview with Lavinia. Still, nobody else seemed to know he was in London so I said nothing. However, as I was leaving to return the children upstairs, I heard Benjie say to Mr Angerstein: 'You might have your Winter Gardens man back yet. I heard today that Reiss is in London and may be tempted up north.' I did not hear the reply, for I was busy brushing crumbs from Zillah's pinafore before hastily making my exit and before anyone might see that I blushed or trembled.

I was tired of all this waiting and trembling and praying and wondering, and longed to go home and try to forget about it all. Would Daniel go to Lavinia? Surely he would wait a little. I imagined the letters which he might be sending to Lavinia and their effect on Barbara. I imagined their clandestine meetings down near the old summerhouse where we had gone – or at least I tried *not* to imagine them and told myself firmly that they would not go there in winter and that Lavinia would probably find some way of putting him off from coming in any case. I wished I had the power to invite him to the Hall, purely as a friend of the family at Harrogate, but that was not feasible. I felt like the actor in a play to whom the manager has forgotten to give the lines and she wanders vaguely across the stage trying to pick up clues from the words spoken confidently by others.

So it was with a sense of shock the next day, when I crept down to look at the post before Emma could bring it up, that I found *another* letter addressed to me. It was unmistakably in Barbara's hand. What on earth could *she* want of me? It was quite absurd. I was trembling again. I should have to take some of Mr Angerstein's waters for my nerves if a letter from Barbara

Stott could start me shaking. But it, too, was short – and initially I could not understand it. I thought at first that Daniel must have gone straight up to Rooks Nest and been rejected once more by Lavinia. Then I knew that was impossible, for Barbara's letter was of yesterday's date and Daniel's had said he would come up to Yorkshire in a few days. Barbara's letter said only this : 'You will be glad to hear that Vinny is back where she belongs. We are to entertain over Christmas, as your Aunt may have told you. This is to extend an invitation to you too, as we hear that you are to spend the Christmas holidays at the Hall. RSVP B Stott.'

Had Lavinia discovered something about Daniel and me which had in some way made her leave Mannheim ? My speculations went even further. If the latter were the case, she must have told Barbara about it. Was Lavinia trying to do me a good turn ? Unlikely surely ? It was more likely that she did not return Daniel's feelings and had had her own reasons for staying on at first in Baden. But perhaps that had fallen through too and she needed a different excuse for Barbara – perhaps that 'Meta's secret fiancé' had dallied with her and, horrified, she had returned home. Or, more likely, that she had read a letter of mine and communicated its contents to her friend, again using it as an excuse for not accepting Daniel's wooing. What an enigma it all was. And why should Barbara even wish to tell me about it ? I thought that she was being ironic, that she realized I would know about Lavinia's late return and wanted to put in her oar. And how could she know I knew about that ? Perhaps just from my aunt at the Hall, I thought it was possible. She would also know that Rainer had visited me, as news travels quickly in small villages. So perhaps – and I heaved a sigh of relief – perhaps Lavinia knew nothing at all about Daniel and me ? But it still seemed odd.

I read the note again and further unprofitable thoughts followed, but I brushed them away. If Lavinia had her eye perhaps already fixed on some other man than Daniel, then both Barbara and Daniel were going to have a hard time of it. I wondered, not for the first time, if Lavinia had ever loved *anyone*. How invulnerable it made you if you never gave your heart away ! But I remembered that she had loved her mama and had been visibly upset when she died.

I thought about the invitation. Did I want to go to the Nest to a Christmas celebration presided over by Barbara Stott? No, indeed I did not. Surely no-one could make me? But I knew that in the end I *would* go.

Great was the rejoicing every time Benjie came to visit. Naomi now allowed herself to appear 'on his arm', and they were the epitome of the happy couple. I could not help wondering as I suppose we all must wonder, what their intimate moments would be like. Curiously, although I had the most vivid memory of my nights with Daniel – too vivid – I could never think of that act with any other actors. Even to have Naomi and Benjie quietly smiling together almost savoured of voyeurism and they were the most decorous of couples. So decorous that I wondered whether Naomi even knew the facts of life, till one afternoon I inadvertently glimpsed Benjie snatch a kiss, rather ruthlessly, from her bare arm – he had rolled up her long sleeve as they stood together in an alcove under the ground floor landing. I shrank back as though I had been stung. It made me feel quite ill. I could not understand it. But that night I dreamed again of Daniel, of his real physical presence, not the Doppelgänger his letters seemed to make him, and I awoke with tears streaming down my face.

December suddenly seemed to hurry along and hasten towards Christmas. I was torn between wanting to go to the Hall and resume the old ways, if it were possible, and staying on in Harrogate where at least I need not see Barbara. Daniel had not put an address on his last letter from London, so I did not know where to write. The day before I was to leave for home, when Fanny was already beginning to get excited about their own festival, and Rufus had returned and was being unusually taciturn, I plucked up courage and asked Benjie, who was sitting in the drawing-room preparatory to instructing Zillah in harmony (she had begged for a lesson), if he had any idea whether his friend had yet come north. It took all my courage, but I knew from his face that he knew nothing of my relations with Daniel. 'His music is missed,' I said. Naomi was not in the room then as I spoke. 'I believe you said he was in London. Why does he not stay in Germany?'

'Oh, he had some offers from patrons back in Mannheim and Baden – I don't know why he didn't take one of them immediately, but he's always been one to forge his own path. If I could compose like him, so would I,' replied Benjie. 'I can't see Mr Angerstein getting him back in his Winter Gardens, though I believe he *is* to call up north before he returns to the Continent,' he went on.

I thanked him for his information and said I missed the Schubert and the Liszt – there were so few opportunities here to listen to anything of excellence. He was about to take little Zillah on his knee and as he did so I lingered for a moment and, really to say something, anything which might prolong our little conversation, went on : 'I believe you met my cousin, Rainer Moore, at one of the Bradford meetings – or was it at a subscription concert ?

'Why yes, I met Moore once or twice a year or two ago ? I didn't know he was your cousin. A most cultivated man – for a –' He stopped. I thought he was going to say 'for a Gentile' but he went on, 'Most generous too with his time, though I don't think he was always popular with the city bigwigs.'

That sounded like Rainer and I smiled. 'You and Naomi must come over when you are married – my aunt would be so pleased.'

'That is kind of you, Miss Moore.'

'Can I come too ?' asked Zillah. She had been staring intently at the pianoforte, but pricked up her ears when I mentioned a visit.

'If your papa will allow you, Zillah – one day when I've stopped teaching you.'

'You are *not* to stop teaching us,' said Zillah.

'You will perhaps have your own little school ?' interposed Benjie. 'Naomi said something of the sort.'

'Will you teach the piano ?' asked Zillah, looking up at me with those lovely dark eyes of hers which were like glowing brown topazes.

'I can't. I should have to employ a music master,' I replied.

'You could employ Mr Reiss,' said the child. 'He was going to come and teach Fanny, wasn't he, Miss Moore ? And then he went away – and he played such lovely music.'

'He did indeed,' I replied.

'I'll play it for *you,* Mr Hertz,' said the child and slid off his knee on to the piano stool which he had adjusted for her diminutive stature. Without more ado she began on Schubert's *Ständchen.* I stepped back a little and turned aside so he should not see my emotion. I waited till she had finished and Benjie gave her a kiss.

'I must go,' I said hurriedly and touched Zillah's wavy brown hair as I tried to melt out of the room.

Prior to my leaving for Christmas, I gave Emma instructions to post on any letters that might arrive for me during my absence. I took the carrier to Leeds and then changed to a train which would take me to Bradford and another to where Sam Hirst might collect me in Lightholme. Zillah had given me my 'Hannukah present' and it was in my baggage with my best dress and as many books as I could pack in for my holiday reading. I thought I had better try to occupy myself as much as possible when I was home, so that I might avoid thinking about Daniel and being anxious for him. It would all probably come to nothing and I should be left to recover my spirits when Lavinia, my old love, and Daniel, my new and so-quickly-lost love had forgotten me. My lot would be to grow up and grow old. The passions and excitements of life were now over for me. That is how I felt.

I sustained my mood all through the slow journey home. Why had I expected to be happy, expected requited love? It was not for a girl like me – I had been stupid to think it was. I had been even more stupid to throw all caution and decorum to the winds, but not in my own eyes. If I were branded in the world's eyes by sin and wickedness, that was because the 'world' saw 'irregular' love as one of the vilest and most shameful occurrences. But most passion was 'irregular', I thought. I was not going to give in and agree with the 'world' – I would fight to the end over my right to accept advances from, or give myself to whomever I pleased without becoming crushed. One day, ought I not to stand up and tell the world what I thought? Then perhaps I would be punished, but I would not regard myself as 'guilty', would defend myself to the death! Thus I asserted myself in my own eyes, but I knew that though such imagined masochism might be realistic, it was not good or right. If I had the courage of my convictions, that was enough. Why should I fight the world and its conventions? I suppose this combative spirit first helped me to put the pieces of my broken heart together by blaming the world rather than Daniel, and to that extent it was constructive. In the end I knew, though, as I looked out at the familiar towns and lanes as we jolted along, that it was destructive in the end, and that too much fighting would destroy me. Then melancholy succeeded my rebellious mood, a melancholy in which I took an almost grim pleasure. It was Daniel I had lost, not yet the world's opinion. I had thought too much of myself, been forced to it by my ability to see myself as others might see me. I was grieving not for my lost virginity, but for my lost love.

As the pony and trap turned down the road which would lead to Sholey, the snow began to fall and the whirling flakes seemed to cover even my melancholy. If only I could bury the thought of Daniel Reiss under frozen snow and inter my heart with it so that I could stop my suffering. But I could never bury Daniel, I knew that. And the snow was not yet fixed and icy, but whirling and blinding. Sam Hirst had been waiting for me and had helped me drag my boxes into the trap. 'Aye, Miss Meta – what a day for your coming back. Your aunt's right worried. See, she's put the big rug to cover your feet. Try not to get too wet. Old pony'll do his best.' We slipped and slid a little, but the snow was not yet too deep for the pony to abandon his job and we reached the Hall wet but safe.

It was a relief to worry about the weather rather than myself and Martha fussed me as though I had been driven all the way in an open cart. One or two of the boarders were still at the Hall and Aunt was busy, but not too busy to embrace me with great affection and set me by the roaring log fire with a bowl of soup. I felt safe and cosseted and even a little happy. Had I been wrong to reject the easy security of all this to follow my heart? I should be more grateful to Aunt Juby, less concerned with myself. I almost felt that I could give up everything just to be little Meta again and to enjoy Christmas, listen to all the village news and fall back once more into the warm nest of home.

All the news was retailed to me by Martha as I toasted my toes. She sat in the parlour with me – Aunt was no stickler for convention and Martha was even more 'one of us' than before, though she made a pretence of saying she couldn't sit, had too much work to do, it wasn't her place . . . but her beaming face told me she wanted nothing more than to sit and look at me and rest her feet.

'Polly and Ellen will look after the oven,' said Aunt. 'You

have a nice talk with Miss Meta whilst I give the boarders some work.'

So we sat there as the snow went on falling and Martha heard all about Fanny and Zillah and the new hotel Mr Angerstein had bought. It was so easy to make Martha happy. I hoped I would never cause her pain, or hurt my aunt who looked tired, her rheumatism lending an increasing stiffness to her tall upright figure.

'She does too much,' said Martha. 'Eh, it were cold last night – we kept a fire in your aunt's room.'

'And what about you, Martha? Are you keeping well – and your mother and sister?'

'Fairish,' was her reply. She would never admit to being tired. 'Mother's over eighty now you know and can't see none too good, but they keep going.'

'I hope the snow will stop for Christmas,' I said. 'Not go away, but just stop falling so we can go out.'

'Sam's dad says it'll stay on t'ground this time,' she replied. 'We've laid in a good stock of logs.'

'Is my cousin Rainer at home?' I asked idly, hoping that Martha would lead into a conversation about Rooks Nest. I knew she wanted to say something.

'He's coming tomorrow, he said. I think your auntie told me he'll be along for Christmas this year. I suppose you know about this "party" Miss Stott wants to have on Boxing Day?'

I said I'd heard from Barbara and been invited myself.

'I've been asked to help out with the cooking. Seems she didn't keep her last cook – I think it's a piece of cheek asking the Hall folk to a "party" and expecting them to bring their own cook.'

'Oh Martha, you mustn't do it,' I said, surprised that she hadn't dismissed the idea even more forcibly.

'Nay – I shan't. She asked me and my sister to serve too. Your aunt was right mad about it.'

'Who is to be there then, apart from Miss Logan?'

'Seems they've got one or two of Miss Stott's poor relations and struck up some acquaintances abroad. Bessy at Lodge, she says they've laid in enough for a regiment. And they've got one of them butlers now. She's stocked up a cellar of them Frenchy wines – it's not right for a lass to do that sort of thing...'

'Oh, she might as well enjoy her money, Martha,' I replied.

'Your cousin's invited, of course,' went on Martha. 'They say Miss Stott has had offers.'

'Do you mean – that somebody wants to *marry* her?' I was astounded.

'Oh aye, there's always some with an eye to the main chance. What would they want with her but her brass?'

'Well I hope she doesn't accept anybody – at least she's an independent woman. I've never liked Barbara,' I confessed to Martha, 'but I admire what she's done, I do indeed.'

'It's not the life for a young lass,' said Martha. 'Leastways she's not much older than you, Meta, but she looks a good ten years older. Eh you're not a bit changed – you could be fifteen, looking like you do now!'

So Martha saw no change in me. I knew I appeared young for my age, but felt a little annoyed that I should be assumed to look like a child. Still I supposed it was a good thing. Children couldn't have wicked love affairs, could they?

When Martha had gone, leaving me to my thoughts as the late afternoon darkened and before the lamps were lit, I moved over to the window to look at the white scene outside. The sun had set with a round, orange-red banked-up glow as the snow had stopped falling, and now there would be the long, long night before us. I heard the shouts of some children returning from their attempt to toboggan on the common fields as I turned back to the fire which glowed more warmly than the sun and cast those shadows of childhood into the room. The house was quiet now and the boarders were at their evening meal in the schoolroom. I must go and unpack and try to assemble myself ready for this holiday. As I brushed my hair, shivering in the cold bedroom for there was no fireplace in my own room, and looked at myself in Mama's old looking glass, I wondered why experience seemed to others to have cast no shade on my features. I looked changed to myself. It seemed again unfair that no one else should remark any difference. Was I to have no scars on my heart either? What if I had returned home pregnant – what would they have said then, these guardians of my childhood? I knew how lucky I had been that there was 'nothing to show' for my passionate nights with Daniel. But was it luck? Ought I not to have something to expiate? I had been foolish to run that risk which all women take when they go beyond the bounds. I would not do it again. I was not cut out to be a victim. I must take responsibility for myself. I must grow up. If only there were a way of loving without fear. What chance had any woman of finding out her true nature, hedged round as it was with fear of discovery, fear of pregnancy, fear of opinion, fear of loss? It was the loss of Daniel I thought of when I finally drew the blankets round me and tried to sleep in the familar room once more – that loss was what the conventionally minded would call my just deserts.

Next morning I got up almost reluctantly to recommence my struggle with myself. It was a beautiful morning to begin with. The snow was a glittering counterpane in the early sunlight and the drifting had made all the trees in the stone garden into monstrous blind giants. I should go out and do some errands if it were not too deep. Martha remonstrated, but I promised I would not be out long and that if the snow began again I would hurry back. I put on my thick boots and my warm cloak and a bonnet lined with fur, and crunched out to the village. There was a stillness everywhere. Harrogate would have the noises of the horses and shouting servants and the elegant shops crowded with purchasers. Here we were almost in the country; the village was isolated except for the few carts and carriages which struggled up the hill; few people were about, preferring to keep to their own hearths, having providently laid in their Christmas provisions. There were wisps of smoke even from the poorest cottages. Only the children were out in great numbers, pulling their home-made sledges behind them. There still remained a few days before Christmas Day, and then the party at the Nest the day after.

I wondered whether Barbara and Lavinia were out this morning and what they were doing and thinking. And Daniel? Would he come to find Lavinia? Could he even now be tramping down the Coach Road in search of his new love? Curiously enough this thought did not disturb me as much as I had expected. I felt there was nothing I could do. I was condemned to be a passive spectator of all this strange intrigue. Yet I should have liked to cast my eye upon Barbara without her seeing me.

The few shopkeepers I spoke to looked no different from the days when I had saved my pennies for humbugs. The old familiar place had not changed. But something *was* subtly different. It was I who had changed – I realized it as they spoke to me with less forwardness than formerly. I decided not to walk in the direction of the Coach Road. Instead I would walk along the lane behind the village shops near the road which led to Leeds. It was too far that day to go all the way to Wynteredge. I wanted to be alone. I savoured it. I had for so long had to be amongst others, Fanny and the family at Harrogate. Not since my last holiday at the Hall in the summer had I had time to walk alone and let my thoughts carry me where they willed.

The snow cast a strange light everywhere and I felt curiously happy in my melancholy. Yet I knew that one sight of Daniel would bring back all my misery. Strange that love should detract from happiness. Was I a shallow creature, a girl who would rebound up in the air like a ball thrown on the ground again and again in one of the counting games the children played?

Now I saw that the sky was thickening, that the sun was shining more weakly through the black branches of the trees and that there would probably be more snow soon. The trodden snow was a crinkly brown on the lanes from the boots that had stepped on it, and the birds were silent. It was very cold, but I found the cold exhilarating. I felt on the brink of some great discovery about myself. I wanted to create a whole out of all my conflicting emotions and began to feel another, stronger feeling which seemed to arise out of my solitude in all this peace and silence and stillness. It was the place, the familiar landscape, that seemed to be healing me. Shrouded in snow with the warmth of home always within reach, the village and the fields and lanes seemed to partake of something eternal which would be there when I had gone. What did I matter in all this except as a receptacle for a vision of beauty, the partaker of a strange light as though I were stopped for a moment and my heart was waiting – and whilst waiting knew that it would resume its beat; that life – all life – not just mine, would go on and that I would remember this moment: the farms and cold skies seen from the top of the hill and the sun fading over Wynteredge in the distance.

I did not want to dissect my feeling, a mixture of a sudden realization of beauty and peace, and a glimpse of something beyond the everyday. I knew the moment would pass, the sounds return, that I must go on and that this was just one small place which belonged to a changing world, not a world of eternity – yet it belonged to that too, through me. Even the sensation of the warm glancing shadows that would be around me when I returned that afternoon to the Hall was part of the feeling. I felt free, close to some truth, knowing that the moment would come only unbidden and that the only way to keep it was through an attempt later to describe it. It was like childhood, the feelings of everlastingness – and like the time we had gone walking on the moors two years before. Did others too feel these things? Was I then not alone?

The snow had begun to fall again – nothing stayed for ever. The fields lay divided by the black drystone walls like mourning cards. The light was changing all the time but I kept that sensation of something far beyond happiness with me even as I walked back and took up my customary life where I was expected and loved.

Later that afternoon Rainer called. I felt almost abstracted from him and from all the others, and he must have noticed I looked a little withdrawn for he said: 'You look exalted Meta – it must be the snow.'

'The snow casts such a strange light in the village,' I replied. 'I went for a walk and it was beautiful.' He looked at me and said nothing. Aunt came in and asked me to toast some tea-cakes and we let the curtains remain undrawn as the light became darkness and the snow fell again, though not heavily.

I was thinking as I burned the half of my face that was turned to the fire, that if Daniel were here I should be able to share some of my morning feelings. Then I thought, no – these feelings are private. We can't share even our best moments because we can't see into other people's minds. That made me feel lonely again.

Rainer didn't seem to notice my introspection, and then Aunt came in and the talk turned once more to Rooks Nest. 'We're to go over for the whole day – luncheon at one and then an afternoon and early evening looking at the improvements.'

'At least the snow will cover all Barbara's *garden* improvements,' said Rainer. 'I saw some of them when I went over with a message from Widdop last week. I never told you Meta, Barbara had written for some papers of her father's and as I was at his office Widdop asked me if I would drop them in. There was some difficulty with the Mail. Anyway I did so and they were in the new drawing room. Then Barbara took me into her "office" and asked me if I thought Miss Logan was looking well. I couldn't see what she was driving at. I thought Miss Logan looked remarkably well. It was she herself who seemed a little ill, I thought.'

'Oh, she's as strong as a horse,' I said.

'Well, she did look a little under the weather. I believe she has worries over her stocks and Widdop isn't too efficient. She told me she was going to employ the services of another solicitor in Leeds.'

'Perhaps she's writing her will?' I suggested maliciously.

'Oh, I don't think she's going into a decline, Meta. She just looked rather feverish.'

'It's so long since I saw her I shall be quite interested to see how wealth has affected her,' I said. 'And Miss Logan?'

'Oh, there's something brewing there all right, though I can't put my finger on it exactly.'

'We mustn't gossip like this!' said Aunt. 'I hear they are to have quite a few visitors.'

'Yes, I took several letters to the post for them, though I don't know why they couldn't have entrusted them to their servants.'

I was sure Lavinia was writing to Daniel, but I could hardly ask my cousin to whom her letters were addressed. The talk changed to Christmas and the boarders' celebration which I had missed.

It was peaceful after Rainer had gone. I sat by the fire and read while Aunt knitted, an accomplishment she had used to be proud of, but which her increasing rheumatism made difficult – which in turn only made her determined to go on with it.

The two remaining girls were to stay with us over Christmas. They were only eleven or twelve years old and I thought they must be feeling homesick, so the next day I took them under my wing and we had a pleasant day while Aunt rested. Later we went to the kitchen to see the Christmas puddings which had been made months earlier and now brought out of Martha's store cupboard. It was all so peaceful and ordinary I wished it would go on for ever and that I could return to Harrogate without having to see Barbara and Lavinia.

Christmas Day itself was bright and cold and the snow still lay on the paths and walls and seemed to have no intention either of disappearing or of adding to itself. The little girls were as excited as I had been at their age when I unpacked the stocking that Martha had prepared for me with its tangerine and sixpence at the bottom. I remembered the feeling – a little like that feeling I had had in the snow. Perhaps I was just getting old and only nostalgia now could penetrate my heart?

Rainer was to take us in his carriage to Rooks Nest on Boxing Day. We got up early and I dressed carefully, putting on the new chain which Aunt had given me the day before. It had been Mama's and was beautiful. Aunt had intended to give it me on my next birthday, but had thought I ought to have something to adorn me when we visited Barbara, so had given it to me for Christmas. I was most touched and kept looking at it in its box before I dared to put it on. I felt it meant that Aunt saw me now as a grown-up person. And with this came the thought that Mama was only four years older than I was now when she gave birth to me. For over twenty years the chain had lain in Aunt's drawer as I grew up and went away – and here I was back, and the chain had found me. The strange power of inanimate objects. How often had Mama fingered this silver chain with its pendant amethyst? Perhaps Papa had put it round her neck for her? 'Your papa gave it to your mother,' Aunt Juby had said on Christmas Day. 'There is a ring for you on your birthday,' she had added.

Oh Mama, Mama, I thought, as we were slowly drawn through the snow in Rainer's carriage at noon on Boxing Day morning. The chain is going home, I thought. I was thinking of the dream I had had that very night. I had forgotten it till the moment the carriage turned down the Turnpike Road, rutted with sepia snow, and entered the grounds of Rooks Nest, by the 'correct' entrance. It had been again that soundless collapse of the house reflected in the water and the falling stones gliding by me. I shivered and drew my cloak round me. I hoped I was going to make a good impression in my new dress. Aunt and Martha had had it made by Martha's sister for me as a surprise, and to me it seemed more beautiful than any confection from a London dressmaker. It was in yellow silk with great gathers and ruches and although not a crinoline in the sense of having a wooden hoop it had three stiff petticoats which held out the silk, a sort of watery material that changed in the light. I had never had such a beautiful dress in my life and felt like a princess. I had protested to Aunt that it had cost too much, but she told me the stuff had been lying there in her chests for years and that Martha had come upon it and insisted that her sister worked it. They had taken my measurements in the summer from my blue day dress, and so I had had no idea of their plan. I had a muff given me by Rainer and a new pair of glacé-kid boots. All in all I felt unrecognizable; it was the first time I had felt transformed by clothes, for previously they had bored me. Martha was *not* helping out at Barbara's that morning; she had volunteered to stay at the Hall with the two boarders so that Aunt could enjoy herself at this great grand 'do'.

As the carriage came round the sweep of the drive to the side of the mansion near the stables, I could see that there were indeed changes. In the summer I had not noticed the new stabling nor the paving which now continued from the front of the house to the side. The gardens were humped under snow. I wondered whether the lake was frozen. 'Not too bad,' said Rainer, as he helped me down. He was referring to the journey.

'I hope it doesn't start to snow again,' I said, having no wish to find myself snowed in with Barbara.

'Oh, John will take us back at dusk – fortunately we're not invited for dinner,' he answered with a smile and then went to help my aunt who found getting in and out of carriages a painfully slow business.

There was a big door at the side of the house before you came to the glasshouses, a door I did not remember seeing before – but of course all those years ago Barbara and I had gone across the paving stones to Lavinia's mother's 'Pavilion'. 'Oh, they've opened the west door,' murmured Aunt Juby. I suppose she was remembering it as it had used to be in my parents' time. I turned back to look at the garden as we went in. Where was the old summerhouse? I supposed it was too far away on the path to the lake to see from there. I pushed away my memories of that summer day with Daniel. Oh, it seemed so long ago – and yet it was only five months! 'Look, Meta,' cried Aunt as we were just about to enter the loggia where a servant was waiting to remove the guests' galoshes. 'Look, Meta – isn't that pretty?'

I followed her gaze. At the corner of one of the wings a fir tree had been planted in a large tub on the terrace and someone had fixed little candles on it. It was covered in snow of course, but stars and gold baubles were peeping out from the branches. The candles were not lit – they would soon have been extinguished in the wind – but it looked very beautiful. 'Perhaps they'll try to light the candles in the dark – it must be Lavinia's idea,' I said.

We went in and were led up a staircase to a large dressing room at the end of the house where we might disrobe and pay the necessary attention to our hair and face and garments. Rainer had disappeared to another room. There was no sign yet of the owner of the house or of Lavinia.

'Will you please follow me down to the drawing room,' said a maid in black with ringleted hair and an un-Yorkshire voice. 'When you are ready, Madam and Miss.'

The dressing-room walls were covered in dark red damask and there were old chairs and tables and a new-fangled fireplace and several sofas, with some large vases placed at strategic intervals containing artificial bulrushes. It reminded me a little of Westminster Square. I followed Aunt Juby down, noticing how painfully she negotiated the stairs. We might have been in a ducal palace for all the formality in evidence. I heard the sound of voices coming from behind an oaken door covered in scrolls and panels. I gave a final pat to my hair, saw myself in the reflection of a long cheval glass placed on the landing and tried to glide towards the door, holding Aunt's arm. The door was opened by a manservant and I saw through to a long salon where, in front of a log fire which blazed in a large hearth at one end, several ladies and gentlemen were gathered, exchanging occasional remarks and holding shallow glasses of champagne. The chairs were upholstered in dark-red velvet and the thick curtains were of red velvet too, and when a figure detached itself from the group and advanced to welcome us it was dressed in red velvet of the same shade. It was Barbara Stott, the chatelaine of all this glory. I was dazzled by the colour of the furniture and the red flames of the fire and Barbara's dress, like blood against the long snowy windows.

'So pleased you could come,' she said in her queer abrupt voice. 'You were right to come early, Mrs Jewesbury.' She gave a polite bow to Aunt and then turned to me. I felt I ought to shake her hand but Barbara had no intention of doing so; instead she smiled in that secret way she had and then assumed a more formal address with a stiff little shake of her head. I murmured: 'I am glad to see you looking so well, Barbara.' It was not true. She looked rather pasty-faced but with two bright spots of colour high on her cheekbones. A lady and gentleman came up then to be introduced to her and Barbara looked extremely gracious with the air of one born to absolute monarchy. I accepted a glass of champagne and then looked round for Lavinia Logan. The drink was delicious. It matched everything in the room which had obviously been chosen because it was either expensive or 'in the best taste'.

As Barbara passed by me to greet some other newcomers, she murmured: 'Vinny will be down in a moment', as though we were fellow conspirators. Barbara was enjoying herself, no mistake, yet she also had an air of anxiety which she could not conceal from me. The luncheon party had been planned to impress my aunt and myself I was sure. I did not know whether the other guests were there also to be impressed. There was a posse of Stott cousins; no one from her mother's side of the family, but one or two men of the sort one meets at such events in Yorkshire and who turn out to be 'in trade', shortly afterwards to retire to Morecambe. I missed something – and realized I was looking for an older man, a father or a husband, someone who would command the butler and order the servants around. Was I so conventional that I could not accept that Barbara was the man of this house? There *was* an uncle it turned out later, and a silk merchant from Bradford – not a Jewish one! Before she stumped away – she had not altered her deportment – I said: 'It is very fine, Barbara,' to please her, and because in its way it was. Then I saw Rainer talking with every appearance of interest to a young lady in blue – someone they had met in Paris I believe. I saw that Aunt had somewhere comfortable to sit near the fire and she was soon in conversation with the village doctor who, along with the rector, had been invited to the pre-luncheon events.

'Luncheon will be served in the South Dining Room,' said a voice, and I turned and there was Lavinia at my side. She had glided up and was looking resplendent in her jade green trimmed with frills and lace and with a great comb in her hair and earrings of chased silver dropping from those shell-like ears like waterfalls. So this was the woman my Daniel now loved. It was an odd feeling.

'We are surely not to eat yet?' was all I found to say, knowing that 'luncheon' here was usually at one. Barbara would know all the right things to do.

'No, no – I thought you might like to know – do you remember the Pavilion where Mama and I used to be?' she added. I was

292

surprised, not thinking she would wish to refer to her humble past. She was still beautiful – I had to admit it once more. I almost asked after Daniel with the rashness induced by a glass or two of champagne, but by that time she had moved on to speak to the Stott tribe and to be the recipient of many admiring glances from the men.

Somehow the place itself did not feel like my Rooks Nest. Yet it was all very sumptuous. I felt curious to see the other rooms, for the walls of this 'salon' had been repainted in white and gold and even the heavy curtains and furniture could not detract from its impressive grandeur. When I was younger I had never taken much notice of the exact proportions of the house of my birth, being too occupied with looking at Lavinia and the gardens. It was the feel of the place that had enchanted me, not the details of its interior. But Barbara, as usual, had had the wit to see what could be done with it. It was a success. Yet I did not like it. In spite of the grandeur and the champagne and the obsequious servants, I did not like it. Surely Mama and Papa had not lived in this way. Aunt answered my thoughts as she came up on the rector's arm, feeling she must make one round of the room before regaining a welcome chair. Apart from myself and, I supposed, Barbara and one or two others, most of the guests were middle-aged or elderly, I realized. Were there no young men in Lightholme?

'Your parents never opened up this room,' Aunt was saying. 'They used to eat and entertain in the little room behind. It *is* rather grand, isn't it?'

'Very,' I replied.

'And I hear there is to be a surprise after the luncheon,' Aunt went on.

Just then a general tendency to move away from the fireplace was made manifest and I realized that we were about to partake of luncheon. By some curious osmosis the guests were sorting themselves out and moving into the large room adjoining, through a connecting door which I had not seen at first. The Persian carpets of the two rooms were identical and this next room was even larger than the drawing room. Down its whole length was a great table covered in snowy white linen with sparkling crystal and épergnes full of hothouse flowers. The cutlery was silver and a few straggling sunbeams disported themselves over the cut glass and in and among the silver drops of two large chandeliers. We were in all about twenty people who were invited to the luncheon. The doctor and the rector seemed to have melted away. The great casement windows looked out on to the terrace and I saw the fir tree standing close to them on the paved flags.

Almost every possible refinement of luxury was on that table. The women were each given a spray of orchids; the wines were delicious and there were fine cigars later for the men. The food was perhaps not quite so good. (I learned later that a chef had been engaged for a week by Barbara from the new Station Hotel in Bradford.) We had trout, then goose, each dish with its wine, and many side dishes, and mounds of cheeses, fruit and ices, as well as Christmas pudding. Rainer was sitting on my right. On my left was a nondescript Stott cousin who was silent throughout the meal. Towards the end of the long repast I said to Rainer: 'Where will they have the "surprise"?'

'Oh, I believe as dusk falls they will open up other rooms. I hear there is to be music. We shan't have time to see all the improvements if we have to sing carols.' So we were to have a 'traditional' Christmas treat. Had Barbara remembered that Christmas at the Hall when we sang 'Silent Night'?

'I hope she knows how *grateful* we are. Really it is a very fine party, isn't it? I don't suppose Lightholme has ever seen its like.'

'Barbara knows how to impress,' he replied.

'Well I must say she *has* impressed me – it needs a good deal of energy to plan a gathering like this.'

'But she does not look happy on the day of her triumph, does she?' murmured my cousin quietly.

'She should have been a military commander,' I said. 'I should hate to have to supervise a house like this, even with all the money in the world.'

'You are not a social climber,' was my cousin's answer.

I could not see that Barbara had achieved any great distinction among her guests. My cousin was by far the most interesting gentleman present. There was the German manufacturer of silk, a Mr Meinertzhagen, one of her deceased papa's friends I supposed, and one minor baronet knighted for his services in providing blankets in our most recent war, in the Crimea. But there was no one half so interesting or talented as those people who came to the Angersteins', always excepting my cousin.

Toasts were drunk at the end of the meal. The baronet proposed a toast to the two lovely ladies of the house and the manufacturer toasted Rooks Nest – 'which our hostess has brought to life again'. I felt a shiver of distaste go through me.

The afternoon drew on and we withdrew to another sitting room, the furnishings and decorations this time in a dark gold and brown colour, with leather sofas and a roaring fire. We all lolled around as the two menservants carried round nuts and coffee and brandy. (I had the feeling that they had *all* been taken on just for a few days.) All this time I had had no further conversation with Barbara or Lavinia, but plenty of opportunity to observe them. Barbara seemed anxious about her friend, continually proffering sweetmeats or stealing covert glances at her. Lavinia did not seem to have a great deal to say. Then Barbara went out and shortly returned to announce that the music room was prepared and we should take our coffee there. I wished I could clear my head with a walk in the garden, but it was too cold. The claret had not exactly given me a headache, but made me feel strangely distant. How I wished I were at home with my books and a cup of tea. But for the moment I decided to creep away for a moment to press a little rice powder on my nose and arrange my hair and dress. I stole out and up the stairs before anyone could stop me.

There seemed to be some constraint surrounding Barbara and Lavinia and I thought I understood exactly why. I knew a little of what Barbara must have been feeling during these last few months. Still, Lavinia *had* returned. The sumptuous house contrasted greatly with the atmosphere in it. None of these people was saying what was in his or her mind – that was it. I knew I was not. It was an elaborate charade to show off Barbara's possessions, including Lavinia who hardly looked at her. The guests, apart from her cousins, did not seem close to either of them. I looked across the snowy expanses of the terraces and lawns when I had finished my toilette; the light was going and there was a moon in the west above the farthest elms although it was only about half past three. No one had lit the candles yet on Lavinia's tree. I was determined to go down and speak to Lavinia, so long as my cousin and aunt were not likely to hear me. Oh, how I should like to walk out of the long windows below, out over the snow to the lake. Whatever was going on here was not to my taste.

When I returned they were all filing into the music room. Lavinia was by herself at the drawing-room window. All evidence of the party had disappeared, cleared away by the ubiquitous, but silent servants. I approached her and asked: 'Are you not coming to the music room, Miss Logan? Are we going to sing carols – and when will you light the candles on your tree?'

She turned quickly and looked at me closely in a way I remembered from long ago. 'Do you think, Meta, that I engineered any of this?' she said. I thought she meant the jollifications in this house that might once have been mine, but she did not, for when I said 'I wouldn't want to live here *now* – ' she interrupted me. 'Not that,' she said hurriedly. 'You will see.' And swept away with that distant look she used to have when I made a bad translation from the German.

I was puzzled until I joined Rainer and my aunt in the music room, for there sitting on a stool before a grand piano at the far end of the room, was Daniel Reiss.

Seven

ROOKS NEST

Everything and everybody around the figure of Daniel, my Daniel, my lover Daniel, was at first a blur of noise and shadows. He had not seen me come in at the back of the high-ceilinged room, but his face was upturned and pitched at an angle as though he were looking for someone. The candle brackets on the piano cast half his face into darkness but I saw the soft wave of that hair I had so often caressed and I saw the beaky nose in the gloom and I saw the high white cravat shining in the darkness, that cravat I had so often loosened! Stop it! Oh stop it! I wanted to scream to my imagination. Don't remember, don't remember! *This* must be a dream; only the other was real, the other Daniel who lay by my side in summer. I stood at the back of the room scarcely aware of the others who were pressing in behind me and then I must have moved automatically aside. Barbara was now at the front of the room near the piano speaking to Daniel, but he was not listening to her. She seemed to be leaning away from him with a sort of guarded passivity. I could see from the way she was standing that she was holding herself back; some great emotion was being held on leash. My conscious thought even then as I stared at him was, why had she invited him, why on earth? Then I found myself shaking uncontrollably as the waves of my first shock receded. I must take a hold of myself and find some distraction. I must try to pretend I felt nothing, when all I wanted was to rush to him and throw myself in his arms and bear him away from the house, away over the snow, back to summer, back to happiness.

The guests were sitting on little spindly gold chairs set in rows. There was my aunt and there was Rainer, chatting quietly to each other and looking out for me. Lavinia was just behind me and heard my sudden gasp, but she took no further notice of me nor of Daniel and went to sit next to the baronet. Then the man who had turned out to be Barbara's uncle, a short thick-set, elderly gentleman whom one would hardly notice, was saying that we were lucky to have today the renowned musician who had been such a success in Harrogate and Baden to play for us before the fireworks were let off on the terrace. Fireworks! This was the first I had heard of any fireworks. *That* must be the 'surprise'. I went to sit down next to my aunt. She bent over to me and said: 'Did you hear this young man in Harrogate then, dear?' Rainer was looking at me with a neutral expression. Had Daniel seen me?

I summoned all my reserves of strength and replied: 'Indeed. He is a wonderful pianist and a friend of the Angersteins. I did not know he was to come here to play for Barbara.' What was Barbara plotting? Surely she would not throw together her beloved Lavinia and the man whom she knew to be in love with her. Had Daniel plotted himself for this? If so, he could surely not have known that I too was to be there.

There was some perfunctory clapping and the sound of clinking coffee cups. He would be used to that at least! I noticed that many of the guests looked rather the worse for wear and was glad I had been to arrange myself. I must not let Rainer see how deeply affected I was by Daniel. I hoped he would put it down to the effect of the music if my voice appeared wobbly. Oh, what a torment it was, a renewed torment to see him there – that beloved man who had held me in his arms, and was nothing to me as far as anyone else knew. But I realized that Lavinia must have known something about me or she would not have said what she did. Barbara went and sat down next to her friend and the room became quiet. The gas candelabra had been lit. I could almost imagine I was back at the Winter Gardens in those happy days a year ago.

When he began to play I looked away and the strain of Liszt's Consolations stole round my ears. The music was too much to bear. I wanted to cry. I *must* speak to him – perhaps I should never see him again, if Lavinia returned his love. But Lavinia was looking away with an expression of slight boredom on her beautiful face. Barbara was looking at him though and her expression was not pleasant. Who had invited him? After the Liszt he played a light piece of Mendelssohn's Christmas music and then rose and bowed. He was looking thinner than in the summer, but just as handsome. I had been concentrating so much on not betraying my feelings that I had unconsciously dug quite deeply into my arm with the nail of my right hand. Oh let them all get up and go. Let me not be asked once more if I knew him! Rainer turned to me as Daniel bowed again before disappearing. There were a few feeble requests for an encore, but these people were not music lovers and would have been just as pleased if he had played some medley of sentimental songs.

Aunt though was delighted and expressed her delight to my cousin. 'Better than carols, after all Christmas *is* over. I wonder we heard nothing of this young man before. Do you know him then, Meta, if he is a friend of the Angersteins?'

'Oh, yes, Aunt,' I replied quickly. 'He is a friend of Naomi's fiancé Benjie – he often played at the Gardens. Cousin Rainer heard him, didn't you, Cousin?'

'I did indeed,' replied Rainer. 'A most remarkable sensibility. I wonder how Barbara got hold of him.'

'Oh, I believe he often plays in private homes,' I replied.

We were now all to go out on the terrace to see the fireworks which the butler was to set off.

'We really must go soon,' said Aunt Juby. 'I wonder if Sam has yet come for us. I expect it will be hard going in the snow and I shouldn't want to put him to any trouble.'

'No. You are to return in my carriage,' said Rainer. 'I told Sam to take the rest of the day off.'

'Then you must stay with us, Rainer. I wouldn't dream of having you go off again. There's a bed for you at the Hall.' Rainer agreed and they moved away together, chatting. Aunt said she would watch the fireworks from the windows. Cloaks were brought in and the rest of us went on to the terrace.

I walked out of the long French window to join the others. The girl in blue from Paris was gushing over the music to the silk manufacturer. Barbara was nowhere to be seen. Lavinia was surrounded by the rest of the guests. I took my chance and went back through another door to look for Daniel. What did I care for fireworks? Where could he have gone? Then I remembered his habit of scrubbing his nails after he had played. He took great care of his hands. But I could hardly look for him in a bathroom. I was sure he had not seen me in the audience as our group had been sitting at the back of the music room. I knew Rainer had deposited his cloak in some ante-room where there was probably a washstand so I went in search of it and waited in a dark corridor behind the long inner corridor from where all the rooms went off in the centre of the house.

How could he have come here to this house, knowing it was where he had been with me? He must be – besotted, was the word – with Lavinia. The way *I* had felt about *him* – and about her too once upon a time.

I did not have long to wait. I was trembling so much I tried to take deep breaths to calm myself and prayed Barbara was not about. My legs felt like jelly and my heart was jumping like a crackerjack. Daniel came out from the further room – I saw his silhouette in the shadow cast by the light from a little lamp on a bracket. Then he came into the main corridor. It reminded me of the Winter Gardens and our first meeting. I stepped forward and he nearly collided with me.

'You – Meta!' he cried.

I said, 'Daniel,' softly, holding on to the wall with one hand. 'You said you might come north.' I half-gasped, half-whispered. '*I* came to Barbara's party, that's all.'

'We must talk,' he said. 'Where can we go?' He took my arm and his touch sent shivers down my spine.

I looked into his dark eyes. 'They're all watching the fireworks. I have to go home soon. We could go to that room in the Pavilion if you like – at the end – I know the way.' Something lent me the courage to move away and he followed me down the long corridor to the old quarters where Lavinia's mother had lived. It was where we had looked in that summer day, but there was no light, only the moon now. I stood there in the darkness with him praying that Rainer and my aunt should think me out watching the fireworks. I could hear the sizzle and plop of a rocket as it swooped and flowered, and as I looked out of the un-curtained window I saw a hundred green stars softly dissolve against the trees.

'She spares no expense,' he said.

'Daniel, do you love Lavinia?'

He took my hand which was cold as ice and drew me to him. 'Yes, Meta – but she does not love me.'

'Did you tell her – about us?' I asked hoarsely.

'A little.'

'And Barbara Stott – does she know?'

'Barbara has probably been told everything,' he said. 'She's got her back – that's all.'

'And Lavinia, did *she* invite you here?'

'Oh no. That was Barbara – to show me that I had no hold over her friend.'

To what machinations did Barbara not stoop? She must not only crow over me and over Aunt but show Daniel too that she would keep Lavinia. 'Then why did you come?'

'To see Lavinia,' he replied simply. 'She would not see me in Leeds – and then Miss Stott wrote to me knowing I was in the north. I got the letter only on Christmas Eve – and I thought, why not? I didn't know *you* would be here. Your letters were so kind, Meta. I have been almost distracted.'

'You really love her!' I said.

'Forgive me.'

'Then I know *you* suffer, Daniel,' I cried.

He held my hand. 'I read your letters over and over,' he said. 'I was going to wait and see you at the Angersteins'. I have been so busy in spite of it all – I've written the best stuff I've ever done.'

'Did you realize when you were coming to Rooks Nest that it was where we were in the summer? Oh, Daniel.' I could not help sounding reproachful. How I loved him, even though I knew in my bones there was no hope for me.

'Meta, it doesn't cancel out anything we did or felt, but I – I – can't stop thinking about Lavinia. She's cast a spell over me I think.'

I thought of the spell that I believed we had cast over each other, Daniel and I, and was silent.

I wanted to say 'Did you love her the way you loved me?' but I could not. It seemed a greater betrayal that he had come to the Nest just to see her. 'If she loved *you* like that, you would not love her,' I said.

'No, perhaps not – we can't choose, can we?'

Now I saw it the other way round, so to speak. I was confounded.

'Daniel,' I whispered, 'perhaps we *can* go on . . . knowing each other? But be careful of Barbara. If she thought there was any danger of Lavinia going away with you again, I don't know what she would do – to you. She is a strange girl. I've known her for years and I've never understood her – but she likes power over others.'

'How can I have anything to fear from her when she knows Lavinia will not have me?' he replied.

'She may not be sure, dearest,' I said, and flinched at my own words. Of course I was jealous but I knew there was no need to be ashamed of it. It was I who had been badly treated in all this – through my own fault. 'I must go now. Are you staying here?'

'Yes. I am to meet a friend of Vinny's – someone from Bradford tomorrow. They are to have a house-party.'

'Daniel,' I said. 'Go *now*, go away and don't come back! Don't meddle in the lives of these women!' He made no answer. I knew it was useless my asking him. I said: 'Kiss me, Daniel!'

He was moved, I think, for in answer he held me close and kissed my forehead as though I were a child. 'You will marry someone who loves you, Meta,' he said and then he kissed my hand and was gone. I gathered myself together and crept back to the main corridor. The fireworks were just finishing when I returned. I leaned against a pillar on the terrace. Daniel had disappeared. I thought Barbara looked rather closely at me when the light from a golden fountain lit us all up, but it may have been my imagination. Lavinia was standing on the flagstones near her little Christmas tree whose candles had been lit, but were outshone by the fireworks. She looked beautiful and remote. I paused for a moment, but I had nothing to say to her. I went in to find my aunt who was still sitting in the drawing-room with a few others.

'Was it good from the terrace?' she asked.

'Oh, very fine,' I replied. I seemed to have a hollow where my heart should be. If he would have had me I would still have followed Daniel Reiss across the world, and I wished I had done so in the summer. I felt my life was over.

Rainer's carriage was waiting for us in the stableyard and we took our farewells of Barbara Stott. Those of her other guests who were staying on were having cold supper set for them. Neither Daniel nor Lavinia was in evidence as we waved our final greetings to our hostess. Barbara looked pinched and worn as though all the cares of the world were upon her, not as though she had successfully performed her duties as hostess which we agreed, as once more the carriage pulled us home, had been well conceived and carried out, though there had been no walk round the rooms and no carols.

The night was dark and still and the ruts in the Turnpike a problem for the coachman, but we arrived at the Hall about three quarters of an hour later and I was glad to fall into bed at last. Rainer was given the room under mine that had been Frances Green's in the old days.

I could not sleep at first but lay reliving my conversation with Daniel and weeping softly from time to time. Finally, about four o'clock I must have fallen asleep, because I woke with a start.

The dawn light was not yet coming through my window and I lay wondering why I had awoken. Then I heard a knock at my door and Rainer's voice. 'Meta, Meta, will you get up – there is something not right over at the Nest!' I jumped out of bed, threw my warm dressing-robe around me, and opened the door. Rainer was standing there fully dressed and looking as though he had not been to bed at all.

'What is it? What did you say?'

'I was up reading when Sam Hirst came knocking at the door,' he whispered.

'Sam Hirst?' I echoed stupidly. 'But what did he want? It's not yet dawn.'

'Hush, he's gone now. He was up early for the milking and he says he saw a glow in the sky over by Rooks Nest.' He paused, weighing his words. A cold serpent of fear seemed to worm into my vitals.

I was no longer half asleep. 'What shall we do?' I asked. 'What is it all about, Rainer?'

'A fire,' he answered briefly. 'I shall harness the pony and trap and go to see.'

'Then I shall go with you,' I replied. 'It won't take me a moment to dress.'

'I'll leave a note for Augusta,' he said. 'It's a good thing Martha's deaf. Hurry now. Hurry!'

I was filled with foreboding and could hardly drag on my clothes, but as it was so cold I had gone to bed in my chemise and old petticoat under my night attire and that helped me to be quick though my fingers were numb and trembling.

The cold was deathly when I stepped out of the back porch. Rainer was waiting beyond the gate, already in the pony and trap. I trudged across the snow in my old boots and he helped me up into the cart. He took the reins and then we rounded out into the lane over the crisp snow, the pony picking his way carefully.

'What do you know about them all at the Nest?' he asked as we went slowly along.

I did not know how to reply. How could I tell him suddenly in the middle of the night that I was in love with a man who was in love with Lavinia Logan? As I fumbled for words he turned the corner by the lane that led up to Sholey and we went on towards the village and in the direction of Rooks Nest. As I looked about me, I did see a strange glow in the sky, beyond the trees. It was not yet dawn and a few stars were still out. Rainer tightened his hands round the reins.

'*I* don't know what it's all about, Meta, but I know you have to go through with it,' he said. I remembered these strange words later. Was it that I was needed to save someone's life? Who was in danger? I kept praying: 'Daniel, Daniel – let him be safe.'

It was a strange, urgently slow ride along the very lanes we had traversed only nine hours earlier. 'I am sorry. I am a lot of trouble to you, Cousin,' I said. I don't know why I said it. I had not caused any fire.

'Someone has to take care of you,' he replied.

'Rainer, I am frightened of something terrible,' I said quietly.

'Yes,' he said. 'It was in the air all through yesterday, wasn't it?'

I had not thought he had noticed and was surprised. All I dared say was: 'I think it may have been something to do with Daniel Reiss.'

'Ah – Daniel Reiss,' he said and then fell silent.

As we came up to the Turnpike Road and turned down to the Lodge, we saw some activity there. Carts were drawn up at the lodge gates and as we turned in, the glow in the sky over the dark trees became ruddier.

'Wait a moment,' said Rainer and reined in the pony as he spotted Bessy Taylor at the lodge door in a nightcap and a strange grey gown. I began to think that we were all in some theatrical production and that I should wake up in a minute. But it was all really happening.

'Has anyone come up from the house?' shouted Rainer.

'No, sir – only them two earlier like in the carriage. It hasn't come back. I sent my Jim to ride over to the militia and the fire-cart – they've got it down by the lake now, they say, but it's frozen over.'

'*Who* went in the carriage, Bessy?' I shouted.

'Only that Miss Logan and a gentleman,' she shouted back.

We did not wait to hear more but set off down the winding drive, now under several inches of snow, and drove under the parapet that carried the Coach Road slung over it. Lavinia and Daniel, I thought with relief – at least they were safe. He had persuaded her to go away with him. Suddenly, as we came round the final curve of the drive, what we saw would have stopped us in our tracks, but the pony went on picking his way. The far side of Rooks Nest was all on fire – it looked as though it had been burning for hours and as we came into the yard at the back, flames were at the front licking at the Pavilion. A man shouted: 'Over there! Keep clear!' Rainer jumped down and led the pony into the safety of some trees at the side furthest from the flames. Running figures were lit up by the glow, as were those standing in huddled groups. 'Get them all to the Lodge,' a man was shouting. It looked like the constable from Lightholme. A woman came up to us. It was the girl in blue from Paris – it seemed an age since we had sat opposite her at the luncheon.

'All our things are in the house – except for the clothes we stand up in,' she complained. 'The fire is only on the other side – can't we go back for them?'

A man approached, one of the Stott cousins, I believe. 'They're frightened it will spread because of the floors,' he explained, and I remembered the grainy wood of the corridor floors. But where was Barbara? We went round to the front lawn. It was like a scene from Dante's *Inferno* – leaping flames, completely enveloping the far wing now and Lavinia's little pavilion, and some firemen with their cart and panniers trudging towards it with buckets filled from the kitchens. 'Lake's frozen,' said another man. 'And their hoses aren't long enough.'

'Rainer, we must find Barbara!' I cried.

'Wait,' said Rainer and went up to the man who seemed to be directing operations. Several other people followed Rainer, as he looked purposeful. Other guests were wringing their hands. I had never seen anyone do this before. I saw on the terrace Lavinia's Christmas tree, fallen now and singed brown.

'They're assembling two carriages at the back,' a woman said, coming up to us. 'Now perhaps we shall be able to go to the inn and finish our night's sleep.'

'Where is Miss Stott?' I asked her.

'We can't find her – '

'Is everyone out of the house then?' I asked. Thank God Daniel is with Lavinia, I kept thinking. But – my lovely house, all burning, burning!

'No one knows – there were so many of us. That man over there is going to call a roll, he says, but we didn't all know each other so we don't know who is here.'

I saw that there were several people who had not been at the luncheon the day before. 'Have you seen Miss Stott?' I asked another woman.

She shook her head.

I asked another man the same question, the uncle, I think, though I hardly recognized him in his Turkish dressing-gown.

'No, nor that Miss Logan either. They can't still be in the house.'

'Where was Lavinia sleeping?' I turned and asked the blue girl.

'In the part where it's burning – but they say she went to call the alarm. We can't find Mr Meinerzthagen or Miss Stott either.'

Just then, as Rainer came back, I saw servants rushing out of the west door carrying silver and a chair I remembered from the crimson room and some ferns and then some menservants with a rolled-up carpet. All these things were dumped unceremoniously near the stables, and they went back in for more.

'They must think the fire will spread, then?' I asked Rainer as he came up.

'Meta, they think Barbara might still be in the house – '

'Oh no! Rainer – ?'

'Meta, where would Barbara go? If she wanted to run away?'

'Run away?' I said stupidly.

'Yes – where would she go?'

I looked at him carefully, but his face was impassive, lit by the eerie glow of the fire.

'They say the rest will collapse and they might not be able to save the wing either.'

'*I* know,' I said suddenly.

'Meta, don't go near the house,' he cried, as he saw me turn.

'No – I'll find her for you – away from the house,' I cried, and as the constable was making his way to Rainer, whom he knew and obviously wanted to consult, I darted back into the shadow of the trees. I could see the faint break of dawn in the grey sky away from the house and I knew – yes, I knew where Barbara would be – and I thought I knew why.

Rainer had turned towards the policeman and I took the chance and ran across the newly paved garden, slipping and slithering on the snow. Then I turned and ran across the wide, wide lawns towards the lake. No one saw me go. It was as though I had had a message and must go to an assignation. When I got to the bottom of the lawn, I looked back for a moment and saw the top of the mansion's pediment crash down as great tongues of flame leapt up to engulf it. The air, even in the garden, was thick with smoke. I turned at the bottom and saw the dawn, weak and pale, slide into the sky as though a water colourist had mixed the faintest white into grey. *I knew where Barbara would be.*

I knew it would soon all be over and that my nightmare was coming true. The summerhouse at the end of the lake would tell me whether I was right or not. Thank God Lavinia had escaped, even if she had taken my love with her. I stopped running and began to walk slowly towards the little building whose silhouette I could now see ever more clearly as the sun rose – Mama's summerhouse where Barbara and I had talked with Lavinia that afternoon of our special visit, and where I had sat with Daniel on a summer day. I went towards it as the sun rose over the meadow and neither felt any cold nor heard any noise from the house. All was silent as now I advanced slowly. I called 'Barbara! Barbara!'

There was no reply, but she might not want to see me. Yet she would have some sort of message for me, I was sure. I knew who had started that fire and for whom it had been intended. I came up to the little building and went round to the front of it. Once more, but this time softly, I called: 'Barbara?'

Then I took another step and looked in at the little door of the octagonal building, a door that was half open.

I saw her sitting upright on the bench, staring at me fixedly. In her hand there was an envelope.

I opened the door and went towards her. I thought she must be frozen as it was so cold. Then I realized as I went on staring at her that she could never feel cold again.

Barbara was dead.

A long prickling shiver went down my back, and scarcely realizing what I was doing I took the letter from her hand. She was stiff and it was hard to prise the envelope from her dead fingers. She must have been sitting there for hours.

I turned and ran and ran back to the house over the snowy lawns, stumbling and gasping. Rainer came towards me. There were fewer people now at the side of the house. I saw in the distance two firemen carrying a window shutter and one of the servants holding a little dog.

'Come away, Meta, come away – more of the stones might

309

fall.' He pushed me under the trees and I said: 'Barbara – down there – you told me to find her – she's dead. Rainer, she's *dead*!' I thrust the letter into his hand. It was now quite light and we heard the low growl of brickwork as some more of the house came down. He seemed to take no notice of my words, but half pushed me towards the stables. A few carriages were being harnessed and there was a small knot of people.

'Oh my God! Meta – but . . .' He hesitated and seemed to look at the envelope almost casually. In Barbara's large, backward-sloping writing, I saw: 'To whom it may concern', written in black ink with a flourish under the words.

'You don't believe me – she's *dead*!' I said again. For answer he took my arm and steered me away from the group by the stable.

'Meta, I'm afraid something else has happened.'

'Something else?' I said stupidly.

'Yes. I'm afraid – Meta, dear child, I have to tell you – they found another body under the staircase near Lavinia's room.'

I knew straight away, and I screamed, 'Barbara killed him! Barbara killed him!' and a few people looked over at me from their business with the carriages. I looked round wildly and saw again the two firemen, still carrying the improvised stretcher but on it there was a hump under a blanket.

'Is that him? Is that him?' I cried out and tried to follow them. But Rainer pulled me back.

'Don't go, don't go, Meta!' I tried to burst from his restraining grasp, but he was too strong for me.

'Where is he? Let me go! Let me go!' I screamed.

'No, Meta. *No!*' He held me back as the two men passed round the stables. 'Hold on to me. I'll get you home.'

I saw him put the letter in his pocket. Then I suddenly went limp. He dragged me to one of the carriages and I don't remember any more.

He must have got me home and into bed, because the next thing I remember is waking from a nightmare and seeing Martha leaning over me. But behind her, just as real as Martha's face, was the sight of Barbara and the two men with the shutter walking endlessly round the room in the light of the fire.

A little later I woke again and Rainer was sitting on a chair by me and I saw I was in Aunt's bedroom and the fire was the fire in her grate. There had been a fire . . . then I remembered again and with awakening consciousness I began to shiver and moan. Then it was all gone again and I plunged back into another nightmare. I had to save Papa. Papa looked like Daniel. Then Lavinia came to me and said she was my mama now and Papa was safe with her. Papa's face, which was the face of Daniel, disappeared but a figure in a summerhouse was shouting: 'Let me go! Let me go!' I awoke to find my face streaming with sweat and that it was myself shouting. Doctor Pitts was leaning over me and I was screaming: 'Go away, go away! I want to die!'

I did not die but slept again after they had forced water down my throat and I remember Rainer's voice saying: 'Of course it was all over by the time we came on the scene.' I tried to sit up in bed when I was properly awake and I knew that reality was worse than any of my dreams. I could not move.

'Is there no hope?' I asked quite clearly. Rainer and Aunt were sitting by my bed. Now my mind was perfectly clear.

'Meta, precious, are you a little better? You were delirious. How *could* your cousin take you out in the middle of the night like that? Though I understand you insisted, he says. You might have caught pneumonia. What a terrible thing to happen...' She went on shaking her head and then Martha came into the room and peered at me.

Perhaps they wondered why Barbara's death had affected me in this way – but then, of course, that would be a shock to *anyone*. Aunt put her hand on my forehead and I tried to struggle up to a sitting position but could not. I looked at Rainer. Then Aunt and Martha went out of the room.

'How long have I been here?' I asked my cousin.

'A whole day and night have passed, Meta.'

'I didn't save him,' I whispered and at last I burst into loud sobs. 'It is all a confusion in my head,' I said, after weeping a long time.

'Hush, Meta. You are just to rest. You've had a ghastly shock. We can talk about it later, but only if you wish.'

'Is it all my fault?' I whispered and the tears seemed to have a life of their own and to trickle down my cheeks against my will.

'Nothing is your fault,' he said soothingly. 'Have a little soup when Martha brings it up and then sleep again and we will talk. There are some friends of yours coming soon from Harrogate. Things have to be done.'

311

'Oh, Rainer, I am so weak. I have so much to do. Where is Barbara's letter?'

'Safe with me,' he replied.

After that I did drink a little soup and I think I slept the next night through, because I remember that the following morning the snow had stopped falling and the winter sunlight was gilding the whitewashed ceiling. I felt once more that it had all been a bad dream, but only for a moment.

Three or four days had gone by and I just could not summon the energy to get up although some power came back to my limbs. My youthful constitution was fortunately on my side. Then finally when I wanted to get out of bed, I found my head swam.

'Please send my cousin Rainer up,' I begged and Martha clicked her tongue and looked disapproving. Of course they would still be blaming him for taking me out that night. 'I shall be well again soon,' I said. 'I want to know all that has happened.'

How strange that my body had done some mourning for me, preventing me from taking charge of myself.

'I am feeling better, Cousin,' I said when Rainer came quietly into my room, looking, I thought, rather frightened. 'I must have had a weakness for several days,' I began.

'Four,' he replied shortly.

'I couldn't move, but now I feel a little better. Please tell me what happened.'

It was strange, I couldn't cry – not then. Rainer was silent, not looking at me.

'Rainer – where is he? Where is his body – what have they done with him?'

'He will be buried after the inquest. Your friends, Miss Hertz and her fiancé, will see to it all – they called and will call again when you are strong enough to see them.'

'Oh, why didn't you wake me up? I wanted to see them – why did you not tell me?' I cried.

'You were in a strange sleep,' he said. 'We were so worried, Meta. I should not have told you like that – about Mr Reiss at the fire. Read Barbara's letter if you are strong enough. Oh, Meta, what a shock you gave us all!'

'I'm sorry, I can't seem to think straight. But I must know *everything*. Please tell me, Rainer, if Lavinia was with someone, who was it? Barbara set fire to the house herself, didn't she? To Rooks Nest – to kill Daniel?'

'It seems she did set fire to the house, but whether to kill your friend – no – I don't think so.'

'I *must* read her letter. But Daniel, poor Daniel.' I moaned and he held my hand and said nothing. 'I loved him, Rainer. I loved him – and he loved Lavinia,' I whispered finally.

'Meta, I'm so sorry.'

'How much do Aunt and Martha know?'

'Only that I took you out to the Nest – they haven't forgiven me for that – and that you found Barbara and that Mr Reiss died in the fire.'

I tried to push the thought away of *how* he died.

'And the house – is it completely ruined?' I asked. It seemed important to know that.

'Not entirely – but not worth rebuilding either I shouldn't think. Rest again, *please,* now,' he said. 'And then if you can eat something and feel stronger, I'll come up again with a copy of the letter you found.'

'Oh, Rainer, it was ghastly – she was staring at me. Did they find her in the summerhouse like that?' He didn't answer but pressed my hand.

It took me longer than I had expected to recover. I knew by Aunt's face and Martha's and from what the doctor said that they were puzzled by the excessive nature of my reaction for I had been able to speak but unable to move and had scarcely taken more than a sip or two of water, and the soup.

Once I was able to drink and eat a little my body began to re-cover and when I was able to get out of bed, Rainer gave me the letter. The doctor said I had better know it all and then I might get over it more quickly, for Naomi and Benjie were to visit me soon. I *wanted* to get well for I had a strange inability to mourn Daniel and this continued for some time. I tried to explain to Rainer, not to the others, and he said it was shock. 'But I do not regret you took me there, to Rooks Nest that night, Cousin,' I said.

Who was guilty? Who could be blamed? It was not the same thing.

Lavinia had not started the fire. The guilty one was dead. Who to blame? And Daniel, Daniel – he could not be *dead* – yet he was.

I opened the envelope which I had taken from Barbara's frozen fingers. How had she died? I had never thought to ask. Even though I now held a copy of her letter in my hands, it did not seem real. I opened it. It said:

TO WHOM IT MAY CONCERN:

I believe each man kills the thing he loves. And each woman too. We shall be together in hell one day, Lavinia. Why did you let that boy admire you? He is a foolish young man. I heard him talking this evening in my green room to Meta Moore. You will *not* go away with him. I leave my house and all its contents to Meta Moore whose parents once lived in it. That is all I have to say. B. Stott.

Although I had known in my bones that Barbara had set fire to the Nest, this strange communication was past my comprehension. To want to kill *Lavinia,* and to have by some terrible fate to have killed Daniel. But I still found it hard to believe in some part of me that Daniel was dead – I had seen no body, only the stretcher and the hump on it. Naomi, Benjie, they all knew he was dead, didn't they? Why did I not *believe* he was dead, though I *knew* he was? But if he were alive he would not be with *me.* Perhaps he had asked Lavinia to marry him, and she had refused. To *marry* him! Was it, could it, be true? Lavinia was not of his race or of his religion. He had just been a smokescreen for her other affairs. I said as much to Rainer when he came in.

I did not care any more that he knew of my feelings for Daniel. What did it matter? I could not even take in that Barbara had left that smoking ruin to me. What did anything matter now that Daniel was dead?

I was not told by Rainer for some time exactly how Daniel died. I think he wanted to spare me, for he blamed himself for my collapse, but I was daily becoming stronger. My body wept blood for me. It was not the right time of the month for it.

Perhaps one day I might begin to mourn properly for him, in my heart.

Naomi and Benjie were to visit me soon and before they arrived, I asked Rainer to tell me of the manner of Daniel's death.

'Was his body burned?' I asked. 'Is that why you did not wish me to see it?'

'No. He must have been looking for Lavinia. He could not get down the stairs. A beam fell, blocking his way. It must have dislodged another – Barbara had not yet had all the repairs done. The second one fell on him and must have killed him instantly. The fire had not reached that staircase. Of course, Lavinia had gone off in the carriage with Anton Meinertzhagen – we shall never know the exact sequence of events.

'Then he did not suffocate and his face was not burned?'

'They found him under the staircase. I could not let you see, Meta – I knew what he had been to you – I mean, I had some idea. I should never have burst out with it but I felt it was better you knew straight away. But – coming after the shock of finding Barbara . . .'

'I loved him with all my heart – and with everything,' I said in a small dry voice. 'But what does that matter now? I would have died for him and I could do nothing.'

He was silent, looking out of the window.

I thought, So she has gone off with another man – and perhaps Daniel would have come back to me in the end.

Naomi and Benjie arrived in mid-afternoon. I was up and sitting in the parlour. I still felt as one does after a long illness, but the initial shock was wearing off, as Rainer had said it would. When Naomi came in on Benjie's arm and came straight to me, and kissed me with tears in her eyes, and gave me a little bunch of violets from Fanny – then I did cry, but only a little and not for long. Benjie too was visibly upset at the death of his old friend and seemed to have some difficulty in understanding how it had come about. But Rainer took him off into the sitting room to discuss what should be done now. I went on sitting motionless on the sofa holding my violets. Naomi was speaking to my aunt in a low voice.

'The coroner said Mr Reiss's death was misadventure due to the fire. He had a letter from Miss Logan from Germany explaining that she had woken to a fire smouldering in her room, had met Daniel Reiss on the landing and had gone to raise the alarm, whilst he went back for clothes and her jewels. She had thought he was following them downstairs. The coroner said it was a great tragedy.'

I sat there with my head bowed, listening, as Naomi spoke to my aunt. It all now seemed nothing to do with me, a curious feeling. She could just as well have been speaking without me in the room. Yet it was I myself who had brought Daniel and Lavinia together. Would he still be alive now if I had not gone to him in London? I could not feel anything – that torpor crept over me again. I could not even feel guilty. I said to myself, Oh please let me feel again, please. Naomi glanced at me and her look was full of compassion.

I closed my eyes and I saw Barbara again in the summerhouse. I opened them again to chase the sight away and I forced myself to think of the fire. Lavinia would have known how quickly fire would spread on those wooden floors. I remembered Martha telling me, years ago, how a hundred years earlier the wood had been floated down the river and the canal from the Baltic.

Aunt went over and stood at the window, looking out across the garden.

She turned and sighed. 'It is all *most horrible*,' she said.

'Poor Barbara!' I found myself saying and they looked at me in surprise. 'She is dead too,' I said.

When they had gone away I went up to my room and I forgot coroners, and Barbara, and Naomi's pity and I stood too at the window and I thought of my Daniel, gone for ever.

And then the tears came, out of a deep well.

It was February by the time I returned to my employers with a clean bill of health from Dr Pitts. Aunt had put down my collapse to the shock of finding Barbara; she had made her peace with Rainer and Rainer had said no more to me about my relations with Daniel Reiss.

I don't know how I got through the rest of that spring. The children were good to me and Naomi and Benjie were as kind to me as anyone could be. Naomi seemed to understand how I had felt for Daniel, although I never told her exactly that I had been his lover. They mourned him as much as I did, and one day in spring took me to see the cemetery where he was buried. His grave had Hebrew letters on it and I put a great bunch of lilac on the stone. But all this seemed to pass in a sort of dream from which I would just occasionally awake.

I came home for a late Easter. One thing I felt I had to do was to go again to Rooks Nest which I had not seen since that December night. I wanted to see where Daniel had last been alive. Rainer had been down there of course already and reported that the only remaining wing – that near the stables – was unsafe. I wanted too to go to the summerhouse to expunge from my mind the awful memory that had begun to haunt me in spite of my grief for Daniel – the sudden sight of that staring, stiff figure sitting on the bench holding the letter in the ghastly dawn light. I told Rainer of my wish. 'Don't tell your aunt – just say we're going for a drive,' he said.

So he drove me there a few days later and he walked down to the lake with me with the spectre of the ruin behind us. Workmen, the same who had been painting it in the summer, were now dismantling some of the tumbled stones. 'You must look at it, Meta,' he said and turned me round to face it. 'It is only a building,' he said. Then we walked to the summerhouse and I clutched his hand. I still saw Barbara there. 'There is no one there, Meta,' he said.

'I feel as though I shall never feel anything again. What is there to live for?' I said. 'I don't want the house now. It's just a *ruin*. Barbara only wanted me to have a ruin,' I went on, my voice choking.

'Turn your face to the lake,' he said. 'There are trees growing there – they will go on growing when the house is gone.'

'And the rooks will still nest there,' I added. 'What is it all for, Rainer? Daniel is dead. I shall have to go away – there never was anything for me here – my dreams told me that.' I spoke a little of my recurring dream as we walked back. 'Soon no one will remember Daniel,' I said.

'Let us walk a little further, Meta – I have something to say to you.' I looked at him – his voice seemed strained. 'I should not say this now, Meta – you will need more than three or four months to get over all this. But if I do not say it now I shall never say it.' I waited and thrust my hands in the muff he had given me. 'I want you to know, Meta, that wherever I am there will always be a home for you.' I looked at him stupidly, thinking: Aunt Juby is going to sell up and there will be no more Hartsedge Hall and she has asked him to tell me.

'You are very kind,' I said. 'Is it Aunt – her rheumatics? But I can always find work away.'

'No, Meta – not your aunt. Just that I want to say to you – and I know it's the wrong time and place, and you are upset by this terrible tragedy, but perhaps it will help you – that I *love* you, I have always loved you. And when you get over this affair – for you will – may I tell you again?'

'I shall never "get over it",' I said. And then: '*You* love me!' I repeated dumbly.

'I know it sounds indecent, but how else can I say it?' he said. 'Just remember I said it – don't think about it, just remember. You'll need to be brave to recover. Go back to work and I'll write to you.'

'I don't bring luck to anyone,' I said. 'Why should you want to love me?' I stood and stared at him in puzzlement.

'It has nothing to do with all this misery.' He pointed to the desolation around us. 'I knew long ago you were in love with that young man,' he said. 'And I saw you with him in London.'

'You saw! And you never said anything to Aunt!'

'Why should I? *I* was young once. It was sheer chance. I was walking on Oxford Street and you passed me looking so happy – and when I saw you looking like that, I envied that man and then I knew I'd loved you for a long time. And of course if all this hadn't happened, you may never have known. I was frightened people would say it was a fatherly feeling, since I'm so much older than you. When you were little I didn't want you to take me for that absent father of yours. I think I felt something for you even then. You can't say I haven't been discreet.'

'And you kept coming to see me because you *loved* me.' It all fitted in, but I was amazed.

'I came to see you because I liked your company – isn't that enough? I want to *give* you something, Meta – you don't like to receive, do you?'

I was silent.

'Go away and try to forget all this – not your young man, I know you'll never forget *him* – but the sordidness of it. I don't want you connected with it at all.'

'I loved Lavinia Logan too,' I said and burst out crying.

'Don't cry about that, Meta. I said it to give you a little bit of cheer.'

'Did *you* love Mama, then?'

'Why, no! Don't tell me you've been suspecting *that* all your life! She was a lovely girl and your papa and she were very well suited. I was a little younger than your mama but *much* younger in good sense. I had years and years to learn to love someone – but not your mama.'

318

'And Papa – do you think *I* am like him then?'

'Not really, Meta – and because you are a woman you will make different mistakes. He was never anchored after Mary died. You will anchor yourself Meta – somewhere.'

We were walking across the field now, near the old Coach Road, and I showed him where I had jumped into the grounds when I was fourteen. 'It still says "Trespassers will be prosecuted",' I said. 'I used to think it said persecuted – and that was true, wasn't it?'

He helped me jump down and we were walking up the lane back to the Turnpike to find our carriage again. 'I was perhaps wrong to say it – forgive me. But remember when you are sad – and you will be very sad – remember,' he said quietly.

'*Will* you write to me?' I said.

'If you want me to.'

'Yes – please write to me and – if I can, later – I shall write to you. I think I should go back to Harrogate again soon, Rainer. I am – grateful for what you've said.'

He did write when I returned once again to mourn my loss in Harrogate. I might as well be there as anywhere, I thought. It did not seem to matter.

At first I was amazed at Rainer's lack of taste in saying to me what he had. And then I thought: He is a little like me – it is not an insult to tell someone you love them. Had he just begun to 'love' me because he saw I loved Daniel Reiss? His words had been understood by part of me, but did not seem to have touched the right place. Was he not just being kind? He had never even kissed me! Love was not like that surely? He was sorry for me and he was noble and good and kind. I told him as much when I wrote to him and he replied that he was not at all good or kind and that he was a very jealous man. He added: 'I shall tell you what I told you at Rooks Nest every summer for the next ten years or till I am too old for any young lady to hear it.' His wry irony and his sense of paradox had always puzzled me, but gradually I came to see that they were a defence against his own feelings.

At the end of June I had another letter from Aunt Sophia and this time I seriously considered taking up her offer. The Angersteins were thinking of sending Fanny away to a girls' school when she was twelve to prepare for going to London to the school where Naomi had been educated, so there would only be Zillah left and Zillah wanted only to learn about music and to play it. Many a time she would play to me 'Daniel's tunes'. The children had been awestruck by his death and seemed to understand how I felt without being told. I put off my reply to Sophia till I should have talked about it to Rainer. He had wanted to come to see me in July, but I was not ready.

Before that, though, a wonderful thing happened. The agent who had gone to Baden and to Mannheim in search of Daniel's lost manuscripts, came upon a great pile of manuscript music books in the keeping of the Margrave of Würtemburg, who had been much distressed by Daniel's death and the manner of his passing. These were handed over to Pinkelheim and he was ecstatic. They were given to Benjie to transcribe. There were songs, studies, sonatas, a veritable cornucopia of music, inspired by Lavinia.

'It is marvellous stuff,' said Benjie.

I had time and plenty to think of all that Daniel had meant to me, and all he could have been apart from me. Over and over again I relived our summer week and the last talk I had had with him at Rooks Nest. I read and re-read his letters. As I thought about it, grieving alone, sometimes all night in my room, I came to see – though slowly – that he had loved me in his way but that I should have had more suffering as time went on. I still could not understand how he had so suddenly changed from loving me to loving Lavinia, but this had ceased to hurt me. I mourned only his passing. How long had I really known him and how well? A year and a half – and then only for short periods. Could I ever have known him in the way Naomi was getting to know her Benjie with the promise of a lifetime together? But had I really wanted a lifetime? I thought I had, but now I was not sure. It was something I should now never know and so I could never now be disappointed, only for ever bereaved. I had been punished in the wrong way. I could have got over my unrequited love in time, I suppose, but how does one get over a real death, not just a death of the heart?

Rainer wrote to me often, but he always said he would not come to talk to me unless I wanted him to. The idea of his loving me began to disturb me – I was incredulous, but the knowledge of his being in the world for me whenever I wanted was comforting and at last I thought I could see him. I put it to myself that it was for his sake too. I must make it clear to him that I could never love him, that that part of my life was really over. Some spring had been touched by Daniel, but it had dried up.

I heard from my cousin about what was happening at the Nest of course. Barbara's affairs had apparently been in none too good a state at her death – she had been far too extravagant.

I was still mourning my lost dead love, but some stubborn residue still remained in me, petrified. I think it was a part of me that could not feel enough to mourn, which sounds paradoxical. I needed strong emotion to release that other buried feeling. I had made a bid for love and lost.

I wrote to Rainer in July about the possibility of my taking Aunt Sophia at her word – just to get away from the places and people whom Daniel had known, to make a new start. I had almost decided to do it, but Rainer begged me to wait and reconsider. 'Why cut yourself off from everyone who loves you – you will only be more unhappy, or, what is worse, learn to do without, and that at your age would be terrible,' he wrote. I expressed guilt to him then, a guilt that would not let me go and he replied: 'It is not *your* fault that your mother died, nor that Lavinia Logan led a young man on and allowed him to fall in love with her, nor that your Daniel was accidentally killed, nor that Barbara's nature was as it was.'

The thought of Daniel was still too raw to be smoothed away with words. Only music released a little of my anguish for him and I used to creep down to listen to Benjie's playing when he came up north every two weeks from London. After he and Naomi left there was not even that.

Rainer came on an afternoon in early August and we went out for a walk on the hills round the town rather than visit the Winter Gardens. Even there on the hills I was remembering Daniel and that walk to the sulphur wells. We sat down on a little wooden seat provided by the town for travellers to admire the view and for a long time we said nothing. Then I tried to explain myself.

'You must not "love" me, Rainer,' I began. 'You don't know the real me. I must be by myself and learn to live with myself. Sometimes I feel I want to spend the rest of my life in a dream – though the other dreams came to nothing. I want to be left alone. I have to work my destiny out for myself.'

'You want to be free,' he replied, looking straight ahead as though he were scrutinizing the fields and the hills. 'I have always wanted to be free too, Meta – but none of us is free. Yet you know I love you. Perhaps I don't know "all of you", as you say, but I am willing to find out. I love what I know and what I can imagine of you – and even if I were wrong about you I could help you to live in freedom, not a living death in the past.'

I was silent. It did feel like a living death very often. Was not work and solitude the cure for that?

'Are you not just sorry for me?' I muttered. 'How could you feel for me what I felt for Daniel? I'm not worth it.'

'If we loved only those who are "worthy", Meta, we should all receive short shrift,' he replied and went on: 'I know what you felt – and perhaps still feel. I know you must preserve your inner life – and it is hard for a woman, I do know that. But the world is stronger than you and men must help women, not hinder them.'

'I know you are right and not many men would agree with you. But to be "free", I have to earn money – go and work for Sophia, or take over Juby's school, look after her, teach . . .'

'I don't want you any different, Meta,' he said. 'Even if you grew away from me, it would be worth the risk. I can't keep you unchanged, but you make my life worth living, you know.' I began to cry and once I started it seemed I could not stop. It seemed I was crying for Mama and for Papa and for Daniel – and even a little for my old self.

'I know I have been blind and self-important,' I sobbed. 'But did I have to be punished like that?'

'You are only twenty – sorry twenty-one – ' he made me smile a little as I blew my nose. 'You have only just begun. People like you don't find life easy – you live on your nervous energy. But I know, Meta, that you could be very happy. It's because you have been so unhappy. You are not a hopeless case.' All this time he had not taken my hand or touched me or anything and I was grateful. 'Old Mother Nature has a way of healing, you know,' he said. 'Why not try it? I don't want to clip your wings,' he added quietly when I said nothing. 'I just want to look after you. If you go to London I'm sure you will find people to notice you and some to love you, but they couldn't love you more than I do.'

'You always took more *notice* of me than anyone else did,' I said in reply. 'But you see – I knew Daniel in a way that men wouldn't approve of for a woman they wanted to love...' I went on, hoping he would understand.

'Yes. I had known that too of course. He would have kept you a prisoner of passion as long as you loved him "more" – for you did love him "more" didn't you?'

'Oh yes.'

'Do you know what I want to say to you?' He took my hand and I turned to look at him. I had never been so close to him – or to anyone else except Daniel.

'I don't know, Rainer. I think I know that you "love" me – whatever that means.'

'It means that I desire you and it also means that I want to marry you,' he said, and then he looked down at the ground. I thought, We are very alike. I could not believe that he wanted me.

'I am so frightened of loving again,' I said in reply.

'I shall ask you every summer, as I said,' he repeated lightly, 'till I am too decrepit to dare.'

'I spoiled my happy days through self-will. I wanted to give, not to receive – I don't know how to do that – except with Martha and Aunt. How could I receive your love and love you properly?'

'You will always find something to love, Meta. Wouldn't it be better to love someone who loved you – or just to forget about the *word* and give yourself up to life, and not worry about it? I realize of course,' he added with a smile, 'that this is special pleading.'

'Do you really want to marry me, Rainer? You know what I think about marriage.' Then I remembered that I would have been quite happy to marry Daniel – if he had asked me – so perhaps I was not as unconventional as I thought.

'Do you know this is a most strange conversation?' he said. 'And just to seal it I am going to do something even more strange, unless you stop me now.'

I looked up into his eyes, so different from Daniel's dark ones. Rainer belonged to a different species. I did not stop him. I was not worn down, just grateful that at least someone loved me enough to want to understand me. Then he kissed me over and over again – little kisses all over my face. 'You are so very adorable,' he said. 'I have been' – (two kisses) – 'wanting to do this' –

(two more kisses) – 'for so long, when you were too young to be kissed even. But I shall not go on kissing you until you decide if you want me or not – this is just a foretaste, I hope.'

I took his hand and held it comfortably. I was not frightened of him – perhaps I should have been – but there were reserves of strength and passion which I could sense just by holding his hand and feeling the sinews of his wrist.

'I don't want to be "looked after",' I said. 'I mean, only if I can balance it by looking after you. Why do I always want to look after people? You are a most unlikely person for anyone to want to look after – you always seemed so self-sufficient. Were you not?'

'I have always been terribly dependent on women,' he smiled. 'But now I want only to be dependent on you. It would be a good "bargain", little Meta – you wouldn't have to be in love with love any more. I think men and women *should* look after each other, don't you? Perhaps it was because your poor mama and papa died and did not look after you, so you felt you must look after them, by proxy.'

'Yes, perhaps,' I answered, seeing everything in a novel perspective.

'And you need not give me your answer for years and years if you don't want. Come now, we'll go down to the town and sample a cup of your father's "cup that cheers".'

'Poor Papa,' I said. 'I don't expect he was a bit like you.'

'No, he was more like your Daniel,' he replied. 'But without that great musical talent, which I expect made Daniel what he was. I want to be your lover, Meta,' he said again as we turned to look over the far moors before walking over to the stile.

'What on earth would Aunt say?' I said, struck with a feeling of incongruity.

'I don't think she would be surprised. I know she'd be relieved – not about the lover part, but about the husband part. There is something else I must tell you.' I stopped and he took my hand again. I thought, He is going to say he once loved Lavinia – I am sure he is. 'Lavinia Logan,' he said. 'Your father *did* have a love-affair in Germany – it was with her.' That took me utterly by surprise. 'Poor Papa,' I said lightly, but everything in my internal kaleidoscope seemed to shift shape and colour.

'I never cared for her myself, as you know,' he said and took my arm again and we walked down to the town and for the first time for months I even had a tiny intimation that I might one day begin to feel again.

I didn't go on being optimistic long nor did I begin to forget Daniel for one moment but, finally and for good, I did decide not to accept Aunt Sophia's offer. I would wait and hope that time would heal me and in the meantime decide nothing else. Rainer wrote to me constantly from wherever he was. I think at first he still remained worried that I should see him in the role of an absent father and never be able to see him as a man, but that was not my worry at all. I wanted to say 'yes' to life, and I wanted in the end to say 'yes' to him – not out of despair or weariness or fear or to 'forget Daniel', but because I did like Rainer so. I had always liked him, but been a little in awe of him. I knew there must be some simple way into that magic land of love on the path I had trodden with Daniel, or some other equally dear path, but I was not sure what it was. Sometimes I would think of my poor dead papa – how well I understood the feelings he must have had for Lavinia!

I went home uncertain of my plans. Fanny was definitely to be sent to school in the autumn and I promised I would let the Angersteins know what I should do myself. Then I had the idea that Aunt's school would be just right for Fanny, and Mrs Angerstein came over with the child and seemed to like what she saw. I didn't want to go back to Harrogate again. I knew I should offer to help Aunt Juby now.

Rainer and I spent long late summer evenings together – he was busy in Bradford and had moved his things to a little house he had rented in Shibden Dale, having given up the Halifax chambers. We were so often together that I thought comment would be made about it. I began to realize that he wanted me as a woman. So long as he did not think I would spring to him because of the other trajectory I had been on, which had thrown me to the ground!

One evening in late September he came over to collect me for our customary walk. Aunt had never commented on Rainer's visits and I was getting a little uneasy about it all. We always talked to each other a great deal and behaved very circumspectly, and I was wondering if it ever could change now. He had scrupulously avoided kissing me again after that first time in Harrogate. It was as though we were both waiting for something. I wasn't sure whether we were being fair to each other. I kept insisting on independence and he never spoke again of love, but trusted his looks to speak for him. I knew that I must learn to accept love – I wanted to – but I was frightened of losing some vague ideal, that 'in love' rapture I had had when I loved my dead Daniel. I 'knew' now that Daniel was dead – I was resigned to it, had accepted it. I knew Rainer had the feelings for me which I had had for Daniel and I admired his constancy and his restraint at the same time as wanting that 'something else'. But would that something else be a compromise? I worked it out that as I was a woman I was expected to go to whoever had these feelings for *me* – I had not believed at the bottom of my heart, perhaps, in 'equal' love, only a mutual rapture of the senses. Perhaps Rainer, too, had fashioned a new Meta out of the feelings he had for me – but that was not all. Because he was a man and perhaps because he was older, the love would balance itself – that is what I dared to hope. Perhaps romantic love was a luxury and one day women would hold their destinies in their own hands.

I still had my own inner life which was full of private feelings like the ones I had had in the snow. I tried to tell Rainer of them. He had the same sort of feelings too, he told me. They were not shareable but it helped to know someone else had them too. I knew what he meant. Rainer quoted Wordsworth and called them 'spots of time'.

So that evening we walked over to Rooks Nest again. 'I think we *must* go there again now,' he said and I had expected him to say that.

When we arrived at the old Coach Road we hesitated for a moment and I said: 'Let's go this way again – over the wall by the Trespassers' notice.' He made no reply, but took my arm. So it was that having scaled the wall we found ourselves once more in that field down by the lake with all its memories for me of happiness and sorrow. I was thinking, To be *able* to give I must be able to receive, and I was ready to receive.

I had been blind to Rainer's feelings for so long, but now – I do not know how it came about – as we stood looking at the lake, not without pain and not without grief, the mist seemed to be wiped away from my eyes. He had said he would ask me to marry him every summer and that itself seemed long ago. I had grown older myself in the interval. I knew I had begun to trust him. He was not an idol for me or a figment of my imagination, but another human on an equal level to mine. Perhaps we could grow even closer together? He had never invoked God or society or propriety to me – he did not want a demure young miss at all. I knew that I wanted to try to put him first in my life now, but I needed help to do it, if I were to risk the rest of my life in the arms of one man. I might have to get along without magic, without illusion. Yet would I be giving up anything he himself was not giving up? I do not think that in the whole of England I could have found anyone who understood me so perfectly and it was a wonder to me that he was not married himself, since he was now thirty-eight. Yet what I might begin to feel for him was so different from what I had felt for Daniel – how could I call it love?

We came round to the path and I forced myself to look at the house. There was still one shorn wing standing in the distance, but the path went on to the summerhouse just the same, and the lake. We turned our backs on the house and stood by the lake again, looking over to the little wooded island and I said: 'We've missed the lilacs, but some late roses will be all over the garden on the other side.' We walked over to that part where Barbara's gardeners had never been, and it was heavy with the scent of roses. They had not been pruned in the spring and were rambling everywhere.

I had been told a few days earlier that as Barbara had died by her own hand I could not inherit from her. I had never expected to. The garden and the ruin and the lake and the summerhouse belonged to no one at present and Sam Hirst was wanting to use the land for hay. I hoped that what remained of the house would be taken down. I did not need it any more.

Rainer broke into my thoughts. 'Augusta wants you to take over the school, Meta.'

'Oh! I don't think I . . .'

'You could employ another teacher. Your aunt is tired. She wants to retire to Manchester with her friend, Miss Walker. Martha would stay on with you of course.'

'Why did she not speak to me about it?'

'She thought you'd been too upset recently. Before what happened here at the Nest she was going to ask you. It was to be a surprise for your birthday. Mr and Mrs Angerstein have given her such glowing reports of you.'

I said nothing, so he went on: 'When she heard you were uncertain about staying on in Harrogate, she asked me to put it to you.'

'Did Aunt ever guess about me and Daniel?'

'No, I don't think so. Of course she realized that you had a fondness for him.'

'And does she know about you and me?' I asked, turning to look at him.

'What should she know, Meta?'

I looked up at him. Here at Rooks Nest was where everything seemed to happen to me. I took a deep breath and said, and it came out like a croak: 'Only that I *will* marry you, Rainer. If you should ask me again!'

He spoke not a word but took me in his arms and then he kissed me, not this time with those little kisses of comfort and affection, but a long kiss like a sigh, as though as he kissed me and I returned his kiss, all in one, we were sealing a bond.

'*Will* you ask me again, then?' I murmured.

For answer he kissed me again and again and in between the kisses he was saying something about a special licence and Italy ... and, oh, my darling! Then he drew away for a moment. 'Unless you want to wait,' he said, a little frown appearing on his forehead.

'No, I don't want to wait – *you* have waited, it seems, a long time!'

'Then I shall "settle down",' he smiled.

We walked over to the summerhouse and it had no power now to frighten me. 'Mama used to sit here,' I said. 'Would you live with me at the Hall if I kept on the school?'

'I need you so, Meta,' he replied. 'I would live in a hovel with you – I can write anywhere. But yes, that is what I thought – you must keep on with your work.' He had thought it all out. We sat in absolute silence for several minutes.

After that, he kissed me again and then we got up from the seat in the summerhouse and walked over to the long grass near the rose garden and we leaned against the garden wall. It was a perfect summer evening and so still and quiet. I saw at last the way he did need me – and I him – there are no words for that. I think I was, just for a moment, as purely happy as human beings are ever allowed to be, forgetting for that moment sorrow and fear and guilt and grief. He put his arms around me and rocked me. It felt blissful. I hoped that bliss would always return whatever happened to us. With all my bruised and yearning heart I had accepted him, for he accepted me. I did cry a few tears of happiness – and so did he. I saw the desire he had for me and it was like a key which perhaps could unlock those bits of myself which had remained shut up and mute ever since Daniel had stopped loving me, taking away the key even before he died. That key of desire could unlock my heart again in a sweet turning and would restore not only love to me but, it seemed then, my childhood and my parents and all the lost things. I wanted him because he wanted me.

We went back to the Hall and we told Aunt Juby straightaway. She was a little surprised I thought, but not for long. Martha was not surprised, and *that* was a great surprise to me. She bellowed her joy in a mixture of delight and sobbing whilst Rainer smiled and smiled and looked quite foolish! They both seemed to have forgiven him for taking me to Rooks Nest that night. I saw and marvelled how it was in my power to make four people happy, including myself. Aunt brought out a bottle of champagne and Rainer and I acted the part of two conventional sweethearts, rather embarrassed at seeing the pleasure our own pleasure had so clearly brought to my two guardians.

Of course, my story does not end here, for marriage is the beginning and not the end of a history like ours. But I have almost finished my account now, that part of it I wanted to tell, and as I sat at the parlour window that evening being toasted, with Rainer holding my hand and so far defying the conventions as to place his strong arm round me, I pondered on all that had happened to me in my first twenty-one years, and thought that in spite of it all I had got more than I deserved.

Today it is snowing as I lay down my pen to go out into our stone garden to feed the birds. I have the school now at Hartsedge Hall and a husband and two children. Still though, when I am alone, I sometimes go into the garden and hear the wind blowing from over the moor and think of my two old loves.

I see Lavinia Logan as she was in my girlhood in her green silk gown against the flowering lilac at Rooks Nest. She is most probably still turning faraway hearts to love and jealousy. We never saw her again.

I think, more often, of Daniel Reiss who lies in the Jewish

cemetery in Leeds. If Lavinia had believed in him she could have been rich beyond her dreams for the music he left is played all over the world.

Sometimes I think of Barbara. I believe I understand her now.

I dream no longer of the house of my birth. The nightmare of its reflection falling soundlessly into the lake is with me no longer, for now the vision is true and the house has gone. The grounds have all been ploughed over and sown with grass and the hay-fields now stretch up to the old carriage drive. Not a stone remains to tell the stranger that a great mansion and its garden once stood here, except for the small headstones of the dogs' graves, now buried in waving grasses, and a few wild roses which still return every year.

The rooks still home in the elms and the place has not lost its name. In winter the wind tears the dark-green seams of the lake apart, ripping little waves off one by one as they arrive on its shore. When the winds die down in summer, butterflies flutter over to the island or haunt the grotto, searching for flowers. The summerhouse is pulled down.

Rainer, my life's companion, turns to me as I go out to my own garden. It was he who encouraged me to lay my ghosts. Those ghosts have lived again for me in the tale that I have told. But it is time to bid them farewell for ever as I go towards Rainer and try to return the love he has so steadfastly given me, and turn to the light the blind side of the heart.

THE END